In Hollywood
Where They Vied for Sex,
Power, and Wealth
They Were Safe
Until They Fell in Love

Belinda Glassman was the fabulous rich girl who used
men to satisfy her passions, but kept her heart unattached
. . . too hurt by her powerful father to risk falling in
love.

Jack Ford was the year's fastest rising star, with a big-
money film contract after a hit TV series . . . and not
into a serious relationship with anybody but the lady
called Success.

Then fate brought them together on a movie set . . .
and into the pitch-black heat of a Laguna Beach bedroom
where the sex got so hot someone was bound to get
burned.

LOVERS AND LIARS

**Their passions felt like heaven on earth,
but their hungers could damn them . . .
straight to hell**

P9-CQD-637

QUANTITY SALES

Most Dell books are available at special quantity discounts when purchased in bulk by corporations, organizations, and special-interest groups. Custom imprinting or excerpting can also be done to fit special needs. For details write: Dell Publishing, 666 Fifth Avenue, New York, NY 10103. Attn.: Special Sales Department.

INDIVIDUAL SALES

Are there any Dell books you want but cannot find in your local stores? If so, you can order them directly from us. You can get any Dell book in print. Simply include the book's title, author, and ISBN number if you have it, along with a check or money order (no cash can be accepted) for the full retail price plus $2.00 to cover shipping and handling. Mail to: Dell Readers Service, P.O. Box 5057, Des Plaines, IL 60017.

LOVERS
AND
LIARS

Brenda Joyce

A DELL BOOK

Published by
Dell Publishing
a division of
Bantam Doubleday Dell Publishing Group, Inc.
666 Fifth Avenue
New York, New York 10103

ISBN: 0-440-20323-6

Printed in the United States of America

Published simultaneously in Canada

September 1989

10 9 8 7 6 5 4 3 2 1
KRI

Prologue

February 1988

*L*ies.

All lies.

The pain was still so raw. How many days had it been? Two, three, four? A week? God, she didn't even know. She was drifting in a cloud of hurt, drifting, like the snowflakes outside . . .

It was hard to focus on anything other than the betrayal. How had it happened? She, who had never needed anyone, not even her parents—not that they had been there for her—and certainly not a man. She, who had had more men in her life than she could count, who had played the singles game more callously than the worst playboy, had not just taken the plunge. It had been a freefall without the chute opening.

God.

Jack Ford.

Hollywood's Golden Boy. Sex symbol nonpareil. Hot. As in hot property. One of the hottest in town. And notorious. Oh, so notorious . . .

The truth agonized.

He had used her to avenge himself on her father.

Dear God. If only she would wake up and find that all this was just a horrible dream.

A knock sounded. She started. The dogs barked. She thought she must be imagining things—no one knew where she was, where she had escaped to, where she was hiding, in this cabin at Lake Tahoe. But there it was again.

She got up, shoving aside strands of blond hair, squaring her broad shoulders, and opened the door. Outside, the wind howled, pine trees swayed, and the snow began falling more heavily.

"Belinda Ford?"

She was the daughter of Abe Glassman, whose multi-billion-dollar conglomerate spanned two continents, one of the most powerful men in America—and she recognized the press ID before she could make out the cardholder's face, shadowed by the hood of his parka. Oh, no, she thought. Oh, no, not now.

And the name he had used in addressing her. *Ford.* It was still unfamiliar. She wanted to deny it. She couldn't. "Yes?"

"I'm with the *National Enquirer.* Can I come in? It's freezing out."

"No, I'm sorry, " Belinda said, starting to shut the door.

But he jammed his Gerry-clad shoulder into it. "When did you and Jack Ford get married, and why keep it secret?" he asked quickly. "And is the rumor true? There's already trouble between the two of you—you're estranged? Have you left him?"

"No damn comment," Belinda said, coldly furious.

"You must have a comment to make on the article in the *Star.* Or is that why you left him? It must be a helluva shock to think you've married a movie star, only to find out he's a porn star too."

Belinda was stunned. What was he talking about? Jack —porn? She recovered. "Please leave before I have to call the police."

"You didn't know!" He was triumphant. "Then there had to be another reason you left Ford just days after the wedding. He's infamous for his women. Is that it? Another woman? Or *did* you know—*was* it because of the porn? And what about all this publicity—your husband's about to take a fall? His career is on the line, maybe finished—"

"Get out!" she shouted. "Just get out!"

"Ford was seen last night with Donna Mills. Do you have something to say about that?"

She succeeded in finally pushing him out the door and slamming it shut in his face. She was breathless. It couldn't be true, could it? Jack and porn? And Donna Mills? God, he couldn't possibly be in her bed, could he? Were there already others? And why—why did it have to hurt so much, and why did she have to even care?

So many lies.

Every second of every moment—another lie.

She inhaled deeply. And faced the biggest questions of all.

What was between her father, Abe Glassman, and her husband, Jack Ford?

And why had Jack used her as the instrument of his revenge?

PART ONE

Strangers

July 1987

1

*H*eads turned.

Today she didn't just look like a star, she felt like one. She was on top of the world—the world was at her feet. "Adam!"

She made a stunning figure. She was not as tall as one thought, five feet six or so, taller now in high-heeled pumps, clad in a pencil-thin black skirt that showed off strong, muscular legs. Her shoulders were broad under an even broader neon-orange jacket, as straight as the skirt, and her golden hair fell in glorious, disheveled waves to her shoulders. Her face was model-perfect, with high cheekbones, straight nose, full, sensual lips, and a strong jaw.

Adam Gordon rose as she made her way among the tables of the Bistro Garden. "Belinda, you're dazzling today."

She grinned, allowing him to seat her, once again impressed by his old-world charm. She had forgotten it still existed. "Adam, we are celebrating. I want the best champagne in the house. My treat," she added quickly. Normally she would never be so extravagant in a town where extravagance was the norm, for she could not afford it. But today she was three hundred and fifty thousand dollars richer—*three hundred and fifty thousand dollars!*

Adam, tall, dark, and slim—and not her type—took her hand. She was still surprised that she had agreed to go out with him and told herself it was *not* because he and her father seemed to dislike each other so intensely. "Share the news," he said. His look was warm.

"My screenplay has sold! God! Finally! North-Star bought it. In fact, they're picking it up as a vehicle for Jackson Ford. Do you know who Ford is?"

This was Hollywood. And Adam was a lawyer in one of the largest firms in L.A. Among the firm's numerous clients, both corporate and otherwise, were the likes of Charlton Heston and Joan Collins. It was his business to know everything about the entertainment business. "Of course. He's on that television detective series—or *was*. The show's been canceled and North-Star grabbed him. He's a very hot property right now, maybe the hottest. Congratulations, Belinda," Adam said, smiling, but he was wondering if this was going to interfere with his plans.

"Oh, Adam, I've waited so long for this—so damn long!" She thought about the one screenplay she had sold two years ago, the one that had never even made it into production. But this time was different. This time North-Star was the producer, not some small independent; this time it was a vehicle for a super-hot property; this time it was going all the way. "I think I've finally made it, Adam. All those years of listening to 'Why don't you go and get a real job?' "

Adam smiled. "You have made it."

"There's more. They're interested in another product of mine, so I'm crossing my fingers. We may be making another sale soon."

"Then this is definitely cause for celebration."

Belinda started to bite a long red nail, then promptly stopped. "I think Ford is hot," she said tensely. "But can he *act . . .*"

It was a rhetorical question, so Adam ordered a bottle of Cristal champagne.

"I mean," she mused, "he has been nominated for Best Actor in a Dramatic Series every year since he got the show, but so what, right? Has he won?" she demanded. "I mean, granted, he has the greatest ass and an even better smile, but . . ." She sighed. "I'm so nervous, Adam. I want everything to be perfect. I can't help it—this is my ticket to success. If the box office is good for this, God, imagine if it was one of those weekend multi-million-dollar grossers! Damn! I wish Mel Gibson was doing the role. Everyone knows he can act."

"Ford will sell tickets," Adam assured her. "He is very hot right now." Belinda gave him a grateful smile, but her mind was light-years ahead.

Production was scheduled to start in December. Thinking about it made her stomach twist into knots. This was her first sale (the other not counting), and *Outrage* was her baby. She was determined to ride this ticket all the way down the pike. She wanted to be in on all the rewrites. If she managed to stay in—and she'd been in this town long enough to know how rare that was, for writers were changed as easily as a pair of pants and discarded with less thought than pantyhose —there would be a lot of ass-kissing and compromising. She wanted desperately to stay in. She wanted this film, *Outrage,* to be better than good, to be fantastic.

She could not concentrate on Adam or lunch. She wanted to be back at home, at her IBM PC, polishing up the climax of her third screenplay—just in case.

Home was a weathered gray beach house in Laguna Beach, a good hour's drive south of L.A. and Hollywood. The house literally hung over the beach, on stilts. It was small and traditional on the outside, eclectic on the inside, with breathtaking views of Catalina and the surf. The floors were faded pine, the ceilings high and beamed, with an enormous skylight over the living room. There was barely any furniture, just the basics—a couch, a few chairs, a pine chest serving as a cocktail table. An oversized painting that was a birthday present from her grandparents dominated the room, taking up all of one wall. Done almost in a Fauvist style, with vivid colors and contrasts, it was a scene of a yacht and a navy destroyer in the New York harbor during the bicentennial celebration. Belinda had fallen in love with the painting in a San Francisco gallery. She had never dreamed she would own it. Next to her IBM PC, it was her most cherished possession.

A big black Lab greeted her at the door as she walked in, and she bent to scratch his head, then began to shed her shoes and hose in the middle of the living room. She thought about her parents. Shouldn't she call them?

Her father didn't give a damn.

Not that she cared. Maybe once, a long time ago, but not anymore.

Still . . . The biggest moment of her life, and she really had to face it, she had no one to share it with except some casual date. That or Vince.

If she looked too hard at that fact, she'd have to face some inescapable conclusions, so Belinda quickly paced to the huge glass doors that slid open onto a deck, bare except for plants and a waist-level glass windscreen. She stared out at the calm blue water, the surfers, and the boats with their white-and-blue sails flapping in the breeze.

After just a few minutes she turned and looked at the phone. So what if her father didn't care? Didn't she have some kind of inalienable right to share the biggest moment of her life with him? She crossed to the phone with long, aggressive strides.

The receptionist put her right through. The next phone rang four times before it was answered by one of the dozen secretaries working for Glassman. As usual, a tone of harassment seeped through the veneer of professional courtesy.

"Mr. Glassman, please," Belinda said, wondering if her own voice sounded tense. For some reason the phone had gotten a bit clammy in her hand.

"Whom may I—"

"Belinda. Glassman. His *daughter.*"

That got the secretary off balance. She heard the indrawn breath. She never called her father, ever, not at work, not outside work, and she hadn't been to his office since she was fifteen. But now, after a three-minute pause, the secretary informed her that she would have to call back later. Mr. Glassman was in a meeting and could not take the call. "Would you like to leave a message?"

"Forget it," she said quickly. She hung up. Just as well. It was a bad idea.

Should she call her mother?

She started to think about the night ahead. She wanted to celebrate. Too bad today wasn't Friday, because there was that North-Star party she had been invited to and had no intention of missing. But today wasn't Friday, and she had always been a loner, even as a child, and it never bothered her—except at times like these.

She suddenly had a nostalgic longing for Dana—her best friend as a teenager. They had drifted apart when Dana had gotten married, and now she was a mother three times over. Belinda guessed that marriage and motherhood suited Dana, but she couldn't imagine herself ever in that role. It wasn't because she was such a loner and just couldn't get close to people; it was rather because she knew men too well and had long ago given up her childish dreams of finding some kind of Prince Charming to share her life with. Most men wanted one thing, and Beinda knew exactly what that was. But that was okay. Belinda wanted it too. It was the lies that she could live without—and she intended to do just that.

Still, this moment cried out to be shared with someone special.

But there was no one, so Belinda shrugged the need away. Of course it would have to be a man. Her mind formed an image of massive male pectorals, thickly matted with black hair. Sometimes there was nothing interesting at all out and about. Other times they all came out of the woodwork.

She hadn't had a really good fuck in too long. What she needed was to be super turned on.

Thinking about men and her needs made her look at the answering machine, and sure enough the light was blinking. She already knew who it was. Vince. Vince was good in bed, but . . .

She found her black book and flipped through. Rick, Ted, Harry (who in hell was Harry?), Brad, Tony . . .

Tony. Tony was very, very good. A bar pick-up, because Belinda didn't believe in attachments. They were all one-nighters or short flings. Tony was really good. The more she thought about it, the more she remembered how much he liked giving head.

But somehow Tony didn't appeal to her just then, and she threw the phone book on the chair across the room. To hell with it. Tonight she would work; she could celebrate anytime.

He couldn't even leave a goddamn meeting to talk to his daughter . . .

2

Abe Glassman ignored his secretary, who was on his heels, striding rapidly down the thickly carpeted corridor and toward the oversized rosewood doors at its very end. His craggy, hawkish face was grim. "No calls, Rosalie," he snapped before slamming the door in her face.

Rosalie knew that that meant he did not want to be disturbed, and her job depended on it.

Abe Glassman stood six feet tall, broad-shouldered, and lean, except for a paunch. But then he was over fifty—and every man, he thought, had a right to a little slack by then. He walked behind his desk to stare through the wall of glass at the panorama of Manhattan spread at his feet. New York. His city. Where it all began.

"Fuck," he said very succinctly.

He could not believe that little prick. Who in hell did he think he was? He was nothing more than some smart-ass, baby-faced kid practically fresh out of diapers. Damn! Abe could not believe he had really turned down the money— that he had actually handed back the envelope filled with ten grand in sweet green cash. Damn! And he'd even had it in his hand. Abe cursed Will Hayward for being such a fucking idiot as to get himself into so much trouble that he, Abe

Glassman, had to try and bail him out by paying off some two-bit cop. Jesus! He'd paid off fucking senators, for crissake, and now some bratty detective was getting moral on him, in a city without morality? New York City was filled with a hundred thousand dirty cops, and it was just his luck to try and grease this one!

Would Detective Smith do something about it?

Fucking nigger, Abe thought, had better keep his trap closed, or he won't know what hit him. And that was a promise.

Abe remembered growing up in a crowded apartment with an ill father, who had suffered a massive stroke right after the Crash in '29. His father had been a shoemaker from Russia. He had done his business right out of the apartment, in the front room. Abe had spent most of his time playing hooky from school and fighting wops and niggers in the streets who'd jeered at his clothes and his heavily accented speech. It was okay. He hated them too.

He had one brother and two sisters and they had always been hungry. Hunger was something Abe had constantly lived with as a child. Even today he would always clean his plate. He could not stand for anything to be wasted.

With his father ill, there had been only a bare income from his mother's efforts as a seamstress. Abe, the eldest child, was a good thief. He had to be. He would steal fresh produce and meats from the vendors to bring home. His mother had never said a word, but she knew. And Abe knew she had silently prayed that he wouldn't get caught.

At thirteen, Abe got his first real job. The local bookie on the corner was a reed-thin giant named Eddie. Abe picked up the slips the bets were written on and delivered them to Nathan Hammerstein, farther uptown. Nathan lived in a pleasant apartment—a palace in Abe's eyes—and he wore suits and polished brown shoes and sported a fine mustache. Now, in retrospect, Abe could laugh at the airs Nathan had put on. But back then he had looked up to Nathan, vowing one day to have a suit just as fine and an even better home.

The job paid well, a few dollars a month, and it kept

food on the table for his sisters, his brother, and his mother. His father died of a second stroke in the winter of 1944.

Abe was not yet eighteen. Because of his age he had missed the draft, which was fine with him—he'd wanted nothing to interfere with his plans. Like everybody who didn't go to fight, Abe had found himself working in the factories of a newly mobilized economy. But with Abe there was a difference; he continued to pick up slips on the side. A man named Luke Bonzio offered him Nathan Hammerstein's job, but Abe had politely declined. Bookmaking was not in his future plans.

Nobody understood when Abe went to college. His two sisters were married at the ages of sixteen and fifteen, and his younger brother had taken over Abe's old job of picking up slips. His mother had looked at him and said nothing, stitching by candlelight. He had chosen a public school, made only one friend, and took his studies very seriously. His friend was Will Hayward, a clean-cut handsome boy, a distant relation of one of the oldest families of New York, the Morgans. Hayward was nothing more than a party boy, already showing signs of alcoholism, but Abe knew that he could use Hayward and his society connections, that he would be important to him.

The alcoholism and the gambling did not bother Abe. To the contrary. He filed that information away.

Abe graduated from City College of New York June 3, 1948. He was almost twenty-two. Hayward had already gotten a job with a bank, thanks to a push from one of his distant relatives. Abe had no job, but he wasn't without offers. He was approached by Luke Bonzio again.

"You got brains and determination," Bonzio had said. "We could always use somebody like you. You could go far with us."

Abe smiled. "I'm gonna go far, all right, but on my own."

Bonzio shook his head. He was angry. "Someday you're gonna need us, and you'll be sorry."

Abe made sure he didn't smile until Bonzio had turned away.

He waited two weeks before he went to the bank where Hayward worked. That was the first time he had ever laid eyes on Nancy Worth, a cousin of Will's, just as she was leaving his office. She was not only beautiful but elegant, even at eighteen—an elegance that had been fostered through many generations. Abe decided then and there that he wanted Nancy Worth, and it didn't matter that she was from the other side of town. "I need a loan," he said to Will.

Hayward looked incredulous. "With what as collateral?"

"My mother's shop," Abe said.

"How much?"

"Three thousand dollars."

Hayward started laughing. "Abe, we're good friends, but I can't give you more than a hundred or so for that!"

"Let's go have lunch," Abe said firmly.

Turning on all his personal magnetism, which was considerable, Abe offered Hayward a partnership in return for the loan. Hayward capitulated, as Abe had expected. They made up a list of fraudulent assets, which they both signed, and Abe got his three-thousand-dollar loan. He promptly put the three thousand down on the corner candy store, which was worth fifteen, buying the lease. He turned around and sold it a few months later for twenty.

The next lease he acquired was a restaurant's, and when he sold that, he made double the profit he'd hoped for. Soon he had several leases going at once, all in Brooklyn. He also had his eye on some property that he wanted to develop in Brooklyn. He knew he could make a fortune putting up an apartment building if he could only get the zoning laws changed. He had Hayward approach a couple of the city councilmen, to sound them out. Hayward told him they'd be amenable to bribes.

Abe built his first apartment buildings.

His ambitions expanded across the river to Manhattan. The economy was booming. The value of property was soaring, and Abe wanted to build offices in the heart of the city. But he would have to tear down some tenements on one of the lots, and this time he couldn't move the city council, not even with the color of his money, because there was an Historic New York movement afoot, led by a couple of fat society matrons.

Bonzio told him he could get the council to approve Abe's plans. Abe wasn't a fool. "What do you want in return?" he asked.

"Just a piece of the property," Bonzio said. "Just a small piece, six percent of the profits."

Abe regarded him with suspicion.

"And you come in on a deal with us in Florida," Bonzio went on. "We need somebody like you with a good head for real estate."

Abe didn't want to do a deal with the mob, but he was starting to get overextended—he had five loans going at once. And his ambitions were uncontrollable; he wanted very much to make another deal—this one even bigger and more lucrative than the rest. And the thought of expanding his reach into new territory was heady and exhilarating. He agreed.

Bonzio, as promised, got the council to remove their moratorium on the building in the district where the historic houses were located. Abe, as promised, went in on the deal to build a hotel in Fort Lauderdale. When it came to his attention that the wife of one of the New York City councilmen had had a serious accident and was hospitalized for six months, he frowned and shrugged the incident away as coincidence, not blackmail.

She had been the victim of a hit-and-run.

3

*N*aked, Belinda sat on the edge of the massive Victorian bed with its half canopy, thick rosewood legs, huge headboard, and antique lace spread. It had been her one major purchase, and it dominated her otherwise empty bedroom. She carefully pulled on a stocking, fastening it to a black garter. The mate followed. Belinda stood, stepping into three-inch heels, reaching for a purple leather skirt. She shimmied into it, forgoing underwear—she never wore panties when she was in this mood. The skirt clung to her strong curves like a second skin. A gold silk blouse followed, and she was braless, of course. The blouse molded to her firm, full breasts. She added a dozen gold bangles, huge gold hoops, a couple of chains, and ran her fingers through her hair, increasing its disheveled appearance. She spot-sprayed it.

She had decided to go out, after all. Cruising. Why not? The adrenaline flow had not ceased. She was feeling powerful. It was a feeling unlike any she had ever had before—a feeling of being able to accomplish almost anything. She was launched. Her career was about to take off. Like a rocket.

She wanted this second sale so badly she felt she could will it to come true. It *would* come true. She knew it. She had no doubts. Even her agent, Lester, seemed confident now that she was *in.* And once that sale had gone through, she could relax, breathe a little, feel secure . . .

Maybe even take a vacation.

She was having a delicious fantasy. An Oscar for Best Dramatic Screenplay. Belinda got goosebumps just thinking about it. She knew the odds were against it, so she tried not to dwell on it. But imagine: Two sales and a multi-million-dollar box office and an Oscar . . .

She tried to picture Abe's face. As he sat there in the audience while she received the silly little statue. Maybe just once he would tell her she was great. "Great job, kid," he might say. No, he'd say, "Belinda, I'm so proud of you." And he'd even hug her.

Jesus, she thought, frightened suddenly. I still need his approval after all these years.

The thought was so upsetting that she willed herself to the other extreme. I did it all on my own, she reminded herself. I did it without their support. That alone makes me a success, now, today.

It had taken years to get an agent, by which time she had half a dozen screenplays ready but no one to handle them. It was a catch-22. You couldn't sell without an agent, but you couldn't get an agent without having sold something first. Then she had lucked out, meeting Lester at a bar, of all places. They had talked, and he had agreed to read one of her screenplays. And that was it. She hadn't even slept with him.

She had taken the hard way. She could have gone to her father. Abe Glassman had connections with everyone who was anyone on both coasts. He was close friends with several of Hollywood's biggest moguls, including the head of Olympia, a studio that had been around since the days of Davis and Gable. Belinda knew she could have gone any one of several routes, from a direct loan from Abe to finance her own independent production of *Outrage,* to even an Olympia production. Not that her father had offered. But he would have just loved for her to come crawling to him, begging for his help. He loved wielding power—she had figured that out when she was thirteen. The worst part of it was, she had been tempted, out of sheer frustration, more than once. Thank God her pride had kept her from that.

Thank God she hadn't succumbed.

It really couldn't be a better start for her. North-Star produced quality films, and if they intended to make a first-rate star out of Jackson Ford, the odds were they would succeed. And he probably could act. Belinda didn't watch television, but getting nominated three years in a row for an

Emmy had to mean something. With him in her film, it probably would do well at the box office, even if the director and producer destroyed it.

That should have given her confidence, but it didn't. She didn't want anyone to ruin her product. She wanted a good director, good cast, good technicians . . .

The phone rang.

"Hello, Belinda," Abe Glassman said.

Belinda almost dropped the phone. "Oh, hello."

"Rosalie says you called."

She was now thoroughly regretting that moment of foolishness. He didn't care, wouldn't care. And she wasn't going to be soft; she wasn't going to allow herself to be vulnerable, not when she knew him so well. He had never forgiven her for moving to California. He had never forgiven her for not marrying according to his wishes and giving him a male heir. He thought writing screenplays was an aberration. He thought she was an aberration.

"I didn't call," she said smoothly. "Your secretary is mistaken."

There was a heavy pause. "Oh," Abe said. Then, "How are you?"

"Just fine," she said.

"Are you gonna get a chance to come east for a weekend this summer? There's someone I want you to meet."

"I'll try," she lied. Thinking, Oh, no, not again. Because, of course, the *someone* was a man and eminently marriageable. Then before she knew what was happening, she said, "I sold a screenplay." And she could have kicked herself.

There was a moment of silence. "To who?"

"North-Star."

"How much?"

"Three fifty."

"Congratulations," Abe said. "Now that you've proved you can write those damn things and sell them, why don't you come back to New York and settle down? Dammit, I'm fifty-three, Belinda."

"No, thanks," Belinda said on a deep breath.

"You've proved yourself," Abe said angrily, his tone louder now. "What more do you want? I'm gonna die one day, Belinda, and who's gonna run all this? Jesus—you're almost thirty, and if you wait much longer you're gonna have mongoloid babies!" He was shouting.

"I don't want children," Belinda grated. It was, at the very least, an untruth. "Or would you like me to go out and oblige you by getting pregnant tonight? I'm in the mood to get laid anyway."

"Christ! You know that's not what I mean," Abe said. "Why do you have to get so defensive? Every normal woman wants kids."

"Thank you," Belinda said. "But I already know you think I'm abnormal."

"That's not what I said."

"My career is taking off," Belinda said furiously. "And I'll be damned if I'm going to stop pushing now! I've sold one screenplay, and as you damn well know, that means I have an in. They're already considering another script."

Abe was silent.

Coming out on top with him was rare, but Belinda plunged ahead. "North-Star is using this as a vehicle for Jackson Ford. He's one of the hottest properties in Hollywood right now. The box office should be good, or great, depending on how much North-Star wants to put out. If *Outrage* does well at the box office, I'm hot; and I'll be selling like crazy." She sounded more confident than she felt. She had learned a lesson a long time ago: Never expose your jugular to Abe.

There was another moment of uncharacteristic silence. "You know that industry is nothing but ifs," Abe finally said. "Nobody can predict what sells at the box office. And an actor that's hot one day is in the crap heap the next. C'mon, Belinda, even you know that."

"Thank you," she said, "for the vote of confidence, and yes, even I know that."

"What?" Abe exchanged a few words with someone off

the line. Then he spoke back into the phone. "I have to go, Belinda. Will Hayward just walked in, and he says hello."

"Good-bye, Abe," Belinda said.

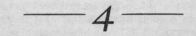

"*T*his dialogue is shit."

"Cut! Cut! Jesus Christ, Jack!"

Jackson Ford stood on the stage, golden and glowering, ignoring his costar, a typical California blonde, who was by now used to this kind of outburst. Silence was replaced by grunts, groans, and a hum of conversation as lights flicked on and cameramen stepped back from their equipment.

The assistant producer, Nickie Felton, small, rotund, with a huge nose and glasses, mopped at his bald head frantically. "Jack, Jack, what's wrong?" he cried, running over in a panic. The star was upset, and that absolutely must not be allowed.

"This dialogue is complete shit," Jack said, carefully enunciating every word.

"Don't worry," Nickie Felton said, perspiring. "We got writers, plenty of writers. You want changes—we'll make changes."

Without a word in reply, Jack spun on his heel and left the stage, disappearing presumably to his private dressing room.

"That man is impossible," breathed Edwina Lewis, a gangly assistant director. "Nothing is right, ever."

"Impossibly gorgeous," drooled another woman.

A tall, lean man strode over. "We are twenty fucking weeks behind schedule. I can't take much more of this. If Ford doesn't shape up, he's out."

"Now, calm down, John. Calm down," Nickie said

quickly. John Price was the director, so his threat was empty —he had no control over hiring and firing. "Ford is right. That particular scene is, well, poorly written."

"Quit kissing his ass. He's a fucking TV star who thinks because he's making a movie he's big-time. Well, he's not. I have about had it up to here with coddling Mr. Star."

"John, John, don't worry. We'll change a line or two, and in no time we'll have this scene done. I promise."

"No one is going to give a shit what they're talking about," Price growled. "They're either going to be looking at Ford's bare chest or Leona's tits."

"At least he doesn't ask for Dom Perignon and caviar on the set," Edwina said. Her aside was loud enough to be heard. "He could be worse."

Felton shot her a look. If Ford wanted Israeli olives, now, this minute, he'd get them, because North-Star had plans, big plans, for him. "True," Nickie said to Price. "But why don't we see if Goldman can't touch up some of that dialogue, make it a little less stiff?"

"I'm going to blackball Ford. I'm going to blackball him and throw him off this film!"

"Now, John, we've only got a week left to shoot. Come on, you don't really want to blackball Ford. He's our meal ticket. And he is good."

"Temperamental son of a bitch."

"I'll find Melody," Edwina said, hurrying off, leaving the two men in their conversation. She spotted the redhead in a corner where she was staring at Price and Felton. "Melody! Please, can you cajole Jack into doing this scene?"

Melody stood, all bosom and red hair. She glanced again, worriedly, at the assistant producer and director. She nodded and hurried off the set. She knocked sharply on Jack's door.

"Yeah?"

"It's me, Mel."

"C'mon in."

Melody walked in, and although she had been Jack's personal manager, assistant, and best friend for seven years, the sight of him at his desk—head bent over, the perfect profile, sunlight dancing on his dark golden head—took her breath away, sent shivers down her body. She closed the door behind her.

He looked up and smiled.

That Jackson Ford grin. It reached his green eyes, made them sparkle devilishly. "Come to smack my hand?"

"You're not funny, Jack. It's just a damn love scene."

"It's my love scene," he said grimly. "William is my character. I intend to protect his integrity."

Melody came over and placed a light hand on his shoulder. "I understand," she said.

"Do you?" His eyes snapped furiously. "They all think I'm a hard-ass troublemaker, but dammit, I was in this goddamn business for eleven years and no one ever gave me the fucking time of day! Now I'm hot, and I intend to stay that way. And I won't—not if the critics laugh my product right off the screen." He stood and paced angrily. "Shit!"

"I hate seeing you get this kind of rep."

"I know you do," he said, softening, squeezing her shoulder. "Anyway, I was just rewriting the scene. Give me a few minutes, and I'll be done."

She watched him slashing out lines. "Jack?"

"Yeah?"

"I know a lot is riding on this flick. But if you get a bad rep, now that the series is canceled . . . even with this contract with North-Star . . ."

He looked at her. "Thank God for that!" Sanderson Horne was a great agent. At first Jack hadn't wanted to sign an exclusive three-picture deal with North-Star. But as Sanderson had pointed out, with his series being nixed, three years as a TV star, no matter how hot—and he was hot—guaranteed him nothing, absolutely zero. "The public is like a whore, Jack," Sanderson had said. "Completely faithless. And this town is worse. You have to work, Jack, and you have to work now, or a year from now you'll be just another one-shot has-been. Get the picture?"

One-shot has-been. Another thing about Sanderson, the man was eloquent. "A bad reputation isn't half as bad as being laughed out of the industry if I can't make this dialogue sound good. Besides, I wasn't exactly an angel on the set of *L.A.P.D.* My reputation, I fear, precedes me." He flashed her a grin. But then his face set into heavy lines of worry.

Melody clasped his shoulder, rubbing it. "You're great. You're going to knock 'em dead. I know it."

"God," Jack said, looking at the script, "so much is riding on this. I've got to make this good, Mel."

"You are good, Jack," she said firmly. "And I have some good news—I just got a call from Sanderson."

Jack looked at her. "Don't keep me in suspense."

"North-Star just picked up what they think is a very hot screenplay for you, and they want to start production on it in December."

Jack let out his breath in a long exhalation. He couldn't believe it. "Already? What kind of film?"

"Similar to this. Chuck Norris with a touch of Rambo. It's action-packed, with character development. The money boys are drooling with anticipation. I heard from the grapevine they're going to increase PR for the release."

"Thank you, Sanderson," Jack said, feeling excitement grow. This shoot was almost finished. Next he had a morning talk show in New York, PR for *Berenger,* the film he was now shooting, and then a Bob Hope special in Hawaii. He was on the verge of major success, something more than being a television star for teenyboppers. He knew it. He could feel it. Not only did he think so but both Melody and Sanderson agreed. The momentum was now. He was rolling. And he wanted it so badly he was exploding with need.

"They're Fed Ex-ing it," Melody said. "Its title is *Outrage.* And you have an interview tonight with that reporter from *US.*"

"Oh, shit," Jack said. "Call Diane and tell her not to come by until ten."

Melody shook her head. "You should be in bed by ten."

Jack grinned. "I intend to be."

Melody didn't smile. "Majoriis's secretary called twice today. You haven't RSVP'd the North-Star party for Friday night."

"Ah, shit."

"Jack, you have to go."

"I know, I know. Okay, RSVP me." Just how he wanted to spend his Friday night, ass-kissing and promoting himself. But he had no choice. Not when there was his future to think of. "RSVP us," he said.

"Okay." But Melody grimaced, making no move to leave.

"What is it?"

"Well"—she took a breath—"Jack, I have some, uh, bad news too. Well, maybe not exactly bad . . ."

"Spit it out."

"There's a woman. She's been calling your office all day. Trying to reach you."

Jack grinned and shrugged. "So what? The sun rises every day too."

"Jack, she says she's your mother."

Jack felt his insides freeze up. "Really?" he said, coolly, so very coolly. "That's impossible, Mel. My mother is dead."

*O*nce she had cared.

Her first memory of her father went back to when she was six. A big, loud man, always coming and going with the air of a king. Sometimes, if she'd get up very early and peek out of her door, she would catch a glimpse of him as he strode down the hallway, clad in a black suit, on his way to work. A giant of a man passing her door with aggressive, determined strides, while she watched, wanting to make herself known, but afraid to make the first move.

Afraid of rejection. Just as she was at school.

She didn't know why it had been that way, but from the time she was very young, even in kindergarten, the other girls had always shunned her. Belinda had no use for them anyway, and she clung very hard to her scorn, for she'd been a tomboy and she would never have been caught dead playing with dolls. The boys had liked her, and she ran with them until she was ten. They would play football in the park —tackle, not touch—and Belinda was the best quarterback. They would play softball, and Belinda was the best pitcher too. The boys didn't mind. To them she wasn't a girl but just one of the guys.

When she was ten she tried out for Little League along with her friends. They all made it; she didn't. And she was the best player of all. She was furious. It was the coach who told her the rules. No girls.

Belinda had been shocked.

She had gone home and cried.

The housekeeper, a big black woman named Dorothea, had tried to comfort her. Belinda had been embarrassed to have been caught crying, and she had pushed her away. Nancy and Abe were out of town somewhere.

As soon as they came back Belinda went to her father. She had been afraid because she rarely saw him and he was bigger than life, so how was she going to ask him for help? Sometimes, when they were in the same room, he didn't even notice her. At other times he did and sent her out. Belinda minded a lot, but she always obeyed. Anything to make him love her. Because she knew he didn't.

But she had loved him.

The way a person loves God. From a distance, with devout admiration. Belinda knew he could fix it with the coach and get her on the team.

The first time she approached him had been on a weekend when he was dressing to go out with Nancy for dinner. Belinda hung in the doorway, suddenly unable to speak, wishing he would notice her. Finally he did. "Hey, kid," he said. "What are you doing?"

She gulped. "Dad, I was wondering—"

"Nancy, let's go. We're late, for crissake."

End of conversation.

She finally caught him late at night in his study. He was immersed in work. Abe noticed her when she coughed. "Belinda, what are you doing up?" There was a note of irritation in his voice.

"Dad, I have to ask you something," she had said bravely.

"You should be in bed. Does your mother know you're up?"

"No, I . . . Dad, please." Tears had filled her eyes. It was so hard to get him to listen to her. And this was so important.

"All right, what is it?"

She explained about the team, about how she was the best player, about how all her friends had made it, but the coach wouldn't even let her try out, because she was a girl. She had stumbled over the words in her anxiety. But she knew now that everything would be all right. Her father, like God, could do anything. *Anything.*

"And that's the problem?" Abe said, lifting a shaggy brow.

"Yes," she breathed.

He had laughed. "The coach is right. Baseball is for boys. Which you are not, unfortunately. It's time you stopped acting like a boy and started behaving like a girl." He began to write on a pad.

Belinda couldn't believe what she had heard. "You won't help?"

"Didn't you hear me? No, I won't help. Now, go to bed!"

She had run back to her room, trying as hard as she could not to cry, thinking, I hate him, I hate him, I hate him. But once in bed, the tears came.

Football wasn't organized, so in the fall and winter she could still play with the boys after school and on weekends. By now—for she was almost eleven—the girls thought she was a freak and made fun of her behind her back, yet openly enough that she always knew.

She had stopped playing football the day Jay Goldstein

tackled her and grabbed her budding breasts. That day she went home and cried hard, hating what was happening to her, hating Jay, hating all the boys, wishing she were a boy, hating God for making her a girl. She knew, without a doubt, if her father hadn't loved her before her body had begun to change into a woman's he wouldn't love her at all now.

That was the year she had gotten Lady for her birthday. It was her dream come true, and when she saw the beautiful bay mare at the stable and Nancy told her she was hers, Belinda forgave her father and loved him with all her heart. She hugged her mother, a rare display of affection. Her father was out of town, but the day he got back she waited up for him, past her bedtime, to tell him how thankful and happy she was.

He had gazed at her blankly. "You what? You got a horse for your birthday?"

She stared. Her face fell. No, this wasn't happening, it was a bad dream . . .

"Your mother got you a horse for your birthday," he said, clearly surprised. Then he smiled. "Well, maybe it's not such a bad idea."

She didn't cry, not in front of him, not until she was in her room, her haven. Then she sobbed until she couldn't breathe. He hadn't known. He didn't care. He didn't care at all.

From then on she had stayed away from him as much as he did from her. That took no effort at all on her part because she rarely saw him. Worse, he didn't even notice she was avoiding him. Then when she was thirteen he took her summer away from her. She had no friends in the city. The girls openly hated her. The boys wanted only to stick their hands up her skirt. Summer was everything. She had Lady, and her best friend, Dana, who was also a tomboy and her first girlfriend. And she had the ocean and her books. She lived for summertime in the Hamptons. And now *he* wanted her to go to camp instead for two months. No way. Never.

She went.

But not without fighting him with every ounce of

strength she possessed. "I'm not going," she had shouted, crying.

"You're going!" Abe roared. "Just who do you think you are, Miss Princess? Spoiled. Your mother's spoiled you rotten. You're going."

"Mom!" Belinda pleaded desperately.

"Abe!" Nancy, pale, did try.

"Shut up!"

"I hate you," Belinda sobbed hysterically. "I hate you. I'll run away. I'll—"

"You hate me?" Abe had asked, suddenly quiet.

"Yes!" Belinda shouted defiantly. "I've always hated you!"

The slap right across the face took her by surprise, the sound cracking like a whip in the sudden lull of silence. Before Belinda could even comprehend that he had hit her, before she could recover, before the throbbing began, Abe had said, "You hate me? I gave you that damn horse. I give you those damn books you read. Those jeans and that shirt —who do you think puts the clothes on your back? This house—you think other kids get a room like this all to themselves? And the toys—those horse models you've got to play with? Huh? You hate me?"

"I hate you," she said, clenching her jaw, turning red.

His mouth worked. He balled up his fists. "You're going! If I gotta tie you and throw you on that bus myself, you're going! Do I make myself clear?"

Belinda said, "Very," her voice barely audible. Then she turned and ran. She heard Abe saying to Nancy, "Don't you dare go after her." And Nancy hadn't.

Camp was a nightmare. As usual, all the girls shunned her. A friendly counselor tried to tell her it was because she was so beautiful, and they were jealous. Belinda had never heard such a crazy thing, but she took a long look in the mirror, searching to see if what the counselor had said was true. She was also the most popular girl at the first coed dance, held at the end of the second week, and that further increased her wonder. An older boy took her into the bushes, somehow evading the counselors (who were college kids too busy making it with one another to really care) and kissed her, her first kiss, his hands beneath her shirt and on her breasts. She was utterly confused. She didn't want boys to look at her that way. But it was pleasant—more than pleasant.

She didn't go to the second dance at the end of the month. That was the night she ran away from camp, hitching a ride to town and catching a bus back to New York. She had despised camp, and there was no point in staying. She wasn't going to let her father make a decision for her that was so important to her and meant nothing to him.

She would never forget the next day. Hearing those strange noises from her mother's bedroom as she approached to defensively tell her she was home—to stay. The door had been shut, not locked. Belinda knocked, but there was no answer. She walked in.

Her mother had been on her back on the bed, crossways. Her shirt was open, breasts exposed. Her skirt was shoved up around her waist. A man was on top of her, pushing his hips at her rhythmically, braced on his forearms above her. Her mother was making strange noises, and there was a steady slapping sound of flesh hitting flesh. Belinda must have gasped.

The man looked up, and their eyes met.

Belinda had run.

6

*E*meralds went so well with red.

Abe would certainly prefer the emeralds.

Yes, she would wear the emeralds with the red Oscar de la Renta. Satisfied with her decision, Nancy Glassman paused in front of a full-length mirror in the master suite of her Trump Tower penthouse apartment to study her reflection. Everyone told her she was a stunning woman, that she looked ten years younger than her forty-eight years. When Nancy looked at her reflection, she saw the beginnings of faint wrinkles around her eyes and on her forehead instead of the perfectly sculpted oval face framed by shoulder-length dark blond hair. For the hundredth time, she wondered if it was time to have her eyes done.

"Mrs. Glassman," a uniformed maid said, standing in the doorway. "Phone call, ma'am."

It was Belinda.

"Oh, hello, darling. This is a surprise." As always, her pulse started to race. Her brow gathered dampness. She felt warm. She put one hand over the mouth of the receiver. "Ingrid, would you get me a glass of wine, please, and turn up the air conditioner." The maid left. "What were you saying, dear? I missed that."

"I have some really good news," Belinda said.

It was nearly impossible to hear her daughter. There was loud, raucous background music at Belinda's end. Unmistakably, she was calling from a bar. And Nancy felt a sinking feeling—after all, her daughter never called.

"I sold a screenplay. In fact, I just put my John Hancock on the dotted line this morning."

"How wonderful," Nancy said, her tone gushing too much, she knew, but she couldn't help it. She never could, not with Belinda. "How very, very wonderful, dear." Frantically she tried to think of something else to say.

There was a pause. "Lester sold it for three hundred and fifty grand, Mom."

Money was one thing Nancy understood very well, and this gave her and her daughter a common ground on which to meet. She seized the opening. "Oh, my! So much for a movie?"

"It's the going rate, pretty much," Belinda said. "The news gets even bet—"

"Thank you, Ingrid. What, dear?"

"The news gets even better . . ."

Ingrid was pointing at her watch. "You have to get dressed for the party, Mrs. Glassman."

Nancy nodded, feeling guilty relief. She tuned in once more to her daughter, who was now saying something about production. "That's very nice, dear." She sipped her wine, not really understanding what Belinda was talking about— but why should she? When she didn't understand her daughter at all. Maybe the diamonds would go better with the taffeta. Everyone was wearing emeralds this season.

"And Jackson Ford is going to star in it, Mom. He's one of the hottest properties right now."

Her heart actually skipped a beat. Then it began pounding very hard, so hard that Nancy could feel the reverberations throughout her entire body. She didn't know how she managed to speak at all, much less in a normal tone. "That's very nice, Belinda."

"I called Abe." It was a flat statement.

Now Nancy was truly perspiring. Jackson Ford. With supreme effort, she thrust him from her foremost thoughts. She could just imagine what the conversation between her daughter and her husband had been like—and she couldn't handle it, not now. She took a long sip of wine. "Dear, I'm running late. I have to get dressed for a charity cocktail party that your father and I are going to."

"Right," Belinda said. "But just for the record, do you know he couldn't say one fucking nice thing to me?"

"He's very proud of you," Nancy managed.

"Right. Look, Mom, forget it, I shouldn't have said anything. It's not fair for me to put you between us. Go to your party and have a good time."

"Call me tomorrow," Nancy told her, sweat gathering between her breasts. "Belinda, I am proud of you. I—"

"Yeah." The phone went dead.

Nancy hung up and wiped the dampness from her brow. She noticed her hand was trembling slightly. She was having a distinctly bad feeling, like an aftertaste, but this time it wasn't because her daughter made her anxious or because constant the battle of wills between her daughter and husband made her even more anxious. She took another sip of wine in an attempt to calm down.

She didn't understand her daughter. Her daughter was twenty-eight, incredibly beautiful, with a figure to match—and unmarried. With no interest in the institution, and no interest in children. She spent her days writing her screenplays and running, cycling, and swimming. What kind of life was that? She should never have moved to California. It was such a waste. With her background and the wealth that would one day be hers, she could make a truly good marriage. She could have her choice of rich men, sons of Abe's friends. What was wrong with Belinda?

It was terrible, but she didn't know her own daughter. No one did. She was so independent, such a loner, and to Nancy it seemed that she led a very lonely life. Yet it didn't seem to bother her. If she had any friends, Nancy had never met them and Belinda didn't talk about them. Even as a child she had been reclusive, self-sufficient, and introverted.

Nancy didn't even know if there were men in her daughter's life now, boyfriends. She didn't really want to know. Not until one of them became her fiancé. Then Nancy would be overjoyed and so would Abe, who wanted nothing more than a grandson—and soon.

It was hard to believe that Abe had let her move away. But Belinda was one of the few people Abe had never been able to control. Not outwardly anyway. When Abe and Belinda clashed, it was head-on, like two battering rams. At least since Belinda had moved west, things seemed to have calmed down. Abe, surprisingly, didn't seem to worry. He had said, "She'll be back. Odds are a million to one she'll make it as a screenwriter. She'll be back."

As if he wanted her to fail.

Nancy didn't want Belinda to fail, but she would have loved her to move back to New York. As the saying went, it was never too late; she had a desperate need to get to know her daughter. But every time she was around her she was so afraid Belinda would reject her that she couldn't think straight. She couldn't seem to say the right things and always had the feeling that Belinda looked down on her.

Once, a long time ago, Belinda had been very, very angry with her—as only a young child whose illusions are shattered can be. Nancy hoped that incident was too far in the past to affect their relationship now—but if she dared to think about it, things really had never been the same since.

Which made her think about *him*.

She absolutely would not think about Jack Ford and everything that went along with him.

He had ruined her life.

Nancy was not a vindictive woman, but if Jackson Ford were dead, it would be completely just.

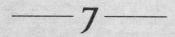

7

*A*be glared at his wife when she opened the door to his library, a vision in red taffeta and glittering emeralds that he was oblivious to.

"Abe?"

He slammed down the phone. "What is it, Nancy? Dammit, I'm trying to get through on an important call!"

"I'm sorry. I just wanted to tell you I'm ready," she murmured, backing out and closing the door behind her.

Abe picked up the receiver again. Where the fuck was Majoriis? He had been trying to reach him all day—ever since he had spoken with his daughter on the phone. He was furious, coldly and ruthlessly furious.

But it wasn't too late.

It was never too late.

There was no way that *Outrage* deal would reach culmination. One way or another he'd stop it.

It was hard to get a handle on which disturbed him more, which disaster was the priority to prevent. Did that fucking son of a bitch Ford think he had forgotten him? If that little prick thought he was going to get the better of him, he had another fucking think coming. "Pick up, damn you!" Abe shouted into the ringing phone.

And if Belinda thought she was about to become some Hollywood dingbat writer, she had another think coming, too.

He hadn't spent his entire lifetime building up Glassman Enterprises into the billion-dollar empire it was, just for Uncle Sam to take it all when he died—nor did he intend to give it away to charities. Damn Belinda anyway, for being the most stubborn broad he'd ever encountered. But there was one thing Abe truly relished, and that was a good fight.

Ford would be easy.

Belinda was another story.

But she was his daughter, right? If he'd ever had any doubts—and seventeen years ago, learning the truth about his wife had given him more than a few of those—they'd long since been laid to rest. She was his daughter, all right. There was no mistaking that. She obviously intended to defy him, out of sheer perversity, until the day he died. Abe knew that was why she was living in that shack in California, trying to make it as a writer, *under a different name.* Just to shove it to him. But—and Abe had to smile—little did she know she was already on the path he had chosen for her. He was going to get his grandson yet.

He toyed with the invitation on his desk in front of him. He'd been to hundreds, no, thousands, of parties. Rosalie had already RSVPed his regrets. Abe smiled. Tomorrow she would call and change that. He was going. Not only was he going to go to this North-Star affair, he was going to bring his wife.

He dialed again.

"Hello?"

"Ted?"

"Yeah."

"This is Abe."

"Abe! This is a surprise. Wait—what's wrong?" A note of anxiety had entered the North-Star executive's voice.

"I just heard North-Star picked up a new screenplay for Ford."

"Yeah."

"Fuck the deal, Ted."

"What?"

"You heard me. Fuck that deal. I don't want Ford doing *Outrage*. Not today, not tomorrow, not ever."

"Abe, the contract's been signed."

"Has there been any financial transaction?"

"The check was handed over at the signing, with a partial holdback, conditional upon revisions."

"Shit," Abe said, but there were other ways to accomplish what he wanted, so he changed focus. "Just when the hell did Ford sign with North-Star?"

"Six months ago, Abe. What the hell is this about?"

"Shit," Abe said. "It's none of your fucking business. Let's just say Ford is on my shit list and has been for fifteen years. I can't believe that little prick signed with North-Star."

How come I didn't know about this, he wondered. It was incredible, unbelievable. Abe didn't watch TV, except for an occasional *60 Minutes* or *Nightline*, or go to the movies. Nor did he shop in supermarkets or K marts where the popular rags abounded. He read only *Time* and *The Economist* and *The Wall Street Journal*. He doubted that a *TV Guide* had ever been in his home. He didn't even know if Nancy read that trash. If he had been a TV watcher or had had to do his own shopping, he would have known that that little, no-good, low-life Ford had actually become a big TV star. Unfuckingbelievable.

And now he was about to become big-time with this North-Star contract.

No fucking way.

"Abe, let me get this straight. You don't want Ford doing *Outrage* or you don't want North-Star producing *Outrage* or you don't want Ford with North-Star?"

"All of the above."

"It's too late, Abe."

"What're the terms of Ford's contract?"

"Shit, I don't know, but I can find out."

"Find out. Fax me a copy of his contract immediately."

There was a moment of silence. "Jesus, what are you trying to do, ruin the guy?"

Abe laughed. "Very good, Ted. Just get me copies of both contracts, for the product and Ford. And keep this under your hat."

"Jesus, Abe, it's too bad you got something against Ford. He's really hot right now. He's in North-Star's best interests."

"You owe me," Abe said bluntly. "Just do it. And Ted, he *was* hot. *Was.*"

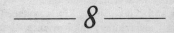

8

"So you're the reporter from *US.*"

"And you're Jackson Ford," she said, smiling, holding out her hand.

Jack took it, delighted and surprised all at once. Linda Myer was a lithe brunette with blue, blue eyes behind square tortoise-shell glasses, an undeniably attractive woman, somewhere in her thirties. "Jack. Welcome." He gestured her past him.

"All the comforts of home," Linda said, glancing around his oversized dressing room.

"Can I get you a drink? Something to eat?"

"I thought you didn't drink," she said quickly. It was a big deal. Jackson Ford was a self-confessed alcoholic and drug addict who'd gone clean seven years ago.

"I don't. But it doesn't bother me if someone in my company does." His green eyes were friendly and admiring. She wore a simple black knit dress, sleeveless, and it clung to

her slender frame provocatively. He liked his women thin.
And tall. Like Linda.

"White wine would be fine."

Jack handed her a glass and led her into a mock living
area. He sat next to her on a plush suede couch. "I never
expected a reporter like you," he said flirtatiously. "I
wouldn't have felt so bad about canceling my date."

Linda knew he was a charmer; that was his reputation.
But she felt thrilled anyway. She was much too old for him
—according to his standards. His women were all eighteen,
or thereabouts. Still, she could feel his interest in her, and it
excited her. She wondered if he was as good in bed as he
looked. "Do you mind if we jump right in?" she said, then
blushed. But he couldn't possibly know what she'd been
thinking.

"Not at all." Jack grinned. He did.

Fumbling and still blushing, Linda switched on a small
recorder. "Jack," she said, firming her voice, "I know you've
been through your life story a million times, but—"

"Two million," he corrected, smiling, his teeth very
white against his bronzed skin.

"Okay. I stand corrected. Two million. But I'd love it
in your own words."

"Okay. Where shall we start?" He noted that she sat
with her legs crossed. They were long and graceful.

Why was he always horny?

"From the beginning," she said. "You were born in
Kansas City."

"That's right. Thirty-seven years ago."

"And your father—"

"My father was an auto mechanic and a drunk who left
us when I was six. My mom was thrilled. She was a waitress.
We lived in the worst side of town. A real *slum*. I played
hooky and stole things and she worked. And never came
home. Or came home with men. Lots of men. Men who left
money on her bedside table. It was always, Not now, Jack.
Can't you see I've got company? Go to bed, Jack. Jack, go
outside and play. Jack! I said go outside and play!"

"Tough life," Linda murmured sympathetically. "Your mother left you too."

"Yep. Just upped and disappeared when I was eleven." No-good cunt whore. He would never, ever forget that day. Even now, just thinking about it made his guts cramp painfully. Coming home to an empty house. Immediately he had known. Hadn't he known all along that one day she would leave him, too, the way his father had? Stunned—both believing it and desperately trying not to believe it, to will the clock backwards—he had stumbled into the kitchen and found half a pint of whiskey that he had finished before passing out. He had never cried. Not over her. And he never would.

Whoever had called him today was not his mother. His mother was dead.

"Go on," Linda said gently.

Jack smiled. He was an actor, after all. "I took off. Hitched my way to St. Louis. Lived off the streets. About a year later I was picked up for hot-wiring an automobile. This big-ass cherry-red Thunderbird." He grinned. "Cops found out I had no family. Shoved me into detention. Best thing that ever happened to me."

"Detention?"

"No. The foster home I got placed in afterward. A real kind old couple whose kids were grown and married and living in New York. They gave me love, or tried to. I was pretty tough, pretty incorrigible, but after that damn detention center, well, I was no fool. I knew I was a lot better off with them. I kept my antics down to running with a gang and getting drunk, getting laid."

"And then you discovered acting."

"Yeah." Jack smiled, running his fingers through his thick hair. "Rather, I discovered the high-school drama teacher. God, she was beautiful!" Tall, beautiful Delia Corice.

"And?"

"I fell madly in love with her. I took all her classes. I wanted her to notice me, so I tried damn hard to be good. First time in my life I ever had any ambition to succeed."

"Go on."

"I was a natural. I mean, don't get me wrong, I was damn awful. But I had natural talent, and Miss Corice took me under her wing, really worked with me. I guess I was a pretty fast study." His lightning grin appeared.

A very fast study.

He would never forget the first time she had made love to him. He had shown up on her doorstep to be "tutored." Well, he had been tutored, all right. It wasn't the first time for him—he had lost his virginity at twelve—but it was the first time he had ever eaten pussy. He loved it. So had she.

"And after high school?" Linda said, interrupting his thoughts. She frowned, looking at her own notes. "According to my research, you spent six years in New York doing repertory theater, then came to L.A. in seventy-seven."

Jack smiled easily, but his stomach tensed at the false bio he had constructed years before. "Right." He confirmed the lie. "I did rep in New York, and when I came out here I did commercials for a couple of years. Then, presto. They cast me in the role of a hard-nosed detective in my own series, and I believe you know the rest of the story." He smiled. What the hell. No one wanted to hear the truth. He didn't want to hear it.

"There's such a big gap in your life from the time you went to New York to when you got the part of the series detective," Linda insisted. "What really happened?"

Jack never stopped smiling as he leaned back casually on the sofa. What really happened? Unconsciously, his fingers went to the slight bump on his nose, the only external scar he carried. He rubbed it. He would never forget the pain of those brass knuckles.

And he would never forget that day. A sunny, cloudless day that had hit 102 degrees in midtown, a real scorcher. Thursday. July 31, 1971. Jack would carry the memory of that day and a chilling hatred in his heart for Abe Glassman until the day he died.

The reporter for *US* was looking at him curiously. He never had given a satisfactory answer to her question. "I struggled," he said lightly. "Just like a thousand other actors and actresses." He shrugged. "It's a boring story."

"I doubt anything about you is boring," Linda said, pushing her glasses back on her nose. "How does it feel to be considered one of the sexiest men in the industry?"

Jack's grin widened. "I didn't ask for it."

"Do you think you're sexy?"

"Do you?" he shot back, still smiling.

"How come you're always smiling?" Linda asked, smiling herself.

"Life's funny." He started to chuckle. "Listen, sweetheart, if you'd been where I've been, you'd be grinning too."

"I guess so. How does it feel to be doing a movie? Inside gossip says North-Star's already lined up another film for you. *Outrage*?"

"It feels good," Jack said. "I admit it."

"During those lean years did you think you'd ever get there? Here, I mean?"

"To tell you the truth, baby, I sometimes wondered." More than wondered, he thought, grimacing unconsciously. He leaned closer, until his face was inches from hers. "Look, I'm bored with this interview."

She blinked. "Uh—just a few more questions?"

"Later. Right now I'm more interested in you."

"What do you want to know?" She flushed.

His voice lowered to a hoarse whisper. "I want to know how you look with those clothes off, how those beautiful long legs feel wrapped around me. I want to know how you taste."

Linda's mouth dropped open, and she stared.

Jack put his hand on her hair and pulled her close, removing her glasses. His lips came down on hers. "You are so hot," he whispered, one hand roaming down her body, pausing over her small, jutting breasts. "Hot, sexy."

As he kissed her his hand descended until it was between her legs. Ignoring her dress, he palmed her. She whimpered. With one hand he unzipped his pants and pulled

his swollen cock out, taking her hand and firmly implanting
himself in her grip. "That's it, baby, that's it."

"Oh my!" she gasped.

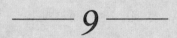

*T*he water was steaming hot.

Melody lay back in the tub, closing her eyes. It felt so
good to unwind, to sink deeper and deeper into the hot,
soothing water, to release all the tension and pent-up energy
of the day. And, God, what a day. She thought she had
placated Price. The man probably wouldn't blackball Jack.
But he probably would badmouth him all over Hollywood.
Jesus. One thing was sure. Price would never direct another
Jackson Ford film.

Jack.

Even with her eyes closed, she saw him in perfect detail.
Thick, brownish hair, wildly shot with gold. Green eyes,
long-lashed, crinkled at the corners from too much smiling.
High cheekbones in a classic face. That killer grin. She
sighed as her insides melted and an old, familiar ache ran
down her body.

Jack filled her days. He was her business.

Jack filled her nights. He was her lover.

In her dreams.

Melody sighed again. She wondered how the *US* interview was going. She hoped Jack was behaving himself. She
didn't feel like facing another day playing cajoler and um-
pire with an irate reporter. One who could do far more damage in far less time than Price. Please, Jack, please, just be-
have.

Fortunately the reporter was a woman. Even if she was

fat and fifty, Jack would be charming—unless she pushed him too hard the wrong way.

Melody stepped out of the tub. She tried not to look at her body. That was easy because she didn't have her round glasses on. She was short, with small shoulders and small hips and huge breasts. Men loved her breasts. They also loved her ass. Compared to the smallness of the rest of her, it was definitely oversized. She considered herself fat.

She also disliked her face. It was plain. Worse. Square. If someone was unkind, they might call her horse-faced. Her eyes were very blue, almost purple, but small, wide-set, and she hid them behind her glasses, which made her face seem less square. A serious, no-nonsense face. One that did not go with her body. Only her incredibly thick red hair went with her body. And on top of everything else she had freckles. Not a lot. But enough. Everywhere.

Jack had never made a pass at her in all the years she had known him. She knew he never would.

In the beginning it was because she wasn't his type. Diane was his type. A nineteen-year-old model with a nothing figure. No breasts, no ass, no thighs—nothing. Tall, coltish. A perfect, breathtaking face. Lots and lots of brown hair, so dark it was almost black. Blue eyes, black lashes. One of a million coltish brunettes that Jack took to bed.

Melody slipped into a T-shirt that came to her knees. She smirked unkindly because Diane had been furious that Jack couldn't see her until later, and she had broken the date instead. Too bad. She was due to be dropped soon, anyway. Most of Jack's women lasted a night. Some lasted a week or two. Usually on a shoot or on location, like now. Melody knew it was convenient. She knew Jack was one of the horniest men alive.

But she understood him. She knew—instinctively at first, and now with the insight of years of friendship—why Jack preferred children and bimbos. He was afraid. Afraid to care about a woman, afraid to love. It was actually very sad. It was because of his mother. Melody knew he made light of her desertion, but she could read past that. She knew that somewhere deep inside he had never gotten over it. He would probably never love any woman.

Was the woman who had been calling actually Jack's mother?

If so, Melody was determined to do something about it. Jack's past still lived with him. It had scarred him. She knew she was making judgments she wasn't qualified to make; after all, she wasn't a psychologist. But she didn't care. She loved Jack.

She had loved him from the first moment she had ever laid eyes on him.

She would never forget it. She had just moved into a run-down studio in West Hollywood and was working in the publicity department of a small firm. She had been living in her apartment for a week and had assumed she had only four neighbors. The fifth apartment on her floor appeared to be vacant. It was Saturday, around noon. She was coming up the stairs with two bags of groceries, and so was he.

He was red-eyed, staggering slightly, unshaven, and smelled distinctly of beer and sex. He was beautiful. His smile was instinctive—and sensual. As she put down her bags she watched him fumble with his keys, cursing mildly, swaying against the wall. Her next-door neighbor was a drunk—but the handsomest drunk she had ever seen.

A week later she had run into him again and introduced herself. This time he wasn't so far gone—maybe slightly high but impeccably dressed, shaved, and cologned. They had wound up chatting. He was, of course, an actor. Their friendship grew in small stages from there, despite the constant trooping of women in and out of Jack's apartment. Sometimes they would share a beer or a joint, if they ran into each other after work.

The night Jack was thrown in jail, it was Melody he had called.

And it was Melody as much as AA who had helped him through withdrawal.

When he had straightened out and she began to realize his potential, it had been her idea to manage Jack on her off-work hours. She had been with him from practically the beginning, and she would be there until the end.

Melody climbed into bed. It was the best time of the night. Once she was under the sheets, she pulled off her T-shirt, letting it drop on the floor. She fondled her breasts and thought about Jack. She closed her eyes, her fingers teasing her nipples into erectness, imagining Jack's mouth on them, sucking and tugging. In her fantasy he was crazy with desire for her, telling her how beautiful she was, how much he wanted her, how he loved her. She slid her hand between her thighs. She could almost feel Jack's mouth, his tongue. She moaned his name when she finally found release.

As she lay waiting to fall asleep she thought about what she really wanted, what she was really hoping for. Certainly not a reconciliation between Jack and his mother. But Jack had to face her and the past in order to leave it behind.

And then what?

Maybe he'd stop fooling around with eighteen-year-old bimbos and find a mature woman he could love and trust.

Like her.

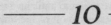

10

*S*he hadn't returned his calls.

Vince Spazzio padlocked the gate on the construction site and sauntered over to his truck. He threw his shirt on over his broad, gleaming chest, heavily slabbed with a dozen year's accumulation of muscle. He climbed in the cab, lit a cigarette, and checked his mirror, pulling out.

Belinda hadn't called. A vast disappointment filled him.

She only called him at work, of course, because of Mary. Maybe she would call tomorrow. He hadn't seen her in four days. He could barely stand it.

He was almost tempted to drive over to her place, but he knew better. She'd have a fit if he appeared uninvited.

He wondered what Mary would have for dinner. He was starved. He was always ravenous after a hard day's work. Belinda. God, he loved eating her. She was beautiful. More than beautiful. He loved and hated her at the same time. He wondered what she was doing tonight.

Didn't she want to see him?

Traffic was usually a steady five miles per hour on the San Diego Freeway when Vince commuted, but not tonight. He had worked until dark, fiercely. It was not so much to avoid going home to Mary as it was to take his mind off Belinda. But that was impossible. He turned on the radio. Maybe she'd met someone else. That thought filled him with panic.

He pictured Belinda naked and wet with sweat on a bed amid rumpled sheets, awaiting some faceless lover. Her own face was glazed with lust. Her breasts, full but high, had hard, erect nipples. Her legs, strong, powerful, curved, were spread and waiting. The flesh between her thighs was pink and swollen and slick.

Vince hit the brakes hard and managed to avoid bumping the car in front of him as the traffic slowed. He was going to have an accident. Every day, five days a week, he drove home and thought about Belinda until he had a hard-on, until he was miserable, because most of the time he couldn't have her. He turned up the station. How long could he go on like this?

He parked in the driveway of his two-bedroom house in Costa Mesa, next to Mary's Volkswagen Beetle. The lawn would need cutting this weekend, he thought. The petunias he had planted were wilting from lack of water. Cursing, he went to the hose, turned it on, and dragged it over to water them. You would think she could at least water the goddamn petunias. He strode into the house.

Mary sat at the kitchen table with another woman, her friend Beth. There was a half gallon of wine between them, almost empty. There was also a sliver of mirror, a vial of coke, mostly empty, as well as a razor and straw. The two women had been talking animatedly, laughter punctuating their conversation, and now they stopped completely.

"Hi, Vince." Mary smiled. She was drunk. She had long, straight dark hair, a roundish face with nice features, big brown eyes. She wore a tank top and jeans. She was about fifteen pounds overweight.

"Mary." He nodded at Beth, who was tall, plain, and slender. He curbed his annoyance at the fact that Mary was high again. "I'm going to take a shower." He paused before leaving. "What's for dinner?"

Mary looked guilty. "I was hoping we could grab a bite somewhere, just a burger."

Vince felt anger rising in him, and it burst forth. "Dammit! I'm fucking starved! I work my tail off all day while you're sitting around on your ass getting fucked up! I'm tired—and hungry."

"Fuck you, Vince," Mary said coolly. She pulled the mirror over and dumped some of the vial's contents out. She started to cut lines.

Vince strode over. "Do you know the fucking flowers out there are dying? Do you even care? And just where the hell did you get the money for that?"

"It's Beth's," Mary said, and Vince wondered if she was lying. Ignoring him, she evened out four lines.

"I can't deal with this," Vince exploded, grabbing her arm and pulling her to her feet. "Look at you! You're a fucking mess! Look at this fucking house! It's a fucking pigsty! I spend a hundred and fifty thousand fucking dollars on a house for my wife, and she treats it like a slum."

"Let go," Mary cried, her voice breaking and tears welling in her wide brown eyes.

"Oh, shit," Vince said, releasing her. He strode into the bathroom. As he turned on the shower he heard Beth say something, then heard Mary's trembling reply. Maybe he had come down too hard on her, but Christ, this was out of hand. How the fuck could he get her to get a job? In the beginning he hadn't wanted her to work. Stupid. Italian macho shit. Now he would give anything if he could just get her out of the house, get her to do something worthwhile.

There had been a time when he had thought she was beautiful. He probably would never forget the day he had first seen her. He'd been building an addition onto a Bel Air mansion that belonged to Mary's stepfather (number two). He had a crew that existed of two. They were still in the framing stages. The wing jutted out from the rest of the house and was only a hop and a skip away from a free-form pool. Mrs. Crandall—Mary's mother—was lying out, as usual, a completely straight woman in an almost nonexistent bikini, nut-brown all over. Even her hair was nut-brown. The first time she had come out Vince and his guys had looked, of course, being normal men. There was nothing to look at though (unless you liked very thin women built like boys), except for her face—which was triangular, nut-brown, and attractive. Still, no tits, no ass—nothing. Vince had quickly redirected his crew's attention to the window they were framing.

"Holy shit, look at that," Fred had said one afternoon.

Vince looked and got an instant hard-on. Mrs. Crandall was in her usual position, which was no big deal—she never came on to them or anything, not like some of the Hollywood wives who loved fucking carpenters. She looked down her perfect, possibly fixed nose at the *help*. But a young girl with long, straight hair, a perfectly grabbable ass, and huge knockers was making her way toward Mrs. Crandall. She was wearing a skimpy halter top and short shorts. Her legs were not bad, a little plump, shapely, really, but who could get past the tits? Vince couldn't. He wanted to look away, but he just couldn't.

"Hi, Mom," the girl had said.

Her name was Mary. She was Mrs. Crandall's daughter. She was in her early twenties and every guy's wet dream. Especially his.

Vince had grown up poor in southern California when everyone seemed to be rich. Or at least richer than he was. He was raised in a slum neighborhood in L.A. He had two sisters; his mother was a waitress; his father had died (or so Mom said) before he was born. He had grown up with rats, yellow water, and peeling paint, just blocks away from movie stars dripping diamonds in silver limos.

After high school it had gotten worse. He took up carpentry and soon was working on their homes. He had his first piece of rich tail when he was nineteen. He was working for a general contractor, who had sent him over to a Beverly Hills house to do some fix-it work. He had to put up towel holders in a bathroom (at thirty dollars an hour). The woman of the house was the wife of a hot screenwriter. She hovered over him clad in a short tennis dress. He was sweating and hard and embarrassed as hell, afraid to stand up, afraid she'd see and he'd lose his job. It was a damn good job. Not only did it pay well—he loved carpentry. But before he had even turned around, trying desperately to will his erection away, she grabbed him—and that was that.

He'd screwed at least a dozen rich broads by the time he met Mary. Mary was different. She was young. Beautiful. Not forty and jaded and bored and looking for a young stud as a kick. She had noticed him that day she was talking to her mother out at the pool. (What woman wouldn't have? He was aware of how good he looked; plenty of women had let him know.) Two days later he had asked her out.

Six months later they were married.

When Vince reappeared in the kitchen, Mary and Beth were in the same position, still drinking and snorting. He gave them both a look of disgust and jumped into his truck. He drove to McDonald's and had two Big Macs and a shake for dinner. Then he cruised around, thinking of Belinda, wishing he were buried deep inside her, pounding away. God, he was so horny.

To his relief Beth was gone when he got home, and Mary was in bed asleep. Or passed out. He sat down on the side of the bed, pulling off his sneakers. From behind, Mary wrapped her arms around him. "I'm sorry, Vince. Please don't be mad."

He could feel her cheek and hair against his bare back.

"Vince? Today just happened. I was so bored and Beth stopped by with the blow and time just got away from me. Please don't be angry." She kissed his shoulder.

He could feel her large breasts against his back, with their pebbly nipples. He imagined Belinda clinging to him like that, rubbing herself erotically against him. He grew hard.

"Vince?" She said his name softly in his ear.

Vince turned around, taking her in his arms. He kissed her, one hand groping along her soft flesh, thumbing already erect nipples. One thing about Mary. Drugs and alcohol seemed to make her hornier. He could never figure it out. He was the opposite.

She moaned and held his head as he took one nipple in his mouth and sucked it. Then he stood, unsnapping his jeans and stepping out of them, kicking them onto the floor. He lowered himself on top of her, rubbing his blue-veined, throbbing prick against her pussy. She wrapped her arms around him and kissed him, her mouth demanding and fierce. Vince closed his eyes.

He imagined Belinda in his arms, so eager and excited. The jolt his thoughts gave him almost made him come right then and there. Belinda. He was careful to keep his eyes closed, determined to hang onto his fantasy. He slid into her. Belinda. He was in her, stroking, in and out, the sensation pure heaven. Gorgeous, gorgeous Belinda. He came.

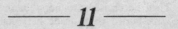

11

Mary rolled over, awareness coming as sleep left. She stretched. Sunlight was forcing its way through the closed curtains, and she reached up to lift an edge and peer out. A gorgeous, brilliant day. A glance at the alarm clock told her it was close to noon. Perfect. Her favorite soap came on at one. She stretched again.

As her senses became fully alert a throbbing heat began

to rise in her loins. She pressed her thighs together, wishing Vince were home. She thought about last night. One thing about Vince—he had a high sex drive, which was fortunate, because she did too. And he was still hot for her after two years of marriage. He had an incredible body.

Her desire increased. Last night had been fun. Booze and coke always made her crazy for sex. The funny thing was, she could never get off. Not that Vince knew. She wished she could tell him, so he could take more time with her and bring her to an orgasm. She just couldn't climax in sex. Even straight. It was always so close, but forever elusive. She'd been faking it ever since she had started screwing around when she was sixteen.

She thought about one of the carpenters on Vince's job, a new guy. Thinking about him made her ache unbearably. She was sure that if Vince were here now, she would come. She slid her hands between her legs and stroked herself, imagining the carpenter standing over her, naked, watching. She climaxed in a couple of minutes.

She got up and padded naked into the bathroom. God, Vince was right—the house was a total pigsty. Maybe she should pick up some coke and get inspired to clean it. She turned on the shower. The scale on the bathroom floor stared up at her. She debated weighing herself. She was positive she had gained two pounds this week. She knew if she got on the scale and saw it there, in bold numbers, she'd get depressed. I won't eat today, she thought. The weekend was coming up and if she dieted hard for a couple of days, she could knock off the two pounds.

The problem was, she'd put them back on during the weekend.

Her mother had called yesterday. She wanted to see her this afternoon. Mary was definitely not going. The first words out of her mother's mouth would be a comment on her weight and advice about diet. Her mother was thin. Maybe anorexic. She lived in Beverly Hills, not on the flats, and she was on her third divorce and working on her fourth marriage. She was a fanatic about health, exercise, diet, clothes, and her looks. Her current husband was only five years older than Mary, some nothing actor. Her last husband had been a hotshot director and closer to her mother's age (whatever that was). Her first husband, Mary's father, produced avant-garde documentaries. Right now he was somewhere in Thailand. Last year he'd been in the Australian outback, the year before in China. Mary saw him once or twice a year.

After a shower she made a phone call and found she was in luck. She drove over to her friend's house. Well, Ben wasn't exactly her friend. Vince would shit if he ever found out about their relationship.

Ben owned a nice home, nothing like the small place they had. It was tastefully furnished too. Ben had made a lot of the furniture. He worked as a carpenter—when he felt like it. He greeted her and led her into the living room.

It had high ceilings and huge windows. In front of a gray leather couch was a glass-and-brass coffee table with a large pile of cocaine, a razor, straw, and a foil packet. "Have a line," Ben said.

"Thanks." Mary grinned. Ben let her do the honors, and she cut four fat lines, two for each of them. She instantly began to glow with self-love and jubilation. Life was grand.

Mary reached into her pocket and pulled out a wad of bills. Vince would die if he could see her now, she thought. She counted them out, three hundred and twenty-five dollars.

Forty-five minutes later Mary was walking out the door. She climbed into her car. Feeling fucking wonderful. Beth was working today. She was a bartender. Mary decided to go down and have a drink. And sell what blow she could.

12

*B*elinda slowed, cruising in her red MR2 at twenty miles an hour, looking for the job under construction. She had to concentrate. Coming here to see Vince for lunch was a spontaneous thing. She had never come down before, and she probably never would again. But she couldn't keep her mind on work. Right now she wanted him. She wanted him pumping away inside her.

Last night had been a drag. There had been nothing interesting, no one she'd even consider taking home. And she had called Nancy from the bar. A few glasses of wine and she always seemed to lose her armor and she knew it. Nancy hadn't ever defended her against Abe, not once in the twenty-eight years she'd been alive, so why did she hope for it now? Besides, she'd been doing well enough, coping with him on her own.

Abe had called back. He had demanded she meet him in Los Angeles tomorrow. He was flying in for a day or so, which wasn't unusual; he frequently came to California on business.

"I can't get down there tomorrow," Belinda said tightly.

"Bullshit. You live forty-five minutes away. Have your ass over at the condo at eight A.M. for breakfast."

"Why?"

"Because we have a discussion to finish and another one to begin."

He rarely presented her with a summons. Belinda hated being ordered around. "Have you ever heard of the word *please*?"

"Oh, Christ! Would you *please* come over tomorrow morning? And your mother wants to see you."

"You're bringing Mom?" Belinda was surprised. Nancy never accompanied Abe on his business trips.

"That's right," Abe said. "I'm taking her to a party."

The construction site loomed before her, across the road. Belinda hung a U and pulled up in front of the chain fence. The house was framed, the roof under construction. A couple of bare-chested, tanned carpenters banging nails up there saw her and whistled. Belinda smiled and slowly got out of the car.

She was wearing a white denim miniskirt, high-heeled sandals, and a thin white tank top that clung to her bare bosom. Lots of gold bangles and black Anne Klein shades. She started through the gate. The hammering had stopped.

She looked up at the three men who were checking her out. "Vince around?"

"He's out back," the blonde called down.

Just then Vince appeared around the corner, bare-chested, his torso gleaming with sweat. He saw her and stopped dead.

She smiled wickedly and sauntered forward. Vince hurried to meet her. "Hi," she said softly, putting her arms around his neck and pressing every inch she could against him.

He groaned, crushing her. "God, what are you doing here?"

"What do you think?" she said in a low voice, sliding her hands into the curly black hair at the nape of his neck. She held his head and kissed him, forcing his mouth open and thrusting her tongue in. Her nipples were hard from the contact with his skin—even through her cotton tank—and she rubbed them sensually against his sweaty chest. He clasped her buttocks and pulled her against a raging hard-on. He returned her kiss wildly, frantically.

They pulled apart. "Shit," Vince said. "What are you doing to me?"

On the roof the guys whistled and stamped.

"I need you," Belinda said. "Badly, Vince. Badly."

He could hardly breathe. "You haven't called. I haven't

heard from you all week—Christ, Belinda, it's been five days!"

"It's been an awful week," she said, sliding her fingers into the mat of hair on his chest. "It's almost noon. There's a motel five minutes from here. Meet me there." She didn't wait for his answer. She turned and started back to her car. She heard him exhale loudly.

He was at the motel at five minutes after twelve—exactly fifteen minutes later. Belinda opened the door, wearing nothing but her tank top, which just covered her hips and left an enticing amount of pubic hair revealed. Vince took one look and grabbed her, pushing her backward onto the bed.

He held her head in his two thick, calloused hands and kissed her again and again. Then he knelt, running his hands down over her breasts, to her waist, her hips. He spread her thighs wide apart. He groaned, raising her and lowering his head.

His breath was soft and warm, his tongue sliding slickly over and between the folds of swollen pink flesh, searching.

"Vince," she moaned.

He reared up and thrust into her powerfully. They clung together and thrust and pumped and pushed and panted.

Afterward they lay together, regaining breath, drenched with sweat. Vince raised his head. "What time is it?"

Belinda looked at her Rolex. "Twelve-twenty."

He pulled off her top and began sucking her breasts. They made love again, starting slowly, leisurely, until Vince's pace became frantic. He always made love to her as if there would be no tomorrow.

"I love you," he rasped as he came violently inside her.

Vince was a regular Romeo when he was between her legs. Men were like that. Spouting Shakespeare.

"When will I see you again? Tomorrow night?"

"I'm going to a party tomorrow night," Belinda said truthfully. Vince had learned about the *Outrage* sale when it was being negotiated. "It's a North-Star party. Maybe Saturday."

"Shit," Vince said. "I could never get away from Mary on a Saturday."

"Oh, I forgot," Belinda said, standing and smoothing down her white skirt. She hadn't forgotten, and she felt a bit rotten. "Well, after the weekend."

"I never see you," Vince said, his jaw ticking.

"I'm not the one who's married."

"You're right." He turned away. "Maybe I'll have to do something about that."

Belinda was aghast. "Don't do anything rash, Vince!"

"I'm sick of sneaking around," Vince said. "Mary disgusts me. Things can't go on like this. Maybe I should just tell Mary—"

"No!" Belinda sat down hard on the bed. "Vince." She stopped and sighed. What could she say? She had always been up-front. Hadn't she made it clear that it was just sex— and that's all it would ever be?

"You're not even jealous," he said. "You don't even care that I spend five nights a week with another woman."

Belinda didn't know what to say, so she checked her face in the mirror.

Vince rubbed his jaw. "What about that party? Can I take you to it?"

Belinda wasn't a liar. Yet she didn't want to hurt Vince. She had never even considered him as her date, and for a moment she felt guilty. Adam Gordon had immediately come to her mind the instant she had learned of the North-Star party. But then she reminded herself that Vince was married, and their time together was stolen, literally. "A friend is taking me, Vince. I'm sorry. But I assumed you'd never be able to leave Mary on a Friday night."

Vince moved away, clearly hurt. Feeling like a heel, Belinda wrapped him in her arms from behind—a sympathy hug. When he turned back to her to kiss her, she could tell she had eased the situation, but she was thinking that Adam was the perfect date for a big Hollywood bash. Adam was slick and elegant and a Hollywood lawyer from a top L.A. firm. He really was the perfect choice.

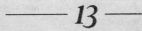

*A*dam Gordon paused at the front receptionist's desk. "I have an appointment with Mr. Glassman."

She smiled. "Please go through."

He knew the way, of course, and was told to sit down in the waiting room near Glassman's private office. He was tall and slim, impeccably tailored, dark-haired and blue-eyed, elegantly handsome. He was perspiring just a touch.

Glassman made him nervous. And mad.

A kind of mad frustration.

Even though Glassman was the answer to it all.

Adam was the fourth and youngest son of the Gordons of Boston. His family were authentic blue bloods, his great-great-grandfather having come over with his bride before the American Revolution. He had supported the British in that war, a fact that the Gordons had fastidiously buried; the current Mrs. Gordons were both members of Boston's Daughters of the American Revolution.

His oldest brother was heir to a small industrially based conglomerate. He was married, with two children, the epitome of Boston society. The second son was an investment banker, having tripled his million-dollar trust already. The third son had died in Vietnam, but only after numerous feats of heroism and even more medals.

Adam had always been the black sheep.

Too young to go to 'Nam, he had been old enough to march in Washington, protesting U.S. involvement. He had dropped out of college as a senior, hitchhiked across the country with a girlfriend who turned him on to all the drugs he hadn't tried, and to group sex, which he loved. They wound up in Oregon on a commune led by a religious fanatic. Adam secretly thought that the Maharajah—as he privately referred to him—was a nut and a con artist, but there was a ratio of about three girls to one guy, and his bed was always warmed, usually by two at once. He drifted through the days in a haze of pot, THC (which they were now saying was acid), speed, and hash.

His father had died of a heart attack ten years ago. Adam hadn't cared then—he had been high on opium at the time—and he didn't care now. His father had always looked down his long, aristocratic nose at his youngest son, had always shown how much he disapproved of him, how much he resented fathering a failure. His mother, ever the obedient wife, followed her husband's cue exactly—when she wasn't doing her charities or going to her dressmaker or the hairdresser. In fact, she had less time for her youngest than her husband did, which said a lot.

It all ended when Adam overdosed and nearly died on his way to Emergency. His older brother flew out and never said a word of recrimination. His face was set with worry and fear—not disgust. Adam had always worshiped his older brother Fred, the ten-year difference in their ages making that easy to do. Fred was everything Adam was not. He was responsible.

Still in withdrawal, Adam had broken down and cried on Fred's shoulder. Fred actually held and soothed him, and Adam at that moment knew he had been a fool. The one thing he wanted to do more than anything else in the world was to make Fred proud of him. He went to a rehab program in Tucson, then to the university to finish up his B.A. Excelling at his studies, he was accepted into law school, and he graduated number two in his class. Fred and his wife came to the graduation, and Fred was beaming. Adam felt it had all been worth it.

Fred got him his first job in L.A. as a corporate lawyer, and four years later Adam joined one of the most prestigious firms in the city, Benson, Hull, and Krutschak. For six years

he had risen through the ranks because he was bright—
something he had always been told but had never believed.
He had never bothered to use his intelligence until he had
gone back to school.

Now he had made it, in a sense. He made two hundred
grand a year, not including the interest from his million-
dollar trust. He wore seven-hundred-dollar suits. He drove a
Mercedes. He had a house in Malibu. He saw Fred and the
family at least twice a year in New York, and Fred came out
to the West Coast at least as often.

It wasn't enough. Before, he supposed in retrospect, he
had been afraid to try to compete, afraid to fail. Now he was
competing, and he was doing well. He was up there, but he
wanted more, much more. He hadn't known he would ever
be ambitious, but he was. Money, success, power, respect-
ability—they went hand in hand. He wanted to be bigger
than he could possibly be as a corporate lawyer.

He wanted to be Fred's equal. He could imagine the
day, the day he walked into Fred's office as chairman of a
powerful conglomerate, controller and manipulator of millions. The feeling of being equal, of having made it, the look
on Fred's face, his warmth, his love.

He had met Abe Glassman last year as they sat at opposite sides of a deal being negotiated here in L.A. Cannily,
Adam had pointed out a few points in favor of Glassman
Enterprises, to Glassman's sharp irritation. Adam then—as
he could now—felt the weight and intensity of Glassman's
black-eyed stare. The man had a charisma that he had never
encountered before. The aura of power—it frightened him,
thrilled him, mesmerized him, and he was unable to deny it.

He knew the call would come, and it had. A discreet
meeting with Glassman in his blacked-in limo. They had
discussed the project obliquely, but by the time Adam was
dropped off, they both knew he had become Glassman's
man. The deal was renegotiated later, without Adam's sharp
and timely interference. He merely gave his approval to the
board.

He thought about the day Glassman would die. With a
smile. The man was fifty-three. Even if he lived another

thirty years, he had to die sometime. Adam could wait—he would wait. He would use the time to increase his power, day by day, bit by bit. For when Abe did die, he, Adam, would be in a position to have it all.

He had never been married, and now he knew why. The right prospect had never come along. He thought of Belinda Glassman, and his smile grew.

And funnily enough, it was Abe Glassman who had suggested it. Strongly.

A marriage made in heaven.

By two mere mortals.

With Abe on his side, how could he lose?

And that was just it. He couldn't.

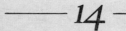

14

She would never forget the summer of 1971.

The aching loneliness and emptiness had begun early in her marriage, a few years after Belinda was born. Or even earlier. Nancy loved Abe. There was no question of that. But she never saw him. He was never there. Oh, he would come home at night, flash a vague smile at her, but then he'd lock himself into his study until late in the evening. Sometimes he'd wake her with his hands and mouth, in the middle of the night when he came to bed. It seemed like those moments were the only times they shared.

She knew she was a fool to complain. She had everything any woman could ever want. She had a dynamic husband who loved her and showered her with furs and jewels and homes. She knew Abe was proud of her. They went out several nights a week. Abe's friends were all business associates; their wives were like her, attractive, dripping diamonds, perfectly coiffed. Abe always had a boastful comment: "Doesn't she look great?" Everyone always agreed with Abe.

Other evenings, Abe went out alone. "Strictly business," he said.

Nancy knew better.

She knew it wasn't always business. She knew there were other women. She told herself she didn't mind. Because Abe loved her and no other woman would ever take her place.

And there was Belinda. Her beautiful daughter. Nancy loved her fiercely from the moment she was conceived. Abe was ecstatic that she was pregnant, for there was nothing he wanted more than a son. During her pregnancy he treated her like a princess, the way he had during their courtship. Nancy had never loved him more, had never been happier. She pretended other women didn't exist. And then Belinda was born.

Nancy knew—although Belinda didn't—that Abe had never forgiven his daughter for not being a son.

He was so disappointed he couldn't hide it. He was so disappointed he was angry. He was so disappointed he was indifferent to the tiny human being who was his own flesh and blood.

Nancy told herself he would get over it. She loved her tiny daughter. She wanted to do everything for her. But she was Mrs. Glassman, and Mrs. Glassman had to have a nursemaid and a nursery and was not allowed to be like other mothers. She was not allowed to change diapers or feed her daughter or answer her cries at two A.M.

Nancy failed to conceive again, and she knew that she was failing her husband. The silent accusation was always there. She gradually became aware that Abe had refocused: As soon as Belinda was old enough he intended to marry her off, so she could give him a grandson.

Nancy had always been faithful to Abe. Adultery was not even in her vocabulary. And though she and her daughter weren't close, when Belinda was forcibly sent to camp that summer, Nancy thought that she might die from the desperation and loneliness of her life that Belinda's leaving seemed to expose.

Just before camp started Abe had hired a new driver. He was twenty-one, a would-be actor named Jack Ford. Nancy didn't look at other men, but she seemed to notice him. At first just a little, then constantly. Especially when they were thrown together every day. Abe was spending a lot of time out of town on business, leaving Nancy with the car and driver at her disposal. That summer was one endless shopping spree. In an attempt to enrich her life and take away the loneliness.

He was blatantly sexy, certainly one of the handsomest men she had ever seen. He held the door for her, said good morning and good night, and she found herself too flustered to respond. She was careful to drop her gaze from his compelling eyes before he could read her thoughts. For she was starting to fantasize about him—and Nancy was appalled at herself.

They had a home in South Hampton, on the beach. They went there every weekend in the summer. Abe would fly out late on Friday nights, while Nancy usually stayed from Thursday morning until Sunday because she wanted Belinda out of the hot city. The weekend after Belinda left for camp, Abe had to go to Los Angeles on business, and Nancy had no desire to stay in the sweltering city alone. She left for the Hamptons. Jack drove her in the limo.

She wasn't really a drinker, but she'd had Jack pull over in Hampton Bays at a liquor store, and she sipped Scotch for the next thirty minutes until they got to the house. She began to wonder if she was making a mistake coming out alone for the weekend. The house was vast—twenty-five rooms— and Nancy was suddenly filled with dread.

She didn't want to be alone.

She still didn't know quite how it had happened. They arrived late; the staff was asleep. Nancy was a little drunk and getting more depressed by the minute. Jack carried her bags in, and she had almost swooned with gratitude when he said, his voice full of concern, "Are you okay, Mrs. Glassman?"

She started to cry, but she managed to stop. "Yes, I'm fine." She looked at him.

He had brilliant green eyes, full of compassion, that searched hers. Waiting. Somewhere along the line he had taken his cap off. His hair was dark gold, streaked with shimmering lighter strands. His tie was loosened, his shirt collar open.

"I'll get the rest of your bags," he had said.

When he came back in she asked him if he'd like to have a drink. Just companionship, she told herself.

And then he took her in his arms.

It felt so good.

"God, you are beautiful. It's so hard working for you, day after day . . ."

His arms were strong, and he wouldn't let her move away. She didn't want to move away. He was kissing her and he tasted so good. His body was hard and hot and Nancy was trembling beneath him—not from fear, but from desire. She needed him desperately, and it was an explosion.

He kept saying things, wonderful things. "You're so beautiful . . . I've wanted you for so long . . . I can't stand it . . . God, you drive me crazy . . . I think I love you . . ."

He thought he loved her.

She wanted him to spend the weekend, but there was the help to consider. And her guilt. And the fact that she didn't know what she was doing. She wanted to ask him to stay at a local motel so she could meet him, but she was afraid to. Instead he left at sunrise the next morning.

She came back to the city a day early. Jack brought her bags up to her bedroom and left many hours later. Monday morning Nancy found out she was pregnant. Five weeks pregnant with Abe's child. He would be ecstatic. She didn't tell him.

All she could think about was Jack.

There was no turning back. They spent the rest of the month sneaking around, usually meeting first thing in the morning after Jack had dropped Abe at the office. Again and again, Nancy postponed telling Abe she was finally pregnant.

And then one morning, when Jack was driving himself deep and thick inside of her, their bodies dripping streams of sweat, slapping rhythmically, he froze.

Nancy opened her eyes, looked at his expression of complete shock, and knew Abe had walked in. She made a strangled sound, pushing him off, twisting, grabbing the bedspread and holding it up, her gaze going to the door.

Belinda stood there, white-faced and wide-eyed. She turned and ran, blond braids flying out behind her.

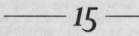

15

*A*be had always loved sex.

He had loved it the first time he'd jacked off in the bathroom at home at the age of nine. He loved it even more the first time he'd had a girl, who was actually a hooker named Mabel who hung out around Eddie's candy store where he picked up the slips. He had been fourteen.

After that he'd become something of a menace. He was always grabbing the girls at school, the older ones who had developed breasts. Fortunately Abe was tall for his age and lean, not skinny. He seemed to have missed adolescent awkwardness. He was magnetic rather than handsome—some might say forceful. He would not accept no for an answer. But he seemed to have a talent for zeroing in on the girls who said yes, and they seemed to like him too. He was both enthusiastic and well-endowed.

At seventeen he became a bit more cautious after he had gotten a senior named Beth pregnant. She wanted him to marry her, of all things. Abe laughed in her face. He couldn't even be sure the kid was his. She married another senior four months later.

The college years were best. There was tail everywhere. Good girls didn't—but so many others did. And Abe knew how to get the borderline cases over the edge. Then, too, there was Amanda Lee, Luke Bonzio's mistress.

She was a blonde and gorgeous, with knockers that would drive any guy crazy. Abe wasn't stupid. He knew she was off-limits. Still, he had to have her. And already, even at the age of twenty, he was used to getting what he wanted. Always.

Bonzio never found out.

Amanda Lee fell madly in love with him.

When Abe grew tired of her, he had trouble getting rid of her. He finally paid her off.

Nancy had been different.

She was a lady through and through. It was why he had fallen in love with her, why he had married her. He knew she was a virgin, just like he had always known his wife would be a virgin on their wedding night. He didn't make love to her until that night, and then he was careful about how he made love to her, careful not to be crude, not to touch her too much. He tried to be gentle, not to hurt her, but, of course, lost control. He had never had a virgin before.

She didn't climax, but then, he hadn't expected her to. She didn't enjoy it, but he hadn't expect that either. Women like her didn't.

Abe desired his wife but not the way he wanted other women. He made love to her as inadvertently and politely as possible. At the office he had a new secretary with a mammoth set of mammary glands, who also gave the best blow job he had ever had. He would never dream of asking Nancy to do something like that.

She was the perfect lady, the perfect wife, and the day she gave him his son, she would be the perfect mother too.

Until that very hot day in July when he had picked up the phone and overheard her conversation.

He had been in L.A. on business. Well, with pleasure

thrown in. California had an endless supply of big-breasted blondes—a bonus to a lucrative deal. His latest mistress was a starlet who was so good he was debating making her into a star. He might buy a studio or buy her a role. He already owned five percent of North-Star, and half the Board owed him. He could get her in there. He was pleased with himself and life in general, having just closed a fantastic multi-million-dollar deal to build a hotel complex in Palm Springs. He was in a magnanimous mood.

He had come home on an earlier flight than planned, and instead of going to the office he decided to make some phone calls from his study.

Purely by chance he had picked up Nancy's line. And would have hung up, except that the man's voice was familiar. He was saying something about "tomorrow," and Nancy said, "We can't. Abe's back."

At the sound of his name he realized he was listening to the chauffeur, the tough kid, Ford. Who was laughing. "So what? That hasn't stopped us yet. I'll come by as soon as I drop him at the office, like always. I've got to see you, Nancy. I *need* to see you."

She was silent. "Jack, I'm worried. What if he finds out? What about Belinda?"

"Don't worry," he said huskily. "I'll worry for both of us. Just hang in there. I'll see you tomorrow, babe." Then, "I'm going to fuck your brains out."

Abe had been momentarily stunned.

He found her in her bedroom, sitting on the bed by the phone. At the sight of him she went white. He reached her in three strides, his arm going out. "No-good cunt," he shouted, and the blow swept her off the bed onto the floor.

Nancy shrank. "Abe," she whimpered.

"I should kill you!"

"Oh, God!" Nancy moaned.

Abe grabbed her, yanking her up, hurting her and not caring. "How long have you been fucking around on me?" he roared. "How long, damn you!"

She was trembling and crying. "It was a mistake, I swear—"

"How long!"

"A few weeks."

"And before Ford?" He had her pinned to the wall. "Answer me!"

"No one," she moaned. "I swear, he was the first . . ."

He wrenched her face back, ignoring her whimper, then threw her on the bed. She rolled when she saw him coming, scrambling to the other side.

"You want it," he had grated, pulling her up violently toward him, "all you had to do was ask."

Abe pinned her on the bed, shoving up her nightgown. He plunged violently into her, again and again, determined to hurt her. Her sobs left him unmoved.

Afterward Abe lay on the bed, his heart raging. He ignored Nancy as she stumbled to her feet and into the bathroom. He closed his eyes. This wasn't happening. Nancy Worth Glassman was not a cheap whore. She was his wife. He kept seeing her as he had through the years—chic, elegant, ladylike. Then he imagined her with the boy, Ford— naked and wet and moaning for him. He was sick. He hated her. He was going to destroy her.

And destroy Ford.

Nancy came out of the bathroom clad in slacks, a sweater, and carrying a small bag. He instantly sat up. "Where the fuck are you going?"

"I-I'm leaving."

He was on his feet. "Oh, no, you're not!" he snarled. He hated her, but he wasn't about to let her go. Oh, no, not when she belonged to him.

She had started for the door, giving him her back.

And it dawned on him. "Just where the hell do you think you're going? To *him*?"

She didn't look back.

And then it was funny. He laughed. "To that two-bit punk? You're leaving me, me, Abe Glassman, for that punk chauffeur?" And he laughed harder.

She wrenched open the door and started running, as if she couldn't bear another moment in his presence.

He had let her go—for then. Ford was just getting his

rocks off, and Nancy was in for a rude awakening if she thought he was her savior. What was she going to do—marry the kid? Live on canned beans and wear polyester for the rest of her life? He would wait. Wait until she came crawling back. And then he'd make sure she lived to regret every day of the rest of her life.

He heard her fall. There was a rolling, thumping noise that instinctively made him run to the top of the long, curved stairs.

She was slowly getting to her knees, bent over from the waist and moaning. He stopped himself from running down to help her, reminding himself of his hatred for her.

Eight hours later Nancy miscarried a twelve-week-old male fetus.

His son.

She and Jack Ford had killed his son.

————— *16* —————

*W*hat really happened?

He had liked his job. Not that driving a Caddie for Abe Glassman was his future, not at all. He'd come to New York to study acting, mostly because he had the face to launch a thousand ships and the pussy panting after him to prove it. Of course, he hadn't made it very often to acting class that summer. But that didn't matter. Glassman was big, as in megabucks, and if he didn't own half of New York City by then, Jack knew he would one day. And maybe he would be there with Abe, riding on his coattails. After all, didn't Glassman trust him?

Jack was certain he did, because he had been tested and had passed with flying colors.

The first time Abe Glassman had given him a sealed

envelope and asked him to deliver it personally, Jack hadn't thought much about it. The third time, he had held the envelope, weighed it, even sniffed it—and knew it contained money. He had taken it up to his tiny grimy room on Broadway and One hundred tenth and carefully steamed it open. He counted, slowly. Fifty thousand dollars in hundred-dollar bills. Then he replaced every single bill, not even tempted, and resealed the envelope. And delivered it.

Of course it was grease money.

The destination of the envelope confirmed it, and Jack began to keep track of his deliveries—city councilmen, CEOs, a secretary in the mayor's office, an aide to a California senator, even a cop. Big stuff.

He began to think how sweet his life might become.

He was making money, good money for those deliveries. And there would be more coming his way.

Then it happened. The kid walking in on him and the gorgeous Mrs. Glassman while he had been driving his cock deep and thick inside her. Shit, that was bad. What if the kid told?

He had sweated bullets, waiting for Glassman to get back from L.A. Unable to sleep, he had tossed restlessly in the heat. Wondering why Nancy Glassman had failed to keep their rendezvous that afternoon, and feeling horny as hell. When he had spoken to her that morning on the phone, she had sounded fine. Had something gone wrong since then?

Abe called a little after midnight—something he often did. Everything seemed the same. Jack had felt vast relief, thinking that Abe didn't know—the kid hadn't talked. He was sure of it when Glassman told him to come by the town house to pick up another "package." He got over there fast. And even in person Abe seemed fine.

The address Abe sent him to was in Queens, not Manhattan. Jack had never been there before, but that didn't mean anything. He had even been whistling as he thought about the nice bonus he always got for these little deliveries, jamming on a rock station as he hit the Midtown Tunnel, fingers rapping the wheel.

He started frowning when he asked directions and was sent into a shabby neighborhood. Not just shabby. More like the kind of place he'd grown up in. An unadulterated slum. Kids in rags playing in streams of water from open fire hydrants. Tumbled-down buildings, some gutted from fires. Pregnant teenage girls sitting on stoops. Old men drunk in doorways stinking of urine. The strains of a ghetto blaster followed him down an entire block.

The address was a store advertising cigars and girlie magazines. This did not smell right. Jack wasn't afraid—he was good with his fists and a broken bottle, if need be—but he was alert. The man inside the store was big and menacing. He looked as if he could break a man's neck with his bare hands. His two customers weren't as big, but they had that same feral look. Oh, shit, Jack thought, locking his door with one motion.

As the big piece of brawn came out toward him, Jack knew. He *knew*.

He rolled his window up and put the car in drive. From the corner of his eye he saw the blurred movement, realizing too late what had happened. The window smashed, glass raining in on him, and a bloody arm the size of a tree branch reached in. Before the car could even accelerate, the man had Jack's throat locked in his arm and was dragging him out. Jack reached for the window, gritting his teeth as jagged glass cut his hands. He tried to pull a piece away. A small, daggerlike shard broke off in his hand.

He was propelled backward, but Jack didn't fall. He regained his balance, crouching. "Come on, motherfucker," he rasped, ignoring his bleeding hand.

The big man laughed.

Jack darted forward, sweeping up with the glass and jumping back. A line of blood appeared on the man's fat belly. He growled.

Jack attacked again, feinting and jabbing with the glass. The man was an ox. He couldn't move to save his life. This time Jack sliced open his arm from elbow to wrist. He blinked salty sweat out of his eyes.

Movement on the periphery caught his attention. The

other two were behind him and approaching from both sides. Then the giant lunged, and Jack had to leap out of the way. Something hit his ankle hard, and as he went crashing onto the ground on his side, he realized he'd been tripped from behind.

He kept rolling, right onto his feet. As he came up he saw the blow coming and heard the man laugh. The undercut to his gut doubled him over, red pain rushing through him. In that instant he knew he was in serious trouble.

Brass knuckles.

His jaw cracked, snapping his head back. Another blow to his stomach, and he cried out. As he hunched over, a knee came up into his groin. The pain was so excruciating he almost passed out. He started to drop. The second knee came up into his face, breaking his nose. Blood spurted. There was an agonizing blow to his kidneys, making him scream. He felt ribs crack. He began choking on his own blood. An excruciating blow to the back of his head, and he crumpled in a heap on the street, a red-and-black haze stealing over him.

"Is he dead?"

"No, he ain't dead, just close, real close."

Dimly, Jack heard and wondered if the man was right. He felt as if he was dying. In fact, according to the staff in the hospital where he was laid up for six months, he had almost died the night he had been rushed into Emergency. And three months after his release, when every door in the city was slammed in his face, when his old girlfriend threw him out, when he was jobless and homeless and forced to sell it just to survive, he knew he hadn't dreamed what the thug had said just before unconsciousness claimed him:

"You're finished in New York, pretty boy. Nobody ever fucks with Abe Glassman."

17

*N*ancy was nervous. It was Friday night. Her insides were twisted into knots. It was silly. But ever since she'd found out that Jackson Ford was going to star in Belinda's movie, she had been a bundle of nerves. Warning bells were ringing. It was like being swept into the past. Worse. He was coming back into her life again, insidiously. Oh, God! Nancy could feel it—the fierce foreboding of a lurking disaster.

She hated him.

She had lain in the hospital too depressed to move after the miscarriage, lain crying and waiting for him to come and take her in his arms and tell her it would be all right, that he was going to take her away once she was better. She waited and waited, for days and days and finally weeks, but he had never come. He hadn't come. She had never seen him again.

God, even now, seventeen years later—how she hated him!

When she had gone home the drinking had started. First an early cocktail hour, then just a white wine with lunch. She never drank before lunch, but from the moment she awoke, it was her anticipation of that drink that got her through the morning. Abe, of course, was rarely home, and when he was his contempt was not disguised. But he never suggested divorce, and neither did Nancy.

She needed a drink now, to steady her nerves.

Why had Abe brought her to California this time, when she hadn't traveled with him in years? Nancy hadn't lived thirty years with her husband not to be suspicious. She knew Abe had brought her for a reason. And she couldn't figure it out. She had been too afraid to ask. And now there was this insistent feeling of fear.

She began to get dressed for the party. Some Hollywood

affair, Abe had said, and he hadn't given her any more information. What if—she began to think, then cut herself off
with a shaky laugh. There was no way! It was ridiculous to
even think it! Hollywood was a big place; it would be the
ultimate twist of fate if Jack Ford were to be there tonight.

How silly.

Relax.

He is not going to be at this party.

A vast, heavy emptiness was weighing him down.

Jack had shot his last scene four or five hours ago. He
expected to crash and he hated it. It never failed, after all the
tension and excitement and creative effort, the striving for
perfection, the actual metamorphosis of himself, Jack Ford,
into someone else, and then—nothing.

Emptiness.

The shoot was over. He had never been better. He
didn't think he was deluding himself—he had been good
enough in this part for an Oscar nomination. Even the cast
and crew seemed to think so. They had actually applauded
today after the final take. A nomination would be the culmination of all his dreams, all his ambitions.

He knew he would never win.

Because everyone in the industry knew how he felt. He
hadn't kissed enough ass. Didn't let the bloodsuckers leech
onto him. He wouldn't play the game. And there was the
jealousy, because his star had risen so fast, burning so bright.

Still, a nomination was within the realm of possibility.

He looked at his watch. He had to get a move on, had
to get dressed. North-Star was sending over a limo and he
was running late. Of course, stars were allowed to be late—
and he smiled. Remembering a time when there were no
limos and no Ferraris and no home in Santa Barbara, no
Rolex, no agent, no roles, nothing.

God, he had come a long way. A long way from the
tough kid chauffering Glassman's limo in New York City.

He was on top.

A star.

He had made it.

* * *

Abe was smiling.

He hung up the phone, anticipation sweet and melting in his mouth. He had been talking to his arb. Schumann had begun the surreptitious process of buying shares and parking them for a hostile takeover. Abe's grin widened. It didn't hurt to be starting out from the strong position of owning nine percent of North-Star. He laughed.

He knew he could count on three men who owed him heavily—he owned them because he could ruin them—to sell him a total of four and a half percent more. One of those men was Will Hayward, who wouldn't dare refuse, not after Abe had fixed it so Detective Smith wouldn't bring charges for possession and dealing. Dealing! Hayward had lost it, he was an idiot! Abe knew he was supporting his habit but that made no difference. Hayward knew too much and Abe didn't trust him, especially now. He had to keep him away from the police and out of trouble. Will was becoming a serious liability.

He would deal with that next week.

Abe stood up and adjusted his tie, feeling very fine indeed. It was time to get his wife and take her to a party.

Beverly Hills.

Belinda was most definitely in the mood. She looked at Adam and smiled. Adam smiled back.

He was the perfect choice, she thought guiltily, in a town where appearances were everything. He looked elegant and handsome, like a young James Bond. She hadn't really been attracted to him in the beginning, but there was no reason for her not to be, and now she could feel the spark kindling as their friendship grew. She was twenty-eight and wasn't it time she gave up hunks? For someone like Adam? Someone successful and presentable and intelligent? She wondered if he was good in bed. Somehow she knew his performance would be just as polished there as everywhere else.

"You are going to turn a few heads tonight," Adam said as he turned his Mercedes into the vast, graveled drive.

Belinda smiled. She was wearing a brilliant orange designer dress. It had a halter that plunged right to her navel, then curved in a skintight sheath to just below her knees. In the back, it was slit up her right thigh—almost as high as the top of her stocking.

"You will certainly be noticed. In fact, some paparazzi will probably think you're a movie star." Adam grinned. "They'll be going crazy trying to figure out who you are."

"Good," Belinda declared. "A little attention never hurts. Especially at the stage my career is at."

They climbed out, Belinda swinging long legs gracefully. She stared up at the neo-Tudor home with the huge lawns and gardens. There were limos, BMWs, and Mercedeses everywhere. A man looking incredibly silly was dressed in armor, sitting on a scarlet-robed horse right by the entrance. Belinda had to smile. Only in Hollywood.

"You'll love this," Adam whispered as they walked past the uniformed maid taking wraps at the door.

They entered a huge stone-floored living room. The ceiling was high and beamed. Shields and pikes and swords decorated the walls. It was right out of a medieval romance. Belinda knew the gossip, just like everyone else: Majoriis's wife, who was thirty years his junior, fancied herself the reincarnation of some Tudor damsel in distress. The party was in full swing and crowded, all dazzling sequins and satin lapels, buzzing with chatter and laughter. Then the whole room became an unfocused collage of colors, textures, and shapes. Everything a blur.

Except for him.

Jackson Ford.

He stood almost smack in the center of the room, golden and glowing, crystal-clear in her vision, his presence a powerful magnet drawing her attention—like the sun at the center of the universe. She stared, not even looking at the group of people he was standing with, because they, too—like everything else in the room—were blurred and indistinct and inconsequential.

He was, if possible, better in person.

Then the unbelievable happened. Or was it the inevitable?

He raised his head and looked right at her.

For a long moment their gazes locked.

18

"*W*ho is that?" Jack asked, staring at the woman in orange as she walked across the room.

Melody followed his gaze. "I don't know," she said, looking at his face.

He tracked the woman with his eyes. She walked with an athletic grace, as if she were very sure of herself, expecting heads to turn, which indeed, they did. She was more than stunning. Incredibly sexy. He could pick up on it all the way across the room. An attitude seemed to emanate from her like a perfume, wafting, enticing, heady, and powerful. "Who the hell is that?" he muttered again.

He chatted with Melody and the starlet who clung to him and the character actor whose face was on every prime-time show although no one remembered his name. He chatted mindlessly, with none of his attention. She wasn't his type, far from it. Too short, for one thing, maybe five seven or eight in heels. Blond, sun-gold blond. He liked dark-haired women. Too old. And too curved, too muscular, almost like a female jock if not for her sensual style, the aura of sex. Broad shoulders, a swimmer's back, but real nice breasts, he could see that. He wished he could get a better look at her legs. There were too many people in the way.

He excused himself from the crowd and worked his way toward her, single-minded now, as if she were a mare in heat and he a stallion. Who was she? An actress, of course, but how come he had never laid eyes on her before? He nodded and exchanged inane pleasantries but never lost sight of her. Twice he caught her eye. Twice he caught her looking at him too. She seemed to be with some guy, a familiar-looking man, but he wasn't sure, and if she was, well, he didn't care.

He finally found himself next to her. By now the party was packed, and she had lost her companion, if he was her companion. He had a knot in his groin, and it had been growing. Everything had been growing. He felt out of control, about to take off. "Hi."

She turned to face him and his best killer grin. A smile curved her lips. Full and pink. She had flair. Style. Jesus, she looked even better close up. Who was she?

"Hi, yourself," she said, giving him the fast up-down. Her voice was husky. Did her gaze linger where he thought it had? His condition wasn't obvious, but if she looked she'd see. He felt like a very hard-up high-schooler.

"I'm Jack," he said, sure it wasn't necessary, extending his hand.

She raised a brow. She didn't seem to recognize him. He didn't know whether to be thrilled or disappointed—he was both. "Belinda," she said, slipping a warm, firm hand in his.

She smelled like something musky mixed with honey-dew and possibly sex. He looked into her eyes, intense brown eyes, and felt a moment of panic. As if he were on the edge of a precipice and knew, absolutely, that he was about to take a fall. But the moment passed, the feeling passed. And was forgotten. Instead there was her mouth, so voluptuous; her breasts, also voluptuous; her thighs . . . Was that the faint line of a garter belt?

What was wrong with him? Why was he in overdrive? She wasn't even his type!

"Who are you, Belinda? I've never seen you before."

"Who are you?" she returned, her gaze locked with his.

She doesn't know who I am! For a moment he just stared, completely off balance. This had never happened—or not in years, not since Success. Certainly not in Tinseltown. He had a flashing kaleidoscope image of the past seven years, all the favor and star-fucking. And he decided instantly that he wouldn't tell her, not tonight. Not until after they'd made it, which he knew they would. Jack knew women. And he knew she wanted him too. "How do you like it?" he finally said, gesturing around.

Her smile was dazzling and genuine. "I love it."

He understood her perfectly then, knew where she was and where she wanted to go. "First time?"

"Yes," she said, holding his gaze again. Her eyes were so goddamn intense. His words echoed in his head, *first time*, and he knew from the way she was looking at him that she was thinking about it too—the first time. Tonight was going to be their first time together. His breathing felt thick and heavy in his chest.

"What do you do?" His gaze slid helplessly down her body.

"What do you do?" she rebutted.

His smile burst forth. "I do a bit of acting now and then," he said lightly. He had never been a braggart, and even though he thought he was glad she didn't know who he was, didn't she watch prime time? Read magazines? Shop in the supermarket? "Now answer my question."

"What do you think?"

"You've got to be a star!—an actress," he said, catching himself before he insulted her. If she were anyone, he would know her, would have seen her.

She just smiled. "Do you always stare so pointedly?"

He jerked his gaze up to her face from where it had strayed, saw the wicked light, and laughed roughly. "Never." A muscle on the side of his face twitched. "Are you wearing anything under there?"

Her gaze locked with his again. "You do tend to jump to conclusions," she said huskily.

"I can think of something better to jump," he said, getting throaty.

"So can I," she said, her glance straying downward.

He took her arm, his hand closing around it tightly, then loosening to slide up and down. Her skin was soft, smooth. Electric. "Let's get out of here," he said. "Is that your boyfriend?"

"No, just a friend," she said, staring into his eyes.

He stepped close. His thigh and hip touched hers. His hand moved to her back. Silk. Her scent was stronger. "Should you tell him we're leaving?"

She shifted her body slightly, but enough. Pressing her hip into his hardness, one breast against his arm. For a moment they stared breathlessly at each other, nerves racing, burning. "I'll have to meet you later."

"Okay," he said, trying not to lose focus. He didn't know what he said. He was aware only of her, her feel and smell—and his intense need to get her into bed.

He swallowed. "In an hour? At Nicki Blair's?"

"An hour and a half," she said, giving him a long look.

He stared at her disappearing back. A gorgeous ass. A glimpse of strong, long legs through the slit. Oh, God. An hour and a half. He could barely wait.

Then he rounded a corner, and there was Abe Glassman.

With his wife.

19

*J*ack and Abe Glassman stared at each other from across the room while Jack fought potent, painful memories.

Jack clenched his jaw so hard he thought he might grind his teeth to the gums. But he didn't look away. He recognized the challenge. And damn, he wasn't afraid of that bastard. Glassman couldn't touch him now. Right?

Jack became aware of how tense he was, and he forced himself to relax, to smile and act cool. As if seeing this man again—who had almost had him killed, who had cost him six months in the hospital, who had then ruined his chances in New York—meant nothing to him.

But the shock of being in the same room with a man he hated made his pulse pound and his brow sweat.

Abe had his arm around Nancy and was pulling her with him as he approached. Jack looked at her for the first time and saw the horror in her eyes, which were riveted on him. She was as white as a ghost—as if she'd seen a ghost. Maybe she'd thought he'd died, after all. Had she once come to inquire about him when he'd been recovering in the hospital? Maybe they'd both thought he'd died—and then Jack immediately corrected himself. Abe Glassman didn't deal in *assumptions*. He had known exactly what he was doing when he'd had Jack beaten up to within an inch of his life. Just as he knew exactly what he was doing now. The fear was just a stabbing, like the prick of a needle. He controlled his expression. He wasn't about to give anything away. *What did Glassman want?*

His heart was pumping erratically.

"If it isn't my old driver," Glassman sneered.

"If it isn't Abe Glassman, Upright Citizen of the Year," Jack said coolly. He couldn't control the trickle of sweat at his temple. But he didn't brush at it.

"You remember my wife," Abe said, holding Nancy tightly by the arm.

Jack met Nancy's eyes briefly and was shocked by the hatred he saw blazing there. For a moment he couldn't look away, and neither could she. "Abe," Nancy whispered weakly, but she didn't take her gaze from Jack's.

"Maybe you two have some catching up to do," Abe sneered.

His cruelty appalled Jack and angered him. "What in the hell do you want?"

"Still the tough punk." Abe grinned. "Once a punk, always a punk."

If it had been anyone else, anyone other than this man, Jack might have been amused. But amusement was the farthest thing from his mind right then. "I don't think we have anything to say to each other," Jack said, turning away.

"Don't turn your back on me, boy," Abe warned.

Jack froze. Then slowly, so as not to appear intimidated, he turned back. "If you have something to say, then say it. If not, I have a date."

"Oh, I have something to say, all right," Abe said, grinning. "I wanted to give you some advice."

In that instant Jack knew. Knew that Glassman was about to go for his jugular. Knew it wasn't over, that it had never been over. Dread filled him. "I can't wait."

Glassman laughed. "Stick to your own league." He laughed harder. "Know what I mean? You're bush league, Ford, and you always have been. You can't make the majors —*you won't.* I'm the Man in this town, just like I was the Man in New York. Ring any bells?"

The sweat was pouring now in a steady stream. "You can't touch me, not now." But he felt as if he were free-falling through space.

Abe laughed. "No? Just wait and see, boy. Just wait and see."

Falling.

God, why?

PART TWO

Lovers
December 1987

20

*H*e hadn't had the dream in years.

Not since he was in his mid-twenties, but he'd been having it recently, and he had it that night. He was a boy—it was years ago. He was walking home. His block stood out crystal-clear in his mind. An empty lot, dirt and debris taking up half of one side, the chain fence partly torn down, so easily circumventable. Rows of rotting, squalid, wood-shingled homes, porches crumbling, paint gone, shutters hanging crookedly. Rats escaping from overturned, overflowing garbage cans. Wrecked and stripped jalopies dotting front yards and the sides of the street.

His own house was on the corner. It was no different from every other house on the block. One side of the porch sagged precariously. White paint had long ago flaked away, revealing green and gray patches beneath. One of the front windows was boarded up; the glass had been shattered. His father had thrown something at it—years earlier—with his mother screaming hysterically and Jack hiding under the stairs. The other front window had a jagged, gaping hole. The screen door had a myriad of tears in it.

As Jack approached the house, getting closer, his mother appeared on the front step. A voluptuous woman, clad in short shorts and a halter top, with dyed blond hair, showing dark roots. She laughed at him.

Jack called to her, wanting to show her something, something important, something that would make her happy, proud, something that would make her love him. He didn't know yet what that something might be. He quickened his pace, and the house started drifting away, with his mother laughing on the porch.

Jack started running.

The house moved away faster.

He ran faster. Calling her.

His mother's laughter grew louder.

Now he was running as hard as he could. He could barely breathe. He tried to shout, wanted to shout, Mom, wait, Mom! but he had no air. The house was moving so fast now. It had almost disappeared from his view.

He woke up.

Sweat covered his naked body. Breathing hard, Jack swung his legs over the side of the bed, flicking on the light. Sweet Jesus.

His hands were trembling. And he could barely breathe —as if he'd actually been running.

He now knew that it really was his mother who had called.

He knew it was her for a very distinct reason—one day Melody had brought her to his office.

What had taken her so long to try and reach him? It was a question that haunted him, a question he hated for its power over him. For the past three years he had been on a weekly TV series. A show that had gotten tremendous PR— even its cancellation had been a major controversy. His face had appeared on the cover of *TV Guide* the first year. Since then he had made the cover of *People, Playgirl, Esquire,* and *TV Guide* again. God only knew how many times he had made the front page of the gossip rags on display at every goddamn supermarket counter in the country. So why now?

What did she want?

What did everyone want? Money. Now that he was a big star, they all wanted money, directly or indirectly. Every guy who tried to become his pal wanted him to read a script or endorse a product or put in a word with whoever for a part. It was the same thing with all the broads. Hollywood was a plastic place. Everyone was on the make. Everyone used whoever they could sink their claws into.

He was on the top of every A party list there was. Turned down invitations left and right, only picking those parties that Melody insisted he go to, to advance himself with the right people. Even he had to play the fucking game. He hated it. And everyone knew it.

But it was play or never work.

Every woman he screwed wanted a piece of the pie.

Now she wanted a piece too.

Well, fuck her.

Jack looked at his watch, a gold Rolex. Eight thousand dollars. He had always wanted a Rolex, during all those years when all the people who now begged him to attend their parties and read their scripts and consider their roles had looked down their phony noses at him and told him to go flush himself down the toilet. He had always wanted a black Ferrari. Now he had both. Now he could look down his nose at most—but not all—of those pricks.

What did she want?

Why had she wanted to see him?

And he still hadn't forgiven Melody for her betrayal, not in his heart, and he didn't think he ever could. He would never forget that day. Even now, for the thousandth time, it was like the rerun of a favorite movie, the images crystal-clear.

"Don't hate me," Melody said from the doorway, taut with apprehension.

"I would never hate you. What's wrong?"

She took a deep, deep breath. "I'm only doing what I think is best," she said, looking as if she were going to break into tears. "Because I love you," she added.

Jack had a horrible feeling. "Mel," he began.

Melody was looking at the door. "Janet, come in."

Jack's mother walked in.

Jack stared, frozen in absolute disbelief.

She looked almost exactly the same. Dyed blond hair that showed dark roots. His perfectly oval face. His green, long-lashed eyes—but on her, made up with tons of dark shadow and mascara. The same overripe figure, clad in tight jeans that showed good legs, no matter how old she was, and a tank top that bared almost everything. She had to be in her early fifties. Her figure didn't show it. Only her face did, because of the garish makeup.

She smiled. "Hello, Jack."

Jack looked at Melody, a murderous expression coming into his eyes. "How could you?"

Melody stepped back. "I just thought . . ."

"You didn't think!" Jack yelled. He turned to Janet. "Get out! Get the fuck out of here—out of my life!"

"Jack, you can't talk to me that way," Janet snapped back.

"Get her out of here," Jack rasped to Melody, balling his fists. His hands were shaking badly.

"I think you should talk to her," Melody said.

"Don't turn your back on your mother," Janet said angrily.

"You're not my mother! All you are is a no-good whore!"

Janet stepped forward and slapped him.

Jack stepped back, his hand on his face, his eyes wide with shock. "Get her out of here," he said again. His heart was palpitating wildly. He felt as if he were having an attack.

Melody was completely shaken. "Maybe we'd better go," she said to Janet.

"No," Janet said, staring at Jack. "Not until he hears me out."

"There's nothing you can say that I'll listen to," Jack snarled.

She stepped close to him. "I have cancer, Jack. I'm dying."

Jack's expression didn't change. "Bullshit," he said.

"It's true." Her eyes pierced his.

"Do you think I care?"

"Jack!" Melody gasped.

"I thought I'd make peace between us," Janet said.

Jack laughed harshly. "You thought wrong, lady! You're going straight to hell!"

"And so are you," Janet said viciously. "You're just like you're father, ain't you? The spitting image, the same drinking problems—oh, I read all about you. He wouldn't have cared either. He never gave a shit about anyone or anything other than himself."

Jack didn't want to touch her. Or he would have thrown her out bodily. He strode to the door and flung it open. "Get out."

She stared, hostility seething in her eyes. "You're a prick, just like he was." She moved to the door. "Don't you want to hear about your brother and sister?"

"No. Now get out."

Janet strode out. Melody hung back, looking at him. When he turned to her, his expression was hard and pitiless. "I'll never forgive you for this," he said, very low.

"Jack . . ."

"Never."

Jack put his face in his hands, his heart racing. She was full of shit, and he knew it. She had left him, and she didn't deserve any of his concern. Even if she was really dying, he didn't give a goddamn. As far as he was concerned, she was already dead.

21

*W*hat a waste, Peter Lansing thought—again.

He had been greeted at the door to Ford's office by Melody, and she looked good. She wore a blouse today— disappointing him, because she wore T-shirts so well—and faded jeans that hugged her small hips and rounded derriere. A great ass. He had the hots for her. He had wanted to make it with her from the first and only time he had laid eyes on her, in early August when he'd been hired to find Ford's

brother and sister. He had thought about her last night quite
a bit. Lansing wasn't used to having the hots for a woman
and not being able to get what he wanted.

That's why it was such a waste.

He had picked up on it instantly. After all, he was an
investigator, trained to observe people and events. But what
he had observed hadn't exactly thrilled him. She had a thing
for her boss—possibly a big thing.

Back then he had wondered if they were sleeping together.

He was wondering it now.

"So," he said, smiling, one step in the door. "How
about tonight?"

"What?" Her blue eyes widened visibly behind the
glasses.

"Dinner. Say, around seven? I'll pick you up." He had
a boyish smile and a good one. He knew it, because women
had told him it was endearing. Almost as endearing as other
attributes—like his hazel eyes, gold-flecked, and straight
brown hair. Like his rugged good looks and his body, which
was a natural Rocky. Of course, boxing was Peter's favorite
pastime, and he had been a middleweight champ in college.

Apparently Melody was immune to his smile. "Peter,
I'm afraid that's out of the question."

He was crestfallen. "Why? Do you have other plans?"

But she was already leading him to Ford's office, speaking over her shoulder. "We go on location tomorrow, and
afterward we're going to Aspen for Christmas. There's a
million things to do."

We. Damn. *We*. He didn't like her use of the plural. His
hands itched to grab that slender waist, and more. Those
fantastic Dolly Parton knockers. He bet she was wild in bed,
once she got there.

He had found Jack's brother, Rick, a month ago, in
between foster homes. He had been running with a gang in
Houston, and luckily for everyone, had been picked up for
assault with a knife—enabling Lansing to locate him. Janet
was Rick's legal guardian, but a judge had been only too
glad to remand the boy over to his half brother. Lansing

hadn't followed what went on, being too involved in locating the sister. But after having investigated the kid, he knew he was running with a bad gang, and no one knew where his mother was. Classic case of abandonment.

Ford was looking very tired and grim. As soon as Lansing came in he rose, extending his hand. A surprisingly strong handshake. Lansing had expected some kind of soft, spoiled actor when they had first met, but it had taken him exactly two seconds to realize that Ford had grown up on the other side of the street—his own side. Peter didn't like him, but he respected him grudgingly.

And did a slow burn whenever Melody turned her moonstruck baby blues on Ford.

To Lansing's annoyance Melody went and stood behind Ford, who sat behind his desk. She hovered like a mother hen. He couldn't stop thinking: Were they sleeping together?

"For God's sake, Mel, relax," Ford half-snapped. "I'm okay."

Lansing felt like punching him.

Ford rubbed his face with both hands, then glanced up. "I'm sorry, Mel."

"It's okay, Jack," she said softly. Then, "Peter, would you like a drink, or coffee?"

"A bourbon straight up would be great," Lansing said, noticing the change in her tone when she addressed him. He was most definitely irked.

"Have you found her?" Ford asked with impatience.

"I'm close."

They studied each other. Ford said, "Spill it. Look, I know what my mother was. She was a whore. Nothing you can say will surprise me. I want to know everything you've found out."

"Okay." Melody appeared with his bourbon. "Leah stopped attending school when she was fourteen. Janet has a rap sheet a mile long. Soliciting. Leah has one too."

"A record?" Ford's voice was strained. Melody was at his side again, her hand on his shoulder. Ford didn't notice.

"First picked up when she was fifteen. Soliciting. She was last picked up two years ago, in Houston, by Vice."

Ford didn't look too good, so Lansing decided to move on. "I found a friend of hers who said she moved to New York. A friend of mine with NYPD is running a check. Odds are if she went to New York, it wasn't for a career change. I should have something concrete for you soon."

Ford was grim. He stood and walked to the window, staring out with his back to the room. Melody regarded him anxiously, and Lansing watched them both. Waiting. After a few minutes Ford turned.

"Find her, Peter, as soon as you can. And I want you to keep me posted on your progress."

Lansing nodded. The meeting was over and he stood, shaking hands. Melody walked him out. "So." He smiled again. "Are you sure you won't change your mind?"

Melody looked at him dumbly. "About what?"

Lansing walked out. She didn't know what she was missing.

What *was* her relationship with Ford anyway?

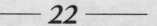

22

"*D*o you know that I haven't seen you in two weeks?" Adam Gordon said.

If he was trying to make her feel guilty, he was failing; if he was trying to make her defensive, he had succeeded. "Adam, I am sorry, but I've been working like a maniac."

They were having lunch in Newport Beach in deference to the unusually springlike day. "I know, I know. The *Outrage* revisions. But you don't work at night. We could have had dinner."

Belinda was irritated. "You know that production begins tomorrow! I've had two frigging deadlines, and I'm under pressure, Adam. I've had to put everything I have into this, every ounce of concentration. At night I've been exhausted. Right now my career is taking off, and it's a priority."

Adam didn't appreciate the lecture, just as he didn't appreciate the pending deal on her second sale, but he didn't let it show. Instead he took her hand. "I know. I do understand. I'm sorry."

Belinda sighed. "No, I'm sorry. I didn't mean to bite your head off like that. I'm stressed to the gills. Do you know I haven't gone out once in the past month? Not once."

Adam was slightly mollified. He squeezed her hand. "You do know that I'm not letting you go today, don't you?"

"What?"

His look was warm, maybe too warm. "Tomorrow you're leaving for the godforsaken desert. For God knows how long. Tonight belongs to me. To us," he corrected.

She had to smile. "It's only Arizona, Adam. You make it sound like Arabia. And I happen to know for how long— we should be on location eight to ten weeks. It's not forever."

Forever. Adam smiled, but that word echoed. This courtship was taking forever. It had been almost five months now, and he had the distinct feeling that he wasn't making any progress. Belinda seemed, and felt, elusive. If he was very honest with himself, he would confess that he wasn't even sure she was attracted to him. But there was her damn career to factor in, and it was taking up all of her concentration and all of her time.

He had complained once to Glassman, who had laughed. "You're not going to have to worry about that much longer!" He grinned, and Adam had felt a rush of exultation. The old bastard was as sharp as they came, and he was definitely up to something. But what? Adam had casually tried to find out. Glassman refused to give. Adam wanted to know what he was doing. Given the right situation, such as being Belinda's husband and accruing power within Glassman Enterprises as Abe's son-in-law, he could wait patiently, indefinitely. But not now. Chasing an unreachable Belinda was not the right situation. Something had to give, and give soon.

Patience. If she was playing a game, leading him on, it was working. The problem was, he knew she wasn't. She didn't flirt. She didn't have to. Her inheritance made her sexier than almost any woman he knew, and so did this prolonged courtship.

"What do you have in mind?" Belinda asked curiously.

She had just finished the revisions, and she felt like cutting loose. She also felt a touch guilty. She hadn't lied when she'd told Adam that she hadn't gone out at all in the past month. She had, however, had Vince over a few times, just for some good sex. In the beginning, she hadn't felt that she owed Adam anything, but now—now that they'd been dating for so long and had become such good friends—she was wondering if she owed him something, like honesty, at least, or fidelity.

But could you owe someone fidelity if you'd never even slept with him? Belinda wasn't sure. She'd only had one relationship, when she was a teenager, and in that one she'd fallen in love, given fidelity, and had had her heart broken. She was an amateur at relationships. She hadn't had a relationship since, not in almost ten years, unless you counted sexual affairs as relationships. Those could not possibly count. But it did seem that four months of dating was definitely heading somewhere, certainly toward a relationship.

She certainly liked Adam and enjoyed his company. And although she wasn't madly lusting after him, the warmth she felt for him had grown in the past few months, and with it, sexual curiosity. But just thinking about having sex with Adam made her nervous. She had never gone to bed with a man she was so friendly with before. If she slept with Adam, would that mean they were now having a *relationship?* Did she want a relationship? Was she ready for a relationship? What if she got seriously involved with Adam and he turned out to be a typical, grade-A prick like her one and only boyfriend had been? And what about Vince?

She would put off making a decision. There'd been too much pressure in the past few months, and right now all she wanted was to relax and kick back. "I suppose I have plenty of time to pack tomorrow," she said.

"You most certainly do," Adam affirmed. "How does Chasen's sound, with dancing after?"

She thought about getting dressed up in high heels and makeup after a month of jeans and bare feet. She grinned. "Adam, you're on."

Adam grinned back. Damn it, but tonight was the night. Before she went out of town he was going to bond her to him with a means as old as time—with sex.

23

She was leaving tomorrow.

He hadn't seen her or heard from her in almost a week.

Vince was going crazy. He was unbearably hard up, thinking about her night and day. And irritable. The guys at work had started to give him a lot of space. Which was fine.

There was a limit to how often he could fuck his wife in place of Belinda.

And Mary these days was impossible. Her drinking was out of hand. The house was a wreck. He couldn't go home without becoming livid. And more and more she wasn't even there. Out. Partying. It was a relief, and at the same time it wasn't.

The thought had briefly occurred to him that she might be having an affair. That should make him happy, make him feel less guilty, but it didn't. It made him furious. After all, she was his wife. What he was doing was wrong, he knew it, but he was in love, and he hadn't meant for it to happen. It just had—he couldn't help himself.

The first time he had ever seen Belinda had been at a party.

A stunning blonde in a skintight red dress, sleeveless, strapless, clinging—and she had looked at him, had smiled at him. With promise.

He knew a come-on when he saw it.

It was totally out of character.

She was a fantasy. *It* was a fantasy.

He had followed her.

Mary was off somewhere outside, drinking and doing lines with mutual friends. They were inside, in the living room, on opposite sides. With another hot, hot look she turned and started up the stairs. Her ass was high and round and perfect for his hands.

He followed.

He had never cheated on Mary before.

But he couldn't help himself.

They did it on the floor, without getting undressed. He shoved her dress up to her waist, momentarily stunned to find that she was wearing stockings and a garter belt and nothing else. He explored her with his hands, his fingers, to find her wet and slick. She deftly unzipped his trousers and pulled him out. "Oh, my," she said throatily. Her only words.

He grabbed her buttocks and thrust wildly into her. She clamped her legs around his waist and arched back. It was an animal rutting—plain fucking. They came within seconds, almost together.

He had watched her as she sat up, adjusted her black stockings, pulled down her dress, stood and smoothed it. Then she looked at him. Staring. He didn't have the foggiest notion what she was thinking.

He knew only one thing. She was the most beautiful woman he had ever seen, and he wanted her again.

Mary never suspected a thing.

Three weeks later Belinda had finally agreed to see him again—the three longest weeks of his life.

Belinda did that. She made time slow down—and speed up.

Just as she made it hard for him to think straight.

He had told her many times in the heat of passion that

he loved her, but he meant every word. He was afraid to say it without the passion to blunt the effect. She hadn't said anything. Not even that she was crazy about him. Nothing. No words of love. No words of affection. Nothing.

He picked up the phone. He was at his local 7-Eleven; he couldn't dial from the house. He called her again, and for the zillionth time there was no answer. Just where the hell was she?

More importantly—who the fuck was she with?

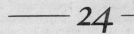

—— *24* ——

*T*he house was a wreck, but Mary didn't care. She took a long time showering and pampering herself, moisturizing all over, then spritzing herself with an exotic, earthy musk. She slipped on shorts and a halter and waited for Beth to arrive.

Beth.

She was hot and wet with desire.

Six months ago she would have fainted if anyone had told her she was going to be having an affair, any affair, much less one with a woman.

Not that she didn't still like men. She did. She still enjoyed Vince, but it was nothing compared to Beth. Vince turned her on—but he couldn't get her off.

She had come the first time Beth had made love to her.

They had been sunbathing outside on lounge chairs. Three weeks ago, during a warm spell. Mary was aware of Beth's eyes, which seemed to restlessly rove her body, dwelling on her breasts. But she didn't think about it. They were both hung over, and Mary was used to the attention her bosom attracted.

Mary had looked, however, when Beth had casually removed her top, revealing round, nice-sized breasts, all tan, the nipples brown and hard. Beth dressed in such a manner that all you ever saw of her was her long legs and small hips. Mary was very envious of her body. It was superb.

When Mary had turned over, untying the string of her top, Beth offered to rub lotion on her back. Her hands stroked the oil into Mary's skin with slow, sensual motions, first kneading her neck and shoulders, then her back.

"You need a massage," Beth had breathed. "You're so tight."

"That feels great," Mary said. It did feel great. She was warm and relaxed.

Beth's hands slid up the sides of her rib cage, grazing Mary's breasts. Mary tensed. The hands moved away. Just when she was relaxed again, it happened again. If Mary had known better or if Beth had been a guy, she would have been sure she was copping a feel. Mary felt depraved. Beth's touch had sent a wet heat spiraling down her body.

Beth's hands brushed her bikini-clad buttocks, and began to massage the back of one thigh. Mary realized she was becoming aroused. Beth's hands, spread wide on her thigh, moved up and down, coming closer and closer to her swelling groin. Briefly making contact. Then a hard nipple grazed her back, and suddenly Beth's hand was stroking her, gently, expertly—and it was like nothing Mary had ever felt before.

"Let me make love to you," Beth had gasped.

Mary's body said yes and her mind said no. Torn, she didn't say anything. Beth slid down, pressing herself against Mary's buttocks, rubbing her nipples against Mary's back, her hands slipping under to capture Mary's breasts. The heat between them was electric and overwhelming.

She slid off and pulled Mary's bikini off, turning her over. Mary closed her eyes. This is wrong, she was thinking. This is really wrong.

Then she felt Beth's tongue probing between her legs, and it was like nothing she had ever felt before.

Ten minutes later, to her complete surprise, she had an incredible orgasm.

Now she sipped a beer. She didn't care that she was bisexual. It was fun—and more. Never had she reached the heights that Beth brought her to. The problem was, Beth had fallen in love with her and was making demands. She wanted Mary to leave Vince and move in with her. Mary wasn't sure she wanted to do that.

What would her mother say?

Mary imagined something like: "If you lost a little weight, you wouldn't have to turn to girls—you could have men for lovers."

But that wasn't right. She had Vince. He was certainly all male.

Still, her mother would find some way, no matter how illogical, to tie her few extra pounds in with her affair with Beth.

Mary hadn't seen her mother in six months. Fortunately, she had been in Paris this fall with some new man. Mary had read in the society column that the divorce was final. Her mother's new lover was even younger than her last husband. It made Mary sick.

She was back in town. Mary had read that, too, in the paper. She was going to call any day, and Mary avoided answering the phone. She wanted to avoid seeing her too, as far as possible. Her mother loved to show off her men. Her mother loved to compare them to Vince. Her mother had never forgiven her for marrying a carpenter. Mary knew it was the ultimate hypocrisy. Her mother's affairs were always with young, poor men. (Well, poorer than she was.) It was okay for her, but not for her daughter. She hated her mother sometimes.

She heard Beth's car and put down the beer. Beth appeared, clad in a sarong-type skirt, tanned and slim and smiling. Their eyes locked. "Hi," Beth said, hugging her.

Mary hugged her back.

Her mother would hate Beth.

25

*O*f course Jack had forgiven her for bringing Janet to him.

But not right away.

The five days following Janet's arrival had been hell.

He hadn't spoken to Melody except for business purposes the next day, the day after he had seen Janet, and he had ignored her at the Cohens' party, still angry, acting like a spoiled child who was holding a grudge. Melody had realized her mistake. Her ploy had turned into a total disaster. Jack was furious. Really furious, in a way she had rarely seen him, and this time he was furious at her.

Her fear was sick and cloying.

The hurt was overwhelming.

Her weekend in Santa Monica had also been a disaster. All she could think of was that she had lost Jack's friendship, his love—even if it was platonic. She had cried on and off, miserable, frightened, depressed. He had returned from New York that next Tuesday, after having done a morning talk show, and they had met at his office in L.A. Jack was cool and distant all day.

At four, just before they were ready to leave for the day, Melody had gone in. "Jack?"

"I was just about to leave." He spoke with none of his old friendliness.

Tears flooded her eyes. "I'm sorry," she said. "I'm here to apologize. I made a mistake."

"Damn right you did," he said tersely. "Don't you ever interfere in my private life again. My private life is just that —private."

Aghast, Melody stood and watched him walk out.

The next morning she was waiting for him in his office

when he arrived. Her eyes were swollen and red. She handed him her resignation with two weeks' notice.

The moment he read it, still standing, he lifted his green eyes, wide with shock—and panic. "Mel!"

She bit her lip and hurried out.

He ran after her. "What do you mean, you're quitting?" he shouted, waving the letter she had so carefully composed.

"Just what it says, Jack," she replied, her voice quavering.

He seemed speechless. Finally he spoke. "You can't."

"Jack, I can't work for you anymore."

Jack's hand, holding the letter, shook. "I thought we were friends. I'm sorry, I've been a prick. I apologize. Melody, you can't leave."

"But . . ." she began, the tears escaping.

"Mel—please. Don't desert me."

She stared.

"You're my best friend."

His eyes were panic-stricken. Like a frightened boy's. How could she hurt him like this, she wondered. He needed her—he always had. And he had no one else.

"I won't leave, Jack," she had whispered finally, her face wet.

He was suddenly upon her, hugging her, holding her tightly so that her face was pressed against his chest. He had never held her so intimately before. She could feel his hands in her hair. And then she felt his mouth—he kissed the top of her head, then the side near her ear. She actually trembled. She was in Jack's arms. The way she had always dreamed of—almost.

He hadn't held her like that since.

Now he was hanging up the phone with barely contained irritation. He had been speaking with the Dean of Boys at Beverly Hills Day School. Melody didn't have to have heard the conversation to know that Rick was in trouble again for fighting. She wondered how much Jack would have to "donate" this time to keep Rick from being expelled. He had already given fifty thousand just to get him in. But keeping him in was proving expensive. Worse, Jack was all torn up over the brat, and he didn't deserve this. He'd already suffered enough.

"Is everything okay, Jack?"

He sighed. "Yeah." Then, "How do you do it, Mel?"

"How do I do what?" She had no idea what he was talking about.

"How do you deal with the nights?"

Melody stared.

"Ah, shit," Jack said. "I have a date with whatshername, and I'm not in the mood. Christ, am I bored. Thank God we start shooting soon!"

Hope surged in Melody. Was he finally tiring of all those mindless bimbos? "How about dinner, Jack? My treat."

He looked at her. "I don't know. I'm so restless. You know, the only thing I hate about this North-Star contract is its exclusivity. Shit, I could have done a couple of commercials, at least, in the past few months. Don't you have plans tonight, Mel?"

She smiled wanly. "Me?"

He seemed to really focus on her for the first time. "You don't get out much, do you? Aren't you lonely at night? Or are you just very discreet?"

Melody looked away, taken completely by surprise. What should she say? The truth? Her heart was thudding. "I'm human, Jack," she finally said.

His beautiful, slightly sad eyes searched hers. "What do you mean?"

"I'm not discreet. And I am lonely." Very lonely. For you.

Jack stared, his face filling with compassion. "I'm sorry."

Melody wanted to lean close and lay her head against his shoulder. As if reading her mind, Jack pulled her close, embracing her with one arm. "Life's tough."

Melody would have given anything to make the moment last forever. She looked into his eyes. Unplanned, the words came out soft and serious:

"Jack, I don't want to be alone tonight."

26

"You got Adam Gordon on the line?"

"I'm sorry, sir," came the cool voice. "He's out of his office for the afternoon."

"What do you mean?" Abe roared. "Try his home. Have you left a message? Doesn't he at least call in for his messages?"

"I've left two messages, Mr. Glassman."

Abe hung up, annoyed and angry. He could picture Adam, tall, dark, handsome in a slick way, so sure of himself, so arrogant. He liked that about Adam. He was man enough to stand up to him, but only to a point. The smart point. He knew which side his bread was buttered on.

Of course, it helped that Abe had a daughter worth billions, if he chose it to be so.

It helped that Adam was greedy.

It helped even more that Abe could ruin him in one second if he wanted to. L.A. was used to perversity, but Adam was a corporate lawyer, working in a big, very big, and even more conservative firm, and if Abe made public some of Adam's inclinations . . .

Abe wanted an update. It had been so easy, getting Adam and Belinda together. Too easy, he realized now. All he'd had to do was make clear that he despised Gordon, and Belinda had practically run into his arms. Yet now it was almost five months later, and he hadn't heard any wedding bells. He was starting to get pissed off. Adam said it was the *Outrage* sale, that all her energies had gone toward that. Which just confirmed what Abe already knew—that if his daughter got her career going, she'd be impossible to control. He'd never get her married off, never get his grandson, his heir . . .

His resolve had never been stronger.

This time, Belinda! he thought with satisfaction.

Soon. It wouldn't be long now before he'd be able to move openly on North-Star. "Hah!" He laughed aloud. Two birds with one stone. He couldn't wait to see the expression on Ford's face when he realized he was now owned by Abe Glassman. Lock, stock, and barrel.

And if Belinda dared to complain, dared to be outraged, (he liked the pun), well, he'd tell her the truth. The truth about her mother. The reason he was destroying Ford. And if she was still upset, so what? In the long run she would adjust, and it would be for the best. Every woman, no matter how "liberated," wanted a husband and family, and one day, one day when her son had it all, she'd thank him . . .

It was so funny. As smart as she was—and grudgingly, he had to admit she was no slouch—she was foolish enough to think she could beat him. To think she had beaten him. He shook his head.

When she had finally graduated college after that two-year fiasco with Rod Barnett, he had had a son-in-law all picked out. Bright, attractive, good bloodlines. The perfect father for his grandchildren. Or so he had thought.

Belinda had met David Shaeffer and quickly picked up on the fact that there was some matchmaking going on. In her usual, blunt, forthright style, she had called him on it. Abe had told her the way it was. "You're twenty-three, almost twenty-four, and not getting any younger. You wasted two years with that schmuck. Where are my grandchildren?"

"I don't believe you," she had said, staring.

"What's there to believe? I don't have a son. I've spent my whole life building up this empire—and not for Uncle Sam. I want a grandson, Belinda, and you won't find anyone better than David Shaeffer."

"I don't love him," she said, stunned.

"So what? What does love have to do with anything? That's bullshit. Lust. That's all it is—then it's gone. Do you know why I married your mother?"

"I'm afraid to ask."

"Because she had everything I wanted in a wife—in the mother of my children. Class, breeding, manners." Or so I thought.

"I'm not marrying David Schaeffer," she said.

And she hadn't.

But not, as she thought, because she had chosen not to. Rather, Abe had found out that David was a frigging closet fairy. Jesus! That's all he needed, a goddamn faggot for a son-in-law. What if his grandson turned out the same way?

So he had dropped the issue temporarily. It wasn't easy finding the right man for a son-in-law. There were dozens of possibilities, but always some flaw—some weakness—that disqualified them. The most important thing was that the man be controllable but not weak. A very difficult balance. The minute he met Adam, he had sensed that he was it—if he could find some way of controlling him. He hadn't had to look very hard.

With Belinda, it was harder. Damn the Worths for giving her that million-dollar trust anyway. It gave her just enough financial independence. But it hadn't stopped him from manipulating her through other means. Rod Barnett had been easy: money. Abe had finally paid the bum to walk out of her life. That and the threat of some physical impairment. Other manipulations had to be psychological, as with Adam Gordon. And then there was her career—her would-be career. By ruining the sale, he kept her vulnerable. One day she'd have to turn to him for help with her career—and he would gladly make her a success. For a price. An heir.

Rosalie buzzed. "Will Hayward's here to see you."

Abe felt irritation. A quick glance at his calendar told him Will didn't have an appointment. Now what in hell did he want? "Send him in." His instincts were warning him that this was no social call.

Will walked in, a slight, slim man with a receding hairline. "Hi, Abe." His smile was quick and nervous.

"You look like shit, Will," Abe said, meaning it. "You'd better get off that damn cocaine and booze, or you're gonna wind up six foot under."

"Abe," Will said, wringing his hands. "Abe, I need a favor."

"Yeah?"

"I need a small loan. Five grand would do it."

Abe started laughing. "You gonna give me some bull-shit about how you're gonna take a vacation in the Carib-bean?"

Will just looked at him.

"After the way you fucked up, *after Detective Smith,* you expect me to support your drug habit?"

"It's not for drugs," Will said intensely. "Abe, please. We go back a long way."

"Will, you go check into some rehab program, and then I'll think about it."

Will's face hardened; his nostrils flared. "Abe," he said trembling, "I've done a lot for you."

Abe threw back his head and laughed. "You've done for me! That's funny! Real funny!"

"All right," Will said, his voice hard. "Look at it this way. I know about Smith, what happened—in detail. And I know about other things too. I mean, take Senator Wilkie, for example. Take the Lazarus contracts with the Pentagon. Take—"

"Are you threatening me?"

"I need the five grand, Abe, but I'll pay it back."

"You're blackmailing me?"

Will took a step back. "You fucking owe me, dammit!"

"You know, don't you," Abe said, his face red with rage, "that if I fall, you go down with me?"

"Not necessarily," Will stammered.

They stared at each other, Abe's rage and incredulity growing. Hayward was threatening to go to the cops, the Bureau, the DA, whoever, and make a deal. Turn state's evidence and make a deal. The fucking idiot. The no-good little prick. Abe smiled. And reached for the intercom.

"Rosalie, bring me five G out of petty cash. Now."

27

*J*ack cruised the black Ferrari slowly down the block, approaching Beverly Hills Day School. Kids were streaming out, fanning away in both directions, mostly walking in groups of two and three, maybe four. His eyes scoured them all, looking for Rick.

He thought about Melody. He was no longer shocked. Now he could smile slightly. She had been red as a beet, saying she didn't want to spend the night alone. She had fled his office. Later she had apologetically told him it was just stress, making her say something so strange. Jack understood. He'd said and done a few things under stress too. Still, to be practically propostioned by Melody . . . It was so unbelievable he had to smile again.

Thank God he was on his way to Tucson tomorrow. He was dying to get back to work. It had been almost five months since the *Berenger* shoot, and he wasn't the type to adjust well to prolonged vacationing. In fact, he hated it. How much fund-raising could he do? Five months, and he was sorry he was locked into an exclusive contract, but it was almost over . . .

Five months.

He couldn't help it, but every time he thought about finishing that *Berenger* shoot he thought about the North-Star party and he thought about *her.*

Her. The blond broad who had stood him up.

The cockteaser.

It was the first time in his life he had ever been stood up, and even now, months later, he was furious just thinking about it. Just who in hell did she think she was? Just who in hell was she anyway? Shit! Not that he gave a goddamn!

He remembered waiting and waiting at Nicky Blair's.

His anticipation had never been so high. He'd been so intense and so focused on her that he hadn't even been able to flirt with the women who'd tried to come on to him. He was having a lot of fantasies, explicit, graphic fantasies, the foremost one being his holding her head in his large hands while he prodded past her lips with his huge cock . . .

The anticipation became sprinkled with slight foreboding. Souring. Anxiety drifted over him. He began scanning the entrance. Every time the door swung open his spirits lifted, only to come crashing down when it wasn't her. Until he knew. Until he knew the bitch was standing him up.

She had stood him up.

First she hadn't known who he was; then she had stood him up.

Unfuckingbelievable.

And he didn't even know who she was. Not that he cared. He could find out her identity in one minute if he did care, but he didn't, so he wouldn't even bother.

He spotted his brother just coming down the steps of the school. The cool-down that began was a relief. He was leaving for Arizona tomorrow, leaving Rick behind. He was worried not just because Rick needed guidance and parental authority, not just because he didn't quite trust him, but because the kid needed him, Jack. He needed someone to spend time with and show him some caring. Rick was indifferent most of the time, and the rest of the time he was hostile, but Jack understood.

He didn't know why, but after Janet's unwelcome visit he had started thinking about what she had said, about his having a brother and sister. At first, whenever his mind had dared to veer in such a direction, he had purposely, adamantly shut off his thoughts. He wasn't interested in *her* kids. No way.

Except, wasn't he her kid too?

There was a blood connection. It seemed to compel him. He had finally given in and hired Peter Lansing, considered one of the best free-lance private investigators in L.A. And Lansing had come through quickly.

He had arranged for a top lawyer to handle Rick's case

separately from those of the other kids involved in the gang fight. And the same lawyer had arranged for Jack's custody prior to legal guardianship and also for Rick's probationary release into Jack's custody prior to his hearing.

The first time he had met his brother had been in Juvenile Hall. Jack felt a tremendous pang upon entering the cold corridors and was swept back against his will to another time, another place, when he was twelve and tough and alone and frightened. Not that he'd shown anything but bravado to the cops and lawyers and social workers who refused to leave him alone. And all for stealing a car! Thank God he'd been caught. It had changed his life as surely as Rick's life was going to change now.

Rick had been sitting in tense and hostile defiance with the lawyer and a police officer when Jack walked in. The resemblance struck him first. Rick had the same face, the same green eyes. Unlike most adolescent boys, his face wasn't gawky and out of proportion, but perfectly formed—beautiful in youth. He stared at Jack with open anger.

"Hi," Jack said softly, momentarily overwhelmed. "I'm your brother—your half brother."

"Fuck you," Rick said. His eyes blazed.

Jack looked at the lawyer and the officer. "Can I see him alone?"

"He's all yours," the lawyer said, with a shrug.

Jack sat down across the table from Rick. "Whaddya want?" Rick snarled.

"I want to help you," Jack said honestly. He was stunned because of the surge of warmth he was feeling for a brother he'd never laid eyes on before. The feelings were new and strange, wonderful and frightening, the kind of feelings he'd never had before, not for anyone—love. The kid's a delinquent, he warned himself. Trouble. Stay on guard.

"Fuck you," Rick said. "I don't want shit from you."

Jack leaned back. "Do you want to go to a detention center? I mean, I can throw you to the wolves, and you can spend the next few years locked up in a prison for kids. Or I can buy your freedom and give you a home, while all you have to do is go to school and act civilized and stay out of trouble."

"I hate school, and I hate you too," Rick said, but with less hostility. Jack could feel his mind working.

"Well, I don't hate you, and I don't know why you should hate me. After all, I've never done anything to hurt you."

"Where were you—Rich Man—when me and Mom and Leah had no money and no food and got kicked out of our place? Huh? Where were you then—Mister Big Star!"

Jack leaned forward, intense. "I didn't even know about you and Leah until four months ago, Rick. Your mother— my mother—walked out on me when I was eleven years old." He felt his anger rising. "I was like you, kid. I had no money and hardly any clothes and I spent all my time stealing on the streets. Janet entertained all her johns and didn't pay any attention to me. One day I came home and she was gone—just fucking gone—her and all her things. I was eleven, Rick. Eleven and completely alone."

Rick stared.

Jack was on a roll now, and he pointed at Rick, his voice hard. "So I know all about you, kid, and don't think I don't. I know who you are because I was you! And the reason I didn't know about you and Leah until recently was because when Janet left me, that was the day she died, as far as I was concerned. Whether you believe it or not, that's the truth. Now, I was smart. When the cops threw me in Juvie, I knew it was definitely not the way to go. I got placed in a foster home, and I played it cool so I wouldn't have to go back to the slammer. If you've got any smarts, you'll throw your lot in with me."

Rick was silent for a few minutes. "So what's the deal?"

"I want you to come live with me. I'm filing for legal guardianship. You have to go to school and pass your courses and stay out of trouble."

"What do I get out of that?"

"You get food and clothes and a roof over your head."

"Shit!" Rick spat out. "I got that without you!"

"You'll have freedom, Rick."

Rick was silent, and Jack felt he could read him like a book. He knew the kid didn't trust him, but he also knew he had already seen the light. Finally Rick shrugged. "Why not? I've never lived with a fat cat before. What the hell do I got to lose?"

"Nothing."

Now, driving along the street, Jack watched him. He was the only kid walking alone, a tough and pathetic figure in black jeans and a black denim jacket, striding hard past all the laughing camaraderie he so clearly wasn't a part of. Jack felt his heart tighten in pity. Even kids who noticed Rick gave him a wide berth. Jack slowed even more as he pulled alongside. Before he could speak, Rick saw him. A dark, wary glance.

From somewhere undefined, there was a female shriek. "Jackson Ford!"

Jack frowned at the sudden hysterical chorus of his name. "Get in, kid!"

Rick jumped in just as a swarm of teenage girls came rushing to the car, crying his name. Pandemonium was about to break loose. Jack stepped on the gas amid cries for his autograph and hands on his car. One redhead jumped aside, and they were free.

God—he would never get used to it.

He would hate it if he didn't keep his sense of humor.

Rick was staring straight ahead, his jaw working.

"They don't bother you, do they?" Jack tried.

Rick still didn't look at him. "I get lots of requests for your autograph," he grunted.

Jack glanced at him. He hadn't been aware of that. "That bother you, kid?"

Rick threw him a belligerent look. "No, why should it? I don't give a shit."

Jack stopped at a red light. "What happened?"

"Nuthin'."

"Don't hand me that," Jack said sternly. "What the hell happened today?"

Rick shot him an angry glance. "It wasn't my fault!"

"It's never your fault, is it? I seem to recall you saying that the last two times."

"They're nothing but a bunch of candy-ass faggots," Rick grated. "They cross me, and they learn fast not to do it again!"

Jack placed a hand on his shoulder. The kid was a coiled bunch of steely muscle. "C'mon, Rick," he said soothingly. "Tell me about it. I'm on your side."

"Fuck!" Rick glared. "You're not on my side. I got you all figured out."

"Now what the hell's that supposed to mean?"

Rick ignored the question.

"Look, you've got to learn to control your temper. You're not living on the street anymore. If you hurt someone, there could be criminal charges and you just might have to go to jail. Money can buy a hell of a lot—but not everything." Jack was grim.

Rick glanced at him, and Jack saw that he seemed to be listening. "Yeah, well . . . It wasn't my fault," he muttered again.

"I hate to see you spend another Saturday in detention," Jack said truthfully.

"Tell them I'm sick!"

Jack hesitated. "I'm afraid I can't do that, kid," he said.

Rick slammed his back hard against the seat and stared straight ahead, arms crossed tightly. "You're no different from all the rest."

"Yes, I am," Jack said. "But you won't give me a chance."

28

"Adam."

"What?"

Belinda took a breath against his shirtfront. His body was warm, hard. His hands on her back felt good. His cologne, now familiar, Lapidus for Men, was most definitely delicious. "Adam, you do know I'm buzzed?"

He spoke into her hair. "Umm. So am I. You smell good."

She felt his mouth brush her temple. Desire, warm and tingly, pulsed gently through her. I'm not madly attracted to him, she thought. But with the wine and the stars, it would be so easy, and she knew she would enjoy it. Wasn't this overdue?

But what about their relationship afterward?

"Belinda," Adam said, lifting her face.

For a moment, their eyes met. He is handsome, she decided. Very handsome, impeccably handsome. "I don't know . . ."

Adam kissed her. He had an erection. She definitely liked the feel of that, and there was an answering swell in her own groin as he pulled her hips against his. She knew she had to make a decision. His tongue probed past her lips, and she let him.

Too much wine, she thought, opening her mouth to him. He was a very good kisser. An impeccable kisser. Not too insistent. Too much French kissing with a man she wasn't mad for turned her off; somehow it seemed more intimate than the act of copulation. Adam sensed it with his impeccable timing and knew just when to withdraw. *So impeccable.*

She leaned back. "I'm buzzed. And I have to get up early. I don't know, Adam."

His body went tense beneath her hands. "It's still early," he said. "Belinda, you're so beautiful. I want you. I've waited. Please."

She was unsure of everything really, except that his thighs against hers felt strong and male and good. She closed her eyes, letting him pull her back hard against him. "Tonight is our night, Belinda."

"Tonight it's the wine, Adam."

Their gazes met, and she saw that he was angry. "Damn, I'm too blunt sometimes. I'm sorry. Adam, I like you—you know I do."

"Do you? Then show me, Belinda."

She hesitated. "We've never really discussed things. Discussed us. Discussed what happens afterward."

"Let's discuss us now."

"Is there an us?"

"God! I'm crazy about you! You must know it!"

She blinked at him. "What do you want from me?"

Adam hesitated, but only briefly, and when he spoke his voice was strong. "More than just your body, Belinda, more than just a night. I want lots of nights. And lots of days like today. I want to wake up every morning and reach for you and find you there. I want you in my life."

She was stunned out of inebriation. Thoroughly stunned. "What are you saying?"

"I want to marry you."

She stared.

He cupped her face. "Belinda, you must care for me—don't you?"

"Of course I do," she said instantly. "We're friends. But I'm not in love."

"Give me a chance," he said. "You haven't given me a chance. You've been totally preoccupied with your career. You've held me at a distance. Let me into your life, Belinda, and I guarantee it will be good. We'll be good."

But will you let me down? she thought. Her heart was racing. She was feeling something suspiciously like fear. And she knew she didn't love him. But hadn't she been keeping him at a distance on purpose? Hadn't she been keeping all men at a distance on purpose? Ever since Rod had walked out on her she'd erected impenetrable walls, preferring men like Vince, men either married or not intellectually on her level, so that there was no question of ever facing the possibility of commitment and betrayal. It was almost ten years since Rod. Damn. Did she want to be alone forever?

I don't mind. Really I don't, she told herself.

Liar!

I have my work. I have myself.

Everybody needs somebody. It was a cliché, but true.

"Belinda?"

She looked at him. What harm was there in sleeping with him? She'd slept with hundreds of guys. It was a step in another direction, because Adam was eligible, but she could still keep him at a distance if she chose. Couldn't she?

She smiled slightly. She gave him a look. An unmistakable one, one she'd perfected years ago. Adam's eyes went hot. Belinda reached for her keys.

29

"*B*elinda, I tried calling you all night last night."

Belinda turned her back to the doorway, thinking, Oh, shit. Vince had better timing than Adam. So that had been him ringing repeatedly last night? She had disconnected the phone the third time, while Adam was expertly and insistently tonguing her clit, bringing her repeatedly to the brink of an orgasm, then refusing to take her any farther, until she couldn't stand it. Until she was reduced to a quivering, begging mass of jelly. Now guilt assailed her. How come Vince had the knack of making her feel guilty and Adam didn't?

And how come, even though Adam knew all the right moves and had superlative timing, there was something missing in his lovemaking, something that Vince had? And what was she, thirteen, to be comparing the two men? And just what in hell should she do about Vince? Or for that matter, about Adam?

Thank God I'm leaving for location today, she thought. It was the coward's way out. She could postpone a decision until she returned.

"Vince, I'm sorry, I wound up celebrating yesterday. I got home buzzed and shut the phone off."

"You're leaving today." He sounded both hurt and panicked. "I thought we were going to spend last night together."

"I never said that."

"I just thought . . . Look, I'm working, but let me drive you to the airport."

"No, that's okay," Belinda said quickly. Right now she couldn't handle him, especially being alone with him. If he drove her to the airport, he'd probably wind up giving it to her in a rest area. And that she didn't need.

"Then stop by the job on your way out."

"Look, I'm running late." She glanced toward the hallway. Adam was still dressing in her bedroom. She really felt like a shit with him there and Vince on the phone like this.

"Belinda, I want to see you."

She knew Vince. Although he was responsible, as far as she went he was like a pit bull. She imagined him leaving work and barreling over to her house to catch her before she left. "Okay, I'll stop by." Just as she hung up Adam came walking out. Belinda began to blush.

"Who was that?"

Belinda looked at him levelly. "Somebody I've been seeing."

Adam stared. "I didn't know you were seeing anyone."

"You never asked. It's not serious, Adam."

There was a long pause while Adam gazed at her, making Belinda feel naked. "Are you going to keep on seeing him?"

"That's not fair, Adam. We haven't discussed anything, and I haven't thought about it." Her tone was sharp. "I have to start packing." It was strange, but she realized that she didn't feel any closer to Adam today than she had yesterday.

His about-face was immediate. "Call me from Tucson so I have your number," he said, looking at her warmly. He gave her a long kiss. Belinda couldn't help it, her impatience was overwhelming. Finally, finally, he released her and was out the door and gone. His Mercedes was still turning over when she dragged a suitcase out of the closet. And began to face the knots suddenly twisting in her stomach.

She sat on the side of her bed and took a deep breath. Her nerves grew in intensity instead of dissipating. She was so tense, she almost felt sick. Why am I feeling this way? It was like being afraid. And she had to face it—she knew why she was suddenly sick with anxiety. It wasn't just because she was going on a shoot for the first time in her life. God.

He probably wouldn't even remember her.

She had stood him up. He would remember, all right. Once he saw her, at least.

What did she care? So what if he was upset or angry.

So what? He had to have a monstrous ego. No, he did have a monstrous ego. Not only did she know it from meeting him once, but she had heard all the stories about how difficult he was on the set, how demanding he was, how impossible to work with. And she had stood him up. He was the *star*. What if he insisted on a new writer? What if he got her thrown off the production? Damn! If he was holding a grudge, he could really damage her, really damage her career. Maybe he would be totally indifferent. Maybe he would be graceful about what had happened. Maybe he really wouldn't remember her.

Jackson Ford.

Jackson Ford and her mother.

30

*S*he had no idea what time it was.

She thought she was going to die.

Mary moaned and rolled over, her heart going wild, her head throbbing, her throat dry. Water. She desperately needed water. With a great effort she sat up and looked at the clock. How in hell had she gotten so fucked up last night?

Vince.

It was all coming back . . .

She had spent the afternoon with Beth. Then . . . laden with guilt, and a little high—she had gone to the store, come home, and fixed Vince a perfect dinner. He had been hours late, and when he had arrived he hadn't even been hungry. Mary had been hurt and furious.

And the more she thought about it the more she realized she hardly ever spoke to Vince these days. Sex was less frequent, down to about once or twice a week, and he was constantly distracted. She knew there couldn't possibly be another woman—could there?

Vince was not the type to have an affair.

He was home most nights; six out of seven were spent with her. That one other night, well, he deserved that one with the guys. That was only fair. But . . . no, he had to have been with the guys that night.

He couldn't possibly know about her and Beth.

Or could he?

Wouldn't he confront her if he knew?

Mary got up and took a shower, starting to feel better but still horribly hung over. Cocaine hangovers were the worst—they left her physically depleted. With rising panic, she kept thinking about Vince. Come to think of it, when *was* the last time he had made love to her? She thought and thought and decided it must have been two weeks ago. That definitely meant something was wrong. She knew him too well. His sex drive was as Taurus as the rest of him—steady, consistent.

For some reason the thought of losing Vince terrified her.

Her mother would laugh and tell her she'd never hold a man unless she lost weight. That, of course, was bullshit. Or was it?

Beth would be thrilled. Beth was crazy to think she'd even consider it. Fooling around with a woman on the side was one thing; living openly with one was another. Besides, she loved Vince.

Didn't she?

Thoroughly worried now, Mary threw on one of Vince's big flannel shirts and padded into the bedroom. She opened her underwear drawer and sorted through the cotton garments, then pulled out a tin box. In it were vials, a mini-scale, straws, razor, cash—but no foil packets.

Fuck! She was out.

She'd had no idea she was getting so low.

Quickly she counted the cash—one hundred seventy-five dollars. She couldn't believe that figure either. An eighth was three twenty-five. She had nothing left. How in hell was she so short? She certainly hadn't done up all of what she was supposed to sell, had she? If she remembered correctly, she had dipped into what she was selling twice—two half grams. That didn't make sense. Had she fronted that stuff? And if so . . . damn, she couldn't remember to whom!

She began to think up lies in order to get some money from Vince. They needed groceries—she had invited friends for dinner this weekend. Perfect. Except she'd probably only get fifty or so out of Vince.

There was her mother. Her mother—shit.

Her mother would give her the balance, that was no problem. But she would gloat. Smirk. Because her daughter had to come for cash to her instead of Vince.

Her life was falling apart. She was out of blow. Vince was tired of her. Maybe he was having an affair . . .

First things first. She would go down to the job and see if she could get some cash from him. Then she would call Ben. Maybe he would let her owe him—he had done that before. If she could remember who her customer was (and it would come back to her), she would call him and pressure him. And there was always her mother . . .

First she would go see Vince.

He hated school.

"C'mon, Rick." Jack was shaking him. "Time to get up. Hey, kid!"

"Ah, shit," Rick mumbled, sitting and rubbing his eyes. When he opened them Jack was gone.

He hated school, he always had, but he especially hated this one. They were all faggot pansies and snobs, every single kid there, looking down their Valley-girl and Valley-boy noses at him. Shit. He stumbled into the shower, full of dread, the same dread he felt every morning when he woke up. At least in Houston the dread had only been once and a while—not like this.

But he knew what it felt like to be in a cage, and that was the worst kind of dread you could feel.

He pulled on torn and faded jeans, black, a pale green muscle shirt, a faded black denim jacket. The standard garb. Already he was smoking a Kool. Jack hated his smoking and had told him he was forbidden to smoke anywhere except in his room or on the balcony. Fine. When Jack wasn't home he smoked in the living room, drinking beer and watching the big-screen TV.

Now that was one helluva TV!

But then again, so was everything in the three-bedroom condo in Westwood that Jack owned. He hated L.A., true, but he liked the condo almost as much as he liked the ranch house in Santa Barbara. Both homes were small compared to the mansions that lined Rodeo Drive and the rest of Beverly Hills, but to Rick they were palatial. Just living in digs like these justified the school shit.

He finished the smoke and felt in his rear pocket, pulling out a five. Damn! He was short by forty bucks. Jack gave him a decent allowance—fifty a week—which was supposed to cover transportation, food, cigarettes, and anything else— such as albums and a new shirt and movies. But it was barely enough for the cocaine Rick liked freebasing. However, the other day he had tried crack for the first time and had liked it. For ten bucks he could get enough crack to stay high for a couple of hours. Maybe he'd forget about freebasing and stick with crack. It was a lot more affordable.

He knew if he asked Jack for more money he'd want to know whatever it was he needed it for. He'd already spent this week's allowance. Jack was too fucking sharp and suspicious. Fifty bucks a week! The guy could afford to give him twice that.

Rick sauntered out into the kitchen, where Jack was placing a bowl and coffee cup in the sink. Jack gave him a friendly smile, which Rick knew was phony. After all, the guy was an actor, wasn't he? Why should he care about him? Some kid off the street? He still couldn't figure out his angle. He guessed it might be guilt.

"I'm leaving in a few hours," Jack said. "I hope you're going to stay on the straight and narrow, Rick. I'm trusting you. Please don't give Ruth Goodman a hard time."

"Yeah, sure," Rick said. Jack didn't trust him, and he knew it. Ruth Goodman was evidence of that. Christ! A babysitter!

"I'm going to try and fly back next weekend," Jack was telling him. "Please be nice to Ruth. And no playing hooky. I mean it, Rick."

Rick mumbled an affirmative. He was thinking about

how, if he could get extra money, he could buy crack and beer and skip school and just party out all day every day and Jack probably wouldn't find out for a couple of days. On the other hand, then the shit would hit the fan. Jack might even fly back immediately to deal with him. Shit. He'd have to be careful. There had to be something around here that Jack wouldn't miss if he pawned it. The guy had so much stuff.

"I won't see you later, kid," Jack said, looking him right in the eye. "You need anything, you got a problem, call me in Tucson, okay? The number's taped by the phone."

Jack hesitated, then finally left. Rick debated what he wanted to do. He would go bananas if he had to stay straight another day. The man would be around today and then not again until Friday. Not that he couldn't score off the street if he had to, but it was easier this way. He walked into Jack's room and stood looking around.

The room was completely modern, all white except for the bed, which was king-sized and black. Black-and-white striped comforter, black-and-white striped sheets. Jack and women in and out of it constantly, explaining to him the second night he was home that he had a lot of women friends. Friends. Right. The noises some of them made kept him awake half the night. If there was anything he admired about his brother it was his love life—he had it in more than out. Rick was definitely envious on that score.

Rick found the gold-and-diamond cuff links he'd seen Jack wear once. They were tossed carelessly in a crystal ashtray that contained all sorts of odds and ends—some single dollar bills and change, receipts, a silver bill clip, a gold tie clip with a diamond in the center, a tie, matches . . .

He debated between the tie clip and the cuff links. And finally opted for the latter.

32

*J*ackson Ford and her mother.

Even now, with the wind whipping her hair as her red MR2 barreled down the freeway, the knowledge was devastating. It made the knot in her guts expand, choking her. There was no reason she should care. None. But she did.

It felt like betrayal.

Belinda took a few deep breaths. She was impossibly wound up. How could she be a professional on the set when she was so agitated? She was sorry she had ever followed her mother to the powder room at that damn party. Sorry she'd ever gone. Sorry she'd ever laid eyes on him—on Ford.

And the worst, the absolute worst part of it, was that she had wanted Ford. Badly. Really wanted him. He exuded total sexual magnetism. A woman was helpless under his onslaught. If he chose to turn it on. She knew that instinctively. Had her mother been helpless too?

She had been anticipating leaving Majoriis's party to meet Jack, trying to figure out how to get Adam out of the picture tactfully. Her gaze, unfocused, had wandered and then, startled, she realized she was looking at her mother and her father and Jack Ford in a distraught conversation from across the room.

There were no smiles. Belinda thought, puzzled, Do they know each other? Then Abe grinned, but there was nothing pleasant in his expression; rather, it was volpine and triumphant. Jack turned abruptly and rigidly away; and then Nancy was suddenly running across the room in her Jourdan heels and Ungaro silk, disappearing down a corridor. Belinda got a glimpse of Nancy's face—enough to see that her mother was upset to the point of tears. She looked back at Abe. Ford was gone, but her father was pleased. What has he done now? Belinda thought grimly.

She found her mother in the powder room. "Mom, let me in. It's me, Belinda." She could hear her weeping through the door.

Finally the lock turned, but Nancy barred the entrance, her makeup streaked. "Belinda, please, not now . . ."

She was a pitiful sight, and Belinda was stunned. "Mom, what is it?"

Nancy crumbled anew.

Belinda shoved into the bathroom and stood, unsure, wanting to hold her mother, but she'd never comforted her before. So instead she laid a tentative hand on her shoulder. "Mom? Do you want to talk about it?"

"I hate him," Nancy raged through her tears. "I hate him!"

"What has Abe done now?"

"Not Abe! Him! Jack Ford!"

Belinda stared, shocked.

The story of their brief love affair tumbled out amid Nancy's sobs.

Belinda still, for the life of her, could not picture them together, even though she had seen them together. And now, thinking back, she remembered how he'd looked her right in the eye when she'd barged in on them as they were fucking. Now, thinking back, she saw his eyes the way she had at the party, and there was no more doubt as to the chauffeur's identity.

Nancy had fallen in love with him.

Belinda clasped the steering wheel, now wet beneath her hands. Impossible to believe, another facet of the betrayal. Her mother in love with Jack Ford? Carrying on her secret affair? And what about Abe? It was one thing to screw around, it was another to love someone else. That was the ultimate violation.

But didn't Abe deserve it?

God! Imagine if Abe ever found out—he would kill Nancy! He would probably kill Ford too!

Belinda wasn't heartless. Despite her shock, she had

tried to understand at the party, just as she was trying to understand now. But for some damn reason compassion was elusive. Though she could empathize with Nancy's loneliness and imagine how Ford would be impossible to resist on a daily basis, she almost hated them both. Maybe she did. Thinking of them together made her sick.

If only she hadn't gone to the North-Star party, she wouldn't be in this damn spot!

Thank God she had learned the truth. Thank God. Because she had been anticipating the evening ahead with more enthusiasm than she'd felt in a long, long time. Now, knowing how close she had come to sleeping with her mother's ex-lover, well, she couldn't handle it. She expected a man to want her exclusively, just as she expected him to walk away and remember how good it had been. Belinda did not try and fool herself. She knew it was not ego, not really, but more of an insecurity. After she'd been so badly screwed over by that faithless prick, Rod, the aftershocks still rippled and demanded an extreme opposite effect. She had thought Rod had loved her, but one night he had just disappeared without a word. Six months later he had married. The betrayal had been devastating. She knew that was why she had avoided relationships ever since. But Ford attracted her so strongly that she would want him for more than a night or two. Even though she knew that the last thing in this life she needed was to get involved with a man like Ford, her instincts warned her that if she slept with him, she'd be lost. And if she had gone to bed with Ford and *then* found out about her mother, it would have been another terrible betrayal.

She almost missed the exit for the construction site. As Belinda whipped off the freeway she said a short prayer of thanks to whomever might be listening, for the fact that she hadn't slept with Ford, that she had stood him up. She resolved to be completely professional with him, no matter how unprofessional he was with her. She would not lose her cool; she would not show contempt; and she would pretend that she had no idea that he and her mother had once been lovers. If she had to, to keep her job, she would kiss his ass.

No matter how much she hated doing it. Yes, that would be her operating principle—kissing his ass. Because seeing this production through to the end was the most important thing in her life.

At least she had learned the truth before it was too late. And at least the truth had doused all her desire for him.

If she looked at it that way, she was one lucky broad.

33

Mary had been down to the job on several occasions. Now she parked in front of the open chain gates, next to a red Toyota. She stepped out of her car, clad in jeans and a sweater and sneakers. The sweater was tight, and sure enough, she got a few interested looks from the carpenters as she walked up to the house. She had chosen it especially for Vince; it was one of his favorites.

She kept running a dialogue in her head: Vince, honey, I've invited Jim and Barbara over for dinner Saturday, and I want to really do it up. I need a hundred dollars . . .

He was going to wonder why she needed so much.

Worse, even if he gave it to her—what would happen when there was no dinner party?

"Where's Vince?" she asked a man fitting Sheetrock across diagonal supports.

"Inside," he said.

She stepped into the house, over a pile of debris, glancing past two carpenters banging nails in a corner.

It was her. She knew it the minute she saw them, Vince looking upset and angry, a woman with a Raquel Welch body clad in a red knit dress, talking to him with her back to Mary. A blonde. Superb.

Her.

She knew it.

Vince grabbed the woman by her shoulders, such an intense look on his face that Mary felt sick. Then he looked up, past the woman, at his wife. He instantly dropped his hands, a look of absolute shock crossing his face.

Her instinct was to turn tail and flee.

Instead, Mary walked over slowly, steadily, trying to breathe naturally—not as if she'd just run a marathon. But her head was throbbing. She desperately needed a drink. "Vince."

"Mary," Vince croaked.

Mary looked at the woman, who had turned and was looking at her equally carefully. She was beautiful. Thin. Not thin-thin, but there wasn't an ounce of flab on her. She had a body like an aerobics instructor. Mary knew she couldn't compete. Not with this. Sick desperation rose up in her, and she wanted to kill the woman, or at least scratch her eyes out.

"Hello," the woman said somewhat curtly. "I've been admiring this house for weeks, and I was trying to get the foreman to show me around. Are you the owner?"

Mary knew it was a lie, bullshit. This woman was Vince's lover. This woman and Vince were sleeping together. She knew it. "The foreman is my husband," Mary said tensely.

"What are you doing here, Mary?" Vince quickly said, taking her arm.

Mary barely looked at him. She couldn't stop staring at the woman, who was watching them although pretending not to. "Mary Spazzio," she said. "You are—?" She had to know.

There was a brief hesitation. "Belinda Glassman. Well, thank you, Vince, for the tour. Nice meeting you, Mary."

Mary watched her leave with a long, strong stride, and then she looked at Vince. Before he had seen her watching him there had been naked hunger on his face—and desperation. She suddenly couldn't cope, couldn't be near him—hated him, hated her. Mary turned and hurried after Belinda.

"Wait," she said as Belinda was about to get into her car.

Belinda stopped and turned.

"Stay away from him," Mary cried. "Stay away from him, or I'll kill you!"

Belinda looked at her. "I'm afraid you're mistaken," she said and slid into the Toyota.

"You bitch!" Mary said, but the car was already gone, a red blur through her tears. "You bitch!"

34

With great reluctance—a vast understatement—Vince turned his Ford pickup into the driveway of his home.

He had run over the awful meeting of his wife and lover a hundred times in his head, and he thought Belinda had pulled it off. She had been perfect. She had given no clue. Her explanation had been logical, flawless. Then why hadn't Mary believed her?

Vince climbed out of the truck and stopped to water the primroses. Methodically he plucked a few dead flowers, not looking at the house, but his ears were burning. Finally, unable to delay the inevitable, he walked in.

She was sitting at the kitchen table, her eyes red, her face flushed, spitting fury. "How long," she demanded. "*How long,* you bastard!"

"Mary, what are you talking about?" He tried to bluff. He didn't know why he didn't just confess the truth—it was what he had been wanting to do for months. Somehow, though, cowardice and the instinct for survival won out.

"You know what I'm talking about," she shrieked, standing. "You're fucking her—Belinda Glassman. Aren't you?"

"No," he lied. The instant the word was out he knew she saw the lie.

"I hate you!" she screamed. And before he saw it coming, she had picked up her wineglass and thrown it at him.

He ducked just in time. The glass flew past his right temple and hit the wall behind him, shattering. "Jesus!" he said.

"How long has it been? I want to know how long you've been fucking her!" She was screaming, and Vince realized she was heavily sauced.

"Mary . . . I don't know what to say."

"Pig!" She threw the saltshaker. "Cocksucker!" The pepper mill followed.

"Damn it!" he exploded. "I'm glad you found out."

She froze. "So it is true?" Her voice quavered with hurt, and she looked so young and vulnerable that he suddenly felt awful. Hadn't he loved her once? He hadn't meant to hurt her.

"I . . . it just happened."

"What about me? I'm your wife." She was sobbing.

"I . . ." There was nothing to say.

"Do you love her, Vince?"

He hesitated.

She stared.

"Yes."

"You motherfucker." Mary stood up unsteadily. "She's a rich broad. Abe Glassman's daughter. She's got millions. What do you think she wants with a carpenter like you? Huh? What? All she wants is your ass, Vince."

It hurt. He knew she wanted to hurt him, but the fact was, she was right. And the truth, while he had known it all along, was awful. Because he did love Belinda, against all his better judgment. "I'm sorry."

"I hate you," she shrieked, and she grabbed a glass from the drying rack and hurled it. He ducked just in time. Missile after missile followed, along with a string of the worst curses he had ever heard. She's crazy, he thought, frightened suddenly; and he slipped out the door and back into the night.

"I hate both of you," she screamed after him. "You're both going to be sorry, you and Belinda Glassman, both of you!"

35

Jack walked in with only a perfunctory knock. His spirits were higher than high. They had just checked into their rooms, and he had his script in his hand. (Not that he needed to go over his lines—he already knew them by heart.) On the way out from the airport, as they were driving through the saguaro-studded desert to Ventanna Canyon, where half the crew was staying, he'd had a major inspiration about the character of the hero, Nick Ryder. He wanted to run it by Melody.

He stopped short.

Melody sat abruptly upright, wiping her red eyes.

"Mel!" Jack gasped. "What's wrong?"

She turned her face away. "Please, Jack, not now."

She was crying. Why was she crying? In all the years he'd known her he'd only seen her cry once, over some schmuck who'd hurt her. "Mel, are you okay?" He approached instinctively, touching her shoulder lightly.

"No, I'm not," she said heavily, pathetically. He couldn't see her face, but her shoulders shook. His hands closed over them. "Tell me what's wrong?" he whispered. "I can't stand seeing you like this."

She moaned and was suddenly embracing him, her face nestled in his chest. Jack sank onto the bed and held her while she sniffled and clung. He stroked her back. "It's not something I did, is it?"

It took her along time to answer. "No. God, Jack,

sometimes it's just . . . I get so depressed . . . sometimes I can't stand it anymore!" She started crying again.

He held her and rocked her. "Tell me about it, Mel, I want to help."

"It's the loneliness." She sobbed. "I'm so alone. I hurt from the loneliness. I have no one. No one at all."

"You have me," Jack said, tightening his hold.

Melody was shaking. "Don't you see, Jack? It's not the way it is for you. I'm not pretty and I'm not a star. There's no one in my life, no men, no man to be with. I haven't been with anyone in years. I have needs just like anybody else. Not only physical needs but emotional ones too. I hate being alone. I hate the nights!"

She collapsed against him.

"God," Jack said, stricken. "I take up all your time, don't I? And leave you with nothing for yourself."

Jack felt awful, and guilty. "I'm so self-absorbed I never even bothered to think about you, about what you need," Jack said. "I make a lousy best friend, don't I?"

Melody didn't answer.

He thought of all the tail chasing him and tried to imagine how it must be for Melody. He could barely relate. He couldn't imagine not getting laid for a week, much less a year or more. How could she stand it? And was this his fault? He knew that it was, at least partly, for monopolizing her. And now he wondered if she'd really meant it when she'd propositioned him the other day. She must have. Her loneliness and physical pain must have driven her to turn to him, her best friend. He knew he could make her happy. He wasn't attracted to her, but he was assailed by so many feelings, some of them tender ones, that it was almost like wanting her. And what was the big deal? After all, they were good friends. Sex was, after all, only sex. And it was because of him that she had no free time to take care of herself.

He shifted her in his arms and brushed his lips against her temple. For the first time he became aware of the fact that she was soft in his arms, soft and all woman, her heavy breasts crushed against his chest. He nuzzled her cheek with his. "Mel, I don't want you to be unhappy," he said huskily. And he meant it.

She lifted her face, her eyes wide and vulnerable and confused. "I can take away the loneliness for a little while," Jack said, pausing long enough for her to understand. Her eyes widened, her mouth parted. Jack kissed her.

She opened her mouth, and Jack gently inserted his tongue.

Melody's hands were twisting suddenly and wildly in his hair. She was somehow on her back; he was on top of her. Her mouth was open, aggressive, voracious. Her thighs were clamped around his hips, pulling him into the cradle of her groin. His reaction was immediate; his cock grew thick and hard and heavy, pulsing against her. Melody moaned, flinging her head back, and Jack's mouth found her throat.

Her explosive passion surprised him only momentarily. It fueled him. He forgot it was Mel. The woman beneath him was soft and warm and trembling with need for him.

He undressed her with fluid, practised ease, freeing her breasts, surprised again with the abundance beneath his hands, against his face.

"So good. So soft, so hard," he groaned, tugging on a large nipple.

He slid into her, his mind registering heat, wetness, wonderful tightness. The woman beneath him writhed uncontrollably. His mind vaguely observed, detaching itself, and he recalled that this was Melody—what a surprise. "Jack!" she gasped as he drove his huge organ into her. "Jack, Jack," she chanted.

She came, crying, "Jack!"

36

"*A*be, thank God you're in town!" There was a note of panic in Ted Majoriis's voice.

"God ain't got much to do with it," Abe said lazily, leaning back in his chair in his Los Angeles office.

"What's going on? The Board's going crazy! Rumors are flying like shit on a fan!"

"Whaddya mean?" Abe asked, smiling at Ted who was wringing his hands. "It's a free country, ain't it? A man can't buy up a few shares of public stock?"

"Abe," Majoriis said nervously. "I heard you got thirty percent of the company. That's a few shares? Look, there's a lot of speculation. Speculation about a takeover."

Abe laughed. "A takeover? Ted, I've been a major investor in North-Star for almost twenty years."

Majoriis hesitated. "There's a big difference between eight percent and thirty percent. I don't have to tell you that."

"No, you don't have to tell me that." Abe laughed silently. "Look, I ain't planning a takeover, so relax. My daughter sold that screenplay to North-Star, remember?"

"Yeah, they're in production."

"They go into production tomorrow," Abe corrected. "I'm just backing her up a little, protecting her interests with a few extra shares, that's all. You shouldn't have come all the way across town, Ted—I could have told you over the phone."

"Oh. Yeah, well, I guess that makes sense. You're not kidding me, Abe? You know you can trust me—I wouldn't say a word."

Abe spent another five minutes reassuring him that he was not planning a takeover, knowing that the rumors would not stop now. In fact, they would increase because of the monkey wrench he'd just thrown into the works. Finally he got rid of Majoriis. "You got Adam Gordon on the line yet?"

"Yes, sir."

"Adam," he boomed.

"Abe—er, Mr. Glassman. Hello."

"Where the hell were you yesterday? I was trying to reach you the whole goddamn day! I'm in town, and I want to see you tonight."

"I was with Belinda."

Excitement suddenly coursed through Abe, and he leaned forward. "All day?"

"All day," Adam said, sounding smug. "In fact, I just got home a while ago."

Abe laughed with pure delight. "So you finally got into her pants, huh? Took you long enough. I was beginning to fucking wonder what was going on. Where do you stand? Is she falling in love with you?"

There was a moment's silence, during which Abe could clearly see Adam, rigid and annoyed, maybe even angry. But, Christ, it had taken a long time! Abe had begun to wonder if he should do something about Adam's extracurricular activities, if they were interfering with his pursuit of Belinda.

"She's resisting," Adam finally said. "She's a stubborn woman."

Abe laughed again. "Don't I know it! You better head up to the shoot this weekend, boy, and follow through." His easy, amiable tone became hard and filled with warning. "You got the edge—don't lose it."

He hung up and stretched, grinning with satisfaction. He imagined Adam chasing after Belinda in Arizona. Striking while the iron was hot. He chuckled. He was feeling great.

He buzzed Rosalie. "Send Helga in."

He always felt great when he was on top, when he was winning. That thought made him think about Will Hayward, and he grinned. Fucking Will had to be an idiot, had to try and blackmail him. Will had just sacrificed any loyalty Abe had felt for him based on their past relationship. No one fucked with him, not ever, not even an old friend. Will had just become a liability.

Will had just written himself off.

Helga appeared in the doorway, a tall voluptuous blonde, a Nordic beauty. "Shut the door," he said. "And come over here."

She came over, a knit dress clinging to full, erotic curves. Abe pulled her onto his lap, taking her hand and placing it on his rapidly stiffening member. "You ready for this, doll?"

37

"*I*'m starved."

Melody couldn't take her eyes off of Jack. She was still on the bed, holding the coverlet over her breasts. Twilight was settling over the desert, etching it in rainbow hues. Against the window Jack was boldly outlined by the setting sun as he pulled his trousers up over green-and-black briefs. He was breathtaking; he was magnificent.

And he had just made love to her.

Just the way she had imagined.

Still shirtless, he straightened to catch her staring. He grinned then sheepishly, running a hand through his hair. "Crazy, huh?"

Oh, God, I love you, Melody thought. She wanted to shout it to the world, to him. She wanted to tell him how fantastic making love with him had been. Instead she stared helplessly.

Jack shrugged on his shirt. "I hope the food is decent

around here. Hey, Mel, I almost forgot, I wanted to run something past you."

Instantly Melody was sitting up very straight. "Jack, why don't you wait and we'll grab something to eat together and we can discuss your ideas then?"

Jack's gaze as it touched her was warm and relaxed. "Okay."

Melody scrambled out of the bed, grabbing her clothes, her heart pounding with excitement—now they were going to have dinner together!—and she fled into the bathroom. Jack watched her, affectionate amusement lifting the corners of his mouth. He'd been with enough women to know she didn't want him to see her body, as if she had something he hadn't seen before. For a moment he couldn't believe he had really slept with her. Then he shrugged it off. He turned to stare out the window, his thoughts full of the shoot now and the character he would be playing. He was so immersed in reflection that he didn't even hear her when she returned from the bathroom, fully dressed.

"I'm ready," Melody said almost shyly.

"Mel," Jack said in the hall, "I had this great insight yesterday. That this is Nick Ryder's last chance at salvation, his last chance to rediscover his compassion, his humanity. To rediscover himself as a man. What do you think?"

Melody blinked. "What?"

"We're talking about my character," Jack said impatiently, then repeated what he had just said. They had entered the vast terra-cotta–floored lobby. Indifferently he scanned the area without making eye contact with anyone, a feat he'd long since perfected, despite the fact that most if not all gazes were trained on him. There were a dozen or so guests in the lobby, including a woman who was checking in with her back to him, and two of the crew, Jack's hairstylist and his boyfriend-assistant. Then Jack eyes went wide, zooming in to the woman in the fitted red jacket and straight black skirt, to the mass of disheveled blond hair cascading over her broad shoulders.

No way.

Jack stared.

There was no way it was her.

"Thank you," she said to the clerk, and Jack's heart jumped. Even before she turned, just from the sound of her voice, he knew who it was.

The broad from the North-Star party. The broad who had stood him up.

She was reaching for her bag when she saw him, and she froze in midmotion.

Jack couldn't look away. Neither could she.

For a long moment their gazes locked.

She was even better than he'd remembered. He had forgotten the impact she'd had on him. It was like being jolted by an electric current. He had forgotten how strong and sexy her body was. The black skirt fit like a second skin, clinging to her long, strong legs.

Then she straightened, smiling as if she didn't have a care in the world. "Why, hello," she said. Casually, oh-so-casually. As if she hadn't stood him up. "We've met before, I think."

She thought? What, she couldn't even recall that they'd met? Was he so forgettable? He, Jack Ford, superstar and sex symbol to millions of women? *Millions.* Which reminded him of the fact that she didn't even know who he was.

Jack couldn't believe it, couldn't believe her. His jaw was as tight as a vise, but he managed to get the words out. "Oh, we've met before, all right," he said. "I remember it very well."

38

*L*ansing knew exactly where to find her at this time of night. He wasn't really in the mood to be doing this. He had had to cancel his date with that hot little blond receptionist, and that irked him completely. She had a great ass, shown to perfect advantage in the tight knit dress he'd seen her in yesterday, and a pair of knockers that begged to be played with. Instead he was cruising downtown to have a chat with a hooker. Too bad he was repelled by the thought of being with one—at least that would take the edge off. Now he'd have to wait but, hopefully, only until tomorrow. Then he'd have lunch with the receptionist—what was her name? Melody . . . yeah, that was it. Pussy for lunch. Why not?

Feeling increased aggravation—or was it frustration?—a very clear image of Melody as she must have looked, sitting at her desk, talking to him over the phone, invaded his mind. Now this was a truly incredible situation, he thought sarcastically, braking hard for a red light.

He had the hots for her, and it was getting worse.

And she was completely indifferent to him. It irked him. Frustrated him. He was not used to this. Women always fell into his lap (and into his bed) when he turned on his considerable charm.

But not Melody.

She was infatuated with her boss.

Christ!

He pictured, as he had dozens of times, her lush body naked, pink-and-white, wonderfully curved, her full bottom in his hands, her even fuller breasts against his chest as he plunged into her—damn, damn, damn.

Of course he had an impossible hard-on now—just what he needed when he was going to have a possibly unpleasant conversation with a hooker.

He shoved Melody out of his mind.

Leah worked out of a stable run by a pimp named Ramon. He was typical: tall, black, overdressed, swaggering. He seemed to have three other girls in his stable, but Lansing wasn't positive. The girls all worked a couple of blocks between Twentieth and Twenty-fifth on the West Side in Manhattan. They lived in a deluxe accommodation uptown —if you considered Harlem uptown and deluxe. Ramon had a sheet a half an arm long and carried a piece. He also carried a ten-inch silver hunting knife strapped to his left ankle, in a snakeskin boot.

He spotted Leah walking out of an alley at five minutes to midnight. She had just blown a john, obviously. She had dark blond hair, a shade lighter than Jack Ford's, permed, frizzy, and shoulder-length. An incredible body if you liked them tallish and slim, which he didn't. Lansing slowed the rental car and cruised alongside her, leaning out his window. "Hey, doll!"

She saw him and sauntered over. "Hi, *doll,*" she mimicked. "Fifty bucks I blow you in the car." Her voice had become a purr. Her face was heavily made up, so he really couldn't tell what she looked like. "Extras are my pleasure—but they cost more."

"I'll take it," Lansing said, opening the other door. He watched her move around the front of the car, shaking everything deliberately. Braless, of course. Round and firm in one of those spandex tops with a matching miniskirt.

She got in, slamming the door. "You can touch," she said, taking his hand and holding it to her breast, "but that's an extra." Then she reached out and found him through his trousers.

He had lost it, fortunately, but to his dismay it jumped right back up. "I guess you're ready," she said enthusiastically. "Got quite a package there, eh, bud? Those balls must weigh a ton!" She cupped each one, then ran a long fingernail up and down his penis. "My, my!" she breathed. She actually seemed excited.

"Look, Leah," he said briskly, grabbing her hand tightly and lifting it off but not releasing it. "I want to discuss some business with you—and I don't want a blow job."

"You prick!" She struggled. "Let go! I don't talk business, not with you or anybody!"

"I'll give you the fifty," Lansing said, yanking on her. "Just be still and listen to what I have to say."

She watched him warily.

He held out fifty dollars, watching as she counted it. "I'm a private investigator. I was hired by your brother to find you and bring you home. He's real concerned about your welfare."

Her eyes widened. "Rick?"

"No, Jack Ford. Although Rick is living with Ford. In L.A."

Leah stared. "What does he want with me?"

"He wants to help you out, I guess. Better yet, why don't you fly out to see him and ask him?"

Leah stared, then laughed. "Help me out, huh? Does he know what I do? That I'm a hooker?"

"I told him," Lansing said evenly. "We can leave tomorrow night."

"Why should I leave? I've got everything I need right here. Besides . . ."—she grinned—"with the right guy, I like what I do."

"You don't have to be afraid of Ramon."

"I'm not afraid of anyone. If I wanted to leave, I would. But I like this setup. I make five hundred a day, easy—no sweat. I got a great pad and jewelry and plenty of blow and all the clothes I need. You tell me why I should leave to go meet some faggot brother who thinks he has to save my soul? Fuck him!"

"Look at it as a paid vacation," Lansing suggested.

She snorted. Then her eyes dropped to his crotch, and she was quick as a snake. She had him in her hand, his pants unzipped. "Good Lord, what a meaty one!"

Lansing tried to breathe. All his mental resistance was crumbling fast. "I haven't ever paid for it," he said, "and I have no intention of starting."

"I'll bet you don't pay for it," she murmured, and suddenly she was ripping open a rubber with her teeth and rolling it on.

It was hard to breathe, but he tried one last time. "Leah, you could start over. Ford has money and power—he'll help you."

She pulled up the spandex skirt, revealing shaved bareness. Oh, Christ! was all he thought. He slid onto the middle of the seat and lifted her onto him. They both gasped at the same time.

"Suck my tits," she said, shoving a suddenly bare nipple in his face.

He obliged.

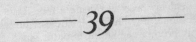

39

*R*ick was used to it.

Everybody was talking and laughing in the corridors at eight A.M., waiting for the first bell to ring. Everybody had somebody, except him. He leaned against a locker, glaring at anyone who happened to look at him. Not too many kids did. There was a nice two- to three-foot radius surrounding him—as if he had an invisible wall protecting him from intruders. No one breached it. Sometimes a couple of girls swung past, looking, pointing, and giggling. Making his ears burn. He knew they were making fun of him.

The bell rang. Five minutes until class started. Rick went into the men's room and lit a Kool. A jock was standing over a urinal, shaking his thing, while two preppies combed their hair in front of a dirty mirror and dirty sinks. Rick leaned against a corner, inhaling. The jock zipped up and left. A long-hair with gangly legs strolled in, pulled out a joint, and proceeded to puff. He was oblivious to all of them. Already stoned.

Rick knew the two preppies. The blonde was Ben Froth, a senior, one of the most popular guys in school with the freshmen women. His buddy was Dale something. Froth was the son of Big Money—everyone knew his father was loaded—and it showed in his Calvin Klein and Ralph Lauren clothes. Dale was well off too. He was also popular. Not that Rick gave a shit. It was pretty funny the way the freshmen girls swooned and screamed and batted their eyes and gossiped about the two of them. They thought they were real hot.

"It's the punk," Froth said, looking at Rick in the mirror. "Hey, punk, don't you ever change your clothes?"

Rick gave him a cool look. Froth was on his case every time their paths crossed, which was once a day at least.

"Why should I?"

Froth held his nose and made a face. Dale guffawed. "Maybe we should buy him some clothes," he sneered.

"His big brother can afford to outfit him," Froth said, turning. "Ain't that right?"

Rick stared evenly and stubbed out his cigarette.

"Maybe we should clean him off," Froth said, grinning.

Rick stepped close. He dropped the butt on Froth's white tenny.

"You little shit," Froth yelled, but Rick laughed and was out the door.

He ducked into his history class just as the second bell was ringing. Froth and Dale were the ones he'd been fighting the other day. Them and two other buddies. Four against one. Nice odds. How come he was the only one to get in trouble? This school sucked.

The class was boring and interminable. Rick didn't pay attention. He stared out the window until he became aware that the prettiest girl in the class—and maybe in the school —was looking at him and giggling, obviously talking about him to her friend, who was also pretty and also giggling. Rick flushed. They were making fun of him, most likely. The first girl's name was Patty. She was a blonde and fully developed. He'd seen her in shorts and a tank top once and hadn't been able to take his eyes off her. She went out with Froth, of course. She was a freshman.

Patty made him think about sex.

He'd lost his virginity to a friend of his mother's when he was thirteen. Discovering sex had added a whole new dimension to his life. He liked it—a lot. Since he'd come to California he hadn't got laid once, which meant he had to jerk off in the bathroom—too frequently. In Houston he screwed whatever he could, mostly hookers, sometimes pretty Mexican girls who were willing and didn't want money and who hung out on the same streets he did.

Class was finally over and he got up, trying to be discreet as he watched Patty's ass ahead of him. He had turned the corner on his way to a study hall when he was suddenly grabbed and slammed against the wall. He looked into Froth's face first, then at Dale and another guy.

"You little asshole," Froth sneered. "You just won't quit, will you?"

Rick was aware that Patty and her friend had backtracked, eyes wide, to watch the entertainment. A few other kids had gathered. Twisting wildly, Rick struggled to get free. Dale and the third guy grabbed him, holding him immobile.

"Don't you ever fuck with me," Froth hissed, punching him hard in the abdomen.

Rick doubled over, gasping from pain, tears blinding him, only to be yanked upright and punched again in the same spot. He bit through his lip so as not to cry out, and then he was released and fell to his knees, clutching his stomach. He was aware of quiet, tense whispering, and through it all he heard Patty say, "What did he do?"

"Come on," Froth said harshly.

Rick looked up to see Patty putting her arm around Froth's waist as they walked away. Shit. He was panting painfully.

"Are you all right?" He heard a voice that was extremely husky, almost hoarse.

Rick managed to sink onto his hip, sitting awkwardly, and looked up into very brown eyes and a dusky face.

"Are you all right?" the girl said again, touching his shoulder. "I'll get the nurse," she said, suddenly standing.

"No!" Rick put up his hand. He didn't recognize her and wondered what the hell she cared.

She sank back to her knees. "Froth is such a jerk," she said.

Rick leaned back against the wall, releasing his belly. She had short black hair, just a bit longer than his, and she was a bit chubby, maybe, depending on one's view—he wasn't sure. She wore a baggy red sweatshirt and loose jeans and beat-up Keds. "Who are you?"

"Lydia. What jerks! Are you sure you're okay?"

"What do you care?"

"I happen to care about people and injustice," she said with a touch of passion. "Someone should kick Froth in the balls!"

Rick smiled then. Their eyes met, and he saw a startled look appear in hers; then she was smiling too. "You look just like him when you smile."

His smile faded. He knew exactly who she was talking about. He stood up, and feeling rude but not knowing what else to do, he walked away.

40

"What am I going to do?" Mary wailed.

"Slow down," Beth said, hugging her. "Vince is having an affair with Belinda Glassman, and he wants a divorce?"

"Yes, yes, yes!" Mary couldn't cry anymore. Her eyes were red and swollen. She had been eating and doing coke and drinking nonstop since yesterday, it seemed. She knew she had better cool it, or she'd gain fifty pounds.

And Vince had come home way after midnight last night, slinking in.

She had ignored him, and he had slunk into the bedroom. Where had he been all that time? She knew. With *her*.

"Is that what he said? Mary?"

She focused with great difficulty. Then she moaned and put her head in her hands. "No, no. I mean, he didn't say anything about a divorce. But he loves her, he told me. He's going to leave me, I know it." She started crying again; the tears were inexhaustible.

"Why do you care? You have me." Beth was affronted.

"I love Vince," Mary snapped, outraged. "I don't want you—I want Vince!"

Beth stood rigid. "You just can't accept the fact that you're gay, Mary. You haven't come to terms with it. I understand. Once you learn to accept it, you'll realize you don't love Vince, just what he stands for."

"That's not true! I think I might kill fucking Belinda Glassman!"

Beth wrapped an arm around her and walked her to the couch. "I can give you everything Vince can't."

"Not children," Mary said, hysterical.

"You don't even want children," Beth said tolerantly.

"Of course I do! Every woman wants children."

"Well, that's certainly news to me."

"I really hate her," Mary snarled. "The bitch!"

"You're just feeling rejected. It's for the better, Mary."

"Oh, you'd say that. You want me all to yourself."

"I won't deny it," Beth said. "I don't want to share you with anyone, not Vince, not another man, and not another woman."

"At least you love me," Mary moaned.

"Why don't you move in with me?" Beth said, her tone giving away her eagerness.

Mary frowned and moaned again. "I can't believe this. God! How long have they been fooling around, Beth? Oh, damn her!"

"It's just as much Vince's fault."

"Bastard!" Mary spat out.

"Are you going to move in with me?" Beth searched her face.

"Not unless I have to," Mary said. "This can't last. She's just playing with him. It can't last!"

Beth frowned and walked to the window. "Belinda Glassman. It's hard to believe. Why would she fool around with a carpenter?"

"Vince is gorgeous," Mary said tersely.

Beth looked at her. "Honey, isn't Belinda Glassman the daughter of that millionaire, Abe Glassman? If she is, believe me, there's no way you can compete with her. If she wants Vince, her daddy will buy him for her." Beth smiled wryly. "Not that she seems to need to buy him."

Mary was suddenly riveted. She ignored what Beth said as she was struck with the beginnings of an idea. Last night on the news there had been an item on Glassman Enterprises, and the newscaster had mentioned that Abe Glassman was in L.A. There had even been a shot of him exiting a long silver stretch on Wilshire Boulevard.

Abe Glassman was in town.

Mary wondered just how hard it would be to get through to Belinda's father.

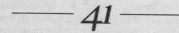

She wanted to kick herself. Hard.

Why hadn't she apologized immediately for standing him up? Why had she played it so cool? Damn! He was angry; it had been obvious. Angry—and still dripping sex appeal.

Belinda jammed her hands into the pockets of her jeans. She was standing in the shadows of a truck and pulley deep in the canyon. It wasn't even seven in the morning, but the crew was already running cables for exterior lighting and setting up props. It was freezing out this early, and her jacket wasn't providing any warmth. She stamped her feet and shivered.

Don't even think about that man as a man, she told herself. Think about saving your ass when he finds out you're the writer—and that you know who he is.

Double damn.

She cast a glance at his trailer.

The first takes were scheduled for nine A.M. She had

been instructed to appear on the set at seven. She wondered if Ford was even in his trailer. He was probably back at the hotel, all nice and cozy with the busty redhead. Not that she cared. Not that it was her business. The moment she saw him and had the chance, she was going to start kissing his ass.

Her heart sank when she saw the director, Don Mascione, in a sheepskin jacket, trudging across the desert, head bowed to the frigid breeze, toward Ford's RV. He saw her and lifted a gloved hand. Belinda watched him knock, thinking, So he is here. She ducked her head when the door to the trailer swung open. But a peek confirmed what she'd thought she'd glimpsed—the redhead. Mascione disappeared inside.

"Coffee's over there," offered a friendly gaffer. "You look like you're freezing." He had his hands full with a drill and extension cords.

"Thanks," Belinda said as he marched past with a grin.

She was halfway to the catering van when she heard her name. She turned to see Mascione on the steps of Ford's RV, waving her over. Her insides twisted into knots. Head up, lady, she told herself, going over, her booted feet crunching on sand and pebbles. The worst that can happen is you eat dirt and get canned.

"We wanna make a few changes in the first scene," Mascione said. "Hey, honey, you need a coat."

Belinda managed a grimace that was supposed to be a smile. She couldn't reply. She couldn't even remember what the first scene was—and she knew this script inside out.

She stepped inside, not at all surprised by the plush suede couches, the heavy wood desk, the wet bar, and kitchen. At the same time that she realized she was clutching the script, Belinda realized that he wasn't there. She started to relax.

"The way I wanna do it," Mascione said, "is with more emphasis on the action, ya know? Less words and more impact—until the end of the scene. So we just need to cut out a few lines up until Ryder says, 'We're not friends, Derek—and we never have been friends,' et cetera."

Belinda focused. Mascione sounded like an idiot, but supposedly he was talented and maybe he had a point. Then a door opened and she whirled around. Her own wide, startled gaze met Ford's.

"Have you met the writer yet, Jack? Belinda—uh—"

"Belinda Carlisle," she said, using her professional name.

"Yeah, Belinda here's the writer; and this"—Mascione grinned and smacked Ford's stiff, unyielding shoulder—"this is the *star*."

Ford wasn't smiling and he wasn't moving. In fact, he was so still he could have been made of stone. After the initial expression of surprise, there was nothing, nothing at all. Belinda took a deep breath. "We've already met—sort of."

Ford didn't say anything. But the corners of his mouth had lifted slightly, maybe in a smile, more likely in a grimace. His nostrils were flared. He turned his back on her—rudely and obviously. "What do you have in mind, Don?"

"She's gonna cut a few lines. More action, more subtlety, until you say 'Derek, we've never been friends,' et cetera. Then it'll hit real hard, ya know? Their relationship. I like it."

Ford nodded, opening his script.

What a fuck, Belinda thought, furious that he would treat her as if she weren't even in the room. She slowly took off her jeans jacket. She didn't have to look at him to know that his gaze had done an Olympic sprint to her person. She was wearing a tight red turtleneck sweater—braless. Her jeans were a second skin, tucked into her favorite navy snakeskin cowboy boots. She sat down slowly, crossed her legs lazily, swung a foot, and opened the script. She placed the end of the pen in her mouth and nibbled it.

Jack stared. Belinda was perversely pleased to have his undivided attention but forced her focus to change. Quickly she made the decisions on what to edit out and began slashing the lines.

"Hold it!" Jack ordered. "Just what are you cutting?"

Belinda paused and looked up. Then she ignored him

and turned to Mascione. "How many lines do you want me to cut?"

"Eight to ten. But it's still gotta be a coherent whole, honey."

Belinda nodded and scanned the scene, then glanced back up. "It's done."

"Just like that?" Ford lifted a brow. Sarcasm laced his tone. He reached down without so much as a May I? and took the script out of her hand. Furious, Belinda bit down hard on a response. He perused the pages, his own jaw tense, a muscle jumping visibly. Then he lifted his green gaze slowly to hers.

Here it comes, Belinda thought. The nuclear war.

He rolled the script up and tossed it onto her lap; it fell against her crotch. The rolled-up script suddenly seemed very phallic, and Belinda wondered if he'd delivered it that way on purpose—and when she met his gaze, knew he had. The sexual challenge was unmistakable. And undeniable. It was cool in the RV, but that wasn't why her nipples were hard.

His gaze drifted over her with deliberate insolence. He said, "It's satisfactory."

Two could play the crotch-staring game. "Umm," Belinda murmured with a glance at his groin.

Ford slammed into the bedroom. "Call me at nine."

Belinda leaned back and closed her eyes. She realized her heart was thudding crazily. What a prick.

No pun intended.

42

*S*ecurity had thrown her out.

Mary was furious.

She had walked into the building, no problem. Taken the elevator to the top floor, no problem. The receptionist had looked at her as if she were a pile of shit. And queried in a cool tone, "Do you have an appointment?"

Mary had said, "No, but—"

The receptionist had informed her that she would have to leave. Mary refused and strode aggressively past the woman. Only to realize she had no idea which way to go. She guessed and went right.

And that was when two huge men from security had thrown her out.

Mary did a line, then hurried back to the front of the building, parked herself on a bench. She would wait all goddamn day if she had to. All day.

And she nearly did. An hour passed, then a few more before he finally came out.

Abe Glassman.

Now he was coming down the steps of the building, broad-shouldered, tall, expensive-looking, moving toward the waiting silver limo. This was it. Now or never. If anyone could stop Bitch Belinda, it was this man. Her marriage and her life depended on it. She raced toward him to cut him off.

She was wearing skintight jeans (she must have gained a pound or two) and a knit top that clung to her voluptuous breasts. Her long hair streamed out behind her. He saw her and grinned, his eyes on her bouncing breasts. He stopped to watch appreciatively.

Dirty old man, she thought. "Mr. Glassman, wait, wait!"

He was surprised; then his grin broadened. "Do I know you?"

Mary was thrown off stride. His gaze was hot, and for an old guy he was really something. "It's your daughter. We have to talk about Belinda." Desperation edged her voice.

"About Belinda?" he said, looking at her face carefully. Then he grinned again. "Perfect timing, wouldn't you say?" He said it to no one in particular. "Let me give you a ride."

She couldn't believe her luck, or how nice he was. Bitchy secretaries! The driver was holding the door open, trying not to look at her, or rather, at various parts of her anatomy, and Mary climbed in. Abe followed. The door shut. Mary bit her lip, clasped her hands, and looked at him.

His warm gaze was caressing her openly. It made her nervous; it made her start to tingle. The knit had rubbed her nipples into erectness, and she was very aware of them and how he kept looking at them. He's attracted to me, she thought, and it was heady indeed. This man was one of the most powerful men in the country—and he was fucking her with his eyes.

"You are . . . ?"

"Mary. Spazzio. Mary Spazzio."

"What can I do for you?" he said as the limo pulled away.

"Your daughter . . ."—she hesitated for a breath—"is having an affair with my husband."

"And your husband is . . . ?"

"Vince Spazzio. He's a carpenter, a foreman for Joe Butler, a GC."

"That's very interesting, Mary." He pressed a button. A panel slid open in front of them, revealing a bar. "Would you like a drink?"

"Yes."

In silence he poured her a glass of white wine and himself a beer. He looked at her again with that hot black gaze. He grinned. "Foolish Vince."

She blushed. "Can't you—"

"Can't I what?"

"Stop her? He's only a carpenter. She's rich. It's just a diversion for her—but it's ruining my marriage."

"I probably could," he said, grinning again and sipping his beer. "But why should I?"

She felt panic. "Please. I mean, your daughter is an heiress. You don't . . . what if they get *married*?"

He laughed. "They won't. You have to give me a better reason for stopping them."

Mary looked away out the window, in consternation. Then she felt his hand on her midthigh, and almost dropped her wine. She looked at him as he was leaning closer. "Make me want to stop them," he said softly, huskily.

She shot a look at his groin. The old buzzard had an erection, and from the look of it, it was big. A wonderful warmth filled with wetness and fear shot along her, racing to the pit of her groin. She couldn't. Could she?

"I don't do anything for nothing," he said, sliding his hand up the top of her thigh, pausing, his fingers splayed and almost reaching her crotch. It was swelling.

She opened her mouth to speak, but no sound came out.

He chuckled. "You have a body like none I've ever seen," he said; and his hand went up to her breast. Mary closed her eyes and leaned her head back as he started kneading the soft, lush flesh.

"Make me happy, Mary," he said, "and I will gladly take care of your little problem."

She opened her eyes. His fingers were strutting across her nipple, and her underwear was soaked. To her shock, she was incredibly turned on. She wanted, desperately, this old man. This powerful, rich man. Not so old—and randy as a goat.

He lifted her top, baring both huge breasts. He buried his face between them. He nuzzled. Then he took one hard, pointed nipple in his mouth and began to suck.

Mary reached down to touch him. A long, throbbing length of flesh, rock-hard. Incredible, she thought, at his age.

"Yes," he encouraged her. "Oh, yes, doll, take it out, touch it." He unzipped his trousers; it sprang against her hand. She grabbed him, exploring the hard, hot length.

He pulled her down, rubbing the glistening head of his erection over one nipple, then the other. Mary thought she might have an orgasm before he even entered her. She fumbled with her jeans, opening them, while he rubbed himself over her breasts, between them, thrusting against her mouth. Then he yanked at her jeans, and they peeled away like a wrapper.

"Oh, baby," he said, grabbing her buttocks and spreading her legs with his knees. One of her feet found the floor for balance, and she had a crazy thought. What about the driver? Could he see?

But it didn't matter. He entered her, big and hard, Abe Glassman, one of the richest, most powerful men in the country. She came.

A huge earth-shattering orgasm.

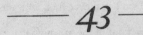

43

Rick leaned against the tree in the parking lot. He was standing a few yards from a sparkling, gleaming red Porsche. It belonged to Froth, and it was spanking new. The way the sun was casting shadows, he was nearly invisible. Unconsciously he rubbed his tender abdomen.

He heard Patty's laughter first. She and Froth were walking hand in hand toward the Porsche. School had let out at least forty minutes ago—Rick idly wondered what they'd been doing. He imagined Patty in Froth's arms, French-kissing, her voluptuous body straining against him, Froth with one hand kneading her breast. He shoved the image away grimly.

Behind them he could make out Dale and Patty's girl-friend. Rick watched them approach out of narrowed eyes.

Froth had opened the car door, and both girls had just

climbed into the back. Dale was standing by the car's rear bumper, waiting. Rick burst out of the shadows, grabbed Froth by the shoulder, spun him around, and kicked him right in the balls.

Froth went down with a howl.

Dale came forward to meet him with an aggressive right hook. Rick ducked, grinning like a madman, and popped up, landing a solid blow to Dale's jaw. Dale's head snapped back, and he was momentarily off balance. Rick swung again, connecting with Dale's soft belly. As he doubled over, Rick kneed him in the face. Dale crumbled. Rick kicked him once for good measure in the ribs, hard enough to bruise but not to break. He wasn't crazy. He had learned long ago that if you fight, don't turn your back until you're positive your enemy is down and out. Rick relaxed. He was positive both Froth and Dale were exactly that.

Froth was groaning and clutching himself on the ground, and he twisted to look at him, his face deathly white. "You'll be sorry!"

Rick smiled. "Don't you ever fuck with me again," he warned.

Patty had climbed out of the car, now that the fight was over, and she knelt beside Froth. She looked up at Rick, her expression confused. Rick glared at her with contempt and turned and strode away.

He wouldn't think about tomorrow.

Froth had a whole school full of allies.

He had no one.

But he wasn't a coward, and he never had been. He would fight until they killed him.

44

"*W*e're not friends, Derek—and we never have been."

An absolute silence descended over the saguaro-studded set, not even broken by a bird's trilling. Ford stood rigid and strained and grim, eyes dark, warning—the perfect hero, Belinda had to admit. Mascione yelled, "That's it! Fucking fantastic! Print!" Belinda also had to admit that Ford was playing Ryder perfectly. At least in this one scene.

He hadn't looked at her once since that morning, and it was almost one o'clock.

What was she—invisible?

The sun was high now, and true to the desert's extremes of climate, the day was warm and springlike. Belinda had shed her jacket hours ago and pushed up the sleeves of her sweater. She watched Ford striding toward his RV, Mascione trotting alongside, blabbing away at a mile a minute. The two of them disappeared into the trailer.

For the first time that day Belinda found herself able to relax. She could feel the tension—emotional, physical, sexual—draining from her body. And she had to face it: She was in deep water. Ford was only going to be on the set for two weeks, then they would all break for the holidays. But it was going to be a long two weeks unless she could get her reactions to him under control.

Under control?

Just how in hell did one control an inferno?

And the worst of it was, it was one-sided. Other than the fact that his ego was sorely wounded, he didn't give a damn whether she was there or not. No, Belinda corrected herself, he was attracted to her—somewhat. If she shoved it in front of his face. It's better this way, she told herself, the tension, anger-laced, rising again. The last thing I need is to wind up in the star's bed. Remember Nancy. Think about your career. I mean, don't I have enough problems?

"Hey, Belinda," the assistant to the assistant director said. "The King has called."

Belinda, about to purchase a sandwich, went stiff. "Excuse me?"

"You are summoned to the King's court." The assistant grinned. She was a lesbian and one of the few females on the set impervious to Ford's appeal. Now she was pointing at his RV.

"Mascione wants me?" Her throat was dry.

"Uh-uh." The assistant to the assistant shook her head. "*He* wants you."

Belinda stared at the RV.

Mascione had left.

Jack's gut was tight, cramped. And his body, well, his body was alive, pulsating with awareness. It had been that way all day—since the moment she had entered his RV that morning.

She was the fucking writer.

He couldn't goddamn believe it.

She was the writer. She was a screenwriter. A Hollywood screenwriter. That meant she had to know who he was —she had to have known who he was at the North-Star party. Back then she had been playing a game. She was playing a game now. Who in hell did she think she was?

Jack ripped off his shirt, balled it, and threw it in a corner. Where the hell was she? He'd told Mascione's assistant's assistant twenty minutes ago that he wanted to see her. *Who in hell did she think she was?*

Strutting around in that tight, tight sweater with that great pair of tits, in those tight, tight jeans with that high, round ass, long, strong legs, legs perfect for fucking, for wrapping around a man's hips . . . He was getting a hard-on.

He had told the assistant to the assistant that he had some dialogue to discuss with her. Right. The script was open and waiting on the table. He wanted her open and waiting, legs spread, pussy glistening, for him. It was hot now, and he began shoving open windows. He relished the physical release. If he wasn't careful, he'd break a window.

Shit. She was doing it deliberately. Teasing, leading him on—he knew a come-on when he saw it. Just as she'd done it at the Majoriis party. Was that how she got her kicks? Getting a guy all fired up with no place to go?

She was a screwed-up broad.

She was impossibly sexy.

There was only one good thing about this entire setup. Her being here had fueled his performance like never before. Never had he been so good, so intense. His acting was taking on new dimensions, new depth. For her. Jesus Christ, he was performing for her. Because the entire time he was out there, on his mark, he knew, *he knew,* she was out there, too, watching him. He didn't have to look at her to know it. He could feel it.

I'd like to perform for her, all right, he thought grimly. In bed.

She knocked.

Jack hesitated but only for a fraction of a second. Every muscle in his body was tight and wired. He opened the door. The expression in his eyes when he opened it was derisive—and mostly meant for himself.

She looked at him.

All self-derision vanished. She knew how to look at a man. Gazes riveted, locked. His body increased its throbbing awareness, and he was sorry he hadn't left on his shirt. He was half hard and growing. He made an easy gesture. "There's some dialogue I want to discuss."

Belinda moved into the RV, her gaze taking in the script on the table, aware of Jack close behind her, aware that he'd shut the door. "Is there something you have a problem with?" She turned to face him.

His eyes blazed. "You might say that."

Belinda lifted her chin. She knew what was coming—and it had nothing to do with the script. But she could play the game—his game. From under her arm she pulled out her own script and once again became aware of the sexual connotations they'd attached to it. She stared at it and thought about Jack—naked and huge and aroused, standing over her. Don't fantasize now, she told herself, breathless and tight, and she lifted her eyes to his.

He was staring at the rolled-up script in her hand, and again his gaze met hers. Belinda knew, without a doubt, that his mind was on the same track as hers. "You have a problem with some dialogue?" Too husky.

"Yes, you could say that," Jack said, his slight smile sarcastic.

Belinda opened the script. "What page?"

It was an explosion. He grabbed it from her hand. "You know damn well it's not on any page in there—although you're the one who wrote it!"

"I'm tired of your yanking the damn manuscript out of my hand—"

Jack threw the screenplay on the couch. "You knew who I was at the North-Star party!"

"All right, yes!"

"You lied. You were playing some kind of game with me, and you lied!"

"No, I didn't lie—"

"Just what would you call pretending that you didn't know who I was?"

"Why the hell is it so damn important whether I knew or not?"

"Because you're playing a game!"

"You don't like games?"

He tensed, then smiled suddenly. He abruptly closed his hands on her shoulders, tightly, ruthlessly. Belinda tensed, her blood pounding. She knew she couldn't move free of him unless he let her. His smile was not pleasant. He had pulled her closer—so close that their bodies almost touched. "Oh, I like games, all right," he said softly. "You want to play games?" His breath was warm.

"I'm not playing a game," Belinda managed.

"Good—then neither am I." It was one little movement, a slight pull but with iron strength, and she was there. Against him, touching him from her knees to her breasts.

Hot, hot currents raced between them. Her jeans had never been so tight, and she could feel the heat of him, huge and aroused now, against her own plump, swollen groin.

"Why did you pretend you didn't know who I was?" he asked huskily.

"I didn't want to stroke your ego."

She felt his anger as his hold tightened; she was pressed more solidly against him. "How in hell would you know anything about my ego?"

"We all have egos," she managed.

When he spoke next his voice was a sensual rasping, meant to caress, seduce. "I want to stroke your ego, Belinda."

She forced her gaze from his mouth to his eyes. The tightening in her chest was instantaneous. "Jack!" Protest or plea? She didn't know.

"Let me stroke your ego," he said, his hands sliding down her arms. His large palms cradled her buttocks, holding her tightly against his swollen penis. "I want you, Belinda . . . I want to make love to you, want to worship every inch of you . . . in bed, baby, that's where I'm going to stroke your ego, stroke it . . . fuck it . . ."

On fire. She closed her eyes, pressing her hips hard against his. His hands tightened on her buttocks, lifting her closer. She was clinging to him. He was grinding against her. She was going to have an orgasm soon, any second. "Touch me," she demanded.

He reached down and grabbed her between her legs. Belinda gasped. His mouth covered hers, hot, urgent. His hold on her crotch tightened. Belinda cried out.

The door opened and shut. "Jack?" Melody said. *"Oh!"*

45

*M*ary felt sexy.

She felt exquisite.

Sated.

Revenge.

She sat propped up in Abe's huge bed, not bothering to pull the covers over her bare breasts, one calf and foot also exposed. She heard him in the bathroom. God, who would have thought? It was the first time she had come with a man —and what a man. He'd made love to her for hours last night; so it was true—old guys could really hold it. And this morning . . . She smiled.

"I'm running late," Abe said, coming out of the bathroom in his trousers, buttoning his shirt. "Because of you, doll." He grinned.

She smiled back.

"You can stay as long as you like," he said, reaching for cuff links. "Damn, I wish I didn't have to go back to New York tonight. Wish I could bring you."

"When will you be back?" Mary asked innocently.

"Want more, huh?" He was obviously pleased, and he came close to fondle her breasts. He rolled a hard nipple with his fingers, watching her face.

The stabbing of desire was incredible.

"I want to see you the next time I'm in town. Give me your phone number."

Mary was quick to comply. She wanted to see him again—God, she did.

"You've got the best knockers I've ever seen," he said, reluctantly pulling away.

"Abe, wait."

He shrugged into his jacket.

"What about Belinda?"

"Leave her to me," he said, flashing a white smile. He winked and left.

Revenge.

Sex.

Abe Glassman.

God, she felt good.

46

Yesterday all he could thing about was Belinda.

Today all he could think about was Mary.

Where the hell had she been last night?

He was going to kill her.

He had called Beth at two in the morning. Beth had no idea where she was and was instantly frightened, thinking Mary had been in an accident. Vince had pumped the information out of her. Mary had gone into L.A. yesterday to see Abe Glassman. Vince was horrified at the thought. She was mad, totally mad! Just what in hell did she think she was doing?

Beth said Mary was going to get Abe to break them up.

Vince was furious. No one would keep him away from the woman he loved, not even Abe Glassman. After all, what could he do?

And he was really going to kill Mary.

Unlike Beth, he was almost positive Mary hadn't been in an accident. She had probably closed down a bar somewhere and passed out. But if she had passed out after fooling around with some guy, he was going to kill her.

Red-hot jealousy.

He didn't analyze it—it was too potent. Too overwhelming.

Today he had actually hit his thumb with a hammer. That would be funny if the circumstances were different. He had rushed home—as fast as five-mile-an-hour traffic would allow. And she wasn't there.

He paced. He cursed. He put his fist through the wall. That hurt, but he didn't care.

And then he had heard her Beetle.

He met her at the door. "Where the fuck have you been?"

She was carrying groceries—*groceries*— and she smiled. "Shopping. I'm starved."

He grabbed the bag out of her arms and threw it on the couch. "Where were you last night, Mary?" It was a roar.

"None of your fucking business, Vince," she said sweetly.

He clenched his fists so he wouldn't hit her, although he felt he was truly provoked and the right was his. She gathered up the groceries, carried them into the kitchen.

"I want to know where you were last night," Vince demanded, following her.

She turned to him. "Why do you care—lover boy? You have Miss Rich-Ass."

"You're my wife," he said, and it made perfect sense to him.

"And you're my husband," she said, tossing her mane of brown hair.

He grabbed her and she winced. "Did you sleep with somebody last night? Did you?" He was seeing red. He had never been this angry, not ever, but he had never had a wife before who might have cheated on him—openly.

"No," she said quickly. "I love you, Vince, and I'm going to be here for you when that bitch dumps you. You'll see."

There was something in her eyes and a glow on her face that made him unsure whether to believe her. His hands went from her shoulders to her face, cupping it hard. He kissed her. Hard, hurtfully, angrily. One arm went around her waist, like a clamp; his other hand found her breasts, grabbing crudely. She kissed him back.

He pushed her onto the floor of the kitchen, yanking at the snap of her jeans. Her face was white with . . . surprise? . . . fear? He didn't care. She was his, and he half knew she was lying—she had fucked around. But he was throbbing and hard and ready to assert his power over her. He pulled her jeans off, kneeing her legs apart.

"Vince!" she cried.

He grabbed her buttocks and thrust in hard.

It was animal rutting, and he came very quickly.

Afterward Mary got up and calmly began to make dinner.

*T*he shower was hot, too hot, a welcome relief for her tired body.

Thank God, she thought, turning off the faucets. Thank God that redhead had interrupted them when she had.

Belinda began toweling herself vigorously. She now knew that the woman was Ford's manager and personal assistant (did everyone in Hollywood have an assistant?). The fact that she wasn't his girlfriend and latest lay pleased her. A lot. Although any idiot could see that Melody had very protective, possessive, and jealous instincts for her boss. Ford probably needed that kind of attention constantly, she decided.

His ego probably needed it.

"Just what do you know about my ego?" His words echoed.

Belinda smiled, slipping on silk Natori shorts and a matching tank, both black and trimmed with white lace. "I know your ego, buddy," she told her reflection, visualizing Ford in her place. "And I know you."

She had almost made a serious mistake. Serious, as in *fatal.* Sleeping with Ford on the set, when he had the power to make or break her? What was she, crazy? Look at the power he'd already exercised over her—ordering her to his RV to "discuss some dialogue." He'd ordered her over there so he could get into her pants—Belinda had no doubt about that.

Just as she had no doubt that if she wanted to stay on this shoot, she had better stay away from Ford.

As far away as possible.

No matter how magnetic the man was.

For you and a million other women, she said to herself, combing her wet hair. *Including* your mother.

Well, she only had thirteen days left to make it through, until they broke for the Christmas holidays, and when they reconvened, it would be without the star. Perversely she couldn't imagine the set without him there, intense and silent, watching everything and everybody (except her), supremely autocratic. There were long stretches where he never said a word, and then suddenly, *wham!* The ax would fall. The lighting was wrong. The camera angles were wrong. The marks were wrong. So-and-so should move left, not right. When the King spoke, everyone shut up and listened. Then Mascione made the changes.

In all fairness, Belinda had to admit he'd played autocrat only twice today—and it did sound as if he knew what he was talking about. Still, it was obvious that everyone around here kissed his ass, including Mascione. Everyone except stupid her.

He hadn't looked at her once since the interlude in his RV. Grudgingly Belinda had to admit it annoyed her, yet it impressed her as well. Her own ego wanted his attention, while her professional self had to admire his own professionalism.

There was a knock on her door, room service, of course. Perfect timing, because she was ravenous. Belinda slipped on a matching wrapper, barely belting it as she went to the door. She opened the door with a smile, then froze.

Jack Ford smiled back. "Expecting me?"

For an instant she didn't move. His warm gaze slid over her languidly, confidently. Her toes curled into the rug. "I believe you have the wrong room," she said tersely, then wanted to bite her tongue. This was one time in her life when she should not be a Mack truck!

"No," he said just as tersely. "I have the right room."

Her eyes widened as, with incredible presumption, he moved past her and into her bedroom. "Oh, I see—you want to discuss some dialogue."

He flashed her a heart-stopping grin. "The dialogue can wait. Come here, Belinda."

His silky tone was almost irresistible. "We have a six A.M. call tomorrow," she said, breathless.

He was staring at her breasts. "You have a beautiful body, a really beautiful body." His gaze lifted. "We have something to finish. Come here, Belinda."

It would be so easy . . . Belinda shut the door, then leaned against the wall, arms at her sides, letting him admire her chest and her legs as the robe came unbelted. His eyes were hot, devouring her right down to her toes, searching, seeking, stroking . . . His gaze lingered on her crotch. When he looked her in the eye again, he was smiling with promise and anticipation and the certainty that she had capitulated.

"Why me?" Belinda asked. "Why not any one of a hundred broads on this shoot?"

His smile widened. "What a foolish question," he murmured. "Why are you asking foolish questions, Belinda? You know I wanted you the instant I saw you. Just as I know you wanted me in that same instant—and that you want me now."

"Desire has nothing to do with this," Belinda said, giving up her provocative posture. "I don't want to go to bed with you. Not now. Not here, not today."

"What a liar you are."

"Oh, I want you physically," she said coolly. "But I have my career to think about, and I'm not about to jeopardize it by fucking the big star. A fuck is a fuck, and in the long run it can't compare to what I want—success."

He was standing very still. No longer smiling. "You think," he said, slowly, "I'll hurt you if we sleep together?"

She realized her mistake, that he was taking this as an insult. She blushed. "It's happened in this business."

"Then," he grated, "you must realize the converse is true too. Right?"

Belinda stared.

"If you don't sleep with me . . ." He trailed off. His eyes were blazing with anger.

"I have to protect myself."

"You really think I'm some egomaniacal asshole."

"I have no idea who you are."

"No?" His tone was hard. "Damn right you don't! So don't you go judging and labeling me—lady!" He was on her in two strides, but he didn't touch her; he just towered over her, furious. "And the next time you wiggle your ass around me, I'm going to take what's being offered. Is that clear?"

"I don't—" she started, when there was another knock on her door. Saved!

"Like hell you don't," Jack spat out. "I'm only reading the lines the way you write them, baby." He was at the door, flinging it open, barreling through.

Belinda's heart was slamming. She didn't turn around but fought for some equilibrium. "You can put the tray on the table."

"What was he doing in here?"

Belinda whirled. "Adam!"

48

She really thought he was some kind of prick.

He couldn't get over it—over her. If he were the bastard she assumed him to be, he'd force her to sleep with him with the threat that he'd have her thrown off the production if she didn't. Never, ever, in his life had Jack coerced or had to coerce a woman into his bed. And he wasn't about to start now.

No matter how much she provoked him.

Because that was definitely what she was doing. Provoking him. As in provocative. Purposely. Jack knew it. He knew women too well not to know it. The real problem here, he decided, was that he was eating it up.

Because if he could manage not to be an attentive audience, it wouldn't matter how often she wiggled her ass in front of him.

Jesus. She had turned him down.

First she had stood him up. Now she was turning him down.

He had a terrible, stabbing thought: Maybe she really wasn't attracted to him. Maybe it was just a game to lead him along like some dumb, hard-up adolescent. And he was playing right into the palm of her hand.

Forget her, he told himself. Really forget her. She may be a good screenwriter, but she's nothing but a cockteaser, and that you don't need.

It was easier said than done. He couldn't sleep. Her boyfriend was here, the same guy she'd been with the night they'd first met at Majoriis's. Were they fucking right now? A very graphic fantasy assailed Jack, of her boyfriend thrusting a massive prick into her while she writhed in orgasm. He turned onto his stomach, hard now, and angry. Right now she was with that nameless nobody, when she could be with him. Not only had she turned him down, she had turned him down for someone else.

This was unfuckingbelievable.

"Adam, you have no right to grill me."

"Have you slept with him?"

"Am I an idiot? I want to stay as far away from him as possible!" She meant it. The truth must have sounded in her voice, because Adam relaxed and took her hand. They were sitting on the bed.

"I'm sorry, Belinda. It was just a shock to see him leaving—with you dressed like this."

"It was a shock when he appeared here too." She looked at Adam, but she was trying not to worry about Ford's warning that he could hurt her for *not* sleeping with him. How come she hadn't thought of that herself? And now what was she going to do? Would he apply the screws? "Just as your appearance here was a shock—is a shock."

He smiled, drawing her hand against his chest. "Don't be upset. I missed you."

"In one day?"

"Yes."

"Adam, you can't stay here. I'm working. I've got enough problems right now."

"I'm a problem?"

He was, of course, but Belinda couldn't say so. "No, I didn't mean that. But it's not professional for you to be here."

"I only came for a few days. What's a few days? Today's Wednesday. We'll have the entire weekend."

"No, we won't," Belinda said. "We're working through this weekend and the next because Ford is here only for the two weeks before the Christmas break and we've got to shoot all his scenes. Adam, I'm sorry, but there's no way you can stay. I wish you'd asked me first, before flying out."

Adam's jaw tensed; but then he relaxed again. "I can't think straight where you're concerned, Belinda. I should have called."

"Look, Adam, why don't you spend the day sightseeing tomorrow, and then we can have an early dinner. And then you can go back to L.A."

He frowned, but as usual capitulated gracefully. "I suppose that's better than nothing. Belinda, will you be going up to Aspen for Christmas?"

Her relief was short-lived. "How did you know I go up there for the holidays?"

He smiled. "You told me you're a skier, and your parents have a condo there."

She had forgotten. She had to tread cautiously. In fact,

she hadn't even thought about Aspen, she'd had so much on her mind. "I don't know."

"I'm going. I've been invited to the Kellers'. You must know that their bash is *the party* of the Aspen season, and that everyone who is anyone will be there. Come with me."

Of course she knew all about the Kellers' annual Aspen Christmas party the fifteenth of December. She'd never been invited herself, although because of her connection with Abe, she could have gone if she'd cared to wrangle it. But it hadn't been important to her. Now that she was a rising star in her own right, she thought of all the connections she might make. "Well . . ."

"Professionally speaking," Adam said, "you shouldn't miss it."

"Okay." Now there was only one hurdle left. "Adam, I've been up since five-thirty this morning. It's ten o'clock now. I am exhausted."

His disappointment was obvious.

"I'm sorry. I wish you'd phoned."

"It's okay," he decided. "I admit I want to make love to you, but I didn't fly all the way out here just for sex. I really wanted to see you, be with you." He touched her cheek.

Guilt raised its head. Had she given Adam a single thought since she'd last seen him? "So we can call it a night?"

"As long as we're on for tomorrow."

"We're on," Belinda said somewhat wearily. She ushered him to the door. She dutifully accepted his kiss. And when he was gone she fell into bed; and her last thought before sleep claimed her was, of course, Jack Ford.

Smiling and oh-so-sexy.

49

*A*bsolute silence reigned.

It was midday, even warmer than the day before, fluke weather, actually hot. There wasn't a cloud in the November sky. Trucks, vans, generators, cables, lights, fans, special-effects backdrops, and masses of other equipment ringed the one empty space where they had been shooting all morning. It was a dry arroyo. Now Jack Ford and his costar, a stunning brunette, stood there motionless.

"Cut," Mascione said without any enthusiasm whatsoever.

The brunette backed away from Jack. Ford stared hard at the ground, shoving his hands in his pockets. Very slowly Mascione approached. "Relax, Jack, it's okay. You'll get it this time, I'm sure."

When Ford looked up, his face was like a thundercloud.

Belinda, watching, bit her lip.

"Look," Mascione said with a smile, "this time, when you say—"

"No."

The one word, uncompromising in its tone, rang out in the desert's quietude. The murmurings of the crew, just started, hushed. Mascione was silent. Belinda had known this was coming. He had been so magnificent yesterday, but today they'd been shooting the same take since eight this morning. And he wasn't getting it. He wasn't convincing. He wasn't Nick Ryder.

"Jack?" Mascione asked.

"This dialogue isn't right," Jack said, and for the first time he looked at Belinda. "It's not convincing."

Everyone looked at Belinda.

She couldn't help it, she began to flush.

"What do you mean, Jack, it's not convincing?"

"It's not convincing. Nick Ryder wouldn't say these lines."

Belinda gritted her teeth.

"Okay," Mascione said. "Everyone, take twenty. Belinda, come here honey."

Trying not to reveal what she was feeling, Belinda strode into the clearing. As if she hadn't been able to hear every word, Mascione turned to her. "I think this dialogue needs a little fine-tuning. Why don't you give it a try, honey?"

Belinda smiled—after all, it was easy to kiss his ass— and turned to Ford. He was staring at her. When her glance met his, something sparked between them. "What exactly would you like me to do?" Her tone was as sweet as the name Mascione had been calling her.

He stared. His eyes were intense, hot flames just beneath the surface. Belinda knew in that moment that he was remembering last night. Maybe, like her, he'd never stopped thinking about it.

"It's stiff," he said.

"It's stiff. Thank you, that tells me a lot. Could you elaborate?"

Once his gaze was on her it seared and stuck, unmoving. "Ryder wouldn't say this to Adrienne."

"I see," Belinda said, trying to control the combustion about to take place. "If you're the expert on Ryder, why don't you tell me what he would say?"

"Honey," Mascione said quickly, "don't get all peeved. We're all trying to make a good product."

Belinda ignored him, waiting.

"I don't think," Jack said, his gaze unwavering, "that he'd say anything. You'd see how he was feeling, from his eyes, his expression, his body."

"You're telling me," Belinda said quietly, too quietly, "*me,* what Nick would do, what he'd say?"

"That's right."

They stared at each other.

She managed to stay calm. "I'm the writer."

No response.

"I created Nick. Nick came from my heart, my soul. And you're telling me you know him better than I do?" Her voice had tipped up.

"Honey, there's no need to go on the rag!" Mascione interjected. He was starting to sound frantic.

"Yes," Jack said, raising his own voice. "Nick wouldn't say that to Adrienne. Believe me, I know. Nick's a *man.*"

"And because you share that particular male appendage with him—you know what he would say and do?"

"He sure as hell wouldn't slobber all over Adrienne the way you have him doing!"

"He isn't slobbering! He's showing concern!"

"You can tell this was written by a woman," Jack shouted. "It *reeks* of being written by a woman!"

"Time out!" Mascione yelled.

Belinda and Jack both turned, as one, to glare at him. Jack grabbed Belinda. "We're going to discuss this scene in private."

"Oh, great!" Belinda cried, half running to keep up as Jack half dragged her out of the clearing and toward his RV. Around them everyone stared; and behind them everyone began whispering.

He almost threw her into the trailer. Belinda stood ready to fight, everything perfectly clear now. He slammed the door shut. Hard. The RV shook.

"Is this what it's going to be like?" Belinda demanded.

He was panting too. "What are you talking about?"

"You . . . wielding your power over me . . . any way you can."

"Ah, shit," Jack said fiercely, slamming his fist on the table. The coffeepot jumped. He glared at her. "I meant what I said. Nick wouldn't act like some pussy around Adrienne."

"Nick is no pussy, believe me. He's all man."

"How would you know?"

"Believe me, I know a man when I see one."

Jack laughed. "Yeah, right! Like that fancy boyfriend of yours? If that's your idea of a man—"

Belinda clenched her fists. "Adam has nothing to do with Nick."

"Trust me, I'm a man. Ryder would not say all that shit to Adrienne."

All that shit? "Nick is my character!" Belinda cried. "I created him! No one knows him the way I do!"

"Wrong!" Jack yelled, jabbing with his thumb. "Wrong, lady, wrong! Nick is my character! I am Nick! From now until this shoot is over . . . *I am Nick Ryder!*"

Belinda stared. "Right," she said quietly. "You are Nick Ryder, and you are the King." In one motion she pulled her sweater over her head and dropped it onto the floor.

Jack's eyes widened as he stared at her full white breasts.

"Let's get this over with," she said. "You can have what you want, and then we can act like normal, professional adults." She reached for her jeans and unsnapped them.

Like iron, his hand clamped over hers, stilling her. "Put on your sweater." His tone was steel.

She looked at him.

His gaze was ice—smoldering ice.

Belinda, why did you just do that, she thought. Way too late!

His gaze dropped to her chest. "You really get a kick out of pushing me," he said, his tone as coarse as sandpaper. "I must be a saint. You've got three seconds. After that, I don't give a fuck—I'm going to live up to all your worst expectations."

Disappointment or relief? Belinda picked up her sweater and pulled it on. "Then why did you drag me in here?"

"To hammer out this scene," he snapped.

She studied him. "You really think it's too soft for Ryder?"

His gaze flew to her. "Yes."

"I wanted the audience to understand him, to really understand him here."

He was all attention. "They will. I can do it, Belinda—

you watch. And I don't want to take out all of the dialogue, just the fifth through seventh lines on the last page."

"You have a script around here?"

"Yeah, of course." Jack grabbed another copy, opened it. Although it was impossible not to be aware of him as a man, Belinda came close to concentrate on the page.

"Here," he said, pointing with one long finger.

"Yeah, I see. You are really good at conveying emotion without dialogue," she mused.

Their gazes caught. "Thank you."

She shrugged. "I never said you weren't a good actor."

He looked at her.

She turned away. "Why not? It's only three lines. If you can do it, the audience won't miss anything."

"Belinda."

She had her hands in her pockets. She lifted her glance.

"You are a helluva writer."

She stared.

"I know this is your first sale. It's really good, really intense—and you didn't sacrifice character development for the action. It's really good."

She couldn't help it—she smiled. Really smiled. "Thanks."

Suddenly he grinned. "And you have great fucking tits."

Now she was on familiar turf. "I know."

"I'll bet you do. You sure you don't want to rewind a bit—back to the part where you take your sweater off?"

She couldn't help it. She gave him a look. His smile faded. "Shit," he said. "Belinda . . ."

She knew now that it was disappointment—that regardless of common sense, she wanted him. "Jack . . ."

He crossed to her, his face strained, his large warm hands going to her arms. "Oh, baby," he said, "you're going to drive me crazy."

She touched his face, trying very hard not to think about the consequences of what they were going to do. To her surprise, he shuddered.

The door flew open. Mascione took them in with a

glance and was unfazed. "Shit! Jack, I got bad, bad news! Honey, you'd better leave!"

Jack was still holding Belinda, and his grip didn't relax. "She can stay. You got great frigging timing, Don. What is it?"

"Jack, shit, I'm sorry, you should really sit down."

Jack didn't move.

"Jack—it's your mother."

Jack didn't blink.

"She died this morning."

Jack's hold on Belinda tightened. But only for a moment. Belinda thought she glimpsed surprise, but then there was nothing. In a man whose eyes were such beautiful mirrors of raw emotion, she saw nothing but dark shutters. "Yeah?" he said casually, and he moved away.

And that was all he said.

Two hours later he was on his way to the airport.

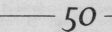

50

*M*elody made all the arrangements at Jack's short, unemotional request. Janet had been in L.A., had died in bed in a grimy, run-down apartment in Santa Monica. Apparently she had refused to be hospitalized. She had been having chemotherapy treatments. The funeral would be tomorrow.

Melody's heart ached for Jack.

She was no longer angry, no longer upset. In the face of Jack's crisis, she forgot her own. She forgot how she'd felt when Jack hadn't turned to her again, hadn't even acted as if he remembered making love to her—and had been panting around that blond bitch like a rutting stud.

What was he thinking? What was he feeling?

He didn't want to see his mother. He didn't know who

her friends were and he didn't care if there was a wake or not. He didn't want a funeral service. "Just see that she's buried somewhere, anywhere, for God's sake," he'd snapped, finally showing some emotion, this one close to anger. "I don't have time for this," he said brusquely.

He hadn't wanted to leave the shoot. Even Mascione hadn't been able to talk any sense into him. It was Melody who had swayed him. "Jack," she said, "if the press gets wind of this, that you didn't even go to your mother's funeral . . ." She hadn't had to say any more. He'd boarded the next plane back to LAX.

How could Jack be so cold? After all, no matter what, Janet was his mother. Had been, she silently corrected. And now when he needed her, Melody, he was pulling away, becoming impossible to get close to.

Melody had already tried to leave a message in New York for Peter Lansing. She doubted he would be able to find and bring Leah back in time for the funeral. Now it looked as if he had already left New York. Well, that was that. She had more important things to worry about.

And what about Rick? When Melody had asked Jack how he was going to break the news, Jack had almost turned vicious, he had become so angry. "I don't know," he growled, and taking the hint, Melody had disappeared.

The funeral was tomorrow. And she was going to be there, right at Jack's side to comfort him in his time of need.

51

*T*here should have been something, he supposed. Anything. Guilt, joy. Relief, anger. But there wasn't.

Nothing.

There was nothing.

His mother was dead.

So what?

He thought about the shoot. About Belinda. About having to leave in the middle of production—about having to leave her just when they were finally going to make it. And that brought forth anger. Lots of anger. Even in death she was fucking him over. Even in death she couldn't leave him alone.

His mother was dead.

So she hadn't lied. She really had been dying. Selfish to the end. Coming to him because she felt his forgiveness might gain her salvation.

And he hadn't lifted a finger to help her.

Maybe his money could have bought better doctors and prolonged her life. She hadn't even had medical supervision—she had died alone, somewhere that could have been anywhere.

What did it matter? She had died a long time ago—for him.

The same numbness he had felt when Mascione had told him the news overtook him now. He really didn't feel a damn thing for the woman who had called herself his mother. And why should he?

Somewhere deep inside there was the damn pinprick, a kind of faint, indistinguishable ache, piercing. He shoved it back down to wherever it had come from. Whatever it meant, there was no fucking way he was going to pay attention to it.

He was relieved that he had Melody to take care of the funeral. But what about Rick? He had to tell him—he couldn't put it off—and he had no idea how the kid would react. Janet was one topic they never, ever discussed.

Something pricked him again. Harder this time.

He ignored it. He would go to the goddamn funeral because of the kid and because Melody was right—not to go would mean bad press at a crucial time in his career. But then he would head up to Aspen for some hard skiing. Mascione had told him they were rearranging the shooting schedule, that they wouldn't need him now until after the holidays. It was a damn good thing he always went to Aspen for Christmas. As if he wanted to sit idle when he'd been idle the past five months. But at least he was going back to work. That was all that counted.

Everything was perfect.

Just perfect.

52

*J*ack hesitated. Rick had just come home from school, and as usual, he had made a beeline for the refrigerator, undeterred by Jack's sudden return. Jack watched him, starting to lose control, a well of deep, dark emotions starting to simmer and roil. He didn't know how the kid would take it —he hadn't the foggiest idea whether Rick hated Janet or loved her. "Kid?"

"Yeah," Rick said, busily making a peanut butter and jelly sandwich.

"We have to talk," Jack said softly.

Rick stopped what he was doing, knife poised over bread, and looked at him with a wary, hunted look. "I haven't done nuthin' wrong," he said sullenly.

"I know," Jack said and saw Rick relax. "Come here," he said, putting his arm around him and leading him toward the couch. "Let's sit down for a minute."

"What is it?" Rick demanded. "What's happened?"

"Rick, there's no easy way—Janet died last night."

Rick went white and sat frozen.

Jack put his hand on Rick's shoulder. "She had cancer —there was no hope." He watched Rick's face; he saw the grief rising and the struggle to quell it. Rick leapt to his feet as his eyes grew watery, and he bolted. He ran into his room and slammed the door shut behind him.

Jack didn't think about it. He went after him. He got his hand on the door and threw it open. "Ri—"

"Get out," Rick screamed. "Get the fuck out!"

The kid was standing in the middle of the room, trembling, tears welling but not falling. Furiously he swiped with a fist at his cheeks.

Jack reached him in two strides and enclosed him in a massive bear hug. Rick went stiff. Jack felt the warmth of his body and the hot surge of a choking anguish. Rick started to tremble. Jack hugged him harder. Rick started to cry.

"It's okay, let it out," Jack said, fighting to push away the pain in his own gut, absolutely willing control. "Crying's okay."

"She didn't even say good-bye!" Rick sobbed.

Jack rocked him and felt guilt. Poisonous guilt. He had known she was dying. He had known and ignored it. He could have done something. He could have let Rick see her. God.

"Why didn't she come and say good-bye?"

"I don't know, kid," Jack said hoarsely. "I don't know."

*I*t was a beautiful day. The sun was bright and warm, with a pleasant breeze pinching at the grass.

Jack wore a dark suit and watched without expression as six hired pallbearers carried the casket toward the open grave. Melody and Rick stood at his side, Melody clutching a black bag, wearing a black dress, and glancing at him nervously. Rick was pale and silent.

Jack looked at the almost black coffin being lowered and didn't really see it. Instead he saw an old kitchen, wallpaper ripping and torn, stained and peeling linoleum floors, a table that wobbled precariously because one of the legs was too short. And the smell.

Her smell.

Thick, cheap musk perfume. Cloying.

Janet.

Janet nearly naked. What did a six-year-old know or care? A sheer red robe over stockings and garters, sending one of her men off. Jack shooting peas at him, laughing. Hitting the fat schmuck in the head.

Jack!

Laughing, racing out of the house.

Too late. Janet had caught him, dragging him up short. A hard slap—right across the head.

You bastard! Don't you ever do that again!

Jack squirming, fighting tears from the pain, thinking, I hate you! I hate you!

I hate you. I hate you.

Something deep and threatening tore at him from far inside, bubbling up. Excruciating tentacles of pain.

I hate you.

His breathing became choked. He couldn't seem to catch his breath. Sweat dripped down his face. Salty. Tears blurred his vision; and feeling panic, he fought them, panting.

I hate you. I hate you.

His heart was pounding wildly. A tear escaped. He brushed at it, struggling as he'd never struggled before. For control. For a mask. To hold back emotions that were growing at an incredible rate. The tentacles were huge knives thrusting upward through his chest, cutting off his air, ripping open his heart . . .

Jack heard an anguished kind of animal noise escape from someone.

Himself.

He turned, stumbling because for some goddamn reason he couldn't see. Tears blinded him. He wasn't aware of anyone or anything. Just the rapierlike pain in his chest, the possibility that he might have a heart attack, the need to find his car. Doggedly he ran.

He didn't hear Melody cry out.

Blindly he found the Ferrari and was in it.

"I hate you! I hate you!"

He was pounding the steering wheel. Tears coursed down his face. He heard huge grotesque sobs. His sobs.

"I hate that bitch! I hate her! I hate her!"

Pounding, pounding, pounding.

She never loved me, he thought, crying into his hands.

All I ever wanted was some love. Just a kind fucking word, one word, one pat—like you'd give a fucking dog—one lousy nice word, one iota of approval . . .

One fucking word.

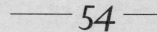

54

*W*hen they got back to the Westwood condo there she was, Janet's ghost.

Jack stared, frozen, feeling faint.

Janet's ghost, only thirty years younger.

She was dressed in skintight gold spandex, four-inch spikes, and black lace. A mane of dark blond hair. All that heavy makeup. Janet's ghost looked him up and down insolently and suggestively, and then Rick shouted, "Leah!" and reality intruded, crystal-clear.

Stunned, Jack watched Rick hug his sister. His sister. Their sister. This . . . whore.

This spitting image of Janet.

He felt sick.

"I got the key from the manager's office," Lansing said, and for the first time Jack became aware of him.

"Hi, bro," Leah said, giving him another suggestive look. "Too bad we're related." She smirked.

Jack got a grip on himself. "Hi," he said, clearing his throat. "Thanks, Peter—I think."

"I'll wait outside," Lansing said, trying to wipe the amusement and pity out of his eyes. Melody ushered him out, closing the door.

A tense silence filled the room.

Rick was watching them both, standing close to his sister—protectively.

"Rick, could you leave us for a few minutes?" Jack asked. He could see it now: Rick was going to side with his sister in any confrontation that occurred, and Jack had no doubt there were going to be many. To his surprise, Rick left without protest. The kid was really shook up over Janet's death.

Leah sauntered close, inspecting him lewdly. "You look just as good in person," she commented. "Maybe better."

"Cut it out," Jack flared up, grabbing her arm. "Cut out the hooker crap. I don't like it." He hated it. This near-image of Janet was making his insides roil.

"Well, isn't that too bad!" She had her fists on her hips and grinned. "You wanted to see *me,* remember, doll?"

He had the traitorous thought that this was never going to work. "Look, Leah, I want to help you start over. There's no need for you to sell yourself on the street."

She laughed. "Sure, I'll take a handout. Too bad you didn't pop up when I was eleven and turned my first trick."

He wondered if he'd throw up. Could he really be related to this whore? Nothing he had done, or ever been, compared to this. "First off, why don't we get you settled in. You must be tired from the trip," he said evenly.

"I'm staying with you?" Her eyes slitted.

He was in trouble—he knew it. "You need clothes," Jack said, unable to delay the topic a moment longer.

"You gonna take me shopping?"

"What's your size?" Jack asked instead. "Seven, eight?"

"Right on. Five ten, one hundred and twenty pounds.

All in the right places, I might add." She patted a round buttock.

Jack clenched his jaw. How was he going to hide this—for her sake as well as his own? "Look, Leah, I have no intention of taking you shopping while you look like you just finished a ten-dollar blow job. I'll have Mel pick you up some jeans and a shirt, and then she'll take you out."

"Do I embarrass you?" Her voice was saccharine sweet.

"You embarrass yourself."

"You got what you asked for, big boy, so don't go laying any crap on me."

"Let's get you settled in," he said firmly.

"When do I get my money? Peter told me you'd give me a few grand to pay for my travel expenses." She grinned. "He make that up?"

"He didn't make it up. You'll get it as soon as you like." What did he think he was doing? Panic punched him like a fist.

"*Now* sounds good to me," she said.

"Tomorrow. Mel will have to go to the bank. I don't have that much cash on me." He paused at the door. "I assume you want cash?"

"Of course," Leah said airily. "I'm a cash-only business —you know that."

55

Mary didn't care what anyone thought.

She had left the downstairs of a friend's house, full of milling people. Tons of coke were going around, and everyone was drinking up a storm. She was high and very thoughtful. She'd walked upstairs and sought sanctuary from the masses.

Anger was better than indifference, she told herself.

What had happened yesterday at least showed that Vince was jealous, possessive. Wasn't that better than nothing?

He had hardly said a word to her since. He hadn't come close enough to touch her either, but it had only been twenty-four hours since he had practically raped her on the kitchen floor. It hadn't been rape, had it? She had been willing finally, if not aroused. How in hell could she get aroused in two minutes?

She thought of Abe. She wished she were with him tonight, fucking his brains out. That man knew what to do to a woman. God, and he could hold it forever. He made Vince seem like a schoolboy. Of course, Abe wasn't built like Vince; he wasn't young and hard and perfectly muscled like Vince. Mary was trying to be fair.

Still, with his money and his power and his cock he didn't need any of those attributes. She smiled. He was sexy in a very different way. And he had made her come.

Hopefully she would see him soon. And hopefully by then he would have his daughter—the cunt—under control. Mary would have her husband back. And then what?

She shoved that problem aside. She concentrated on what she and Abe would do to each other the next time they were together, until her clit was swollen and aching. She was wearing a long skirt and boots, and she wondered if she dared to masturbate before going back downstairs and getting super high.

"There you are."

Perfect timing, Mary thought, looking at Beth.

"What are you doing?" Beth asked.

Mary hadn't told her about Abe. She knew Beth too well; Beth would be jealous and wouldn't understand. "Thinking," Mary said truthfully enough. She patted the bed next to her. "Come here."

Beth came eagerly, sitting beside her. Mary took her hand and placed it beneath her skirt, on her knee. She slid it up her thigh, back down, then up again, this time closer to her wet, wet pussy. Then she placed it there, holding Beth's hand in place, arching her throbbing flesh against her. Beth slipped her hand under Mary's panties, found her clitoris and started to stroke it. Mary gasped.

She lay back on the bed, legs spread, as Beth ran to close the door. "There's no lock," Beth said hoarsely, coming back to kneel between Mary's legs. She threw up Mary's skirt and rid her of her pink panties.

"I don't care," Mary said, moaning as the cool air stroked her nakedness.

With her thumbs, Beth parted the heavy lips of Mary's cunt. She lowered her head and slid her tongue between the folds. Licking and lapping.

They shed their clothes and moved fully onto the bed in extreme haste. Beth kneaded her buttocks as she ate her, kneeling between Mary's plump thighs.

That was how Vince found them.

He had been feeling guilty, of course.

He had been feeling guilty ever since he had taken his own wife so brutally. He wanted to apologize but just couldn't seem to do it. It was easier to be a coward and never bring up the subject again. Except—he still wanted to know.

And now he did.

They were so engrossed they never heard him calling Mary's name. He stood in the doorway and stared at Beth's bare bottom, her twat peeking out as she sucked his wife's pussy with incredible vigor and noise. Mary moaned and writhed, her huge bare breasts gleaming above Beth's bent dark head.

He had an instant erection.

Mary's lover was a woman.

He didn't get farther than that thought. He had already unzipped his fly. This was his secret fantasy—every man's fantasy—and his cock was huge and he had no intention of passing this up. He came up behind Beth silently and watched, fascinated and ready to come, as she lapped his wife's swollen pink flesh.

Mary's eyes opened, and they stared at each other.

Vince grabbed Beth's hips, and unable to wait a second longer, he thrust into her.

They all came at once.

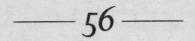

56

*M*elody stole a glance at Jack.

He sat silent beside her in the twenty-seat plane as it began its descent into Aspen. Ten days had passed since the funeral and there were only ten shopping days left till Christmas. But it didn't feel like the holidays, she thought grimly. Jack was staring out the window. He hadn't said more than a dozen words to her since they had left Los Angeles. Rick had pleaded to stay in L.A., and Jack had agreed reluctantly. Afraid to leave Rick with Leah, he had sent her to Palm Springs for a "vacation." Leah was as happy as the cat that ate the canary.

Melody tried not to look out the window as the plane circled mountain peaks, snow- and pine-capped, turning for descent into an impossibly small, snowy valley. She closed her eyes, hands tightening on the arms of her seat. She wasn't afraid of flying, not really, but this was different. Flying some diminutive plane into a miniature hole in the mountains—she felt quite sick.

Poor Jack.

She wanted desperately to comfort him, to hold him, to ease his pain.

It had happened. What she had been hoping for. Jack had broken down at the funeral, and although she had wanted to comfort him then, she had known he wouldn't let her, wouldn't want her or anyone to see him cry and grieve. An outpouring of all those emotions, and she wasn't sure what they were. She just knew it was healthy for him to release them. He had been living with poisons in his system for years, and now he was finally letting them out. Like an infection that had to be lanced, letting all the pus drain away.

Thank God.

It was sad that Janet's death had to be the trigger.

Maybe tonight she would be able to get close to him.

He'd had his hands full with Rick and Leah since the funeral, especially with Leah. They were openly engaged in what seemed to be a constant battle. Melody had offered to take him to dinner, the movies, anything, but he'd always turned her down. But tonight . . .

Jack intended to go to the Kellers' Christmas party with her. Afterward . . . afterward Melody would be there to hold him, to ease his sorrow any way she could. She hadn't forgotten how it had been when they had made love, and she knew he would want to be with her again—she just knew it. And, God, she herself had barely been able to think of anything else since that day.

He hadn't even looked at her with any sign of intimacy since that afternoon. Hadn't flirted (not that he'd ever flirted with her) or in any way intimated that anything had occurred between them. How could he be so dense? So callous? Didn't he know her at all?

Hadn't that night meant anything to him?

She was pretty certain that he hadn't been with a woman since he'd made love to her. That had to mean something!

She could vividly remember everything he'd done to her —intimacies she'd never experienced before. His tongue and lips in her most private places. Oh, God! She didn't want to think that he made love like that to all women. It wasn't possible. It just wasn't. Was it?

Jack cared for her. She knew he did. And he had made love to her and enjoyed it. She had seen his arousal. Didn't that add up to them becoming lovers? It was only logical.

Tonight.

Tonight they would find each other, she was sure of it. The plane touched down, bounced twice, hard, and sped down the runway, brakes screaming. When the plane slowed Melody opened her eyes. Jack was looking at her, and he gave her a smile that was an imitation of his real one. "We made it," he said quietly.

She smiled at him, looking into his eyes—he looked away.

It was about eighteen degrees out. They emerged into fading winter daylight with twenty other passengers, down the stairs, into the warmth of the building, directly to baggage claim. The airport was as tiny as the plane, as the valley seemed—in the midst of the Rockies—improbably small.

Melody saw her coming.

Blond, long, lean, wearing jeans, after-ski boots, a huge Gerry parka. In her hand was a mike. "Jack Ford," she cried, closing in.

Jack turned away, and Melody moved protectively between them.

"I'm with KXIS," the woman said. "Please, Jack, a comment on North-Star's announcement."

"No comment," Melody said firmly, not even wondering what the announcement was, concerned only with shielding Jack.

"According to inside sources, *Berenger* was Oscar material. Why do you think North-Star would cancel its release?"

Jack turned, eyes wide with shock.

"You didn't know!" the woman cried eagerly. "It's the first policy change since the takeover. North-Star will not release films that do not live up to its standards—do you want the quote? Shit—I had it somewhere!"

"What!" Jack said hoarsely.

"No comment," Melody said firmly, grabbing Jack's arm. "Jack, ignore her," she said to him alone. "We don't know what's going on."

But the reporter heard. "You don't know about the takeover?" She was triumphant. "North-Star has been raided by Glassman Enterprises. Do you want the quote on the *Berenger* cancellation?"

Jack stared, shocked.

Falling.

Free-falling through space.

" 'North-Star is canceling the release of *Berenger* because the film does not meet the quality standard that has made North-Star an industry leader,' " the reporter read. " 'It is possible that with further editing the film may be released at a future, unscheduled date.' " She smiled. "Any comments?"

Falling.

God, why now, after all these years?

For a long time he didn't speak. Then he said, his voice barely audible, "That bastard is still after me."

*S*he was stunned.

Not even furious, just stunned.

Even if she hadn't been planning on going to the Kellers' party tonight, she would have come to Aspen now to confront Abe. What in hell was he up to?

It was only yesterday, the last day of the shoot before the holiday break, that she had first heard the rumors. She'd been sipping a coffee and eating a sandwich; everyone was taking lunch. She'd been flipping through *The New York Times,* probably Mascione's copy. Her friend the gaffer had joined her. Belinda paused when she saw a photo of her parents leaving a tremendous New York benefit ball at the Met. Before she could turn the page the gaffer said, "I wonder if it's true."

"What?"

"All the rumors."

She tossed the paper aside and picked up her sandwich. "What rumors?"

"The takeover rumors."

"What takeover rumors?"

"Jesus! Haven't you heard? Word's out that North-Star's about to be raided." The gaffer raised his Coke. "By that guy, Glassman."

Her world became deathly still. *"What?"*

"He's been buying up stock like crazy. He says it's just friendly investing, but everyone I know says he's gonna take over the studio. Can you believe it? We're in the middle of a corporate raid!"

A sick feeling started to well up within her.

Just what the fuck was Abe up to?

"So how's the big-time screenwriter?" Abe asked the minute she stepped inside his Aspen duplex condo.

"Hello, dear," Nancy said, an elegant vision in designer jeans and tons of silver-and-turquoise Indian jewelry.

"Hello, Mom," Belinda said, and then she turned to face Abe. "Is it true?"

"You look like you swallowed some turpentine. Is what true? Can't you even say hi to your old man?"

"Is it true, Abe?" Belinda grated. "Are you raiding North-Star? Are the rumors true?"

Abe looked at her; then he laughed. "They ain't rumors, babe."

"You shit!" Belinda ground out.

Nancy, behind her, went white.

"Don't you talk to me that way," Abe said, hard.

"Why? Why are you doing it? It's me—isn't it?"

"You?" Abe lifted a brow. "Don't flatter yourself!"

He was lying—Belinda knew it. "What are you up to? It's an awfully big coincidence that you're taking over a company I'm working for!"

"Before this raid I already owned eight percent of North-Star," Abe said calmly. "This was strictly a business deal, and you have nothing to do with it."

She didn't believe him. Did she?

"Do you think I'm gonna piss away millions of dollars? I've been eyeing this company for a long time, Belinda. I didn't get to where I am today by making stupid personal decisions. Besides, what in hell would I have to gain by taking over North-Star as far as you're concerned?"

"I don't know," Belinda said. "That's what I'm trying to figure out."

Abe laughed. "Well, you keep on thinking long and hard, and you'll figure out that you don't have anything to do with this."

Belinda looked at him. She knew only one thing—she didn't trust him. She knew him too well.

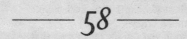

58

"*J*ack, this is silly."

Jack stood bare-chested in the bedroom of the condo he was renting. He rummaged through his suitcase, then pulled out his favorite sweater and pulled it on. "Did you reach anyone, Mel—anyone?"

Mel stood watching him. Why was he insisting on going to this party now? He had just been devastated. He needed to relax. He needed comforting—her comforting. Why did he have to face the vultures that would gather around him at the Kellers? "No, Jack, everyone's gone until the first."

Jack was expressionless, but a muscle ticked in his jaw. "I sure as hell could use a drink," he said more to himself than to her.

Melody's eyes went wide. She bit her lip, not sure what to say.

He looked at her, laughing, not a particularly happy sound. "Don't worry, I need to stay sober to fight fucking Glassman."

"Jack, I'm sure there's a reasonable explanation for *Berenger*'s cancellation."

His gaze, furious, pinned her. "This is personal. Glass-

man is trying to fuck me—personally. Do you understand?"
Before Melody could answer, he was jamming his thumb at
her. "Do you know what that film means to me? To my
career? The difference between being a teenybopper's TV
idol and a frigging movie star! Movie star! I worked on that
film for four months, Mel, four fucking months—and I was
good, I mean, damn good! And now, now he's reaming me,
the son of a bitch."

"But, Jack, why would he do this to you?"

"Because I laid his wife."

She gasped.

"Sixteen years ago, Mel. I was twenty-one, for God's
sake. And she wanted it—believe me—badly. Christ, that
was the loneliest woman I have ever seen!"

"Jack, that's crazy—"

"Yeah, well, you tell the crazy man that. After I got out
of the hospital—oh, I didn't tell you, did I?" He was bitter.
"He had three thugs beat the shit out of me after he found
out. I almost died. After I got out of the hospital, I couldn't
keep a job. I kept getting fired. Glassman had one of his
thugs chasing around after me, paying everyone off to see I
stayed out of work. My spot in acting class had been taken,
and the bitch wouldn't give me another one. A girl I was
shacking up with threw me out. Believe me, Mel, I know. He
paid her off, the cocksucker. I had about ten dollars to my
name, and I was on the streets of New York."

"What did you do, Jack?"

He laughed harshly. "Picked up some rich broad who
paid me for fucking her."

Melody's expression was full of pity and compassion.

"For God's sake, don't look at me that way," he
snapped, striding out of the room, brushing past her rudely.
"Are you going to get ready, or not?"

"Yes, yes," Melody said and hurried into her own room
to find something suitable to wear.

Jack stared at the well-stocked bar. Wanting it. A drink.
He hadn't craved alcohol like this, not in years.

Abe Glassman was not going to drive him back to
drink.

Abe Glassman was not going to destroy him.

He was going to fight—somehow. After all, he'd been raised on the streets, and he'd been born a fighter. No, Glassman wasn't going to win—not this time.

Too much was at stake.

His career was at stake.

59

*J*ack was having a horrible time.

But he was dutifully making the rounds, with a pleasant look plastered on his face.

The Kellers had a mansion on Red Mountain, with two-hundred-and-eighty-degree views of a nighttime Aspen glittering at their feet. The party took up three huge rooms, beginning with a vast stone-floored entryway below a huge skylight. The living room was even larger; it too had stone flooring, and at least a dozen seating areas. There were a hundred people in this room and the dining room, where a buffet that would have done Bel Air justice graced one long, pine-planked wall. The house was typical Aspen, a combination of country and contemporary, stone and wood, huge windows everywhere to show off the magnificent views.

At least a dozen people had mentioned the *Berenger* cancellation, showing just the right amount of sympathy. Half of these dozen people reassured him that with editing even the worst of films could be made palatable. Jack smiled and nodded amiably.

Inside, he was furious. *Berenger* was good—damn good. He knew it. Everyone who had seen the rushes agreed. And he knew he was great in the film—not good, great. Oscar material.

The other half of his consolers prodded and pried into

his feelings, with barely disguised glee, trying to get him to reveal himself. He could feel their panting, bated breath. They wanted him to fail. It wasn't just Hollywood—it was people. They loved a rags-to-riches-to-rags story. It was the best kind of story there was.

And on top of that, there were a lot of people who were jealous of how big he had made it, and how "fast." Eleven years of grunt work before having been discovered didn't count to them. They saw only that he'd had the lead in a series pilot; then eight months later he'd been touted as the Sexiest Man in Hollywood, the network's Golden Boy. He had signed a new contract (reputed to be half a million a year), been seduced by independents, million-dollar commercials, specials, a lead in a six-hour miniseries. Half of Hollywood hated him and tonight that half seemed to be here.

He spotted Melody looking very bored as she chatted with a couple he didn't know. Safe territory, and he headed for it, making his way over to her. "Jesus," he said, taking her aside.

"How is it going?"

"Just great," he said sarcastically, scanning the sea of people swirling around him.

"Jack, why are we here? Let's leave."

"So everyone can think I'm afraid to be seen? No, thanks."

"This is ridiculous," Melody said. "Let's go somewhere quiet and get a bite to eat, just you and me."

"I appreciate the concern, Mel," he said, softening. At least she was in his corner. Melody would never desert him. He took her hand and squeezed it.

And then he saw her.

First his eye caught a flash of gold. As if on cue, a couple in his line of vision moved aside. She stood talking to three men.

Belinda.

He hadn't forgotten her. To the contrary. He'd given her more than a few thoughts since he'd last seen her. To be precise, he had been anticipating returning to the set—returning to her. To continue where they'd left off. To finish what they'd started that night so many months ago.

The gold knit top she wore tonight was very thin, and it clung to her broad shoulders and full bosom. Black leather pants fit like a second skin. Strong and sexy, and tonight she was going to be his.

She was standing as if poised, laughing now, at something one of the men with her had said. It was her fancy boyfriend, but Jack didn't give a damn. His heart was thudding, and he could feel a new tightness in his jeans. How had he ever let her get away?

Nothing was going to stop him tonight.

Nothing—and no one.

This was just what he needed in order to forget *Berenger*. In fact, he had already forgotten.

*J*ackson Ford.

She was already throbbing with sexual excitement, swollen and wet.

Belinda was having fantasy after fantasy of Ford driving his cock into her, of going down on her, and she was having trouble concentrating on anything. Or anyone. Other than him.

He was the most magnificent male she had ever laid eyes on.

And he knew it. There was no doubt of that. The one thing he wasn't was modest. He flirted outrageously, and the women flocked to him.

It increased her excitement.

This was long overdue.

The past two weeks, since she had last seen him, had

been a contradiction. Amazingly exciting—after all, it was her first production. And amazingly boring—without him there. The anticipation, knowing she was going to have him when they went back into production after the holiday, had been so sweet—and so agonizing. Now the waiting was over.

A while ago she had thought he was coming over to her. Finally. But he had stopped just outside her group, to shake hands and chat and flash his liquid-inducing grin with some Aspenites. He had been close enough for her to see that his cock was bulging very obviously against the tight faded jeans. She had lost her breath, mesmerized by the sight of him, the sight of that. Then he had looked past the woman he was talking to, at her. He had smiled, slowly, dazzlingly. With sheer sexual promise.

She drifted away from the group she had been talking to, searching for a ladies' room. She wasn't wearing underwear, and she had been emitting incredible amounts of high-voltage lubrication. She was going to fuck his brains out tonight. Nothing else mattered, not *Outrage,* not Abe, nothing.

Where was he now?

The house was full of bathrooms, almost a dozen. This particular bathroom belonged to a bedroom and was carpeted wall-to-wall. The Jacuzzi could fit six, easily, and the window surrounding it caught the dazzle of night lights from the town in the valley. She stepped inside, and faced the full-length mirror. Her face was flushed.

She patted her face with powdered paper, flicked at nonexistent smudges on eyeliner. Her makeup was very dramatic, to go with her mood—sable brown and gold on her eyes, and red, red lips that would look garish on most women, but not on her. She pulled out her lipstick, about to reapply.

And then she saw him in the mirror.

Their eyes met in the glass.

Jack smiled, his eyes moving to her reflection and then roaming down her back and legs.

She turned around. His gaze settled on her eyes, her

mouth, lingering—then her breasts and their pointed nipples straining against the knit top. And lower.

Belinda swallowed. She was very dry-mouthed. She couldn't speak.

Jack took two steps and placed his hands on her shoulders. She could hear his breathing, feel his breath on her forehead. His fingers dug softly into her flesh, kneading. Then he trailed a barely-there finger to her neck, pausing. He briefly looked into her eyes. His finger glided down her chest and into the deep V of her top.

He ran soft, gentle hands around her back. Setting her on fire. They came back to her shoulders, toyed, moved to her neck. He cupped her face, bringing it close. His eyes, green and hot, held hers. His mouth descended slowly, agonizingly slowly.

The contact sent her to heaven.

His mouth moved with an incredible softness, and shudders racked both his body and hers.

And then he had her in an iron grip, hands moving frantically to her buttocks, pulling her against his massive prick, his mouth bruising hers. Belinda moaned, flinging her arms around him, pushing against him, meeting brutal kiss with brutal kiss.

He had her breasts in his hands. Squeezing, his tongue deep in her mouth. Belinda pulled on his buttocks, rubbing her swollen, wet pussy against his thick erection, finding a rhythm, whimpering, desperate for the orgasm she was so close to. Searching, seeking, determined. Jack's hands moved to her buttocks, helping her stroke him.

He was suddenly gone, and Belinda was bereft. Only to realize he was on his knees, pressing his face against her crotch, his breath fanning her like hot flames. He kissed her through the slick leather, the pressure exquisite, and Belinda was lost.

"Please," she moaned.

She was on the floor, on her back. He pulled off her boots, the hot skins of her pants. With his fingers he parted her thick, wet lips, and then his mouth was there, lapping at her, exploring the deep pink folds. With his tongue he lifted her tumescent clit, trailing along the length of its underside, back and forth. He took it in his mouth, sucking, pulling gently. He flicked the tip of his tongue over it, around it, coaxing it into larger dimensions. Belinda grabbed his head. Moaning and sobbing as the contractions spiraled with a violence she had never felt before. The orgasm lingered for a final, startling explosion and began to fade.

Her heart was still thudding when consciousness returned. Her eyes flew open, and she lifted her head. Jack was staring up at her, on his stomach on the floor, each of her naked thighs draped across his shoulders, his chin lost in the nest of her pubic hair.

"Good God," Belinda breathed.

"You came too fast," Jack said. "I'm not through."

A rush of indignation. Belinda struggled to sit, but he held her down, with a hoarse laugh, and then the laugh was gone. He lowered his head, and his tongue moved restlessly back into her moist slit, sliding lower, stiffening, plunging into her cunt.

Belinda moaned. Sinking into the carpet.

Voices.

Female voices, and even as Jack said, "Oh, shit!" and as Belinda realized that the door was opening, it was too late.

Two women stopped in midsentence, gasping, too stunned to move. Belinda sat with her legs spread and Jackson Ford on his knees, his head poised intimately over her glistening genitals.

The women ran out.

Belinda looked at his golden head. It was bobbing up and down—but he wasn't touching her. Why hadn't that bastard moved off of her? And then she heard a sound. A strangled sound. He was laughing.

He lifted his head, and she saw that he was choking with laughter, tears in his eyes. Belinda smiled. Jack rocked back on his heels. Hysterical.

"Can you imagine!" He sputtered. "Can you imagine!" He was holding onto his stomach.

Belinda began laughing too.

61

*G*oing back downstairs would have amused Jack terribly, if he weren't so insane with desire for Belinda. They didn't have to talk, didn't have to make plans. Jack kept a firm grip on her arm, glancing at her admiringly. Belinda looked like the cat that had lapped all the cream. Not in the least bit embarrassed. In the foyer they waited for her coat.

"Where are you staying?" he asked.

"My place is out—my father's there, and we also have company." She was looking at him out of intense brown eyes. He felt a kind of pang, something deep and tugging and not at all physical.

"I have to go tell my friend I'm leaving," he said. He knew that Melody wouldn't mind.

"So do I," Belinda said, grinning conspiratorially.

Jack found himself smiling back.

Melody just stared when he told her to enjoy herself and that he'd leave the door open. He was wishing he had come alone, so he could have glorious Belinda all to himself for the entire weekend. They would make love all day and all night—to hell with skiing. Maybe once he buried his dick deep inside her he would never come out. God!

His ache was bad. What had happened before was only a tease. He needed more—a lot more.

He wanted privacy. Lots of privacy. Days and days of privacy.

He had the feeling he had just touched the tip of an iceberg.

That he was about to step into a pond, only to drown in an ocean.

No one in Aspen used cars except for the rare times they went out of town to parties like this. The cab came immediately. The tension was so thick in the car he could feel it—and he could smell it. Her smell. The smell of female dampness, of her arousal, of her need for him. It was heavy and heady and delicious.

He put his arm around her, and before he knew it they were making out like kids. With her hand she traced the outline of his cock. "Don't," he whispered. "I'll never make it."

She smiled.

Jack paid the driver; then he took Belinda's arm. He was wearing sneakers, and they both skidded across the icy sidewalk until they made the safety of the stairs. He unlocked the door, and Belinda moved ahead of him into the living room, pausing, proud and graceful and sensuous, looking at him with intense promise. She moved into the bedroom. Jack followed.

With one movement she pulled off the gold knit top.

Her nakedness was perfection. Luscious round breasts, hard-tipped. Narrow waist. She bent to remove first one high-heeled boot, then the other. Her breasts swayed. Round and full and white, they brushed her leather-clad thighs.

He watched her hands, unsnapping then unzipping her pants. She paused long enough for him to glimpse the tangled, damp nest of curls he had tasted briefly. And then she skimmed off the pants, stepping out of them proudly.

She's performing for me, he thought, startled with sudden comprehension. She knows how hot she is. She's not afraid of me, not awed by me, and she never has been. The thought thrilled him. He felt himself being sucked in deeper and deeper, fascination rivaling his arousal.

Jack undressed quickly, and she watched his every motion. He wished he weren't so eager, wished he could give her a show, but he couldn't. He liked the way her gaze roamed over his powerful torso, rippling with every movement. He knew exactly how he looked—he had seen himself on film a million times.

"Jack," she whispered, coming forward.

He closed his eyes when her hands slid over his hard stomach and up into the furring of brown hair on his chest.

She inhaled. Her hand drifted down, moving over the huge bulge in his jeans. Jack was filled with pride. Anticipation.

Fingers found the zipper and slid it down. His cock rocketed out, red, massive, and straight.

She stared.

Jack stumbled out of his pants. As if he had no experience, no control. He was more than proud. All women seemed mesmerized by him, and it was this moment that was perhaps the most exciting of all. He moved toward her.

"You don't wear underwear," she said unevenly.

Jack laughed harshly. "Two of a kind," he said, pushing her back on the bed.

It was an explosion.

One moment they were apart, and the next they were together, straining wildly at each other, entwined, gasping, desperate. He held her face in his hands and kissed her mindlessly, losing all coherence, all detachment, overwhelmed by sensations, by a gaping emptiness he knew only she could fill.

He raised himself up on his forearms and rubbed the head of his prick against her belly, stroking her soft, damp flesh, each stroke taking the straining purplish head lower, until it slid between thick cunt lips, over her clit again and again. The head was huge, growing larger. She made a wild, desperate sound. He couldn't delay a moment longer. He was mad with his need to ram himself deep inside her—and he no longer had any control. For one brief instant he poised the tip of his prick against her cunt, trying to tease, trying to wait. He plunged into her.

This was what God meant when He promised heaven.

And then the unthinkable happened.

He came. It happened so quickly, and he was helpless to prevent it. It was an incredible orgasm, the like of which he had never experienced before. It seemed to last forever, that hot, hot pumping, that emptying. But it didn't matter. He knew she had come too. There was no doubt about that. He had felt every single one of her violent contractions. He looked at her.

Her eyes were closed, her mouth open, her hair very

damp. He reached up to touch a wisp of hair, move it aside. Her eyes fluttered, opened. He locked onto them, drowned.

She smiled.

He smiled.

He lay his cheek on her shoulder and explored her body with his hands. He was suddenly filled with doubts. He was with one of the most beautiful, confident women he had ever seen, and he had orbited in a couple of minutes. Less. What was she thinking? Was she disappointed? Christ! How in hell had that happened? Talk about a straight fuck. He hadn't even said any of those words—love words, sex words—that women loved to hear.

She sighed and sat up, shifting away from him. "That was nice," she said, sliding her strong, shapely legs over the side of the bed.

Stunned, he realized she was about to get up—and leave. "Wait," he said, gripping her wrist.

She looked at him inquiringly.

He didn't know what the hell was wrong with him. He was having trouble finding words. What a time for his charm to desert him.

"I should go," she said carelessly. She gave him an equally careless smile.

He hadn't let go of her wrist. She *was* disappointed. All that build-up, all that anticipation, and then a two-minute bang. "Suddenly in a rush?"

"*Me?*"

He almost blushed. Instead a sound escaped, almost a growl, and he was pulling her back down beneath him. "It was your fault."

Her gaze was serious. "But you're the *man.*"

And he chuckled.

She laughed, looping her hands around his neck. "Do you forgive me—Nick?"

"For what? Being a complete tease or a complete fool?" But he was still smiling.

"For making you come so fast."

"Don't remind me."

"Why not?" Her voice grew husky. "The thought excites me."

He smiled lazily, shifted, and started running his hand down her body. "You like knowing I lost all control around you?"

She arched, eyes closed. "Yes."

"So that's why you're here, to have your ego stroked."

"Umm."

"Just your ego, Belinda?"

"No."

"How about this?"

She arched her breast more fully into his hand. "Yes."

"And this?"

She spread her legs for him. "Jack . . ."

"And you were going to leave."

"I've changed my mind."

He laughed, enjoying his power over her. "Come for me, Belinda, again." His fingers moved slickly against her.

"Jack . . ."

"I want to watch you while you come."

She gasped, eyes wide at the surge of pleasure he had induced. This time, he thought, I'll show her just how good I am—how good it can be for us. He lifted her hair and kissed the nape of her neck, just barely.

She shuddered.

He started to make love to her slowly, sensually, intending to use every trick he knew to bring her to heights she'd never reached before. But . . . his mind stopped working. There was only her and him. He became lost in her. His hands and mouth and body moved without instruction, with need, with desperation. Before he knew it, they were joined, moving with a slow, languid rhythm. And this time he brought her there again and again and again.

Afterward he lay stunned. He had the strangest feeling that for the first time in his life he'd made love to a woman. Made love with his heart and soul, not fucked with his body and mind. It was disturbing.

"God!" she said. It had to be hours later.

Jack's eyes were closed. He smiled with satisfaction.

Then he became aware of something else. Her hand had moved to his face, and he became very still, barely breathing as she touched his cheek, his temple, his ear, tracing the outline of his face. When she had finished, he dared to look at her.

And their gazes met, holding, for an intimate moment.

I might be in deep shit, he thought. He pulled her against his side. "Tell me the truth, Belinda. Why did you stand me up the night we met?"

Oh, God! Belinda did not want to think of her mother —of her mother and Jack—not now. "I can't remember."

His jaw tightened. "So now it's back to games?"

"I really don't remember." Her eyes flashed.

"Okay," he said, releasing her. He stared at the ceiling. "You're the only woman I've ever met who wasn't impressed by who I am, do you know that?"

"Do you want me to be another one of your mindless brunette bimbos?"

He raised up on an elbow and grinned. "What?"

She blushed.

"How do you know I like brunette bimbos?" he asked, trying not to laugh. He was delighted. She was jealous. He hoped. Even if it was just a little.

"Your reputation is impossible to miss."

His grin widened.

"Don't let it go to your head," she warned.

His eyes brightened. "You go to my head," he said while Belinda groaned at the bad joke. "How much do you know about me, Belinda?"

She gave him a dirty look. "I read the rags."

"You really aren't impressed," he said, nose-diving.

"I'm impressed. I'm impressed that God gave you a perfect face and a perfect body and that you had the smarts to cash in on it. I mean, that's impressive."

Instant deflation. "Thanks."

"Why do you want me to be impressed with Jack Ford, the star? Your whole world—all those Masciones and Melodys—is impressed with Jack Ford, the star."

"It would just be nice to know I impressed you a little."

She softened. "I'm impressed with Jack Ford the actor. He's good."

Jack looked at her. "Thanks."

A mischievous light came into her eyes. "And Jack Ford the lover. He's pretty impressive too." She had the audacity to wink at his now flaccid member.

"And Jack Ford the man?"

She looked at him. "I don't know who he is," she said quietly.

"I want you to know who he is," he said.

She regarded him silently.

"Belinda, I want to really get to know you." He meant it.

Her face went tense. "You have some crappy lines, but the delivery's great." She turned, reaching for her leather pants.

He moved then. Before she could even lift them, he had her in his arms. "I'm not letting you leave," he said huskily. "God, I don't know why . . . but I'm not. Not yet. It's too soon."

She stood very still, her back against his chest as if she had stopped breathing. "Spend the night with me, Belinda. Come back to bed."

How could she resist that sexy tone?

"I want to fall asleep with you," he whispered in her ear. His breath sent hot tingles down her spine. "I want to wake up a few hours from now and fuck you again."

Hot, wet heat.

Belinda stayed.

He watched her fall asleep in his arms. Fascinated, wondering all kinds of things, who she was really, the woman behind the facade. His last waking thought was that he would find out everything, everything there was to know about her, Belinda . . . And that he might never let her go.

62

*B*elinda woke.

She was filled with the man beside her in every way but the physical one.

He had his arm around her, and he was snoring softly. His skin was silken on his shoulder, coarse on his chest. His breath gently fanned the top of her head. Even asleep, his presence was vitally magnetic and commanding.

She couldn't believe what had happened between them.

He had made incredible love to her.

She wasn't sure a man had ever made love to her before.

Even now, her heart was doing weird somersaults, and she was starting to tremble and sweat as if she had run a marathon.

Just what she needed right now.

Belinda cautiously slipped out of Jack's possessive arm and sat, regarding him with sheer open curiosity, her eyes wandering slowly, seeking satiation. He was beautiful, no doubt of that—too handsome for his own good. And he had an animal sex appeal. A deadly combination. But of course. That's why he was a top sex symbol.

In sleep, the lines of hardship and the crinkles around his eyes had softened, making him seem much younger. And his body was perfect. She had already seen it—or parts of it. It was a major commercial draw to show a gleaming Jackson Ford torso; hard, broad pectorals, rippling biceps. Was he a natural, she wondered, or did he work out?

Why was she so terrified?

She didn't realize it, but her hand had followed the path of her eyes and was gently caressing his skin, slightly coarsened by a scattered nest of wiry, brownish hair. A nipple hardened under her hand. She didn't want to wake him up.

A hard-on miraculously appeared before her eyes.

The man was magnificently endowed, to say the least. No wonder he was so horny. She smiled, her hand slipping to his belly, soft in sleep. Not padded, just relaxed. He must diet, she thought—or it wouldn't be fair.

Even his legs were the way she liked them; strong and muscled, not thin and not squat either. Just very, very powerful.

I am in deep trouble, she thought. If she had been scared of a relationship with Adam, she was terrified now. And then she felt Ford roll over, pressing himself against her leg. It was too hard to resist.

She slid down beside him, and his arms went around her, his eyes still closed, looking relaxed, asleep. Instinctively he moved on top of her, one knee parting her willing legs, his cock moving with unerring homing instinct, sliding deeply into her. Belinda had been smiling, thinking, Oh, no —even in sleep! But the smile disappeared as the feel of him made her lose her breath and think of only one thing.

His eyes flicked open, hazy and unfocused. He moved gently, with growing fervor. His gaze became lucid. A smile. "Belinda."

She would have died if he'd called her by another name. Belinda closed her eyes, let herself go, let the feelings build. It happened very quickly; the impending rush, the pull, like the tide, tugging her along, sweeping her up, and she whimpered, panted, moaned his name—and then she was gone, hurled away, beyond control, a series of intense contractions racking her body, causing her to lose focus with everything.

When she opened her eyes she met Jack's grin, sort of like a proud boy who had just proved he could climb the highest tree; and then he slid onto his back, with his arm around her and was starting to snore.

Unbelievable.

She looked at him and wanted to scream with joy—and rage.

Why her?

She didn't need this, didn't want it. Why had it been so good? Worse: She was fatally attracted to him. And she knew that was the only way to describe it—fatal. Damn him! To him, she was just another lay, one of hundreds.

She stared at him and tried to see the real man.

He's nothing but a star with a monstrous ego and an insatiable need for pussy, she thought. And I've just become another nameless, faceless fuck.

Maybe I'll stand out in the crowd because I'm a blonde.

She wanted to laugh, and she wanted to cry.

The timing could never be good and had never been worse.

She knew Ford, all right—she knew him very well.

And the last thing she needed in her life was a super-stud actor. A man like that could bring only pain. Lots of pain.

Especially when she had these damn feelings that were trying to pop out of her, incipient and demanding—and very, very threatening.

Oh, she knew him all right!

He was her flip side, her male counterpart.

Her soul mate.

She got up and very quietly gathered her clothes.

63

*J*ack was dreaming.

He knew the dream—and hated it.

The goddamn neighborhood. The empty lot full of garbage. The broken chain fence. The slovenly cottages, the filthy streets, the rats. His house.

He didn't want to be in the dream. He wanted to wake up.

He saw her standing there, on the porch. His mother.

Something was wrong. He knew his mother was dead.

Wake up!

He felt his heart lift in anticipation as he suddenly knew who was standing there, waving, waiting.

It wasn't his mother.

Belinda.

He started to run. His heart was going crazy now, with a kind of insane happiness, a desperate need, a kind of ecstatic feeling that didn't belong in the dream. Belinda was so beautiful, and she was there waiting for him.

But it was wrong. She shouldn't be there, not on his porch. Something was wrong.

He felt afraid.

And then he knew why: Because it was happening, and he had known it was going to happen all along. His house started moving away as he approached.

No!

Belinda!

He screamed, but no words came out. He tried to run, but his legs wouldn't move.

The house was disappearing!

Belinda! Belinda! Belinda!

He couldn't get his voice to work, and his legs were still paralyzed. The house was dropping over the horizon. It was just a speck now, and he started crying.

Jack gasped and sat up, fully awake.

What a dream.

His face was wet. He couldn't believe it. And then he realized the other side of the bed was empty.

He leaned back against the pillows, his heart pounding, waiting for it to slow down, listening for Belinda in the bathroom. Why would he dream something like that? How insane!

He turned his head toward her side of the bed, touching the spot where she had lain, inhaling the heady smell of sex. The sheets were cool, and he frowned, sitting up. Looking down, surprised. He was growing.

He half smiled. All kinds of memories came spinning back to him. Jesus! Never had it been so good—last night made every sexual encounter he had ever had seem embarrassingly poor! He laughed, a husky, smug sound.

They had made love on and off for most of the night, mostly on. He had always been proud of his stamina but hadn't known it was quite this good.

Where was she? Just thinking about her was making him throb deliciously, demandingly. What hadn't they done?

He had a sudden desire to give Belinda a bath. He smiled, visualizing how he would soap her entire body. He stood and walked into the bathroom.

She wasn't there.

He walked back into the bedroom, hitting the lights. Scowling now. Her clothes—the gold top, the cowboy boots, the leather pants—were no longer on his floor.

No way. It wasn't possible.

No woman walked out on him until he told her to leave.

Impossible.

His gaze settled on a note propped up on the bedside table, and he pounced on it:

> Thanks, Jack. It was fun.
> Belinda

He crumpled it in his hand, hurling it at the floor.
Fun? It was *fun?*

Who the hell was that little no-name screenwriter to leave him in the middle of the night and call their evening *fun!*

He couldn't believe she had just gotten up and left!

The no-good cunt.

It was then that he heard a crash in the living room and a hushed curse. Like a shot he was through the door.

64

*B*elinda cursed again, this time to herself, carefully picking up the lamp and placing it on the side table she had knocked over. She couldn't see a fucking thing. Then suddenly the entire room was illuminated—someone had hit the switch. She jumped a foot into the air.

"What a nice note," Jack said. She had her boots in hand, and she looked guilty and furtive.

Belinda straightened, trying not to act like a crook, not to feel like one. After all, it was her right to leave whenever she damn well pleased. "I thought it was a nice note. What was I supposed to do, just leave without a good-bye?"

"You weren't supposed to leave at all," Jack snapped.

"The night is over," Belinda said. "It was nice. Now it's over. Look, I don't have time for this."

"You are one cold lady," Jack said rigidly.

Belinda grabbed the door and swung it open. "Goodbye, Jack."

He grabbed it, and his strength won. The door closed. "Let's talk."

Just who did he think he was? She wanted to go, and that was that. "I don't want to talk, Jack. I want to go home, take a shower, have some coffee, and get dressed to go skiing."

Jack's scowl deepened.

Belinda shrugged.

"It's insulting that you're trying to leave like this."

"I'm sure it is. All those mindless bimbos you fuck wouldn't dare leave until you told them to, would they?"

"So now you want to fight?"

"I don't know you well enough to fight with you," Belinda said, wishing his eyes weren't so expressive and beautiful. Wishing she had made it out the door without his catching her, then wishing he would make her stay.

"If those weren't fighting words, then I don't know what you'd call them."

"Maybe it's just that the truth is hard to take?"

"Don't try and tell me again that you're not trying to provoke me," Jack said.

Belinda turned abruptly on her heel. Damn him, but he was right. She was angry, angry at herself and at him, but mostly at herself, for her feelings, and she was taking it out on him. She did want to fight.

Jack was suddenly there, suddenly had her in his arms, his breath against her cheek. "You're not going," he said in that silky tone of his. "You're not going and we're not fighting, Belinda. You can't possibly walk away now. Not from me."

She pushed him away so she could really look at him. The trouble was, she was melting under his charisma, and she didn't want to go. *But she had to.*

"I want you to stay, Belinda. Just you and me. We'll stay through the holiday, a whole week, just the two of us." His tone was husky, seductive, urgent. It was his smile that decided her, so ripe with cocky promise. Imagine a week of this! But then what? To get thrown out on her ass and replaced by his next bimbo? "No, thanks."

He was incredulous. "You're refusing me? Leaving? Walking out on *me?*"

"Sorry."

"Fine." He stomped to the door of the bedroom and turned. "Just fine, Belinda, just fine!"

She stared, unsmiling.

"You do know what you're missing?"

"I believe so," she said.

"I won't chase after you again," Jack stated, eyes flashing angrily. "I never chase a broad."

"And I never chase a stud," Belinda said, opening the door.

"You're the coldest bitch I've ever met."

"You have an incredible head," she said and then smiled coolly. "Meant both ways."

"I've got millions of broads chasing me," Jack shouted.

"Good! Go after them! I'm not your type anyway."

"No. That you most certainly aren't."

It hurt. It really hurt. "You truly are nothing but a prick."

"And you are nothing but a cunt," Jack snarled. "Shit, I must have been crazy! I got pussy coming out of my ears! And I chase this?" He disappeared into his bedroom, stiff and volatile.

"Like I said," Belinda called sweetly after him, "it really was fun."

Jack slammed the door behind him.

Belinda stepped out into the frigid dawn and felt like crying.

I will not shed one damn tear over that son of a bitch, she vowed. I absolutely did the right thing.

She did not feel better.

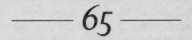

——— 65 ———

*J*anuary 15, 1988

Mary was livid.

That bastard had lied. He had used her and lied.

Worse, after not having seen him since that one night they had spent together, she had gone running when he had called this morning and told her he was in town for the day, before heading back to New York. She had met him at his condo in Westwood, and without ceremony he had stripped her and spent a few hours fucking her. She had moaned and climaxed again and again. Really getting off on the fact that she was fucking Abe Glassman now, today, while her bastard husband had been fucking his daughter last night.

Mary was no fool. Vince hadn't even bothered to come home last night. She knew where he had been, the shit. After sex, she had asked Abe what he was doing about it.

And he had laughed. "Nothing," he had said.

"What?"

"Nothing. The timing's not right now, doll, but what does it matter? You have me."

With a scream, Mary had risen to smack him across the face. Abe caught her hand, his eyes becoming black and deadly. He almost broke her wrist. "Don't you dare," he said, and he threw her back on the bed, hard, so hard that her head hit the headboard, and she was frightened. Then she saw his stiff, straining prick—they were both naked— and when she saw him climb on the bed, all kinds of jolts of desire surged through her. She hated him. He had lied, used her. But when he rammed that long, thick dick into her, she forgot everything. Everything.

Well, she was remembering now.

Remembering and steaming as she did line after line, guzzling white wine on the rocks, on the side.

When she had first been married, when Vince had loved and cherished her, he had insisted she learn to use a gun. Just an average, twenty-two caliber revolver. Now she pulled open the drawer where he kept it, in his nightstand, and she picked it up. It was black and cold and gleaming in her hand.

She shuddered and reached back into the drawer for the bullets.

It was long and black, and it gleamed in the moonlight.

The man holding the revolver grinned, raising it.

Will Hayward gasped. "No, please," he cried, unable to take his eyes off of the instrument of his death.

"It's too late for you, motherfucker," the big man said.

Will managed to take one desperate look around him, but Central Park was empty at this time of night—as he had

known it would be. His gaze flickered back to the man about
to murder him, and he backed up a step. "Please, please!"

"There ain't nowhere for you to go to, fool."

He was right. Sweat streamed down Will's face in the
frigid winter night. The gun loomed larger than life in his
vision, a blow-up, and he could see that trigger finger beginning to squeeze . . .

Will screamed, backpedaling.

And just as he pulled the trigger, the giant slipped on
the icy footing and went down hard, all three hundred
pounds of him. The shot echoed harmlessly in the night.

Will ran.

Panting, his breath condensing into thick puffs in the
freezing air, he ran for his life. The ground was slick with
snow and ice, but Will didn't fall. He knew the giant was
behind him. He could hear him. He hit Fifth Avenue, gasping and doubled over. He threw a glance over his shoulder
and saw him. This time there would be no escape . . .

The yellow cab had stopped for the light. Will lunged
for it, screaming as another shot sounded. It wasn't until he
was inside and huddled against the backseat, the driver ac-
celerating wildly away, yelling in a mixture of Spanish and
English at him to get the fuck out of his cab, that Will could
even begin to think again, ignoring the cabbie's furious,
frightened ravings.

One coherent thought formed.

That bastard was trying to kill him.

For he did not have a single doubt.

Abe Glassman, his oldest friend, was trying to kill him.

Just when things were going so well.

Never had a raid been smoother.

Abe smiled. Belinda was more gullible than he'd have
thought, to have swallowed the crap he'd handed her. Didn't
she understand that there was no way, no way, that he could
allow her success? Didn't she understand that he absolutely
willed it that she come to heel, marry Adam Gordon, and
give him his heir? His patience was finally paying off. She
and Gordon were close. And her career was not going to

interfere with his plans for her and Adam much longer. There was only one thing left—the coup de grace, as he saw it. And it wasn't up to him. "Get her pregnant," he had told Gordon last night.

As for that prick Ford?

Abe chuckled, more than pleased.

He had seen the newsclip on the local Aspen TV station of Ford's arrival and his shock at the news of the takeover and *Berenger*'s cancellation. Abe's smile grew. He had a coup for Ford too. If Ford had been shocked by that little turn of events, how would he greet Abe's next step in his campaign of destruction?

Because destruction it would be.

Total destruction.

Abe couldn't wait. Couldn't wait for Ford to find out that the production of *Outrage* was cancelled. The only question was one of timing—when to let this cat out of the bag?

Jack was in such a foul, rotten mood, he couldn't even read the words on the script in front of him. He shoved it away. He thought of the long-legged redhead he had spent last night with, and he felt angry. He had had trouble getting aroused. Him, Jack Ford, cocksman without peer, was having trouble getting it up. He slammed his fist on his desk and paced to the window.

It had been like that for four weeks—*four fucking weeks* —ever since that uppity cunt had walked out on him. First there had been the lack of desire, not really caring about getting laid. Unless he thought of her. Then he'd get hard in a second—all revved up with nowhere to go. Damn the bitch.

He had skied all day every day with Melody right through New Year's Day. Biting Mel's head off half the time, the other half brooding. Once or twice when he was perched high in the air on the chair lift, he had thought he was seeing her—Belinda. The same hair, sticking out of those ridiculous woolen hats, but in bulky ski clothes it was impossible to tell. Each time he had been wrong.

But the third time he saw her he knew it was her.

It was a warm day. The chair lift had stopped momentarily. Melody had her face tilted to the sun. Jack watched a skier coming down Red's Run, a vast mogul field, the moguls three and four feet high, really cut up, hence the fact that there was only one skier attempting it.

Wearing skintight stretch skipants, bib-style, a sweater tucked into them, a black men's cap on her head, black sunglasses. Her figure was striking and strong: broad-shouldered, full-breasted, small-waisted, long, strong legs. He knew it was her without seeing her hair or her face.

She could ski. Perfect style, seemingly slow, cutting into and hanging over those moguls, as graceful as a ballet dancer. Her legs had to be unbelievably strong. He knew how strong they were—he remembered vividly, tactilely, how strong they were when she had wrapped them around his waist. She skied beneath his chair without looking up, every ounce of concentration on the difficult terrain in front of her, and even as the lift started moving again, he twisted his head to watch her until he could see her no longer.

And he had a hard-on.

An angry one. The bitch. No one walked out on him. No one. Especially not some piece of ass. It wasn't *that* fine.

Now he stared down at Wilshire Boulevard with clenched fists. Obsessed. He was obsessed. He couldn't concentrate, couldn't sleep, couldn't enjoy fucking. If only he were working, but there had been a temporary postponement in production, more shit for him to worry about. Of course, if he were working, he'd be seeing her. He didn't know whether that thought thrilled him or infuriated him. Damn. He had to know. He strode to the door and yanked it open. He had to know where she was. He had to see her tonight. "Melody!"

"Yes?" She looked up.

"Where's the phone book? Do you know if that broad, Belinda Carlisle, the screenwriter, lives in L.A.?"

Melody stared at him.

He actually flushed.

"I can tell you where she lives, Jack."

"How in hell would you know?"

"She's a celebrity in her own right," Melody said. "I read a piece about her once in one of the rags. She's got a place in Laguna Beach."

"What?"

"She's got a—"

"What the hell do you mean, she's a celebrity in her own right?"

"Don't you know?" Melody smiled. "Her real name is Belinda Glassman. She's Abe Glassman's daughter."

Restless.

Bored.

Disgruntled. A good word. Poised, almost waiting, feeling an empty space inside, almost able to grasp what she needed, what she was missing—yet it was elusive, intangible.

Oh, bullshit, Belinda thought. Elusive, intangible? There was nothing elusive or intangible about Jackson Ford.

She had a crush on the biggest prick in Hollywood. Then she laughed. Probably true, but she hadn't meant it literally. Besides, he knew who she was. Had he called? Or tried to coax her into another night? No, he'd given up without a fight, as she had known he would. Spoiled. Spoiled and arrogant. Right now he was probably with one of his eighteen-year-old bimbos.

Red-hot jealousy.

Jesus, I'm in a bad way! she thought.

Outrage was in a temporary hiatus. Belinda couldn't help it, her skin prickled whenever she thought about it. But she'd talked to Mascione, who was unperturbed, saying this kind of thing was the norm after a big takeover and not to worry, they'd be back in production by February—he'd been promised. Fallout from Abe. Unintentional, just fallout, but . . . He was screwing with her career, even if it was inadvertently, and Belinda wished, not for the first time, that he could just be a normal father. In which case she would be on the set right now, working. With *him.*

Eventually they would be working together again. Eventually? February was two weeks away, and that wasn't eventually. Out of the frying pan, she thought grimly, and into the fire. How could someone both dread something and anticipate it at the same time? Somehow, she was going to have to stay away from him.

And, of course, staying away from him made her think of being with him, that night at the Kellers'. It made her think of the incredible passion. And her incredible stupidity.

She hadn't used her diaphragm.

She hadn't even thought about it.

Belinda knew herself: She wasn't stupid and she wasn't forgetful. But she really had forgotten. Except, there was no way she could have forgotten unless it was deliberately. For some perverse reason, her inner self was defying all reason and sanity. For some reason deep within herself she wanted to get pregnant with his child.

Maybe it hadn't happened.

Oh, what have I done?

She, a liberated woman of the eighties, reverting unconsciously to a ploy as ancient as time?

Tomorrow, she thought with dread and disbelief, I'll get a pregnancy test. And when I go back to Tucson, I am staying the hell away from him. He is one dangerous man.

She was going to stick to the Vinces of this world.

Last night had been a disaster. She hadn't been laid since Ford, not in the entire time she had spent in Aspen nor the two weeks following; and last night she had had to fantasize about Ford in order to come while Vince was making love to her. Christ. Poor Vince. The doorbell rang.

Belinda knew with an uncanny instinct that it was Vince. Sighing, she opened the door.

Mary Spazzio smiled and raised a glinting black revolver at her. "You fucking bitch," she said.

PART THREE

LIARS

January 1988

She hated him.

How could he?

And, God, the noises—they had kept her up all night.

And that laugh. His laugh. Low, unbearably sensual, unbearably aroused. He had never laughed that way with her. The bastard.

Melody didn't know if she wanted to quit or die or kill Jack.

"Mel!" he shouted from his office.

"Fuck off," she murmured and felt pleased with her boldness.

"Damn it, Mel, what the fuck is the story on *Outrage?*" He came to the door. "What is this 'extended hiatus' crap?"

At least he looked like he was getting as little sleep as she was, Melody thought sourly. How could he? Didn't he know *she* loved him? Wanted him? Why had he picked up that damn playgirl at the Kellers' when he could have had her—someone who cared? She hated him.

She loved him.

"Ted is returning my call as soon as he can," Melody said calmly.

"That's what his stupid-ass secretary has been saying for two fucking weeks," Jack raved. "Jesus, Mel, it's already the sixteenth! Go down there in person and find out what's going on!"

"We already know what's going on," Melody said coolly.

"It's like they don't even know who I am," Jack grated. "It's like I'm not signed to one of the biggest contracts in North-Star's history. It's like I'm some fucking untried kid —it's like the way it used to be!"

"There's always new policy when management changes," Melody said very unhelpfully.

"New policy? This is a fucking personal war! First the takeover, then *Berenger's* cancellation—and now this! And I'm tied into this exclusive fucking contract! I could kill Sanderson! And I can't get a fucking secretary to even talk to me! *What the fuck is going on?*"

"North-Star has been taken over. *Berenger* isn't being released. The production of *Outrage* has been postponed," Melody recited, watching his face darken again. "And didn't Sanderson tell you to cool your jets? You got paid, Jack."

"What are you, enjoying this?" He gave her an angry look and disappeared back into his office, slamming the door behind him. Melody hoped he was angry with her too.

Once he had been sensitive. No. Once she had *thought* he was sensitive. Now she realized he was no different from any other good-looking actor—selfish, egotistical, and imperious. He hadn't been sensitive enough to know when she loved him, and he wasn't sensitive enough now to know how angry she was.

Angry and hurt.

That weekend in Aspen she hadn't even had this sanctuary of anger. There'd been just a terrible hurt. She had cried herself to sleep each night, soundlessly, because she knew the walls were very thin. Sometimes, sitting on the lift with Jack, with the pain ballooning in her heart, she had thought she would break into tears right then and there in front of him. She had managed not to. But more than once she had been skiing blinded, tears blurring her vision, steaming up her goggles.

She reached for the phone. Ted Majoriis was still in a meeting. Melody flipped through her Rolodex. "Nickie Felton, please."

He was in a meeting, but she knew he would return her call.

Nickie, the assistant producer of *Berenger,* had had the hots for her. And he always knew the inside story. Melody didn't know why she was going after this. She didn't know if it was because of her job or because of something else, something deeper, darker.

"Hiya, sweetheart," Lansing said, startling her. "So how about tonight?"

*H*e sat staring into space.

Staring into space, out the window at the lawn and beyond that to the road—or at the bent head of the teacher, who was oblivious to everything except the book he was immersed in.

This is just great, Rick thought.

He hated study hall. Hated it.

Just great.

A boy who looked twelve was doodling all over his desk. A few of the kids were actually studying. Another guy, a redhead, seemed to be tapping his toe to a silent rhythm. Two girls were talking in sign language, right at his side. When the teacher, Mr. Howard, looked up, the room was hushed. When he looked down, the doodling and toe-tapping and sign language continued. Rick saw that the redhead had discreetly managed to stuff a Walkman headphone into his ear. Now that was unfair!

One of the girls slipped him a note: "Are you really Jackson Ford's brother?" Rick was disgusted, but anything was better than boredom. All these girls were the same.

They couldn't care less about him. All they cared about was his damn star brother.

He got another note: "Are you seeing Lydia Carrera?"

Now where had that come from? Sure, he'd talked to her a couple of times, but that was it. He wasn't *seeing* her.

He scribbled on the scrap of paper: "No." He slipped it back. The girls giggled. Mr. Howard looked up. Sharply.

"What is going on?" His eyes searched everyone. And settled on the redhead, who hadn't managed to get the earphone out of his ear. "Brian Leahy! Take that off immediately, and bring me that radio."

Brian complied with obvious distress.

Ten o'clock. Rick knew he was going to die of sheer boredom. Another minute passed by, second ticking after second after second. Suddenly a movement caught his eye, and he jerked around to look out the window.

Lydia was hanging upside down from a tree, like a merry, delighted ape. Rick smothered laughter. She was making faces. He had to smile. Her shirt was hanging toward her chest, revealing an expanse of flat, brownish belly. He wondered hopefully if her boobs might fall out. Then she made another face, and he laughed out loud. He clamped down quickly, the moment he realized what he'd done.

"Rick Ford! What is so funny?"

"Nothing," Rick said, not daring to steal another glance out the window and still trying not to laugh. He stared at the science teacher in front of him. But a few instants later he had to look out the window. She was gone.

68

*A*dam was no fool.

He stepped into his apartment, closing the door behind him, thinking. He had seen Belinda leave the Kellers' party with Ford. She had told him she had a headache and insisted he didn't have to accompany her. What did she take him for, a fucking fool? She'd used the exact same lines at the Majorises almost six months ago. Twice now, she'd dumped him for that two-bit actor.

He had been livid then, not jealous, just livid—because Ford was getting in his way.

And because that little cunt had chosen Ford over him. Chosen some two-bit stud actor over him.

That was when he had first come to hate Belinda Glassman.

He hated her now.

He had invested almost half a year of his life chasing her, courting her, wooing her—playing the perfect gentleman. And she had dumped him for that nothing actor. It was beyond belief. Even now, just thinking about it, he was having fantasies of grabbing her and raping her, teaching her a lesson, pounding into her mercilessly.

Of course, he wouldn't do it.

He was a man of reason, and reason ruled. He had no intention of losing this battle—and all the spoils of war. Belinda Glassman was not going to escape him.

All he had to do was think of Glassman Enterprises, and the billions of dollars it represented, to know conclusively that she was not going to escape him. He couldn't let her.

"You're home."

Adam looked up and smiled.

Cerisse smiled back, leaning against the doorway to the hall. She was black, beautiful, tall. She wore a nippleless bra and crotchless panties. Adam's prick rose immediately to attention. He walked toward her, staring at hard, large, brown nipples.

"I have a surprise for you," she murmured, dodging his hands as he reached for her breasts.

He followed her into the bedroom, throwing his sweater on a chair. He stopped. Stared.

The woman in his bed was as short and slim as Cerisse was tall and voluptuous. She was Asian. Naked except for black stockings. Her nipples, small and pointed, were rouged the color of red wine. Her pubes were shaven, her legs spread—like the whore she was. Cerisse chuckled.

"Go down on her," Adam said, "while I get undressed."

69

Mary knew she was on the edge of a terrible breakdown, maybe insanity. The phone rang, but she ignored it. She was surrounded by today's newspapers. They'd been opened, read, and tossed aside. Nothing. She couldn't find a thing.

Oh, God!

If Belinda Glassman had died, she knew without a doubt that the police would come knocking on her door. She expected them at any moment—as she had for the past eighteen hours, ever since the gun had gone off yesterday evening. She thought she heard a car in the drive. She jumped, ran to the window, peered through the curtains. No one. Now she was hearing things.

She was sweating.

She would never, never forget the look on Belinda's face

when the gun went off. Belinda had grabbed it. Mary had struggled against her superior strength. Then the blast. Belinda suddenly letting go, face white, eyes wide, staggering backward. A red blossom, small at first, above her left breast, growing rapidly. She had started screaming wildly as she fell to the ground.

Except, Mary realized, it wasn't Belinda screaming—it was herself.

"Call an ambulance, Mary," Belinda had gotten out.

Mary was frozen, standing there, moaning, panting, unable to move, to think, to respond.

"Mary! An ambulance! Please!"

Mary stared and watched Belinda's eyes close, her breathing stop. Dear God! She was dying, maybe dead. That did it! She was jolted into action. She ran down the stairs to her car. Then she thought of the gun—and fingerprints. She ran back up the stairs, panting wildly, and grabbed the gun. She turned and fled to her car, backing out, going over the curb, not caring, shifting into first, gunning it. Sweat poured down her face, blinded her. She forced herself to slow to the speed limit.

What if Belinda was alive?

She stopped at a 7-Eleven and called an ambulance, hanging up as soon as she gave the address and told them it was a shooting. Back in her car, she took off. It wasn't until she was home that she paused, leaning against the seat, her heart pounding crazily, clenching the steering wheel so tightly that her hands were white. She was gasping for air like a fish out of water. Oh, please, don't let her die, she prayed, and it became a litany that she said over and over.

She knew that they were coming at any second for her. They wouldn't care that it was an accident. She would say she didn't think the gun was loaded. The gun. She had to do something about the gun.

But what?

She knew from TV that cops could trace a bullet to a gun. Carefully she wiped off all her fingerprints. How would they ever find the gun? If it was back where it belonged in Vince's nightstand drawer, as if it had never left? It was so

tempting to throw the gun away—into the ocean maybe—
but Vince would want to know what had happened. No, she
had to leave it where it always was, replacing the used bullet,
and sit tight.

Mary was torn. She didn't want Belinda to die. But if
she lived, she would tell the police what had happened—and
then what? Mary would go to jail. Prison. She knew it. She
had seen movies; she knew how horrible prisons were.
Maybe Belinda would die. Maybe she already had.

She turned on the news. Listened to the radio. There
was no report of a shooting, much less a killing. Vince came
home, looking harassed, in a bad mood, but Mary couldn't
face him. She wished he loved her, that she could confide in
him; but if he loved her, none of this would ever have happened. It was his fault.

He wanted to know what they were having for dinner.

"Fuck off," Mary said.

He cursed her back and jumped into his truck and took
off.

Mary started to cry. She was supposed to be acting
normal. Then she heard a car in the drive. Vince returning—
or the cops? She couldn't stand it, the waiting, she just
couldn't. There was a knock. With a moan, she went and
answered it. It was Beth.

Mary collapsed in her arms, sobbing hysterically.

70

"Laguna PD."

Belinda looked up at the plainclothes officer from where
she was sitting in a hospital wheelchair. "It was an accident," she said wearily. She had already told that to a cop in
uniform last night—but her memory was hazy.

"I'm afraid I have to make out a complete report," the detective said. "My name's Hewitt. Now, exactly what happened?"

"Five minutes," Dr. Gould said protectively. "That's it."

She had nothing to hide. "I'm having an affair with a man named Vince Spazzio. He's married. Yesterday I opened the door, and his wife was there—with a gun. She was obviously doped out. She called me names. I never thought she would shoot, and I was angry. I'm a very private person—I hate being intruded upon." Belinda was angry just thinking about it. "I tried to grab the gun. I guess that was stupid. But I'm very strong, so I knew I could get it away. Well—I did. After it went off."

"That was stupid," Hewitt said. "But we can bring all kinds of charges. First and not least, assault with intent to do bodily harm, assault with a deadly weapon, leaving the scene—"

"It was an accident," Belinda said. "An accident. She's a pathetic wreck. I'm not pressing charges." And I'm not seeing Vince anymore, she thought. She didn't need this. Oh no. A biweekly bang was not worth this.

Both Gould and Hewitt gaped. A nurse informed them that Belinda's cab was there.

"I'm sure you'll change your mind," Hewitt said. "Anyway, it's not up to you. The DA will decide whether to prosecute or not. I still have to file my report. Spazzio?"

"Yes," Belinda said weakly.

Dr. Gould wheeled her to the doors of the entrance, hospital policy, he told her. Belinda was very flattered and very grateful that he personally was escorting her out. He slipped his arm around her waist, and she stood. God, she was tired, and her entire body hurt. How was that possible from a simple gunshot wound in the shoulder?

He helped her down the wide outdoor steps and into the waiting cab. "Plenty of rest," he admonished gently. "And I want to see you exactly one week from today."

"Aye, aye, Cap," she managed. She sank back gratefully in the cab, completely exhausted.

Her arm was in a sling, but it wasn't her arm that had been shot. The wound was close to and just under her collarbone. The bullet had gone right through. After having been in the hospital over twenty-four hours, she had insisted on going home. She hated hospitals. They terrified her.

Gould had wanted her to call a relative or friend, both to pick her up and to spend a few days with her. There was no one she could call. She had already realized how alone in the world she was—yesterday, when she was being wheeled out of Emergency, regaining consciousness on her way to a hospital room. Completely, utterly alone. Who was there in her life who cared? Who would be there for her now when she was hurt, wounded physically, shot by some maniac, and all alone in a hospital?

It was the medication, she hoped, that was making her feel sorry for herself.

And of course, not for the first time, she thought of Jack Ford.

What would he do if he knew she'd been shot, and that she was alone now and hurting?

She was appalled at herself. At her obvious need to have him come running to her. As if that would ever happen. He didn't know she was hurt, and even if he did, she knew he wouldn't care, not one bit.

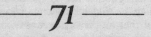

71

She hadn't returned his call.

And she had been discharged from the hospital.

Abe was furious. To think that if some ass-kissing nurse that he just happened to have balled hadn't made the connection between his daughter and him and hadn't been working that day at the hospital—he wouldn't have even known Belinda had been shot.

It didn't matter that her doctor had told him she was fine, just weak and exhausted; nor did it matter that Lieutenant Hewitt had told him the same thing. Abe let the phone ring, and when the answering machine came on he started to shout. He knew she was there. And dammit, he wanted to know what the fuck had happened.

"Don't yell, I'm here," Belinda said, her voice sounding very doped up.

"What the hell happened?" Abe practically shouted. "Are you all right?"

"Abe, I take it you found out I was shot. It's nothing. In case you care, I'm all right. I was sleeping."

"Gould said he asked you to stay in the hospital for a few more days. Christ! For once could you listen to somebody other than yourself?"

"What difference does it make?" she said wearily.

"You're all alone out there, that's what. Anyway, your mother's on her way, and we're sending over a nurse. *Now, what happened?*"

"I don't want a nurse here," Belinda said firmly. "And there's no need for Nancy to come."

"She's coming. For this once, just this once, do me a fucking favor," Abe snapped. "Now what the fuck happened?"

"It was an accident," Belinda said. "The wife of my lover came over high as a kite, and she had a gun. I'm sure she didn't mean to use it. I tried to grab it, and it went off."

"That was fucking stupid," Abe said. "The no-good cunt. For assault with a deadly weapon she can get ten years, and I'll see that she does! That little bitch!"

There was a pause. "Abe, drop it. She needs drug rehabilitation, not imprisonment. Besides, I'm not pressing charges."

"*What?*"

"You heard. I feel sorry for her, I guess. The gun shouldn't have been loaded—no, she shouldn't have even brought a gun—but after all, I have been screwing her husband for the past six months. I asked the police to just drop the whole thing. I think she's more upset and traumatized than I am. She was hysterical when I got shot."

"You can be damn smart sometimes, but sometimes I wonder where you left your brains. You can't let that little bitch fuck with you, Belinda, do you hear me? She's crazy! You think she's learned her lesson? How the fuck do you know? What happens when she decides to try again? Huh?"

"She won't," Belinda said shortly. "Believe me. Look, I'm not up to this, not at all. Good-bye, Abe."

"Don't you dare hang up on me," Abe said.

"I need my sleep—so I can get better and get back to work."

"Forget it," Abe said. "Didn't you get notified? The *Outrage* production is suspended."

"*What?*"

"Relax."

"What do you mean—suspended? I was told we'd go back into production in February. What are you up to, Abe?"

"Nothing," he said. It was one of the few times in his life he'd felt sorry for something he'd done. Not for canceling the show, but for bringing it up now. "It's just a matter of reassessing the budget," he said smoothly.

"I knew you were up to something . . . you are up to something!"

"Look, Belinda, you get some sleep and don't worry about a thing. I'll take care of that little cunt."

The phone went dead.

"Damn!" He slammed his own receiver down. He couldn't believe that cunt Mary was so crazy. And for a brief moment he felt regret—because, God, she sure had been a prime piece of tail.

But no one, *no one,* fucks with a Glassman. With what was his. And Belinda might be a rebel, but she was his, dammit, his flesh and blood, his daughter, and one day the mother of his grandson. Fucking with Belinda was like fucking with him. The challenge couldn't be more direct. He grabbed his phone book and dialed Mary's number.

There was no answer.

What the fuck. He should take care of this in person anyway.

—————— *72* ——————

*H*is phone rang and it was, unbelievably, Majoriis's secretary. "Please hold," she told him.

Jack started to sweat. Then Ted was on, with a falsely jovial hello.

"Hello, Ted," Jack managed in as calm a tone as he could. "You can't deny something's going on. Last week you were personally taking my calls—and now I have to wait two days to get through to you?"

"Jack, sweetheart, relax. *Relax!* I've had some major problems with a film on location in Brazil. *Major!* The two leads were having a hot and heavy affair—offscreen—which made for some fucking fantastic dailies. Now we want to shoot the major scene, and they act like they're worst enemies, not—"

"Ted."

"I mean, half the crew has food poisoning and I may have to fly down there and take Rob Dere by the balls and start squeezing. As for Barbara Sa—"

"Ted, I don't give a shit about some fucking film in Brazil. I had to find out about *Berenger* from a goddamn reporter, for chrissake! You think my own damn studio could call me and tell me what's going on?" He was trying not to shout.

"Jack, baby, everything's under control. Everything's looking great. You have nothing—*nothing*—to worry about, I promise you."

"Then *Berenger* is being released?"

"Uh, at a future date, most probably."

"What is this shit?" Jack gave in and yelled. "And what about *Outrage*?" Then, to make matters worse, he heard a buzz on Majoriis's intercom, his secretary telling him George Masters was there.

"Jack, gotta super important meeting. I'll get back to you. Don't wor—"

"No, Ted," Jack said. "I've been trying to reach you for two days, not counting the times I tried to reach you over the holidays—a feat only a wizard could have managed. Meet me for a drink, lunch, breakfast. *We need to talk!*"

"Christ!" Majoriis said. "Okay, tomorrow, Polo Lounge, at one." He hung up.

"Thank you," Jack said to the empty line before slamming down the phone. He was standing, and he paced angrily around his office. No way Price could have ruined that film. No way he could not have made it into a beautiful thing. Not with a super script, great cast, good crew, and Price himself.

Majoriis had better not stand him up tomorrow.

One thing about this town: When you're hot, you're hot. It's ass-kissing all the way. And when it stops, you most definitely know your ass is no longer being kissed. There was no doubt. January in L.A. was cool, but this was an arctic chill. He was being avoided like a leper, treated like a loser— not like a multi-million-dollar hot property. Motherfucker.

Glassman.

Always back to him.

He was North-Star now. If he wanted *Berenger* released in one month, it would be done. He had enough power to make it happen. And the same was true for the resumption of *Outrage*'s production. And if he didn't want it released . . .

Would the man really take a loss of eight million dollars just because of him?

After all these years?

And there was still the biggest question of them all— why? Why?

Jack's heart said yes—Glassman was after him. His

head said no—be cool, this isn't happening; it isn't how it feels.

He thought of *her*.

And became even more angry.

He should be laughing. It was so ironic that of all the women in the world, of all the prime tail, he would fuck *her*.

Fuck her like there was no tomorrow, he thought, and automatically he was remembering every detail. To his increasing anger and dismay, he grew uncontrollably hard. He slammed his fist into the desk, and the pain was welcome.

He was no longer interested.

She wasn't even his type.

Did she have any idea how many millions of women would die to sleep with him?

Not hundreds.

Millions.

It was still unbelievable that she had walked out on him —not once, not twice, but three times, if you included the shoot in Tucson.

Belinda Glassman.

Like father, like daughter.

He was a bastard, she was a bitch.

Used to getting her own way. She really thought she was better than him. He burned—in more ways than one.

——— *73* ———

*T*he silence had lasted one second.

"So when's our date?" Lansing said, grinning and leaning against her desk.

Melody flushed. She had forgotten, what with the trauma of having slept with Jack and expecting to do so again—but instead having to listen to him make love to someone else in Aspen. Then having to pretend to be indifferent while she was alone with him.

"Don't tell me you changed your mind?" Lansing said quickly. "You promised."

She looked at him, smiling slightly. He was appealing in a naughty-boy way, and she had said yes. "Well . . ."

"Pick you up at seven," he said with a dazzling smile.

"Tonight's impossible," she said quickly.

"Seeing the boss?"

She started. "What?"

"The boss. You know, the guy who pays you every week."

"No, I'm not," she said coldly. She was seeing Nickie Felton. Actually, she almost wished she were seeing Peter instead.

"You don't have to play games with me," Lansing said airily. "I don't bruise easily. I'm not the jealous type. I can handle it." But his stare was direct and sharp and penetrating.

"Peter, I have no idea what you're talking about. How did you ever get Leah to come?" She changed the topic with relief.

The long, judgmental stare remained in full force for another moment, then was gone, disappearing into a twinkle of gold-flecked moss-green. "The color of money. And the smell. Nothing like the good old greenback." He sprawled on the sofa, facing her at an angle. He grinned disarmingly. "How about tomorrow?"

Melody thought about that creature who was Jack's sister and how much he hated her being here. She felt a kind of spiteful elation—a far cry from how she would have felt in the past, when she was so ready to run to him with compassion and consolation. "Poor Jack," she said and found that she was smiling ever so slightly. Imagining his discomfort. He deserved it! He had everything too easy—the bastard.

"Oh, shit," Lansing said, frowning. "So much for fucking jealousy."

"What?"

She watched him stride toward the door, looking thoroughly disgusted. Had she done something? Said something?

Jack and Leah walked in. Jack looked as disgusted as Lansing. "Mel, Leah needs money."

"Gotta buy some groceries," Leah intoned.

"What am I, a bank?" Melody snapped.

Leah swaggered over to Lansing and firmly took his arm, pressing herself against him, ankle to shoulder. "You're a fast worker, Pete," she said sweetly. "When do I get to see you again?" Her look was blatantly sexual.

"You don't." Lansing smiled, looking at her face. "I'm afraid my job is done."

Her hand slipped to his waist, stroking. "Take me to dinner tomorrow, Pete. I can promise you, you'll enjoy dessert."

"Why don't you put some of that, er, energy into your family?" He moved away.

"Jesus," Jack said harshly, frowning. "Will you try and act like you're not a hooker, for God's sake?"

"Shove it where the sun don't shine, big brother," Leah said lightly. She stepped closer to Melody. "Have fun, dearie. He *is* good, isn't he?"

Melody was scandalized. *Had they?* She should have known. They were all the same. She turned to stare at Peter incredulously. But he was already gone.

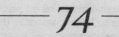

74

She had stood him up.

Vince slammed his hands on the steering wheel and stared at his house. She wasn't even returning his calls. Maybe he should go over there again and wait until she got home. Or maybe she was home. Maybe this was it. Maybe she didn't want to see him anymore.

Last night he had gone over and waited and waited—the wonderful anticipation slowly fading, becoming replaced with frustration, hurt, and anger. Until he had known he was being stood up. Known it and hated her. Almost.

He was losing her. He was sure of it. He hardly saw her anymore, and the other night, after she'd gotten back from Aspen, it had taken a long, long time to bring her to a climax—one single one. And then Belinda hadn't wanted to make love again. She had asked, then insisted, that he leave. Saying she was tired from her ski trip.

Vince got out of his truck. Damned if he'd crawl anymore. Let her call—let her apologize.

But as he walked up the stone path to his house, he was so damn tempted to turn around, jump into his Ford, and drive over. He could be there in thirty minutes. Thirty-five minutes from now, after she had apologized, he could be making love to her.

Mary was sitting on the floor surrounded by newspapers, looking ghastly. "What's with you?" he asked out of curiosity, not interest.

She looked at him as if she were about to cry.

"You on the rag, or what?"

"Fuck off, Vince," she said, starting to weep.

He shook his head and stalked into the kitchen. She looked like shit—he could barely stand the sight of her—and she had a mouth to match. Too bad she wouldn't move out on him, maybe in with her lover, so he wouldn't have to leave. Because once he told her about his plans for a divorce, one of them was going to have to relocate. But he wasn't in the mood now—he was too aggravated about Belinda. He'd tell Mary tomorrow about the divorce.

Then he felt her as she threw her arms around him from behind. "Vince, I'm sorry." She was sobbing. "Oh, please don't be mad."

He disengaged himself and looked at her. "Are you high? Drunk? What is it with you?"

She wiped her eyes. "My whole life is falling apart," she moaned.

He quickly decided he wasn't in the mood. "I take it you're not cooking tonight—again?"

"How can you think about food?" she wailed.

"Shit," Vince said. "I'm ordering a pizza."

Mary walked away, slumped, and Vince felt a twinge of remorse. He wasn't being very nice to her. But, God, couldn't she at least cook him dinner every *other* night? Was that too much to ask?

Belinda would never cook for him.

Oh, she had, two or three times, when they were first seeing each other; but back then the meals had gone cold because they couldn't keep their hands off each other.

Where the hell had she been last night?

Better yet, with who?

He couldn't think about it. If he did, he would go crazy.

There was a sharp knocking on the door. Vince wondered who could possibly be dropping by. As he passed Mary he wondered if she were really ill. She was so white. He opened the door to see two uniformed police officers and a man in jeans. The man in jeans was holding up a police badge. "Police," he said. "You Vince Spazzio?"

"Yeah," Vince said, thoroughly puzzled. "What's this about?"

The detective was looking past him, at Mary. "That your wife?"

"Yeah."

"Do you realize, Mrs. Spazzio, that leaving the scene of a crime is a felony?"

"It was an accident," Mary whimpered.

"What!" Vince exclaimed.

"I'm afraid you're under arrest," the cop said to Mary.

"Arrest?" Vince was stunned. "For what?"

"Leaving the scene, for one. Suspicion of intent to do bodily harm, for two. Possible assault with a deadly weapon. She got a license to carry a gun?"

"Mary?"

"I didn't mean to, Vince." Mary was weeping. "I didn't."

"Lady, anything you say can and will be held against you," Hewitt said. "Come on, I'll read your Miranda rights as we go." He looked at Vince. "Maybe you should call the family lawyer."

"I don't understand," Vince said. "What the fuck happened?"

"Your wife shot Belinda Glassman yesterday afternoon."

*B*elinda tried to wake up. The hands were welcome, reassuring. Soothing, stroking, calloused, a man's hands. She tried to remember where she was. Ah, yes, Aspen. She snuggled closer. Jack. Jack was here; she was still with him; he was saying her name, a hoarse caress of sound.

Something was wrong with the scenario, she knew it. Then she realized and was jubilant. She wasn't in Aspen. That was days ago. She was home. She had been shot. But Jack had come. He *cared*.

She turned her face into his hand. So real. He was really here.

"Sweetheart?"

She sighed. Tried to speak. She was so tired, she couldn't move, not a muscle, not even her tongue. Jack, she thought.

"Sweetheart? It's okay, I'm here."

The lost shrouds of sleep left. Belinda nuzzled the large warm hand that cupped her face.

"I love you. God, I love you."

Her eyes flew open and a vast disappointment careened

over her, like a wave breaking on the sand. Vince. It had just been a dream, just a damn dream. So real, but already the exquisite sensations, the unbearable happiness was fading to nothing but a figment of her unconscious, nothing but a fantasy.

"I didn't mean to wake you," Vince said.

"What are you doing here? How did you get in?"

"The door wasn't locked. I just found out. God, Belinda, I'm so sorry!"

Belinda was too tired, too sore, and too groggy to be angry. She closed her eyes. She felt the bed dip, then felt Vince stretch out cautiously near her, on her good side. This was wrong. It was over. But . . . there was no one else who cared, and she was so alone, hurting and alone . . . Vince cared. "Oh, Vince," she said, but it came out terribly choked. It was the pain-killers, she knew, making her overly emotional, making her self-pitying.

"Shhh, I'm here." He soothed her. "And I'm staying here until you get well."

"Hold me," she murmured, and he did, awkwardly. The heat of his body felt so good, so reassuring, and his hands were so comforting. She fell asleep.

Her dreams were a weird collage—her father, grinning; her mother, accusing; Vince; Mary; the gun. A crying baby. Belligerence became fear. The gun exploded. Fear became pain. Mary was screaming and screaming. Her mother was weeping. Abe was shouting. Abe became Vince. Comforting, solid. And the baby was still there, still crying. Was it hers? Then Vince started to drift away, just when she needed him so badly, and she begged and pleaded for him to stay. Or was it Abe? Then his face changed, became Jack's, twisted with anger. "You're a cold bitch," he said ruthlessly, unmoved by her wound.

A cold bitch.

But I'm not! She was crying. I'm not, really, I'm not!

He was leaving, slamming the door. It was only a dream and she knew it. She willed him back. But it was useless. He wouldn't return.

*"E*veryone knows, Melody."

"So tell me," she said, leaning forward.

They were at Spago. They had just finished smoked-salmon pizza and Chablis—something Melody had thought sounded horrible but was actually phenomenal. Nickie Felton had removed his glasses, the better to come on, she supposed, but now he replaced them.

"Abe Glassman has a hate thing for your boss. And I don't know the particulars. *Berenger* was great. I saw the answer print—so did a lot of people. But Glassman—lunatic that he is—canceled release, and that is the end of that. *Finito.*"

So there was a basis for Jack's paranoia, she thought. "Will it ever be released?"

"Who knows? I will tell you one thing though." He paused dramatically.

Melody waited.

"Price was fucking pissed. I mean *pissed!* Livid. Ready to kill. You know how that bastard is. Hell, I don't blame him."

"So what happened?"

"I have no idea how he was calmed down. Needless to say, Price is about to go on location for a Paramount film." Felton shrugged. "Price was offered our biggest-budget flick for eighty-nine and turned it down. So he may have stopped mouthing off, but I know he's not happy."

Melody leaned back in her seat and thought. *Berenger* was never going to be released—she was sure of it—and Jack didn't know it. It was only a minor setback, really—he had two more films to make. "What about *Outrage*? And exactly what are the budgetary problems?"

Nickie gave her a funny look. "There are none."

"What?"

"Haven't you heard?"

"Heard what?" Melody asked, her heart thudding in excitement.

"The real scoop is that *Outrage* is finished. It's not ever going back into production."

Oh, my God.

"If there's any way—and this is strictly between you and me—that Jack can break his contract and survive, advise him to do it and do it now."

Melody nodded.

"Now," Nickie said, "let's get out of here."

Nickie drove a red Mercedes convertible, the top down, which Melody didn't mind, because her hair was so unruly anyway. She was too absorbed in her thoughts—a tiny idea forming—to pay attention to what Nickie was saying as they sped toward her apartment, which was almost in Westwood. But when his hand drifted along her thigh she jerked back to reality. He grinned at her. Squeezing her flesh.

She removed his hand. "No, Nickie."

"Ah, come on," he said. "A tit for a tat."

He rubbed her thigh again, coming dangerously close to her crotch, and again she removed his hand. He insisted on walking her up to her apartment. Melody knew he expected her to sleep with him for the information he had given. He did deserve something—those were the rules. There was just no way she was going to let him stick it to her. No way.

"Come on, Melody, invite me in for a drink."

"Nickie, it's late."

He persisted; she let him in. They sat on her couch sipping amaretto. Nickie grabbed her. Kissing her, or trying to, and fondling her breasts. She had decided she would give him a couple of feels, make him happy, then send him away. He grabbed her hand and placed it on a throbbing erection. He groaned and grabbed her crotch.

"No," she said firmly, removing his hand.

He groaned again, pressing her hand against him. "You don't put out, do you, Melody?"

"No, I don't."

"Just touch it, okay? I want to come—I'm so hard I'm going to die."

Melody made a flash decision—better her touching him, than him her. She stroked his rather short length softly. He fumbled with his zipper. Melody could not believe she was doing this. He pulled it out of his green bikini. Short and red. And very eager. His head fell back, mouth open, his hand clasped hers, forcing her to grip him, showing her a rhythm.

Melody became quite fascinated, having never had the opportunity to witness how a penis swells and swells. A few minutes later he grunted and came. After he had cleaned himself up he left as if nothing had happened, cheerfully, kissing her good night on her cheek. Melody closed the door behind him and leaned against it.

It had most definitely been worth it.

Now what to do with what she knew?

*V*ince was not home.

Mary had to take a cab home.

She was furious.

Just where the fuck was he when she needed him? She had just spent the entire night in jail, for Christ's sake. *In jail.* She had been allowed one phone call. And Vince hadn't been home.

They had finally told her she was free to go. She didn't understand it, not any of it. All she knew was last night had been the worst night in her life, spent in some small, cold cell —alone, thank God. That was after the questions—the same questions, asked different ways, over and over, until Mary had wept. She told them the truth fifteen times before they took her to the cell.

It had been past midnight when she had capitulated, and now it was almost noon. Mary had never been so happy to see anyone when the police officer had opened her cell and told her she was being released. Dear, dear God. It was almost over.

They walked down the endless, spotless corridor, past sleeping inmates, past a barred door, around a corner, then past another barred door. They stepped into a room bright with yellow lights, filled with desks, detectives, and uniformed officers—and her mother.

Just what Mary needed.

Celia Holmes Bradbury Davis, born Edna Grock, saw her at that precise moment and stood without moving a single poised muscle. Poised in a white silk suit, nails red, lips red, eyes lined with charcoal-black liner but devoid of shadow, hair perfectly curled under in a classic and elegant page, skin tanned neatly to a nut-brown, five-carat diamonds winking from her ears, an eight-carat radiant winking from one finger—she was the picture of haute couture elegance. The diamonds were courtesy of her second husband, David Bradbury, the son of a self-made millionaire who had tripled his father's own fortune—fortunately before the divorce. It had left Celia free to pursue her pleasure without financial cares.

"Mary."

Mary was ready to cry, except that she had bawled for half the night already and was completely dried up—and hung over. Her head ached. Her heart was going like a jack-hammer. Her mouth tasted like shit and was dry as a desert. Her body hurt. Her eyes were puffy. Her hair was dirty. Or it felt dirty. She felt dirty. She hated herself, and she hated her mother. So she ignored her.

The officer led her to a desk sergeant who released her personal possessions back to her. As she was dutifully inspecting her purse to make sure nothing was missing, a man introduced himself as Rob Cohen, her lawyer.

Mary turned and swallowed and looked at him.

"Everything's taken care of, Mary. The DA's dropping charges. You're free." He smiled.

Her mother did not.

Her mother marched by her side in silence out of the police station. Once free of those confines, Celia Holmes Bradbury Davis stopped abruptly, and as if she were attached to her mother, Mary stopped too.

"What is wrong with you?" Celia asked.

"Mom."

"How could you? Mary, what is wrong with you? God, this is all your father's fault! Where is he when his daughter needs him? He never, ever put two cents into your upbringing, and look what happened. What are my friends going to think?"

"I really don't care," Mary said, near tears.

"That is obvious!"

"Mom—"

"Look at you! You look awful. You look like some poor little tramp, Mary. Where is Vince?"

"I don't know," Mary said.

"I don't know if I can deal with this, I truly don't."

"Can you give me a ride?"

"After my driver drops me at the gym. Mary—here." Her mother handed her a slip of paper.

Mary looked at a name and phone number. "What's this?"

"Paul Socarro is one of the best psychologists in L.A. Call him. Today."

She looked at her mother. "You know what?" she said, quivering. "I hate you."

"Mary, don't act twelve. Call Paul."

Mary tore up the paper, furious, her headache growing worse.

"That's it!" Celia said. "I'm calling your father. This is his responsibility. He's off in goddamn Ceylon or Shanghai or God knows where—"

"Borneo."

"What?"

"He's in Borneo."

"Well, wherever. I expect him to take care of this mess."

Mary watched her mother stride effortlessly, gracefully toward the waiting Jaguar with the driver standing beside the front fender. It was illegally parked in a tow-away zone right in front of the police station. Her mother slid in.

Having no choice, Mary followed.

Now she was home. No sign of Vince. When the phone rang she pounced on it, thinking it was him. It was her mother.

"Now what?" Mary asked, ready to cry.

"Mary, how about my sending you to the Golden Door —or any other spa—for a few weeks, a month?"

Mary laughed. Leave, now? When her prick of a husband was in love with someone else? "Am I allowed to leave the country, Ma?"

"This isn't the movies, for God's sake, and you're free to do as you please. And don't call me *Ma*. Well?"

"Forget it," she said sullenly.

"Mary, I am not stupid. I know about the other woman. If you look the way you do, how can you expect your marriage to last? You must have gained ten pounds since last year, and we both know you weren't exactly trim then."

"At least *I'm* not anorexic."

"Don't be silly. My body's perfect—everyone says so. There's a wonderful spa in Arizona, Canyon Ranch. I hear they work wonders with everyone. Besides, you should get away until all the gossip dies down."

Mary hated her mother. Her perfect, thin, rich mother. Her mother who thought that everything that went wrong in the world was connected to your weight, your body. Her weight had nothing to do with Vince's straying.

Or did it?

Was she as fat as her mother said?

Unbearable to look at?

Had she gained weight recently?

God knows, she hadn't gotten on the scale in weeks— she didn't dare.

As soon as she hung up she did a line. Fuck her mother, and fuck Vince too.

Where was he?

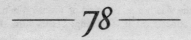

78

Charles Hamilton was a big star. Known to his friends as Chuck, he was six feet two, close to sixty, and still exuded a virile magnetism. He walked into the Beverly Hills Hotel along with Jack, the two of them stopping traffic as they did so. The hotel staff was nonchalantly casual about their presence, but tourists literally panted; and as the two men maneuvered toward the Polo Lounge, a wake of human bodies formed behind them.

Jack and Hamilton knew each other, of course. They had been at a few, a very few, of the same parties in the past three years since Jack had become a star. They didn't know each other well and didn't care to; but upon finding themselves entering the hotel together, they had exchanged the requisite pleasantries. Hamilton had not brought up the cancellation of *Berenger*'s release, which showed Jack that his acquaintance had more class than most of Hollywood's population, and Jack was grateful. He looked around for Majoriis but didn't see him anywhere.

Then he saw Leah and stopped short.

She lounged against a pillar in a skintight black leather minidress and four-inch spikes. The dress was strapless and exposed vast cleavage. Jack wanted to kill. No, she didn't quite look as garish and obvious as she had yesterday when Lansing had brought her into his office, but there was no mistaking her body language. Damned if she wasn't soliciting in the Beverly Hills Hotel!

What was she, crazy?

Leah saw him and smiled lazily. "I'll kill her," Jack muttered beneath his breath, hoping she looked like an over-eager and overabundant starlet, but not really thinking so.

"Who's that?" Hamilton said, following his glance. Leah was appraising Hamilton with recognition and female approbation.

"Excuse me," Jack said. "Nice seeing you again." He didn't wait for a response. He strode over to Leah, refraining from grabbing her and shaking some sense into her. "Just what the hell are you doing?" He forced himself to keep his voice down.

"Brother, dear, you do look *mah-velous,*" Leah trilled, kissing his cheek.

"I can't believe you," he managed.

Her eyes widened. "I'm playing tourist, Jack! Aren't I allowed to do that?"

"I know damn well what you're doing," Jack growled, wanting to strangle her. He knew he had made a dreadful mistake. "Didn't I give you enough money?"

"I intend to invest that," Leah said easily. She took his arm. "Do introduce me to Charles Hamilton. What a fox!"

He tried to shake her off. "You have got to be kid—"

"No, please introduce us, Jack," Hamilton said, having come up from behind.

Jack looked at him and was horrified at the come-on smile. Hamilton's eyes caressed Leah with lazy but tangible let's-fuck interest.

"I'm Jack's sister," Leah said, extending her hand. "And I most certainly know who you are!"

"What a treasure," Hamilton breathed, still holding her hand. "The resemblance is incredible. I think you're actually better-looking than your brother."

Leah tossed her frizzed mane and laughed.

"Leah is visiting from New York," Jack said quickly, wishing that they weren't looking at each other the way they were.

"How long are you in town for?" Hamilton asked.

"Indefinitely. Right, Jack?"

Jack managed a smile.

"Are you an actress, Leah?"

"She's interested in getting into the business," Jack said quickly. "We haven't gotten her a screen test yet. She only got into town yesterday."

Leah smiled, amused.

"She's gorgeous. It's obvious she'll fly past a test. Where have you studied?"

"She hasn't," Jack said quickly. "She's been living in New York."

"What a waste," Hamilton said.

"Yes. Jack agrees." Leah smiled. "He hired a private eye to find me once he knew I existed and now he wants to launch me in a new career. So noble and caring, isn't he?"

"How about dinner? I should be finished in a couple of hours. I'll pick you up at seven."

Jack opened his mouth too late. Leah was already saying, "I'd love it! I'm staying with Jack."

"Great," Hamilton murmured, mesmerized.

Great, Jack echoed silently, just fucking great.

Then he heard the page. His name. And he realized he had known this would happen all along. He didn't have to go to the phone—although he did go—to find out from a secretary that something had come up, a "crucial meeting," and Majoriis wasn't going to show. He had known it deep down all along. He had become what every actor dreads—a Hollywood leper.

From hot to dead.

79

Afterward, he knew he would have been more alert if it hadn't been for Lydia.

She appeared beside him as he was trotting down the

steps after school. "Hey, what would Cheetah be if Tarzan and Jane were Jewish?"

Just the way she said it made him smile. "I don't know. What?"

"A fur coat."

Rick couldn't help it—he laughed.

"Want to go to a movie?" Lydia asked in the next breath.

Rick was so stunned he stopped short. Was she interested in him? The thought was astounding. She wasn't his type—even if she was sort of cute in a very different way. And she was funny. "Yeah, sure," he answered before even thinking about it. He was flattered. No girl had ever asked him out before.

That's when it had happened.

"Rick! Look out!" Lydia screamed.

From behind a tree, four guys leapt out at him, and Rick got a glimpse of Froth and Dale. Two huge football defensive ends grabbed him before he could run. Froth laughed. "Well, well, if it isn't the little twerp from the bad side of town. Hey, brat. Did you really think you could get away with it?"

"What?" Rick said innocently.

"Let him go!" Lydia shouted, kicking one of the football players. He growled.

"This is so you'll know not to mess with us," Froth said. He looked furious, and Rick tensed for the blow. It hurt, right in the stomach, but at least he had been prepared. "Little cocksucker," Froth said, and the next blow cracked a rib.

Lydia jumped on Froth's back like an enraged cat, sinking her teeth into his shoulder. Froth screamed. "Get her off!"

Rick twisted, managing to loosen the hold of one of the football players in his surprise and interest at Lydia on Froth's back, now clawing at his face. Dale was trying hesitantly to remove her, and Froth was cursing and shouting like a crazy man. Rick freed himself enough to twist aside and jam his knee into one unsuspecting groin. With a howl, the boy dropped, clutching himself. Rick sunk his own teeth into the forearm of the other boy, who responded with slow, oxlike reflexes, grunting, releasing him, trying to pull away. Rick kicked his shin and pulled free.

Dale had managed to drag Lydia off. He had his arms around her rib cage in a viselike grip. She twisted futilely, furious. Dale was panting but laughing. "Look what I got!" he shouted. With one hand he squeezed one of her tits. Lydia shrieked in rage.

He slid his hand down and grabbed her crotch.

Froth started laughing. "This your girlfriend, punk?" He grinned, looking at Lydia with interest. He glanced at Rick, who was momentarily frozen. Then he reached out and grabbed Lydia away from Dale, jerking her against him.

Red.

It was the color Rick saw.

After that he didn't remember what he did. He flew at Froth, and in a moment Froth was lying moaning on the ground, clutching his nose, blood pouring around his hand. Dale ran. The football player he had kicked in the groin was still on the ground, whimpering and clutching himself. The ox stood watching, rubbing his shin and his bitten forearm. "Shit," he said succinctly, and he walked away.

"You okay?" Rick asked worriedly, pulling Lydia away by the hand.

She wasn't even crying, and it amazed him. She looked at him with shining eyes. "Thank you," she said, smiling.

Her look, not her words, made him puff out with pride. He felt a hundred feet tall.

80

*I*t was nine A.M. Where was she?

Of course Jack knew where she was—she was at Hamilton's Beverly Hills mansion. He was sick with worry. Leah was so obvious—couldn't Hamilton peg her for what she was? If he'd had any wits yesterday when Hamilton had asked her to dinner, he would have thought of something, anything, to make sure that date didn't come about. He wouldn't be there to block the punches for her, to say the right things. They hadn't even gotten her story straight. Leah was bound to blow it. He was sure. One-hundred-percent positive.

The whole thing made him sick. She was the spitting image of Janet, as far as he could see. He knew he'd made an awful mistake bringing her here. Maybe he should just give her more money and send her packing. It was the brightest thought he'd had that day.

But she was his sister. Didn't he owe her something?

He knew his worries and fears were selfish. He'd had bad PR in the past and had survived. Most of it had been so phony it was laughable, all that trade-rag stuff, and *part* of the truth he had openly confessed—parts of his past, his addictions. He had survived it all. If anything, the pain he'd lived through made him a more endearing hero to the masses.

Why was this different?

Why did his stomach turn over every time he thought of Leah?

He knew why.

It was like being confronted with Janet. It was like going back into the past. Even Leah looked at him with contempt as if she were superior, the way Janet had when he'd been a boy. Leah reminded him of his abandonment. Of the love his damn mother had never given.

But there was more. If the press got hold of Leah, alive and breathing and in the flesh, it would be different from the phony bullshit the rags had glorified in the past. This was real, and he was vulnerable right now. Bad PR could kill him. If he wasn't already dead.

Maybe he should get her her own apartment.

How long was she going to stay in L.A.?

He reached for his phone. Majoriis was not going to call him back—he knew it as sure as he knew he would take another breath after this one. It was very hard to believe he was being treated like this, when it hadn't been so long ago that he had been fawned over, his every wish—no, his every whim—granted by the studio. Pricks.

"Mr. Majoriis is in a meeting, Mr. Ford," the secretary told him coolly.

"Listen, sweetheart," he purred. "This is crucial, a matter of life and death. I have to speak to Ted."

"I'm sorry, he absolutely cannot—oh, hello, Mr. Glassman, yes, please go right in. Good-bye, Mr. Ford." *Click.*

Jack stared at the phone. Glassman. It was too ironic. Too goddamn ironic.

Leah breezed in, still wearing her leather barely-there dress and spikes from the night before. "Hi, Bro."

She swept right past him into her bedroom, and Jack followed her. "Leah."

"Can't it wait? I'm beat."

"No, it can't." He watched her as she stepped out of the heels and flung her purse on the bed. "What happened?"

"My, we are lascivious!" She grinned. Unzipping the front of her dress.

At the sight of her bare bosom, Jack averted his face. "For crissake, I'm trying to talk to you!"

"And I need a bath," she said, stepping out of the dress.

Furious, Jack pulled a robe off a hook and shoved it at her, ignoring her bare body. "What is wrong with you?"

"Too bad we're related," Leah said, slipping on the robe.

"What happened?"

"What do you think? The old goat can still get it up."

"What did you tell him?" He wanted to strangle her.

"Oh, about my past? Don't worry, dear. Our secret's safe. He thinks I've been waiting tables since I was twelve— not giving blow jobs." She walked into the bathroom and ran the tub.

"You didn't take money from him, did you?"

"Of course not! What am I, an idiot?" Her eyes sparkled with good humor. "I actually like the old guy. I wouldn't mind seeing him on a steady basis." She tested the water. "Of course, if he wants to see me, he's going to have to give me something for my time. Don't rich stars clothe their mistresses in furs and diamonds and such, Jack?"

She meant it. She really wanted to know the answer.

"Hamilton is married, you know," Jack said testily.

"Yes, but he likes me." She smiled. "I mean, after last night, he *really* likes me."

Jack was getting a headache. "So you're intending to stay for a while?"

"I can't ever go back to New York," she told him.

He stared. "Why not?"

"Jack," she said, very serious now, "my pimp would find me and kill me."

Jack tried to absorb what she said.

"And he'd take a long time to do it too," she added casually, dipping her toe in the tub. "Umm, perfect. Here, be a dear." And she handed him the robe, sliding into the steaming water.

With immense relief he heard the phone ring. The timing couldn't have been better. It was Melody. "Jack, I've found out something very interesting," she said, a strange, almost gloating tone in her voice.

"What's that?"

"North-Star has no intention of resuming production of *Outrage*. They're dumping it."

He wasn't aware of hanging up. He wasn't aware of anything except the pounding of his heart and the sure knowledge that Glassman would not stop until he had completely destroyed him.

Jack grabbed his phone book, flipped through, very intent. He dialed. Peter Lansing answered on the third ring. "Sorry to bother you," Jack said abruptly. "I need information—immediately. Where does Abe Glassman stay when he's in town?"

It was called the horse's mouth.

And he was going to go straight to it.

81

*I*t was about ten minutes into the movie that Rick became intensely aware of Lydia.

She'd picked him up at seven, arriving in jeans, sneakers, and a baggy T-shirt, not even tucked in. She was brown as a berry, which surprisingly made her big dark eyes seem bigger and darker. He thought she might have lip gloss on her mouth, but he wasn't sure. Her hair was almost to her shoulders but cut like a boy's.

"Hi, Rick," she said with a big smile.

It was funny, but her smile and her good nature brought out an equivalent response in him, and he was smiling too. "Hey, kid."

She frowned. "I'm older than you, boy."

"Yeah, two months."

"Still, that makes me an older woman."

Rick laughed.

"What's going on in here?" Jack asked, stepping out of his bedroom.

Rick immediately tensed. "This is Lydia," he said, no longer smiling, waiting for her to drool all over his brother.

Jack smiled. "Hi."

Lydia said hi politely, then grabbed Rick's arm. "Want to go?"

Rick was stunned. Did she know who Jack was? "Yeah, okay."

"You guys have a good time," Jack said, smiling. "I intend to be home before you, Rick. Can you keep it down when you come in?" He was already at the door.

"Sure," Rick said, still amazed. Lydia had barely looked at Jack. When they were in the elevator, he said, "He's probably going to bring home a girl."

Lydia shrugged. "You look better," she said.

"What?"

"Than when you first came to school. Taller. Not so skinny."

"You look the same," Rick said, then was sorry he'd said it. He hoped she wouldn't be offended.

"We can't all look like Patty Epherton." Lydia was not in the least perturbed.

"You're much nicer than she is," Rick told her, meaning it.

"Anyone's nicer than she is."

Now, in the theater, he was intensely aware of Lydia, and his awareness was resulting in a throbbing hard-on.

Sitting side by side, her shoulder touched his, and when he put his arm on the armrest, his bare skin touched the flesh of her forearm. She leaned closer to whisper something in his ear, and a breast pressed against his arm, becoming crushed. Her hair brushed his cheek. He had no idea what she was saying, but she smelled good, like soap, but lemony maybe, not all perfumed like a whore.

He wanted to kiss her.

It was all he could think about. He stared at the screen and had no idea what was going on, and he didn't know why he couldn't get up the courage to make a move. He had had lots of girls! Yeah, but not like her. They were all paid for, or easy at least. He wasn't sure Lydia had ever been kissed.

Everyone in the theater laughed at the show, except for Rick.

Lydia leaned over and again her soft breast brushed against him, and whispered, "What's wrong? Don't you—"

He kissed her, cutting her off.

She stiffened while he put his left arm around her shoulders, holding her so she wouldn't move away. Then her lips softened.

He had never known kissing was so exciting.

Her mouth opened; she kissed him back. Rick's other arm went around her. Her hands went around his neck, and Rick deepened the pressure, darting his tongue into her mouth. She stiffened again. He withdrew it, kissing her less intimately for a long, long time.

He realized as he was kissing her that he really liked her.

Somehow, he knew she was a virgin.

He knew no one had ever stuck his tongue into her mouth before.

He wanted to touch one of her breasts but was sure she wouldn't go for it.

Instead his mouth played in hers until she pulled away. He was dismayed, until he realized people were getting up and the movie was over. Soon the lights would be going on. Time had flown.

She stared at the credits on the screen, and he could hear her breathing, even though she was trying not to breathe so loudly. Rick felt flooded suddenly with a feeling that was unusual for him. It was warm and caring. She had a beautiful profile. Perfect, really. A sloping forehead, a straight, small nose, full lips . . . which tasted wonderful— he should know, he had just spent an hour kissing them! A pointy chin. He took her hand and held it.

She glanced at him shyly.

"Let's go have something to eat," he said. His voice cracked.

The lights came on. She was looking at him with a shy smile, but her face was flushed—how had he ever not thought she was pretty!—and her eyes were shining. "Sure," she said, her voice a nervous squeak.

They both laughed.

82

*T*he Ferrari took a corner ruthlessly.

Wheels screeching.

Now was not the time to be thinking of Belinda. Jack wanted to shove her not just out of his mind but out of his life. Impossible. The obsession wouldn't quit. Yet she was the enemy—wasn't she?

He should not have to remind himself of how and what she was. The spoiled daughter of his arch enemy—the man he was sure was trying to destroy him—the man he was on his way to see.

He put his arms around her and kissed her.

She felt absolutely nothing.

Belinda let him kiss her for one more beat, out of charity and guilt, then pushed him away. They were standing on her doorstep, outside. She tried a smile and made it. "Thank you, Adam, for a very nice evening."

"Only very nice?" he teased.

"Very, *very* nice."

"You want me to leave?"

Belinda looked at him. He had shown up on her doorstep with flowers and all kinds of sympathy, which in her state of mind had been impossible to resist. Adam was kind. And they were friends. He had been entertaining and thoughtful and the past few hours had flown.

"Adam—my arm," she said. There was no way she could have hidden everything from him. But she had fibbed and told him Mary was a burglar. She wasn't up to revealing the truth.

"We could just sleep together, hold each other."

"Please, I'm not feeling very well."

"I'm sorry. Think about next weekend," he urged. He had invited her to Santa Barbara.

"I promise," she said, and watched him leave. The instant his Mercedes was gone, someone stepped out of the shadows. A man.

Belinda jumped, frightened.

"Who the hell was that?" Vince demanded.

She stared, unable to believe that Vince had been lurking about, waiting for her. "What were you doing?"

"I came by to see how you're doing," he said bitterly. "Expecting you to be in bed—like the doctor ordered. But oh, no! You were screwing around. *Were* you screwing around? How many are there, Belinda? How many guys do you give it to?"

"I don't have to answer that," she said furiously. "I don't owe you anything."

"I love you," Vince raged. "Are you sleeping with him?" He grabbed her.

"Ow! Dammit! That's my sore arm." He released her, and she stepped away from him.

"I'm sorry," Vince said quickly. "Belinda—I'm divorcing Mary."

Belinda took a breath. "That's entirely your decision, Vince."

"Any other woman would be thrilled."

"Vince . . . there's no easy way to say this. It's over between you and me."

"What? Didn't you hear me? I want to marry you!"

She felt terribly sorry for him and equally annoyed that she had to go through this. Not to mention guilty—because this was her fault. "I don't love you," she said softly.

In the dim light she could see his eyes—hurt and anguished, like a betrayed puppy's. "We don't have to get married," he said urgently. "We could keep things the way—"

"No," she said firmly. "I'm sorry, Vince. It's over."

Fuck Jack.

Melody knew she was becoming a different person, but

she was too angry to care. A part of her was appalled at what she was doing; the other part was applauding.

She thought about Peter. Peter had now become important to her. What right did he have to get angry with her? What did he know about pain, heartache, betrayal? She had given the past four years of her life to Jack Ford—a selfish, egotistical, insensitive bastard. What did Peter know—how dare he judge?

He couldn't be angry with her.

Not now, not when she needed him.

She reached for the phone.

"This is Lansing," came the smooth, cocky voice. "I am unavailable now. Please leave all information, and I'll get back to you. *Beeep.*"

Melody exhaled. "Peter, this is Melody. I—I'm sorry. For whatever I did. If you still want, I'm available tomorrow night." Her voice broke and she hung up. Then she smiled broadly. Perfect. God, she should be an actress! He would come around.

He had to.

Because he was part of The Plan.

Lansing was deep inside the sex machine.

Her name was actually Nora. She had already reached oblivion—twice, in fact; and now Lansing felt it was his turn. After all, he had no interest in making this an all-nighter. He was almost there when the phone rang.

With a sixth sense he knew beyond a doubt who it was.

He was thrusting as the message in his machine came on. "This is Lansing . . . unavailable . . . all information . . . get back to you. *Beeep.*"

He was almost there.

Nora was making appropriate noises and motions.

"Peter, this is Melody," Melody said, sounding fragile and vulnerable. He started to deflate. "I—" She choked, her voice breaking. "—I'm sorry. For whatever I did. If you still want, I'm available tomorrow night. *Click.*"

He lost his erection.

Lansing groaned, rolling off Nora.

"Who is that?" Nora asked.

"Fuck," Lansing said.

"I don't think you can, honey," Nora replied.

Lansing stared at the ceiling. She had sounded so upset and fragile and vulnerable. Shit. He had been raised to be a gentleman. He had been pretty rude, even if it was because of jealousy.

He really did owe her an apology.

"Fuck," he said again.

"Well, I'm still game," Nora said, placing her hand on his limp member.

Abe opened the door, smiling. Yes, he had been surprised when the doorman had announced Jack. But he had recovered quickly; he was in control.

And he loved it.

Jack didn't smile back. He stared, willing his face to show no expression but not succeeding in hiding anger—deep, gut-wrenching hatred. "*Berenger* was good," Jack said vehemently.

Abe grinned. "I think it was shit."

"And that means it is shit, correct?"

"You're bright—boy."

Jack tensed. He wanted to punch this arrogant, powerful lunatic, but he didn't dare. "Level with me."

"Gladly."

"This is because of me. It has nothing to do with the product."

Abe laughed. "Very good. Top of the class."

"What do you want from me?" Jack said.

"To see you in the gutter, where you belong."

Jack stared. Abe was no longer smiling. His face was a mask of burning hatred, and it was frightening. He took a step back. One word loomed in his mind. *Psychotic.*

"By the time I get through with you, boy, you're gonna wish you'd never been born."

"And *Outrage*? It really is cancelled, isn't it?"

Abe smiled. "Just try and break your contract, boy. I'm waiting."

It was all out in the open now. *Berenger* would never be released. *Outrage* was finished. And he was still locked into an exclusive contract with North-Star, until he completed a third film for them. Jack didn't have to ask to know that there wasn't going to be another film. He was going to spend the rest of his life waiting for one that would never come through. This was it. He was out to pasture. He could not go up against Glassman. Not on his turf.

Not legally.

"Explain one thing," Jack said tersely. "Why? Why, after all these years?"

Abe bared his teeth in a mirthless smile. "You killed my son."

Jack blinked.

"Nancy was almost four months pregnant. She was leaving me and running to you. She miscarried my son—my heir."

As he absorbed what had happened, Jack opened his mouth to protest. In the same instant he realized that nothing he would say could change what Abe believed—what he had believed for seventeen long years. His jaw worked and he turned and walked away, his heart pumping furiously. Behind him, he heard Abe's laughter—loud, heartfelt, raucous. He rang for the elevator.

Glassman was not just vindictive.

He was obsessed.

Jack was down low and about to be ruined. Abe held all the cards—no one's career could survive Glassman's vengeance. He knew it without a doubt.

It was over.

His career was over.

But his life wasn't. He was a fighter. And this was war. And it had just begun—because now he had nothing to lose.

So he could fight dirty.

The idea formed out of nowhere.

Revenge.

Belinda Glassman.

PART FOUR

LOVERS
January–

February

1988

——— 83 ———

*T*he phone rang insistently.

Belinda was at her word processor, and she ignored it. The new scene was hot, an action sequence, and she couldn't stop. Besides, it was probably Vince, figuring that she had changed her mind since last night about seeing him. Her mother, who had arrived yesterday to take care of her, poked her head into her study. "Dear?"

"Mom, take a message," Belinda said irritably. "I have an answering machine, you should—oh, hell." She stood.

"It's a man, and he won't leave his name. He says it's urgent," Nancy said, frowning. "He sounds familiar."

Belinda picked up the phone. She knew it was Vince. "Vince, listen," she snapped. "I meant what I said last night. Every word."

There was a pause. "Who's Vince?"

Belinda knew that voice. She flushed. "Jack."

"Poor Vince," Jack said, a smile in his tone. "Is my timing off?"

Her heart was pounding erratically, and it annoyed her. What could he possibly want? "Yes."

"If I were a lesser man, or maybe a better one, I'd tell you I'll call back later. But I won't. How are you?" His tone became intense.

"Fine."

"I've been thinking about you."

She didn't respond.

"A lot. That's not a line. I want to see you—soon."

Belinda didn't hesitate. "You still come on like a Mack truck."

He chuckled. "Two of a kind. Maybe it's you. Maybe you bring that out in me. Well? What are you doing to-night?"

His tone was so damn seductive. It was stirring up urgent memories. His breath, hot, on her ear; his hands, hotter, sliding over her breasts. "I don't think so. I'm busy."

"Well, at least I know Vince is out of the running," he joked.

Another silence fell. She imagined his cupping her bare buttocks and pulling her up hard against his massive prick, rubbing against her. Slick, slicker . . .

"How about tomorrow night? Some place quiet and intimate, so we can get reacquainted."

"I already have plans for tomorrow night," she lied. Her tone had gotten husky. "After all, it's Saturday."

"Sunday."

"I don't think so."

Now he was silent, assessing, she guessed. "I get the feeling you're ticked at me. Why?"

"I'm not ticked at you," she said stiffly. Life would be so much easier if she were angry. "Look, Jack, Aspen was fun. Like I said. But this is real life. And I have no desire to get involved with a Hollywood star."

"And you think I lack tact," Jack said.

"Sorry," Belinda said lightly. At that moment her mind decided to play havoc, and she recalled vividly how he had pulled her into his arms after they had made love—and how they had fallen asleep in each other's embrace.

"Come on, sweetheart, break down. Besides, Aspen was more than just fun, and you know it."

"Jack, I'm working. I'm in the middle of a big scene. I'm sorry, but I don't have time for this. Good-bye." She hung up.

"Who was that, dear?" Nancy asked as she strode back to her study.

Belinda stared at her mother, wondering what Nancy

would do if she knew it had been Jack on the phone. "Just some arrogant jerk, Mom. Nobody important."

She had lost the drive, the creative momentum. She wrote another page, then deleted the whole thing.

His damn face kept superimposing itself on the screen.

Her traitorous inner self said, I wish I had said yes.

------ *84* ------

*O*ne thing that Peter Lansing prided himself on was the fact that he was a gentleman.

He could not, in good conscience, forget the sound of Melody's fragile, vulnerable voice on his answering machine. So abject, so apologetic.

Had he been too rough on her?

He returned her call.

About five hours later he was sitting in her living room, watching her carry in a tray of hors d'oeuvres. He noticed she had most definitely gone out of her way to dress for him, in a purple silk dress that was perfect with her hair and her curves, and it was low-cut too. She was wearing contacts and makeup, and the effect was dynamite. She placed the tray next to their drinks and smiled tentatively. He smiled back. She was nervous and shy; he was horny as hell. It made him feel like a heel.

"Peter, I want to set the record straight," Melody said, twisting her hands nervously.

He watched her steadily. She had beautiful eyes. He wanted to hear what she was going to say.

"You're wrong about Jack and me. We're not lovers, and we have never been lovers."

Lansing stared.

"But you were right in a way—I was in love with Jack

for years. But he never knew it. I made a play for him recently and he turned me down, which is why I was acting so strange." She looked at her hands. "I was hurt, and I wasn't ready for another man, Peter. But now I realize it was all just fantasies on my part."

Lansing, with the unerring instinct of an investigator, knew she was telling the truth. For the most part. A sense deep inside told him she was hiding something—something that made him uneasy, but he couldn't pinpoint it. He was too busy thinking—she and Jack weren't lovers. It felt damn good.

"Do you still love him?"

She sighed. Her gaze was level and luminous. "I'm trying, Peter, to put my infatuation behind me. It's hard."

"I appreciate your honesty," he said.

She grilled salmon steaks for them while he kept her company in the kitchen. He enjoyed watching her. Conversation was casual, a touch stilted at first, and Peter knew Melody was embarrassed about having told him such intimate things. He told a few funny stories, and soon had her smiling. He departed early.

At the door she stood poised, waiting, so he kissed her —nothing all-out, just light and short. To his surprise, she pressed against him, her arms going around his neck, returning his kiss and deepening it. He had to remember that she was in love with Jack, and he was damned if he was going to be a surrogate.

"I'll call you soon," he said, and she smiled.

She was smiling even more when she had closed the door and he was gone.

A smile of triumph.

Were all men such fools?

She thought of The Plan and positively tingled.

85

*F*inding out where she lived was easy—she was listed.

He never chased broads. Ever. But this was different. So he was chasing her all the way to Laguna Beach.

Belinda did not have a chance in hell. Not when he was determined, not when he was going to pour on his charm and keep pouring it on, until she fell madly in love with him.

He couldn't wait. He couldn't wait for the day when he would be face-to-face with Glassman. Couldn't wait to see the expression on his face. Maybe he would say: "Aren't you going to welcome me into the family?"

Glassman would look at him blankly.

Jack would laugh. "Your daughter and I were married last night."

Triumph.

Revenge.

He could taste it, and it was sweet.

86

*H*e was the last person she was expecting.

Belinda opened the door and felt a tide of hot, threatening emotion. He looked so good. He had come to see her. She was glad, damn glad. "Jack."

He didn't smile. "Hi."

All her protective defense mechanisms came surging back. "What are you doing here?"

"You're not giving me a chance," Jack said intensely. "It's not fair."

She felt herself weaken and instantly dammed up the softness. "I don't have to be fair, Jack."

"It's cold out—it's about to rain. May I come in?"

It was cold out, just her luck—as if even the weather were conspiring against her. She stepped silently aside. Jack moved past her, and Belinda slammed the door harder than she'd intended. When she turned to face him he was smiling tentatively, looking unsure. Sober. She had never been more nervous in her life.

"How about some coffee?" Jack said.

"Fine." She felt him following her into the kitchen. What did he want? God, how was she going to handle this? "I only have instant."

"That's okay. You have a nice place here."

She shot him a glance to see if he meant it, and he seemed sincere. He also seemed hesitant, maybe nervous too. "Thanks. Is black okay? I'm out of milk."

"Black's fine," Jack said, standing just behind her as she put on the kettle. When she turned she was almost in his arms, uncomfortably close, but he didn't do the polite thing. He didn't step back. She brushed hair out of her face. This is ridiculous, she thought. To be so nervous. To fight to be cold. When I really don't want to be cold at all . . . just the opposite. Inside, she could feel a stirring of arousal.

"Belinda," Jack said, taking her by the shoulders.

She tensed.

"I'm sorry for flying off the handle in Aspen. For the name-calling. I didn't mean it."

She heard herself say, "I know." She was very conscious of his hands on her.

"I wanted to spend the whole weekend with you." He smiled ruefully. "I'm not used to getting jilted—it doesn't happen too often."

"I'll bet it never happens." She smiled slightly, relaxing a little.

"Not in a while," he said modestly. "I guess I'm a bit spoiled."

"A bit," she agreed. She returned his gaze, then found herself looking at his mouth. Oh, damn, she thought, he's going to kiss me. "I shouldn't have sneaked out like that," she said breathlessly, watching his lips part. He leaned closer.

"No," he said softly. "You shouldn't have. Can't we start over?"

"Jack." A feeble protest.

His face was very close. "Just give me a chance. I'm not the bastard you think I am. You don't even know me. It's not fair to judge me based on bad press."

It wasn't fair, and she knew it. She closed her eyes. His mouth touched hers—soft and fragile, brushing. His hands slid to her shoulder blades, but he didn't press her against him. They looked at each other.

"Dinner? Tonight?" He kissed her again, this time more deeply. "Tonight at seven?"

"I don't want to complicate my life," she said.

He suddenly grinned and threw a glance at the ceiling. "Only you, Belinda, would call me a complication. You do know, lady, that you have a way with words?"

"If I didn't, I'd be in trouble."

"Not with me you wouldn't. Never with me. I'll pick you up."

She hesitated only a moment more. "All right."

They kissed again.

Later, after he was gone, she stared out at her driveway. What am I doing? she thought in desperation. She could feel it coming—the big plunge.

87

*N*ancy sat very still in Belinda's vast living room. From Belinda's study came the rapid-fire, staccato typing sounding, a constant background noise. Nancy leaned forward to pick up her Scotch. She drained it and got up to make another one.

She felt sick and frightened inside.

What had *he* been doing here?

She would probably have met him face-to-face if she hadn't seen him approaching the front door and recognized him immediately. She had fled to her bedroom in horror and hatred and cowered there, unable to think.

The man responsible for her life's ruin. Jack Ford.

Once he had been her lover.

And now she hated him.

God, did she hate him!

Jack Ford had ruined her marriage. Her life. It was as simple as that. He had been the pivotal element. Had he not been there that summer, none of it would have happened— her betrayal of Abe, his anger, his turning away from her. The miscarriage of their son—which Abe had never forgiven her for. And he had lied. He hadn't loved her. He had only used her. If he had loved her, he would have come to her when she'd needed him, after Abe found out and she miscarried. And now the man she most wanted to have never existed was somehow involved with her daughter.

Oh, God.

If it was a coincidence, it was too horrible and ironic.

If it wasn't a coincidence—and how could it be?—what did he want? Money? Or was his interest in Belinda somehow tied in to the screenplay she had sold, the one he was going to star in? Nancy knew about Abe's takeover of

North-Star and very clearly recalled that the studio had been the one to buy Belinda's screenplay for Ford. Everything was connected—somehow. Something terrible was happening—she knew it with a mother's eerie intuition. She could feel it.

She wanted to protect her daughter.

And now, when she thought of Belinda with him, she felt sick, about to vomit. She couldn't let this go any farther.

From outside the kitchen she had eavesdropped, barely able to breathe, on their brief conversation before he had left. Jack had been charming. She could hear a note of defiant belligerence in her daughter's tone. It increased her horror. This was not a first time for them. They had seen each other before. Their emotions were too complex, too developed—she had to do something.

She could not let Belinda see that man tonight.

88

*J*ack was whistling when he got back to his apartment.

Things were looking good.

Very good.

He picked up the paper and shook it, tried to read. He saw Belinda's face. Felt arousal. Life was so ironic—she was a pawn now in an ugly game, but she really did turn him on. The front door opened, and although Jack couldn't see the door from the kitchen, he heard voices—Rick's and a husky female voice he remembered from yesterday, belonging to the very pretty dark girl, Lydia.

Rick was saying, "Yeah, but they should have known all along!" And his tone was different from the brooding, hostile one Jack was used to. Happy. That was the only way to describe it.

"What are they, mind readers? Like you, smartass?"

They both started laughing—giggling, really.

Jack had to smile. Rick had never sounded like this— like a normal kid. It thrilled him.

"Oh, Jack. Didn't know you were home," Rick said, stopping in his tracks and dropping Lydia's hand. He flushed.

"Hi," Lydia said, flashing him a big smile.

"Ignore me, Rick, Lydia. Sorry, kid, but I'm going to be in for a while, if you guys can handle it."

"Oh, that's okay," Lydia said quickly.

"We rented some movies," Rick said, holding up a bulging bag.

"You guys gonna have a movie marathon?" Jack asked. Lydia was leaning against Rick. A hand on his shoulder. Very affectionate.

"Yeah," Rick said and shot Lydia a warm glance.

Wow! Jack thought as they disappeared. He decided he'd hole up in his bedroom and do some paperwork there, give them some space. He was so delighted to see Rick with a friend and a girlfriend all in one—especially an obviously nice girl.

The TV was on now, and their conversation had ceased. Jack poured himself a cup of coffee, glad to be distracted. He picked up the paper and stepped out of the kitchen.

They were sitting on the sofa, necking.

Jack hesitated. Break it up? Ignore it? They obviously couldn't do anything while he was home—but what about later? Should he even bother to stop them? She was an innocent girl. He said, "Rick, may I speak to you, please?" and walked into his bedroom.

Rick came in, turned to him, and Jack frowned. He wasn't sure what to do.

"Close the door," he said.

"Okay."

"Look, Rick, I know that you two are going to do what you want to do. I mean, I can make it difficult for you, but eventually you'll find a way."

"Jack—"

"Wait. Lydia is a nice girl. I think you should treat her with respect."

"I know she's a nice girl," Rick said seriously. "A *very* nice girl. Don't worry."

Jack smiled, immensely relieved.

"And she happens to like me too," Rick added.

"I can see that. Listen, I want to tell you something about women—girls—that it took me years to realize. Women are much more emotional than we are when it comes to sex. A guy can screw some broad and not give a damn who she is, walk away, and never think twice about it. But most women can't have sex without becoming emotionally involved. Do you understand what I'm saying?"

Rick nodded. "I think so."

"I mean most regular woman. You've had experience only with hookers. That's different."

"I know."

"Lots of girls at Lydia's age aren't ready for sex—emotionally."

Rick nodded.

Jack was surprised he wasn't defensive. "Maybe you should just be friends with her and use that phone number I gave you."

Rick scowled. "I don't want to screw those whores anymore."

Jack shrugged. "End of lecture. Just wanted to give you something to think about."

Rick nodded, closed the door, and sat on the couch beside Lydia, who snuggled up against him instantly. Making him feel warm all over again.

"Was it bad?" she asked.

Rick laughed. "He told me that you're a 'nice' girl."

Lydia started cracking up, and Rick joined her.

89

*V*ince closed the front door behind him, leaned on it, and stared at the kitchen-living area, which was a shambles as always. Mary would be home any time, he thought indifferently, walking toward their bedroom. He supposed his timing sucked. He pulled a suitcase out from under the bed and opened all the drawers in his bureau. He began piling clothes in.

The stab of pain shafted him again, through a general feeling of numbness. When had the pain started to give way to the numbness? He wasn't really sure.

Last night, facing the overwhelming realization that he had lost Belinda—no, that he had never even had her—had been the most awful, painful time of his life. He had driven around in circles all night, grieving and hurting. He had finally gone home at dawn.

Now he was exhausted, numb, with these intermittent moments of aching. It was time to start over, really start over. That meant separating from Mary. He wanted to get his things out of here as soon as possible. Maybe before she got home. He couldn't handle a scene with her, not today, not when he was feeling so low.

God, had he ever been a fool.

It had been a fantasy for him to think he could have anything more than an affair with a woman like Belinda.

A woman like Belinda.

Independent, strong to the point of selfishness.

A sudden realization of just how selfish she was arrested him in his tracks. Had she ever given anything to him, other than her body, her nymphomaniacal passion?

The answer was an overwhelming no.

Vince paused, a pile of shirts in hand, wondering what

this realization meant. How could he have fallen so deeply for a woman so cold and uncaring? She had used him.

A flash of anger sparked.

And made him feel alive again, like a man.

The phone rang, and he was shocked to hear the voice of Abe Glassman's secretary. She left a message that Abe had called and would Mary please call back. Vince hung up. What in hell was that all about? Why would Abe Glassman be calling Mary?

He packed, thinking about Belinda, trying to see her as she really was for the first time, instead of worshiping the ground at her feet. The picture wasn't pretty. Mostly he kept remembering her selfishness. And the way she had led him around by the nose.

Making him feel insecure, jealous, bestowing her favors like a queen throwing crumbs to a beggar—Jesus!

He had a sudden perspective, one he didn't like. She had made him feel like less than a man.

Anger vied with the sense of loss and hurt.

Out of her life.

The thought rose up to choke him.

He hated the bitch.

He was in the bathroom, throwing his toiletries into a paper bag when he heard a car door slam. He tensed. Bracing. Mary called his name. She appeared in the doorway, looking pale, disheveled, terrible. "Oh, Vince!" she cried, throwing her arms around him.

He hated this. He disengaged her and saw that she was crying. He felt like a shit. "I'm sorry about what happened," he said.

"It was awful, Vince, a nightmare. I spent the whole night there, in jail . . ." She stopped.

Vince sighed. He threw his cologne in the bag.

"What are you doing?"

He hesitated, and her eyes went to the bathroom cabinet, now empty of every single item that belonged to him. "Vince?"

He couldn't meet her eyes. "It's over, Mary. I'm sorry. I'm moving out."

"You're what?"

"Moving out." He walked past her into their bedroom.

"How could you!" she shrieked. "How could you do this to me when I need you!"

"I've wanted to tell you for a long time. Our marriage is a sham—and you know it. You don't love me." He didn't add that he didn't love her either.

"You motherfucker! You're kicking me when I'm already down!"

He slammed his suitcase closed.

"You're moving in with her. With that cunt. Aren't you?"

He didn't answer.

"She talked you into this. To get back at me. Oh, goddamn it!" She sank on the bed.

"Mary, get yourself together. You've got Beth. You've been cheating on me. You've got your mother—and money. You'll do okay. And Belinda and I are through. We broke up. I'm moving in with one of the guys from the crew. It's for the best—for both of us."

He picked up the suitcase, unable to do more than glance at her briefly. "Vince," she moaned.

Suddenly he remembered, and he looked at her directly for the first time. "Abe Glassman called."

"What did he want?"

"That's what I want to know. Why in hell is he calling you?"

Mary paled. "It's something to do with the shooting, I think. I mean, why else would he call me?"

Satisfied, Vince started for the door.

She followed him. "Vince, don't do this. Please!"

He ignored her.

"Is it really over between you and Belinda?" she demanded tearfully.

"Yes," he said, and he walked out without even looking back.

Never had he felt so lonely in his whole damn life.

90

"Are you going out?"

Belinda was sitting on the bed in a short red silk robe, rolling up a stocking and attaching it to a black garter. "Hi, Nancy. Yeah."

"Your arm shouldn't be out of that sling yet."

"It's only for tonight. And I feel fine, pretty much."

"Belinda—*don't go!*"

Belinda looked up. Between her tone and her eyes, Belinda knew that somehow her mother was aware that she was dating Ford tonight. She stood and rebelted her robe. "It's just a date." Liar.

"With him."

"Yes."

Mother and daughter stared, unsmiling, at each other.

"Don't be a fool," Nancy said harshly, for the first time in her life full of certainty and conviction. "He's going to hurt you, Belinda. He's a user. Worse—he's a liar."

Every hair on Belinda's body bristled—in defense of Jack. "What happened between you and Jack happened seventeen years ago," she snapped. "Not only was he just a boy —the past is dead, and I'm not you. And as far as I'm concerned, your affair has nothing to do with me."

"You're going out with the man who destroyed your mother's life, and you don't think it has anything to do with you?" Nancy cried.

"I'm sorry that you fell in love with him, Mom," Belinda said. "So he broke your heart. Well, you know what? You're not the only one who's had a broken heart—we've all been hurt."

"He'll break your heart, Belinda. He'll use you and then he'll walk away, just the way he did with me."

"Like I said, I'm not you. I'm not saying I trust Jack, but I'm not you and my relationship with him is not an instant replay of yours."

"I know that man!"

"You think you know him!"

"You think *you* know him?" Nancy was incredulous and aghast. "Oh, Belinda, stop it now, before it's too late!"

"Look, Mom, I know Jack, all right. I know he's a superstud, I know he's got an ego, so I'm prepared. Okay? I'm a big girl. I've played this game before. I can handle it. I can handle him."

"No, you can't."

Belinda stared at her mother.

"You're a woman," Nancy said. "You can't handle him."

The uneasiness that had begun with their conversation prickled and poked at her. "I'm going to be late. Do you want to have a drink with us? He'll be here any minute."

"Think about what I've said, Belinda. I'm your mother. I love you. I'm only trying to protect you."

"I can protect myself," Belida said stubbornly.

Her mother left.

I am not my mother, Belinda thought grimly.

Jack Ford is not going to use me.

He is not going to break my heart, because I am prepared.

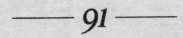

91

*O*f course she looked wildly sensual and stunning.

As they walked in, heads turned, and Jack was well aware of the fact that as she preceded him, she was the one precipitating the admiring interest, both male and female.

That admiration quickly changed to curious recognition as the glances then settled on him. He found himself amused—and a little bemused.

Belinda was wearing a red leather bustier and skirt. The bustier laced up the front, and she had left an enticing one-inch gap. It was hard not to keep looking at what was revealed of her breasts. The skirt zipped at an angle up the back. It was hard not to look at her perfect round buttocks when she walked in front of him. The outfit was more than provocative. It clung to her strong curves like a wetsuit. If she wasn't dressing for him, then for who?

Jack was pleased.

Maybe a bit more so than he should have been.

Jack had half expected her to be out when he came by to pick her up, but not only had she been there she had been dressed and ready to go. She was quiet during the drive, so he found a jazz station and they zipped into town in silence. He knew she was still fighting him. And maybe herself.

Not that it mattered.

The host seated them with a flourish, at a table with great views.

"So tell me," Jack said lightly, though his eyes were fierce, "why *did* you leave like that in Aspen?"

"The coward's way out, of course."

"You, lady, don't strike me as a coward."

"Usually I'm not."

He smiled. "You know what? I'm going to take that as a compliment."

"You can take it any way you like."

"I'd like to take you any way I'd like—and every way."

She arched an eyebrow.

He was sheepish. "I couldn't resist."

She smiled.

"Belinda," Jack said, very serious now, "I want to know why I make you afraid."

She sighed. "Come on, Jack. Don't tell me you've never done that yourself. The old hit-and-run. You know it's easier than facing a stranger on the other pillow in the morning."

"It's different with us, and you know it. We are certainly not strangers."

"No? What are we, Jack? Friends? Lovers? C'mon, Jack! Don't, *just don't,* use your lines on me."

He closed his hand around his water glass and studied it. She wanted the slightest chance to fight. He had to be careful. This was not in the game plan, not the way to get what he wanted. When he looked up she was studying her menu.

Jack intended to break her down. This was going to be a great evening. It *had* to be. It was time to take control and turn on the charm. And so what if it just happened to be easier because what he said was also the truth? "I don't use lines on you, Belinda, not when I'm being serious."

She glanced at him.

"I wouldn't insult you or your intelligence that way."

"Thank you."

He reached out and clasped her hand with his. "Belinda, come on. Please relax, loosen up just a little."

"So you can seduce me and feel macho?" But she was softening; he could feel it and see it.

"Well, I won't deny I want to make wild love to you . . . kiss you all over. Your mouth, your hair, your breasts, your ni—"

"Jack. That couple is listening to every word."

He dropped his voice. "—navel." He grinned. "You already know that. I couldn't care less about the other part."

"No? You deny that your male ego is at stake here?"

"Ah, so we're back to egos now."

She closed her eyes and smiled.

"Do you have an ego fixation, Belinda?"

She looked at him. "What do you think?"

A long silence reigned. "I think," Jack said slowly, "I think it's time my ego got some stroking."

She fought a smile. And she didn't say no either.

"Tell me about yourself," he said after they had ordered drinks, a merlot for her, a Perrier for him.

"What do you want to know?"

"Everything. How old are you?"

"Too old for you," she said.

He smiled. "Twenty-eight?"

"Dead on. What, no flattery?"

"You're too smart and too poised to be twenty-one. And a twenty-year old couldn't write what you've written."

"Thank you."

"So, what about family? I want to know your life's story," Jack said. The hair on the back of his neck started to rise. With guilt?

"My mother and father live in New York," Belinda replied.

"So you were born in New York?"

She nodded.

"Any brothers, sisters?"

"No, just me. That's a big disappointment to my father, believe me."

"With a daughter like you, why would he want another child?"

She smiled wryly.

"He must be very proud of you," Jack said. "You must be very close."

Belinda seemed to choke on her water. "You've got to be kidding. His daughter, a writer . . . give me a break! He can't understand how I could spend my time making up stories. And Abe is close to only one thing—power."

Jack stared, absorbing everything, the quick outbreak of defiance and the bitterness. "That's ridiculous," he said quietly. "Being able to write is a great talent—you're a big talent, Belinda."

"Tell that to Abe."

"I don't see how your father could not respect what you do. Everybody knows that it all starts with the writers."

"Abe is . . . different. His trip is power. Whether it's owning a studio or a refinery, all his assets are just means to an end."

"That's not a very flattering assessment of your own father."

She looked him in the eye. "No, it's not. But I don't owe him anything—not one damn thing."

"You don't get along with him," Jack said, with increased stirrings of guilt.

"No, and I never have and never will. Not as long as he sees me only as a broodmare to get him an heir for his empire." She grimaced. "He wants me to get married. Have babies. Preferably male babies. Soon. I'm over the hill," she explained.

Outwardly Jack smiled. She was being amusing. Inwardly every nerve went on alert. Glassman wanted her to get married.

Glassman wanted a grandson—an heir.

How would he feel when his grandson's last name was Ford?

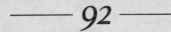

92

*H*e couldn't fucking believe it.

What they said was true—you couldn't get decent hired help these days.

Abe could not believe the colossal fuck-up.

He could not believe Will Hayward was still alive.

"I want this taken care of," he snarled into the phone. "Not today, not tomorrow, but yesterday! You understand?"

"Yes."

"I want that stupid bastard nailed—now." Abe hung up. He did not feel the slightest degree of guilt. Not the slightest degree.

Hayward's days were numbered.

They'd been numbered from the moment he had dared to cross Abe.

93

"*D*amn Vince!" Mary screamed. "Damn him! I don't want a divorce! Damn him!"

Beth hugged her and tried to rock her, but Mary lunged away to pace rapidly around Beth's bedroom. "How could he? *Now?* When I'm so fucking down?"

"I don't know, honey, but give it up."

"What?" Mary turned on her.

"Give it up. You don't love him. Let him go—it's for the best."

"You're right about one thing," Mary said vehemently. "I don't love him—I hate him. I want to kill him!" She sat back down. "Wait till my mother finds out," she moaned. Her mother would tell her she was too fat to hold a man, to save her marriage. She'd tell her that she failed at everything —so what did she expect. All because of a few pounds! Fuck her mother. She hated her mother even more than she hated Vince.

Her mother had called earlier. "Mary, have you called Paul Socorro?" she had asked tightly.

Mary had belligerently said nothing.

"Mary? Have you called Paul?"

"No, Mom," she said rigidly.

"Do you know how many of my friends have called up, asking about you? It's embarrassing! What a terrible *incident.* Mary, are you listening? You cannot go on like this."

Mary's grip on the phone grew tighter.

"I've reached your father. Not personally, but I left an urgent message. He should be calling. Call Paul Socorro. Why don't—"

Mary had hung up.

Now Mary wished she had a line. "Do you have any toot left?" She was horribly depressed.

"No. Mary, you've been doing an awful lot lately," Beth said cautiously.

Mary knew it was true. Deep down she was worried because she knew she had a habit, and she wanted to break it. And she had to face it—she also wanted to lose fifteen pounds. Because her mother was right. She hated facing what she had known all along—her life was a shambles and she was a shambles, all because she was such a fat slob.

"Are you okay?" Beth asked worriedly.

Mary didn't answer her either, and the phone rang again. She just looked at it. When Beth moved to answer it, she said, "Don't. It's my mother."

Calmly Beth picked up the receiver, spoke, listened, then handed it to Mary. "It's Abe Glassman."

Mary felt a tingle of something close to anticipation. But she knew that was impossible. She was angry at that horny old goat—wasn't she? He had used her and lied to her. But she had a flashing image of the two of them entwined, Abe's big, thick prick deep inside, thrusting deeper and deeper, and her groin started a slow swell.

"Hello?"

"Mary, this is Abe. How're you doing?"

Mary took a breath. She knew exactly where she would like to be right now. Under him. "Fine, Abe."

"You're not still pissed, are you, about our little misunderstanding?"

"It doesn't matter anymore," she said truthfully.

"Good. I want to see you. Can you come down to my office tomorrow morning—say, at nine?"

Mary was thrown off balance. When he had said he wanted to see her, her whole body had surged in anticipation. But his office? "Well, yes . . ."

"See you at nine." *Click.*

Mary hung up the phone. Thinking.

"What did he want?" Beth asked petulantly.

"I don't know."

94

*W*hen they got back Jack was finally gone.

Finally!

They had watched two movies, a B-grade sci-fi flick and Clint Eastwood in *Firefox*. Then they had gone out for pizza. Now they had the apartment to themselves. Rick produced a joint and lit it.

It had been the best day he'd ever had in his life. Being with Lydia was fun, nonstop fun, and when she wasn't cracking jokes she was mimicking everyone—including him! —and Rick had never laughed so much in his entire life. He didn't want the day to end.

They sat on one of the sofas in the living room and Rick handed her the joint, relaxing against the pillows. They passed it back and forth in a new, very easy silence. Rick had never felt so close to anyone before, and he was struggling to get a grip on his feelings. He kept feeling as if he were about to burst, a delicious sensation.

"You look so serious," Lydia said, imitating his expression and jabbing him in the ribs with her elbow.

He laughed at her face. "I was thinking," he said.

"About what?" She stubbed the roach carefully in an ashtray, saving it for later.

"I was wondering if you're ticklish," he yelled, pouncing on her.

She shrieked, and he attacked her underarms. She was ticklish. She started laughing, and the more he tickled the more she laughed. "No, Rick, stop!" she cried.

Rick changed his area of attack. She was on her back, and he had her thighs pinned with his. His hands went to her belly, slipping up under her baggy T-shirt. She shrieked and wriggled to get away.

And suddenly the game became more than a game.

Rick had his hands on the smooth, firm silky skin of her belly. He was on his knees, suspended over her, no longer laughing but breathing hard, and not from physical exertion. Looking down into her face.

The moment his hands stopped their torture her own laughter stopped, and she stared up at him, her breath coming in short, fast gasps, her lips parted—and the moment was suspended.

His hands moved over her belly, slowly, enjoying the feel of her.

Breathless, her mouth hung open; her eyes searched his, dark, moist, trusting.

Rick's arms slid around her, and he lowered himself on top of her. She raised her face eagerly for his kiss, meeting his lips halfway. He tightened his hold, his legs parting hers, not deliberately but instinctively, the hard ache of his cock settling in the soft, warm V between her thighs.

This time her mouth parted for his tongue, and she welcomed him.

Kissing her was better than all the hookers and even Patty Epherton put together. It was a dazzling realization, like a bolt of lightning. He loved her.

He had never loved anyone before.

Tenderly he cupped her face with both his hands and searched her eyes with his own, looking for a reciprocal feeling. He saw trust, innocence, desire, and something else— something like wonder. He kissed her with all the love he was feeling.

Lydia kissed him back, her hands beneath his shirt, roaming his back, her hips responding and arching against him.

And then, just like that, it happened. He clutched her tightly and came in his pants.

"Rick?" Her tone was soft, confused.

"Sorry," he murmured, still on top of her, still holding her, wondering if she could feel his heart pounding like a jackhammer.

"What happened? Are you all right?"

"Nothing," Rick said, kissing her.

They kissed for a long time. It was growing dark outside. Rick wanted to touch her everywhere but respected her too much to treat her like a tramp. Instead his hands roamed her back, her waist, even curled in her thick, wavy black hair. His desire renewed itself. He wanted her so much.

Lydia shocked him when she took his hand and guided it to her breast. "Please," she said. "Don't you want to touch me?"

"Yes," he gasped, sinking his hand into her soft flesh. "I didn't think," he said, squeezing her breast and finding an erect nipple, "that you'd let me."

She moaned very softly.

Rick wasn't sure how far to go. But one look at Lydia's face told him he shouldn't stop. Daringly he slid his hand under her shirt, fondling her through her brassiere. Lydia's moan encouraged him, and he slipped his hand beneath the bra, found the bare, swollen flesh, caressed it and stroked it and wondered if he was going to come in his pants again.

"Oh, Rick," Lydia cried. "I've dreamed about this, about you and me."

"You have?"

Her eyes opened and she smiled. "Ever since you first came to school."

"Lydia? Are you—?"

"Yes." She stared at him through long black lashes. "I want you to be the first."

His heart careened madly.

"I am sixteen," she added, sitting up. "Don't you want to? Or don't you like me?"

"I want to," Rick said quickly. "I just didn't think you did."

She smiled. "I thought boys didn't care about what the girl wanted."

"They don't," Rick said. "But I care about what you want—very much."

Her eyes filled with tears.

Rick was confused. "Why are you upset?"

"I'm not upset, you fool," Lydia said. "I'm happy. I didn't think you'd ever like me."

"I like you, all right," Rick said, standing and pulling her up. He held her hand and led her into his bedroom. Rick locked the door behind them. Who knew when Leah might appear?

She looked at him shyly, blushing.

Rick smiled and said, "Don't worry. I'm pretty experienced."

"I'll bet," she said, like the old Lydia.

He stripped off his clothes rapidly, only to find her staring, still fully dressed. He wasn't embarrassed—he was proud.

"I've never seen it quite like that before," Lydia said, staring at his erection. "I saw my father once, and when I was younger, my neighbor. It looks awfully big," she added dubiously.

"It will fit perfectly," Rick said, trembling with excitement but wanting to appear nonchalant. "Are you going to undress?"

She sat down on the bed. "I don't look like Patty Epherton," she warned.

"I don't care," Rick said. "I think you're beautiful."

"Maybe we should wait until it's completely dark out," she said anxiously.

Rick sat beside her, took her hand, tried to think of how to reassure her. He had never said the words before, but suddenly he wanted to, desperately. And he wanted to hear her say them back. "Lydia? I love you."

She stared. Then her face crumpled. She fell against his chest. "Do you really?"

"Yes," he whispered, stroking her back. "How do you feel? About me, I mean?"

"You fool," she said, raising a teary face. "I've been in love with you since we first met—when you only had eyes for Patty Epherton."

"Do you mean it?" He was overwhelmed.

"Yes."

He helped her undress. It was twilight, and the calm

grayness filled the room, giving him just enough light to see. He was stunned as her body was revealed—broad shoulders, nice strong arms, big beautiful breasts that put Patty Epherton and all the hookers to shame. A small waist and hips, long, curved legs, muscular from all the sports she was always doing. Her body belonged in a centerfold, and he couldn't understand why she was always hiding it.

"I told you," she said with a nervous laugh.

"You are so beautiful, Lydia. Patty can't hold a candle to you!"

"You're just saying that."

"Oh, no," he said, lowering himself down on her. "I mean it."

He kissed her mouth, her jaw, her throat. Working his way down to her beautiful breasts. When he tongued a hard nipple she gasped and grasped his head tightly.

"No one's ever done that to me before!"

He suckled her with fervor until she was writhing, until their bodies began to film with sweat. His mouth explored the rest of her—her ribs, her navel, the patch of dark, coarse pubic hair. He slid his hand into the moist V, and she bucked against him, gasping, panting. He wanted so much for her to feel what he felt.

He had tried it once—it had been not particularly pleasant. But now—with his face hovering so close and his fingers spreading apart parts of her that were so different, so new, so exciting and beautiful—the urge to taste her came over him. He lowered hesitant lips and kissed her gently.

She cried his name.

He deepened the kiss. And was surprised at the jolt it gave him and the surge of need it produced. It seemed to have the same effect on her, for she was spread and arching for him, and he experimented. Probed with his tongue. It became a whole new world, a delicious, erotic, sublime experience. He became lost in the taste and smell of her.

Lydia's hands tightened so hard on his head that it hurt. She emitted a strangled cry, arched up, and shuddered convulsively.

Beyond reason, unbearably ignited, Rick was on top of

her, kissing her, probing. He found her entrance, pressed, couldn't even get more than the bare tip of himself in. Reflexively he reached down, guided himself into a space that was tight, not accommodating, but wet, hot. He put his arms around her and pushed. And then he was moving surely, steadily, and she was moving too, eager, but awkward, her rhythm missing his, but it didn't matter—it didn't matter at all.

95

"*T*hat's all right," Belinda said, her hand reaching for the door handle. "You don't have to get out."

"Don't you dare open that door!" Jack flashed, his hand already hard on hers.

"I thought you weren't a gentleman."

"I am when it suits me," he said, jumping out and striding around the car.

Belinda stepped out and they walked up to the front door. She unlocked it and turned. "Well, thanks for a nice evening."

His expression was incredulous. "A *nice* evening? Only nice? Lady, you have a tendency toward understatement. You're not going to invite me in?"

"It was a very nice evening, Jack—don't press it. And, no, I'm not inviting you in."

"You think you're so tough," he murmured, leaning closer.

"Forget it," Belinda said, stepping back against the door, pushing it open.

"Invite me in for decaf," Jack insisted, flashing her a heart-stopping grin. "Don't be afraid," he added in a murmur.

"Let's set the record straight. I am not afraid of anything with a prick."

His grin widened. "So you're going to invite me in?"

"After you," she said. She marched into the kitchen and put on a kettle of water, letting him wander as he pleased. What would he say if he knew her mother was asleep downstairs in the guest room? When he reappeared she turned to him deliberately. "I only have instant."

"Do I care? Are you going to change?"

"No, Jack, I'm not going to change."

"I sort of like that sheer black lace negligee in your bathroom," he said with a kind of pout that, unfortunately, made him close to irresistible.

"My mother's here."

She had to hand it to him: He was a pro, cool as a cucumber, unfazed. As if he didn't know her—intimately. "She asleep?"

"Probably." She waited another moment, but of course he wasn't going to tell her he'd balled her mother seventeen years ago. Why was she disappointed?

Belinda put on a quiet jazz station and glanced at him cautiously. He had taken off his jacket, which was black silk with a silvery sheen. He looked very relaxed and collected— as if this were his home, not hers. He was removing his red tie, and Belinda watched, mesmerized. He caught her eye and smiled.

He knows exactly what he's doing, she thought, but couldn't move her eyes. He drew the tie off and casually let it slip to the couch. He was staring at her as he unbuttoned one, two, three buttons. And then his hands stopped; he patted the couch and smiled.

Such a simple act, but he made it into something incredibly sexy and sensual. "I'll get the coffee," she said.

When she came back she approached cautiously, carrying the two cups. As she handed him his she saw, to her dismay, a healthy bulge in his slacks, which she promptly decided to ignore. But he'd caught her attention.

"Sorry," he said with a soft laugh. "Some things are impossible to control."

She ignored the comment and sat in a chair facing him, crossing her legs. He eyed them—as she'd intended.

"What, do I have a social disease or something?"

"I don't know. Do you?"

"No, as a matter of fact, I don't. Why don't you come over here?"

"I'm quite comfortable right where I am, thank you. Do you think I'm an heiress, Jack?"

"What?"

She smiled. It was nice to see him off balance for a change. "I am not an heiress."

"All right."

"I thought I'd mention it. In case that's what you're after."

Jack laughed. "Sweetheart, I've got enough cash to tide us over for a few years. And I don't mind your being after *me* for *my* money."

"You wouldn't mind, Jack, if I wanted you for your money? Your connections?"

He grew serious. "I was teasing. Of course I'd mind. That's one of the things I like about you, Belinda. Even though it's taken a while to get used to, you really don't care that I'm a star."

"Bravo," she said quietly. She was impressed. She stood up slowly. "Want to dance?"

Jack was already standing in front of her, pulling her into his arms. And then they were swaying to a soulful love song. His grip tightened. She could feel the whole length of his body. He had one hand on the top of her hip, the other on her bare shoulder, and his fingers caressed and burned into her skin. She had her arms around his neck, not exactly sure how this had happened, but it was the most natural thing in the world to close her eyes and lay her cheek against his chest.

This one timeless moment was the most exquisite she had ever experienced.

A kind of smoldering fire leapt and sparked and warmed between them.

It was so obvious. I love him. Terrifyingly obvious. I

would like to stay here, just like this, drifting in his arms forever.

She felt his breath on her temple; then he dusted her flesh with a kiss. His hands pressed, sliding over the soft leather of her skirt.

Belinda didn't open her eyes. Drifting away . . . so warm . . . She could barely breathe.

His lips touched her cheek, another fragile whisper of a kiss. His arms tightened, and she could feel his chin and mouth on the top of her head. He rubbed his face gently into her hair. Inhaling. Another brief kiss.

The beautiful tragic music, bittersweet and melancholy, ended only to be replaced by something upbeat and incongruous to the mood and the fire between them. Jack had stopped swaying, had his hand on the back of her neck, was saying her name in a husky tone, pulling her head back.

"Belinda."

She opened her eyes. His face was inches from hers, his green eyes heavy-lidded and glazed.

"I want a kiss," he murmured before claiming it.

It would be so easy to surrender.

Conscious logic interrupted what they were doing, intruding, ruining everything. In one second she thought of all the men in her life. Of Rod and Vince and all the one-nighters and two-nighters and now Jackson Ford. A huge panicky fear engulfed her.

She pushed herself out of his embrace, wrenching away. "Not tonight."

He stared at her.

"Go away, Jack, you've outstayed your welcome, damn you."

He became incredulous, angry. A long moment passed before he spoke. "Why are you doing this?"

She absolutely could not tell him the truth. So she said nothing.

"We've already been together. I don't understand."

"Just leave."

"Why are you doing this?" he demanded again. "You

want me. And if you think that you don't, you're lying to yourself. And God knows, Belinda, I want you."

"The only thing I want from you, Jack, is something you're incapable of giving me—or any woman."

"And what exactly is that?"

"A real, honest emotion," Belinda returned intensely, her gaze clashing with his. "Pricks are a dime a dozen, Jack."

Confusion started to fade from his gaze. He smiled slightly, lucidly.

"Get out," she snapped. "Just get out, Jack, now."

"I think," Jack said slowly, approaching her, "that you care for me."

Belinda stepped backward, furious with herself for revealing too much and furious with him for being so insensitive and egotistical. "The problem is, Jack, that you don't have a heart—or what heart you have is hanging suspended between your legs."

"Low and mean," Jack said, but he was smiling as he reached for her. She couldn't evade him. "Give me a chance, Belinda."

Eyes locked.

"If you don't give me a chance, how will you ever know if I have a heart or not?"

"I don't know what you're talking about. It's late. Go home. Go back to L.A. Do us both a favor."

"Why won't you listen? I do care about you! I'm falling in love with you, dammit! Isn't that what you want to hear?"

"You misunderstood what I meant. Go home."

He was no longer smiling. "I could get down on my knees, couldn't I, and declare myself the way they did a hundred years ago and you'd still think I was full of shit, wouldn't you?"

"Yes, I would."

"When am I going to see you again?"

She almost gaped. He really had the tenacity of a pit bull. "I don't know," she said cautiously.

"Tomorrow night." It wasn't a question but a statement

of intent. He was heading for the door as if nothing had happened.

She felt disappointment.

And was angry at herself for feeling it.

*F*or the occasion she dressed.

She wore a skintight T-shirt, braless, and a new jeans skirt that was a few inches above the knee. Medium-heeled sandals, silver bangles, and her hair loose. A touch of pale pink lipstick and blush. Mary had to admit she looked great —even if she was a bit plump.

Her legs had a nice shape; in fact, they were her best feature. Her arms were probably her worst feature, but no one would notice because of her breasts and hair. She had even invested in a new perfume, Nicki. She was nervous.

This time there was no wait. The bosomy blond receptionist ushered her straight in. Abe rose to greet her, his eyes flicking over her. Mary decided she was an absolute pervert —she couldn't believe the thoughts that were rushing through her mind.

"Hello, doll," Abe said. "Come on, sit down. Coffee?"

"No, thanks," Mary said, sitting and crossing her legs. Her skirt rode up high on her thighs. Abe looked. He sat casually on the corner of his desk, facing her.

"What was this shit with you drawing a gun on Belinda?" His tone was suddenly harsh, his eyes hard.

And Mary was disappointed. "You lied," she said tremulously. "So I decided to do something myself."

"What are you, crazy?"

"I didn't mean to shoot her," Mary cried, upset. "I just wanted to frighten her away from Vince. That's all."

"Jesus, you could have killed her!"

"She shouldn't have tried to grab the gun," Mary half moaned. "I'm so sorry—believe me. It was the worst nightmare of my life." To her horror a few tears trembled on her lashes.

"Christ, if you'd talked to me, I could've told you to lay low and let it die a natural death. I had plans for Belinda—marriage plans. And they didn't include your husband."

Mary blinked. "You did?"

"Next time you come to me first."

Mary bit her lip. She looked at him. She felt thrilled—he hadn't lied. Hadn't used her. And he wasn't angry any longer, just intent. "I was drunk," she confessed. "Or it would never have happened."

Abe laughed. "No harm's done, and hell, what you did was a response as old as time. Probably something I would have done."

She smiled.

He leaned back and let his gaze roam her leisurely. Her nipples tightened against the ribbed cotton of her T-shirt. He said, "So that chapter's closed now, right, doll?"

"Yes. Vince and I are through anyway. I've had it with that bastard."

He raised a brow. "Quick change."

She lifted her chin. "I'm getting a divorce, and I kicked him out last night."

Abe grinned. "Good for you." He shifted again. And tugged at the crotch of his trousers. Mary's glance followed his movement, and she noticed a healthy hard-on. Their gazes met. "C'mere," he commanded softly.

Her heart leapt while her vulva grew slick and moist. She was on her feet and moving between his thighs. He grabbed her breasts, squeezing. "Jesus," he said.

She clamped a hand on his penis through the material of his pants. It leapt and quivered. "Abe," Mary said.

He pulled up her shirt and buried his face between her breasts, kneading them. She freed his cock. He took a large nipple into his mouth. "Big and beautiful," he said. "I want to fuck your tits, Mary."

And he did.

*F*ear.

Rancid, stinking fear.

Will Hayward sat very still, in the living area of his studio on Ninetieth and First Avenue, listening. Straining to hear. His face was white. Sweat shone on his forehead and trickled past his ear. His arms were wrapped fiercely around himself. Again he heard it, and he leaned forward, concentrating.

A creaking.

Someone was coming.

And now, now there was nothing.

Will knew he was a coward. If he wasn't a coward, he would get up and go to the front door and at least use the peekhole to see who was out there. Who? An assassin, of course. An assassin hired by Abe Glassman.

But he couldn't do it.

He was afraid to even go to the door.

There was no noise now, nothing.

It had been his imagination. Will relaxed slightly, as much as possible with his heart racing a hundred miles an hour and his body wired from all the coke he'd done in the past two weeks. He knew he needed to come down. He wanted to shoot some heroin, or at least do a few Valium. But how could he? He needed to be alert!

Will opened the vial and snorted a few spoonfuls.

Then he heard the elevator—there was no mistaking that sound. He capped the vial, almost spilling its contents because his hands were trembling so badly. He sat once more in frozen, abject fear. It was only when he heard his neighbor's door opening and his neighbor's girlfriend's laughter that he relaxed, closing his eyes and sinking back against the couch.

He couldn't go on this way much longer.

For one thing, he was down to the end of his stash—but he was afraid to go out. He hadn't left his apartment in two weeks, not since he'd almost been killed in Central Park. He hadn't gone to work, and he hadn't answered his phone. He still had money left from the five grand he'd gotten from Abe, so that wasn't a problem—not yet. But what was he going to do about Abe?

He was going crazy.

He knew it.

He had to do something.

He just couldn't go on like this anymore.

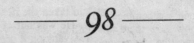

98

Jack finished shaving. He whistled at his reflection in the mirror.

Despite himself he was really looking forward to tonight.

And he was very pleased with himself. His timing, he thought, was impeccable. He hadn't seen her in four days, not since an early morning run (followed by a deli breakfast), and he hadn't called her until last night. While he was making himself clear regarding his intentions toward her, his instincts told him how far and how often to push. His instincts were always right on target when it came to women, and Belinda was a woman—a helluva woman, unfortunately —even if the stakes were entirely different this time.

He thought he had figured her out. She liked to be in control. She had reversed the sex roles by becoming the predator, the provider. Her men were like his bimbos, studs to service her. That was why she was so flighty toward him —she wasn't used to an aggressive, powerful male chasing her. She didn't like not being in control. He had to admit he found her an exciting challenge.

We're not so different, he thought.

He refused to think about all he had learned that other night—about Belinda's relationship to her father. That knowledge was tucked securely away where it couldn't affect him or his plans.

His apartment had been very quiet ever since he had come home to dress for their date. No sign of Rick or Leah, although both of their bedroom doors were closed. As he was dressing he realized he couldn't find his favorite cuff links, diamond-studded antiques. He knew they should be in the ashtray on his bureau, the only place they ever were. Irritated, he then noticed a tie clip was missing. It had been a gift from Tiffany's. What the hell . . . ?

Leah.

He suddenly knew she had taken the items.

Jack was rigid with fury. He was out of his bedroom and at her door a moment later, yanking it open. He stared, stunned. A man was on top of her, humping away, while she encouraged him with soft sex words and her hands and body.

"What is going on?" he roared.

The man leapt off Leah, going beet-red. He was short and paunchy except for skinny legs and a skinny, rapidly deflating dick. He hopped into his pants frantically.

Leah smiled, stretched, and slowly sat up.

"I don't believe this!" Jack yelled.

The man was grabbing his shirt. "I didn't know she was married. I swear we never met before. I swear!" he cried, edging for the door.

"Get the fuck out of my house," Jack snarled, and the man fled with a hasty snatch for his shoes.

"I'm a big girl," Leah said, making no effort to cover

her nakedness. "If Rick can play around with his friend, why can't I?"

"Because somehow I think there's a difference here," Jack said stiffly. He was furious.

"Honey," Leah said, standing and stopping the man from exiting. "Not so fast."

The man pulled out a wallet and counted out a number of bills, Jack watching incredulously, and stuffed them into Leah's hand.

"Later, doll," Leah called after him.

"Put on some clothes," Jack snarled, clenching his fists. She was whoring out of his home!

She slipped on a robe. "What's the matter, Bro? Gettin' excited?"

"I want you and your things out of here by tonight," Jack managed. "I can't deal with this!"

"So now big brother's going to turn his back on poor little sister," she drawled sarcastically. "Did I even ask to be brought here? Did I? And now you're kicking me out?"

"You're incorrigible," Jack grated. "Just like our mother."

"And you're so high and mighty. You got a different piece in here every night—and you pay them just like my johns pay me. With a good word, a favor, a walk-on. You hypocrite! You're no different from them."

Jack controlled himself, because he actually wanted to drag her by the hair and throw her out of his apartment.

At that precise moment the front door opened, and Rick and Lydia walked in laughing, their bodies touching, Rick's arm around her shoulders. Jack ignored them.

"And what happened to my cuff links and tie clip? Are you a thief as well as a whore?"

Rick put his arm protectively around Lydia and backed her down the hall.

"I don't know anything about your damn cuff links," Leah shouted angrily.

"Dammit," Jack shouted and left, slamming her door closed.

"Er . . . hi, Jack," Rick said uneasily, his arm still around Lydia. "What's going on?"

"Nothing."

Rick and Lydia exchanged glances. "Maybe we'd better leave," Rick said to Lydia.

"That's all right."

Leah appeared, her face flushed with anger. "I'm gonna tell you what I think, you bastard!" she hissed. "You come into my life and turn it upside down. You drag me out here. I didn't want to come. And now you're throwing me out. Where am I supposed to go? *Where?*"

"Rick," Lydia said softly, tugging his hand. Rick stared from his sister to Jack, both obviously furious, and he took Lydia's hand and they slipped out of the apartment.

"Back to New York," Jack said.

"You lousy bastard! You think I can go back there? My pimp will kill me—he will fucking slit my throat!"

Jack stared.

Leah had tears in her eyes. "I can't go back there."

"You can't stay here," Jack said tersely.

"You wanted your family, but now that you see what it's like, we're not good enough for you," she said bitterly.

"Not *we,*" Jack said. *"You.* Why, Leah? Why did you have to turn a trick? Christ, I give you money, a place to stay, you had Hamilton—why?"

"It's my profession," she snapped. "What am I supposed to do, sit around on my ass, bored all day?"

"I can't believe this."

"I like it! It turns me on—it's forbidden, and it's always different."

"You're not even going to try and reform, are you?"

"Fuck you!"

"I'll set you up in your own apartment," Jack said. "I'll buy you a two-year lease. Give you some money to get started. But that's it. You're on your own. Unless you want to get into the business in one way or another, in which case I will gladly pull strings for you."

Leah looked at him a long moment, then smiled. "That's a pretty good deal," she said.

"Damn right," Jack retorted.

"Maybe I was wrong. You're okay," she said. "My own place?"

She was just like Janet. Selfish and self-centered. Pathetic. Suddenly, for the first time, Jack felt sorry for her, sorry for Janet. "Look," he heard himself say, his voice surprisingly gentle. "Let's not fight. Let's release the past."

She looked at him as if he were crazy.

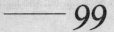

99

*A*nother extension.

Another Beverly Hills home.

"Bill, goddamn it, go pick that up," Vince said harshly, snapping. He watched as the gofer ran to pick up some wrappers one of the guys had left lying around. "Doug, when I said sweep up all that debris, I meant it," he said.

He walked around the wing they had started to frame, making sure they were leaving the site impeccably clean and spotless. Hills people had fits when there was even one cigarette butt lying in the drive—even the service driveway.

He saw a nail and picked it up. A flat tire would be just great. Straightening, he glimpsed long female calves. Standing, he started, did a classic double-take.

The woman was auburn-haired, tall, sleek, perfect in profile, and she was talking to the gardener who had been trimming hedges all day in an elaborate modern swirling design. She was obviously the missus of the house—and what a missus.

Thirty or so, he guessed, maybe close to forty. She had a Jacqueline Bisset look. She dismissed the gardener and turned her head and body slightly. Their gazes met.

Beautiful, stunning, impossibly sexy.

She smiled and strode forward. The way she walked reminded him of someone. An aggressive, confident walk. Her body was strong and athletic. Desire rose.

"Hello, I'm Shanna Jacobsen. Are you the foreman?" Her accent actually had a touch of Ireland. Her eyes were gray, like a winter sea. God, what he wouldn't give to fuck her.

"Yeah, Vince Spazzio. Please to meet you, Mrs. Jacobsen."

She looked right into his eyes. "You can call me Shanna —everyone does," she said.

He hadn't put his shirt back on, but she hadn't looked at his chest once. It was disappointing. "Thanks," he said.

"Let's discuss some ideas I've had since I last saw the architect," she said, smiling and starting toward the framing.

Vince followed eagerly.

*M*elody knew she had to be very careful.

Had to stay in character.

She had thought it all out.

Seduction wouldn't work—it would be too obvious.

"Well," she said, smiling, "that takes care of that." She had just removed the last of their dinner dishes. "More wine, Peter?"

"Yes, please," he said, looking at her intently.

He was sitting on the sofa, relaxed, denim thighs spread. Melody poured the full-bodied Cabernet, leaning close enough to almost touch him. Her hair did. Then she moved to sit next to him.

"Dinner was great, Melody," Peter said, shifting his arm casually behind her on the sofa.

"Thank you," she said demurely.

He was facing her. "Quite a package. Even cooks."

She dropped her gaze.

He caught her chin and kissed her for a long time. He was a good kisser, Melody decided—not that she had very much experience. The kiss was arousing. Not like Jack's, of course. She stiffened at that thought and the timing was perfect; Peter had just slid one of his large hands over one of her large breasts. He removed his palm and moved away, sighing. "Melody."

"Peter, please understand," she said.

He didn't look at her. "I guess I do."

This time she took his hand, forcing him to look at her. "I'm not like most of the girls in this town, and I don't want to be like them. I need to love the man I sleep with."

Peter half smiled. "Yeah. Well, I guess you can't blame me for trying." He leaned closer. His eyes had picked up the tone of his shirt. "You really turn me on, Melody, and that's not a line." He kissed her again.

"I guess I'd better go," he said reluctantly quite a bit later.

Melody wished she could let him stay. She remembered how it had felt to have an orgasm with a man inside her, and God, she needed that again. But The Plan was more important. And he was leaving. *Now* was the time to act.

"Peter, before you go, can we talk business?"

"Sure," he said, leaning back against the couch.

Melody suddenly noticed the outline of a massive erection. The denim hid nothing. Then she realized she was staring, and she averted her eyes, blushing profusely.

"I told you," Peter said softly, "you really turn me on."

Melody met his gaze. The sight of *that* had tightened her unbearably, but The Plan was the most important thing in her life. Melody was not experienced, but she was clever. Right now when Peter wanted her he was most malleable. So she looked away at her lap, where she clutched her hands; and when she spoke, it was in her most fragile, timid voice. "Peter, I need your help."

He thought her eyes were so guileless, so wide and innocent and blue. "I'd love to help."

"I need you to get a video for me, Peter."

Peter listened.

"I know who made it, and he's here in Hollywood . . . well, he lives in Bel Air—or he used to. The thing is, he won't sell it to you or anything. You need to steal it."

"I see." Peter studied her. "Why?"

Melody gulped. "Because I'm Jack's manager and friend and right now he's very vulnerable and the video is very damaging. I want to destroy it."

"Porn?"

"Yes. How did you know?"

"His past is no secret—at least not the drugs and alcohol. The wild parties? It wouldn't be the first time a young, good-looking, struggling actor living on the wild side made a couple of dirty movies for a few bucks."

Peter contemplated the floor, and Melody waited anxiously. "Peter? Are you upset with me?" Her voice was small and childish.

"No." A half smile. "I admire your loyalty. And I'll be happy to help."

"Thank you."

"But my fee is another night like tonight," he said, suddenly mischievous.

"Dinner?"

"Dinner and your company."

Melody smiled. "Well, I think that can be arranged." She hesitated. There was one more crucial thing. "Peter, I don't want Jack to know about this. He's so pressured right now. I don't want him to worry. When it's all over and I've destroyed the video, I'll tell him."

"My lips are sealed," Peter said.

101

*I*t was easy to forget his role—his *goal*— and he let himself, because it was to his benefit to do so. It was easy, too easy, to really enjoy himself in her company. She was funny in a very wry way. She laughed at herself and at him. Making him laugh too. She was intelligent and opinionated, *very opinionated,* but somehow he found it stimulating. They discussed the industry, President Reagan, reincarnation. They argued about everything—with enjoyment. He found, to his complete surprise, that underneath her tough, aggressive facade, she was a romantic; and she found that under his easy, life-is-a-ball charm, he was cynical and wary.

Earlier that evening they had started to get into a conversation that was too risky. She had asked him about *Berenger.* He had tensed, feeling a reflexive anger that he got under control and managed to shrug off. For some damn reason he wanted her to know that the film was good, damn good, and that he had given his best performance ever in it, Oscar-contender stuff. He wanted to share that, wanted maybe to impress her, but he couldn't—he had to pretend indifference.

"Aren't you disappointed?" she had asked.

"Oh, sure." He shrugged. "I got paid."

Later, cautiously, he asked her if her mother knew about him. He wasn't sure, but the look she gave him was funny, pointed. "Why would she know you? She hates cop shows."

"I like the way you stroke my ego, Belinda," he managed lightly. So much for that! Belinda hadn't told him what he wanted to know—if Nancy knew they were dating. "Is she still staying with you?"

Another funny look. "Yes."

This was a problem Jack had been considering. If Nancy saw him, the roof would go down. Belinda obviously had no idea about their brief encounter seventeen years ago. Of course, he couldn't tell her; it would be taking a needless risk that could ruin everything. But why was his conscience crucifying him for the omission?

She asked him about his past, about the long lean years when he'd been struggling to make it. For some unfathomable reason, he didn't want more lies between them. He didn't want to give her the same cock-and-bull bio he gave the world. Instead he casually changed the topic to one he could discuss, one where he had nothing to hide, and he found himself eagerly talking about Rick.

"I'd like to meet him," Belinda said later, just as they reached her house. They had been strolling along the beach, and now they paused on her back doorstep. "He sounds like a carbon copy of you. Imagine, a chance to meet the adolescent Jack Ford! I'll bet you were dangerous even back then."

"Do you think I'm dangerous, Belinda?"

She laughed, a short sound. "Very. Worse—you know it."

He smiled. "I was a terror," Jack said, his mind irrepressibly turning to carnal thoughts again. Carnal thoughts and Belinda. "Because I cared only about myself—about what I wanted."

"And now you care about what other people want?"

"I care about what *you* want," he said, his tone taking on the rough edge of sandpaper.

"Jack."

If it was a protest, he ignored it. His hands found her shoulders. "You know I care about what you want."

She swallowed, tense beneath his fingers. "If you cared," she managed, "you wouldn't push me like this."

"Am I pushing you, Belinda?" he asked, leaning forward, his hold tight now, and nipping her throat. She swayed irresistibly toward him. He emitted a groan. He rubbed his face in her bare decolletage; her hands wove into the thick strands of his hair.

"Jack."

"Let me make love to you," he whispered, languidly rubbing his cheek against the top part of her chest. "I need you so much. I want you." Shuddering, he dropped a kiss in the deep valley of her cleavage. Tonight he wasn't sure he could find the discipline and self-control he'd exercised on their last date. Tonight there would not be any more cock-teasing. "You want me too, Belinda," he murmured. His mouth moved against her breast as he spoke. She shuddered.

"So good," Jack whispered, nuzzling her, his hands moving to her waist. "You know how good I can make it. This time, Belinda, I'll make it even better—I promise."

"I've never"—she gasped as he nipped her breast—"had any doubts about your prowess or generosity in bed."

"Good," he murmured, taking her nipple into his mouth, silk and all. He backed her against the door. Her hands had found his hips and were pulling demandingly; but he resisted, not pressing against her, enjoying the teasing, the frustration, the anticipation. She began stroking hard, tight circles on his buttocks. He moved the silk blouse out of his way. He grasped both nipples between his fingertips, burying his face in her neck. She moaned, her hands sliding to the front of his pants, sliding over his huge erection. It was nearly his undoing.

"Damn you, Jack."

"Who's pushing now," he managed hoarsely, squeezing her nipples, wondering if he might do something very adolescent—like come in his pants. "Lady, this is getting dangerous—we'd better go inside."

The words died a fast death. Belinda had yanked his zipper down, letting his thick organ rocket out. "Ah, shit," he said.

"Show me some caring now, Jack—*now.*"

As he pushed her skirt up to her hips, he had one last lucid thought—right on her back doorstep with her mother inside somewhere—but she was holding him, running her nails over the tip, and he jammed his thigh between hers. "I want to fuck you the way you deserve, Belinda," he said. "Lady, you've got me in a topspin."

She hooked one long leg around his hips, giving him a

view of dark tangled hair and a glistening clitoris. "What are you waiting for?"

He pushed her hard against the door, bending, taking his prick and jamming it against her, thrusting in. "No more running, Belinda."

"I can't run, Jack, not tonight."

Neither one smiled.

She locked her legs around his hips. They were kissing, teeth catching, tongues warring, entwining, while Jack pumped into her. "I'm not going to last," he gasped against her mouth.

"Neither am I," she gasped back.

Moments later they were both crying out, her wet, tight little cunt contracting around him while he exploded, sending blast after blast of hot sperm deep inside her. They were both panting, Belinda slipping naturally to her feet, his face buried in her neck. She smelled so good. She felt so good. Good. It was all he could think. Good. Belinda.

Eventually he became aware of her strokes on his back, on his neck—wonderful love touches—in his hair, on his buttocks. He felt his prick stirring, hardening, growing against her belly. She felt it, too, because she laughed softly. "You're so easy," she whispered.

He bit her shoulder playfully.

"Ow," she cried, pulling away.

He lifted her in one motion into his arms, ignoring her protest. "Is this door locked?"

"No."

He carried her inside, entering on the upper level. He laid her on the big Victorian bed, kneeling over her, kissing her sensually, gently. When he opened his eyes, his mouth still playing on hers, he found himself looking into her brown eyes. For a moment, maybe, their souls—or something—touched. With a brief flash of guilt Jack closed his eyes, nuzzling her neck and licking her ear. "This time we'll take forever," he murmured.

"Yes . . . forever."

102

*T*he first words she heard were "Oh, shit."

Belinda sighed, eyes closed, then felt a pair of strong male arms wrap around her. Someone said, "Damn, I have to leave!"

She became more awake. Jack was holding her, kissing her neck, and a wonderful hard-on pressed against her thigh. The room was light, meaning it was morning (had she gotten any sleep?), and she turned her face to his for a kiss. He leapt out of bed. "I have to go, damn!"

She smiled, quite satiated, stretched, and watched him stride to the bathroom, wonderfully muscled, an Adonis in the flesh. Coherent cognition set in. She knew she was a fool. Oh, the worst sort of fool! But to hell with it. She liked sex—so why not have it with the man who turned her on the most? Why deny herself? She was an adult, a liberated woman—she could handle it.

She had to be able to handle it.

Fool, her inner voice said. Too easy. You were too easy, and now the chase is over. Fool! You just wait and see!

Jack reappeared, eyes bright and wandering over her. "I don't want to go," he said.

"Why are you running like this? Stay." She patted the bed. As if she didn't know the reason for his hasty retreat. Tell me, Jack, she silently commanded, tell me now. Tell me the truth.

"I can't. It's seven. Got a meeting at eight." Total lie.

"Okay, I'm going back to sleep." Belinda snuggled back down, knowing it would be impossible to sleep. She couldn't seem to take her eyes off him. She was such a fool she didn't care that he was lying to her.

He sat on the bed and pulled on his socks. "What are you doing Friday? I know this great spot—you'd love it."

"I have plans."

He looked at her, then stood and pulled on his pants. "Okay. Saturday—we'll leave first thing in the morning. It's out of town." He grinned. "Okay?"

She hesitated. "Jack, I'm going out of town this weekend. I'm leaving Friday, and won't be back till Sunday night."

His face fell. He turned away, picked up his shirt and shrugged it on. "Where are you going?" he asked casually.

"Santa Barbara."

Jack laughed. "That's where I wanted to take you." He looked at her. "I have a house up there."

"Oh."

"Can't you break your plans?" he asked after a pause. "And come with me?"

"No."

"I see." He reached for his belt. "You're going with your mother?"

"No, I'm not."

He yanked the belt together and stared intensely. "Who are you going with?"

She hesitated. There was no point in lying. "It's not really your business, but I'll tell you. Adam Gordon."

Jack stared. Then he turned away rigidly. "I don't fucking believe it," he said, grabbing his jacket and whirling back. "You gonna fuck him too?"

Belinda sat up, clutching the covers. "You don't own me. We've dated a few times, slept together once."

"Twice," he spat out. "Aspen. Remember?"

"I remember. Why are you so bent out of shape?"

"Me? Bent out of shape? I couldn't care less if you go up to Santa Barbara with that faggot. Go right ahead." At the door he paused. "Have a good time, Belinda."

He slammed it after him.

He had just effectively ruined her day.

But maybe it was her fault. Why had she decided at that exact moment to accept Adam's invitation? Adam had been pestering her all week. She loved Santa Barbara, and she had put off telling Adam she couldn't make it. She really hadn't wanted to go—not with Adam. It was her sane self that had just decided to go—her protective self, the side of her that knew she was hopelessly falling for a man who could only hurt her. She should go with Adam. It was not just unwise to let Jack get too close, especially so soon; it was dangerous.

Still, she hated playing games.

She got up, naked, and ran to the window to call him and tell him she'd changed her mind. He was trotting down the stairs, looking furious. She didn't call out. Her pride demanded she remain aloof, even if they were sleeping together. God forbid he should know how much she wanted to be with him. God forbid he should know . . . and lose interest.

She hated herself for being that way, but she was too afraid not to.

Not just because she wanted him so much.

But because there was the baby to think of.

103

"Damn it!" Jack said fiercely, and then a moment later after a fruitless search through his drawers, he let loose with a string of curses. He couldn't find his favorite sweatshirt for running.

He flopped on the bed, tense and coiled. To hell with it, he decided, and put on his least favorite sweats, and then he was out the door and running, right down Wilshire, hard, very hard, until sweat was pouring down his body and dripping off his chin. Forty minutes later, as he stripped for a shower, he realized he did not feel better.

His mood had been like this since he'd left her yesterday morning.

Today was Thursday.

Tomorrow she was going away for the weekend with another man.

Every time he thought of them together he was assailed with hot jealousy and fury. He had been so sure things were going smoothly—better than smoothly. He knew his charm, its effects, how persuasive he could be. He hadn't quite expected her to give in and go to bed with him again so easily, but maybe deep inside he had known she would. And it had been so very fine. Finer than fine. How could she even contemplate sleeping with another man?

His ego was seriously bruised. Worse, this was not the game plan. How was he going to get her to marry him if she saw other men? It never once occurred to him that she would spend the weekend with Gordon and not sleep with him. After all, she was a woman, he a man, and this was 1988.

To make matters worse, Jack was very aware of himself, and he knew he was jealous. Jealousy was not a part of the plan. It was something he had not counted on.

Tomorrow was Friday, and everything was set.

They would leave for Santa Barbara at noon, arriving by two or three if the traffic was good. They would settle in, then walk on the beach before cocktails. Adam had hired a caterer to do an intimate dinner for two, starting with Cristal champagne and canapés, then a delicate asparagus appetizer, a Caesar salad for two, grilled king salmon steaks with an excellent Chardonnay, chocolate mousse for dessert. More champagne after dinner. He didn't intend to get her drunk, just high. A moonlit stroll and maybe skinny-dipping. Or the Jacuzzi. By midnight she would be in his bed—happily.

Although conventional sex bored him, he knew all the right moves, and she was going to receive each and every one.

When he was through, she would never know what had hit her.

He was so excited he canceled his last appointment for the day and went home early.

Where Cerisse was.

The problem was, she didn't care what she brought.

Belinda stared at the open suitcase on her bed with irritation. How had she gotten herself into this? She didn't want to spend the weekend with Adam. Who was she fooling? Oh—right!—Jack. She was fooling Jack, at her own expense. She had too much pride, which was and always had been her problem. A normal person would have backed out, but here she was, committed to a weekend she was dreading. And she absolutely would kill if Adam lay one hand on her.

She threw a sweater into the suitcase, then jeans, sneakers, boots, a pile of G-strings, some shirts. She slumped in a chair.

Maybe she should cancel, stay home, and when Jack asked—if he ever called again—she wouldn't lie, not really; she would say she had stayed home because she had decided at the last minute to work. Now, that was plausible.

She remembered Jack's temper tantrum before he had left yesterday morning, and she started to smile. He had acted jealous. Very jealous. That was a good sign, wasn't it? As much as she hated playing games—and she was now becoming a master game-player—he was jealous, which meant that he cared to some degree. So maybe she had better go, if only to keep his interest up.

Then she grew sick and tired of herself. This was ridiculous. She was falling badly for that playboy bum. Badly? Hah! *Completely* was more like it. And as a result she was acting in a manner completely out of character, resorting to tactics she couldn't stand, losing self-respect and her own integrity. She had even gone and gotten herself pregnant. She wasn't going to play any more goddamn games. It just wasn't her style.

What would Jack do if he knew what she was hiding from him?

Belinda grimaced. The question was pointless. She could never tell him. Ever. It would be the worst kind of manipulation.

And that wasn't her style either.

Mary went shopping.

She went to Giorgio. She didn't find a thing that didn't make her look like a cow. From there she went across the street to Armani. Hours later, she hit Neiman-Marcus. In Vicky Tiel she struck pay dirt.

The dress was a bright royal blue. The bodice was extremely low, strapless, revealing most of her white bosom. Her best asset. The waist was nipped in, making it look smaller than it was. The skirt billowed out, cut on a bias, revealing all of both her calves and ankles, which were perfectly shaped, and then her right knee and half that thigh. Somehow, it was a knockout. She looked ten pounds thinner. Gorgeous.

The saleslady sent her downstairs to a makeup artist at Chanel. Worried about the time, Mary nevertheless had her makeup done from scratch—soft shades of pink for her cheeks and lips, subtly done eyes in a soft blue that she had never known she could wear. It was dynamite with her big brown eyes, making them look bigger and browner. When she went home she showered carefully, so as not to ruin her face, then blow-dried her hair upside down to give it volume. She slipped on the dress, added several dabs of her new perfume, and waited for the car Abe was sending to pick her up.

He was taking her to dinner. He had told her to get dressed up, and when Mary had said she didn't have anything to wear, he had given her a thousand dollars. Mary had tried to protest. But she was secretly thrilled.

"I want to show you off." Abe had grinned, pulling her close and fondling her.

The fondling quickly led to another round of mindless, orgasmic sex. "I can't seem to keep it down around you," he said later, chuckling.

"I don't mind," Mary had said truthfully.

She didn't mind the money, either, or the silver stretch limo that arrived shortly after she was ready.

Wouldn't it be fantastic if they ran into her mother?

The small pickup truck rolled to a stop in front of the closed gates of a Bel Air residence. On the side of each door was written LOS ANGELES MUNICIPAL WATER DISTRICT. A serviceman got out of the truck and rang the intercom.

"Yes?"

"L.A. Municipal Water."

The gates opened. Peter Lansing got back into the truck and drove through.

Bart Shelley was a Hollywood director. He had been around for years. He was still around. He no longer did feature films; he did miniseries for TV. He was well respected in the industry, despite his bisexuality. His reputation for wild parties and orgies was known by all the insiders.

Nine years ago, just before Jack had given up drugs and alcohol, according to Melody, he had been a paid escort invited to one of these parties. The services he performed on several women guests at one and the same time were videotaped. At the time Jack had not been aware of the camera. He had told Melody he was pretty much out of it, the whole thing a blurry haze. It was only when Shelley had invited him back and run the video for him and tried to grab his crotch that Jack realized he'd been filmed. Shelley, being a great director, had gotten some very good shots. Close-ups. Worse. There was another man there who had also been screwing the two women. The man had tried to screw him. That had been easily circumvented. But the way Shelley had put together the film, it looked as if the climax of the orgy was a homosexual coupling.

Jack, of course, had rejected Shelley's overtures. In fact, he had run—literally—from the house at the end of the film.

Lansing knew that the screening room was on the third floor, last door on the right. He knew that all the films were stored there. He stopped the truck in front of a large brick home with huge white pillars in the Greek Revival style, which looked as if it had been transplanted from the antebellum south, along with the magnolia trees gracing the entry and the carefully designed gardens.

"Yes?" The man at the front door was clearly a servant.

"There's no cause for alarm," Peter said slowly. "But there might be some leakage of sodium chloride into the drinking supply of the houses in this area. I need to run some tests on the tap water at various locations in the house."

"Leakage of sodium chloride?"

"Again, there's no need for alarm. However, we are advising that you drink bottled water for the next few days, if you don't already—until we reach a definite conclusion."

"Come right in," the servant said worriedly.

Melody was humming.

Peter Lansing had told her not to worry. He would get the video one way or another. And that was a promise.

She smiled.

Just you wait, Jack.

104

"Are you going to do it?" Lydia asked.

He looked into her wide brown eyes, full of faith, and he nodded grimly.

"I'm so proud of you," she whispered, hugging him. And then she ran out the door, leaving Rick alone with his brother, who had disappeared into his room.

It was Friday afternoon, and this was not how Rick wanted to spend it. But he had felt so guilty ever since he had overheard Jack accusing Leah of stealing the cuff links and tie clip. (Did he notice a crystal ashtray gone as well?)

He had finally blurted out the whole thing to Lydia. She was aghast but not accusing.

"You have to tell him," she said firmly. "Come clean."

He was relieved to have gotten the terrible burden off his chest and relieved that she wasn't too disgusted to love him anymore. "Aren't you . . . don't you wonder how I could have done it?"

"Yes," she said. "Do you want to tell me?"

He nodded. They were walking in the park after school, oblivious of everyone else. "I didn't like Jack. Maybe I hated him. He has everything. He's rich. I starved my whole life. It seemed like no big deal, to take a couple of things so I would have money to party."

"I understand," she said softly. They were holding hands.

"But now I sort of like him." Rick felt embarrassed, so he stole only a glance at her. "And he is my brother."

"And he does love and trust you," Lydia pointed out. That, of course, clinched it.

"Jack?" He stood in Jack's open doorway, very tense and anxious.

Jack looked up, throwing a shirt on the floor. "Can't ever find a fucking thing," he growled. "I'm gonna fire the fucking maid. Maybe if she spoke fucking English, it would help."

Rick wondered why he had been walking around like a wounded grizzly bear for two days now, when for the week before that he had been nothing but quick smiles. "Can we talk?"

Jack sighed, softening. "Yeah, sure, kid. Come on in." He looked at him quizzically. "You look like you think I'm going to bite your head off."

"Maybe you will," Rick said on a deep breath. Then he blurted out, "I took the cuff links and tie clip. I'm sorry!"

"I don't understand."

Rick had never felt so low. "I hocked them. For extra money."

A muscle on the side of Jack's face twitched. "I see."

"I'm sorry," Rick said again.

Jack came forward, looking hurt and wounded. "Why? I trusted you. I gave you just about everything—I would have given you more, but I thought it wouldn't be healthy. Why did you do it?"

Rick faltered. "I needed money. To party. I hated it here at first. It seemed like you had so much. I didn't think you'd even notice or care. I'll pay you back. I'll get a job after school and pay you back."

Jack stared, then smiled faintly. "You don't have to pay me back. You told me the truth, and that's payment enough."

They looked at each other, and Rick flushed under his brother's intense gaze. Then Jack said in his familiar big-brother tone, "So what do you mean by *party*?"

Rick went redder. "Uhhh . . ."

"What? Booze? Drugs? What?"

Rick knew there was no escape now. "Just some brews and pot."

Jack's eyes narrowed. "Diamond-studded cuffs and a tie clip would buy a lot of brews and pot."

"A little coke," Rick said miserably. After all, everyone in Hollywood did coke—except his brother, of course.

"A little coke," Jack said, folding his arms. "You snort, shoot—or what?"

"Just snorting," Rick said quickly. "And a little free-basing—everybody does it."

Jack stared thoughtfully. "Go get your coat," he said.

"But—"

"Get your coat," Jack said.

Rick went and did as he was told, very aware of the fact that Jack had shut his bedroom door after he'd left, and gotten on the phone. He was perspiring, realizing he had gotten off lightly so far. But now what?

They jumped into Jack's Ferrari and headed downtown. Jack never said a word. Rick was afraid to ask where they were going. When they stopped in front of a city hospital, he felt fear. "What are we doing?" He didn't realize he was whispering.

"Come on," Jack said, getting out. "As the old adage goes—a picture is better than a thousand words."

Miserably and apprehensively, Rick followed. All he could think of was that everything had backfired. This hospital had one of those drug programs that were so popular, and Jack was going to make him attend—and maybe stay—and he hadn't even gotten to say good-bye to Lydia. Jack didn't even pause to ask directions but went right up to the second floor to a doctor's office, where they sat waiting in silence for almost a half hour. Then the doctor walked in—a well-groomed, attractive woman who did not look like a doctor, except maybe like one on *St. Elsewhere*.

"Sorry, Jack," she said, pushing strands of ash-blond hair out of her face and peering through large preppie glasses. "An emergency." She looked at Rick. "You must be Rick. Hi. I'm Dr. Edwards."

They shook hands.

Jack clapped a hand on Rick's back, and they followed Dr. Edwards into the elevator and through a maze of corridors and swinging doors, into what looked like a recovery room. Several guerneys were lined up, one suspiciously lumpy and draped with a white sheet. Edwards walked over to the lump and pulled back the sheet. Rick had no choice but to follow, because Jack was pushing him forward.

The lump was a young man, maybe five years older than Rick.

"Is he . . ." Rick felt fresh sweat break out on his entire body.

"Yes," Doctor Edwards said. "He died a few hours ago. We're waiting for the morgue boys to pick him up." She looked at Rick. "He died from a seizure. Do you know what that is?"

Rick shook his head.

"The electrical activity of his brain stopped. Just like that. Of course, he had been doing coke—just snorting it, mind you—not even that much, according to his girlfriend. A few lines. But sometimes it's fatal."

Rick knew he was going to be sick.

"What a waste," Dr. Edwards said, flipping the sheet

back up to cover the corpse completely. She looked at Jack, and they exchanged a silent communication—which Rick didn't see in his struggle not to throw up.

Dr. Edwards came to the rescue with a pan just as Rick could contain himself no longer.

While Rick heaved, Jack met her eyes again and mouthed a silent thanks. Louise had not been thrilled to participate in his scheme, but she had succumbed. Whether to his persuasive charm or to her own love of life, he didn't know—although he suspected the latter.

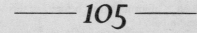

105

"*V*ince, I know it's late and you've finished for the day, but would you mind putting up a picture for me?"

His crew was already in their cars, heading out. Vince paused by the side of his truck, drowning in Shanna Jacobsen's gray eyes—eyes the color of a winter sea, and just as fathomless. She smiled and he smiled back, nodding.

He followed her back to the house. She was wearing short shorts and he could see the bottoms of her perfect buttocks. His pants grew tight. She was not wearing a bra under the thin cotton tank top—that he had noticed several hours before, when she had appeared to watch them work for a few minutes. She had small, young, pointy breasts. Her nipples had been hard, and he had tried not to look, unsuccessfully. Now he watched her swinging ass and wondered how he was going to manage not to blush when she noticed he had an interested erection.

Of course, there was always the possibility that she wanted to seduce him.

But he didn't think so. He had met Mr. Jacobsen several times. He was forty or so and very attractive—tanned, fit, polished, handsome. Shanna wasn't like the other Hollywood wives who had wanted his ass, what with their fat or bald or bizarre husbands. But he grew very hopeful when she started up a huge curving staircase and threw a casual glance over her shoulder, gray eyes seeming soft and amused.

Her bottom swung inches from his face once he got two steps behind her.

He wasn't sure he had ever seen such tight shorts. They were riding high into the crack between her cheeks.

They walked down a hall plastered with modern art—prints, paintings, and sculptures—and then she swung open a door and they stepped into what was clearly the master suite.

He'd seen "California kings" before, but this bed had to be a king and a half.

"The picture goes on that wall," she said, her voice soft and lilting, with a touch of humor. He quickly looked away from the bed. The painting was somewhat abstract, but there was no mistaking the subject—two nude women, done in bold lines, reclining in each other's arms, and a nude man, very erect. A tangle of linear but living bodies.

"Uh, sure," he managed, sweating.

He noticed her crotch. The shorts looked uncomfortable. He could see how her cunt lips strained against the white fabric, clearly and suggestively outlined. "I need to get some picture hooks," he said.

"Good idea," Shanna said, moving forward—to him. She stopped a foot away, smiled into his eyes. Carelessly and, yes, with amusement, she reached out one long, manicured finger. The nail was long and coral, and with it she traced his prick from the tip to its root. Vince emitted a half groan.

She looked up. "But I have a better idea."

106

"*I* want to talk to you," Nancy said.

At her mother's tone Belinda paused. They were in the kitchen; Belinda had been making coffee. "Want a cup, Nancy?"

"No."

Belinda turned to face her mother squarely. She didn't have to be a mind reader to know exactly what was on her mind. "Fire away."

"This isn't funny, Belinda."

"No, I suppose it's not."

"He was here the other night."

"I'm a big girl, Mom."

"He spent the night."

"It's not your business."

"Belinda! I'm trying to protect you! Just how involved are you with him? It wasn't the first time—was it?"

"No," she said, her jaw tensed. She was angry. "It wasn't the first time, and it won't be the last. He's too good to pass up, Mom. Oh, but I forgot—you know that already!"

Nancy paled, then flushed angrily. "Do you know what your father would do if he knew the two of you were seeing each other?"

Belinda was very attentive now. "I hadn't really thought about it."

Nancy laughed. A short and nervous laugh. "Well, he'd certainly do something!"

"Probably shoot Ford," Belinda murmured, something inside her twisting cruelly with dread. "Are you going to go running to Abe, Mom?"

"I'm only doing what I think is best for you."

"Are you going to tell Abe?"

Nancy hesitated. "No. Belinda, you can end this now, before it goes too far."

She almost said, It's already gone too far. But she bit off the words. "Nancy, I don't appreciate you intruding into my private life."

"I'm only trying to protect you," Nancy said. "I don't want you to make the same mistakes I made. Don't be a fool, Belinda."

"I think you've said enough." Belinda was furious. "If you're my guest, you should respect my privacy."

"Your guest? I only came to take care of you! But you seem to be well on the road to recovery, so I think I'll go back to L.A."

"That's a good idea."

Nancy turned angrily, but at the door she paused. "I really have only your best interests at heart."

Belinda watched Nancy leave. She knew her mother was telling the truth—she believed Jack would use her and hurt her. But how many times did she have to hear this tune?

She sat down.

She couldn't tell Jack about their child, and even if she could and did, she had no idea how he'd feel. She guessed he wouldn't care much. She was certain he wouldn't believe it was his.

And Nancy? Her mother would be horrified.

She thought about Abe. She was finally giving him his grandchild and heir. She knew that Abe had known about Nancy and Jack's affair—she had found that out from her mother the night of Ted Majoriis's party. Nancy had said he'd never forgiven her, and that sounded like Abe . . . Belinda bit her lip. She had not contemplated it before, but suddenly she knew her father wouldn't be thrilled that his grandchild and heir was the son or daughter of the man who had cuckolded him. But just how adverse would Abe's reaction be?

I'll just keep it a secret, she thought grimly. Oh, God, how had this entire tangled web happened? She realized her hand was protectively splayed on her abdomen, and she had to smile. Another first. She was about to become a single mother, something no one would have ever predicted regarding her. And she wanted this baby. Fiercely.

Belinda's doorbell rang.

Annoyed, she strode to the hallway and opened the door.

"Hi," Jack said.

Every fiber of her being went tense. Even her heart for one moment; then it pounded madly. "Hello, Jack," she said as evenly as she could.

"Can I come in?"

She hesitated, then stepped aside and let him walk past her. She followed his gaze to her pile of luggage. His face was without expression as he walked farther into her house. He paused, staring out at the surf and sails, then turned to face her. His gaze swept briefly over her tight denim jeans, the skintight black turtleneck. Belinda folded her arms. She wanted an apology but didn't expect one. "What are you doing here?"

"I'm sorry I flew off the handle."

Their gazes met and held. She felt a shiver of anticipation and pleasure. Every time she saw him she marveled anew at how attracted she was to this man. And not just physically. If, she supposed, he stayed away for a few years, she would probably be able to escape his dangerous pull. "Apology accepted," she said, letting her arms drop to her sides. "We had such a wonderful night," she heard herself saying, unable to stop. "It was a shame it had to end the way it did."

"You're the one who jumped into my bed while planning on sharing Gordon's."

"Don't you dare go judging me—you, Mr. Pussyman of the century! And I didn't jump into your bed—you seduced me!"

His fists clenched, but he controlled himself—admirably, she thought. He looked at her luggage, then exploded into three hard, swift strides that carried him to her, his hands like vises on her shoulders. *"Don't go,"* he said urgently.

She looked at him, feeling like a liar, which she was, if silence could be a lie.

"Don't go," he said, his tone becoming less urgent, more seductive. His face came closer; his breath was warm and sweet. She looked into leaf-green eyes and felt incapable of denying him anything. When his mouth came closer she closed her eyes, and the touch of his lips was soft, a baby's breath. He plied his mouth a little harder, and she clung to him.

He pulled away to cup her face in large, calloused hands. "You're not going," he said huskily.

"No," she breathed.

"You're going to take your stuff and put it in my car," he said.

"Okay."

"You and me—we're spending the whole damn weekend together."

"All right."

He suddenly smiled, and so did she. He pulled her closer and she came willingly, burying her face in his shoulder. So warm, so hard, so male, so . . . Jack.

She wondered if she should tell him she had canceled her plans with Adam that morning.

She wondered if she dared to tell him everything.

——— *107* ———

*T*he weekend passed too quickly.

They walked on the beach holding hands and made love. They swam in the sea and chased each other like porpoises and made love. They ate smoked salmon and bagels and cream cheese and stayed up to watch *The Late Show* and made love. They ran at sunrise along the surf; they flew a kite until they dropped; they grilled Pacific king salmon on the deck overlooking the ocean. They made love on the dunes, on the bed, in the shower, in the sand, in the Jacuzzi, and on the kitchen table, among peanut butter and banana sandwiches and frozen yogurt shakes.

It was Monday morning, but still black as pitch outside. Jack lay next to Belinda, unable to sleep, listening to the rhythm of the surf. Mingled with the sound of the waves thundering against the shore was Belinda's steady breathing. He restlessly fixed the pillow beneath his head, tossed uncomfortably, punched the pillow once, then threw it on the floor.

Shit.

He'd been awakened by that fucking dream—the dream about his mother.

Except, once again, instead of it being his mother on the porch of his house, disappearing, it had been Belinda. It was stupid, his unconscious. He didn't know what the hell it meant. He didn't *care* what it meant.

It was growing lighter out. He turned to look at Belinda, beautiful even in sleep. Today the weekend, which had been just perfect, was over. Today was Monday.

Today he was going to ask her to marry him.

The feeling in his gut was like a cramp, the feeling behind his temple a definite ache. He wouldn't think about it. About what he was doing.

He got up and silently made his way into the kitchen. He toasted an English muffin and put up water for instant hot chocolate. He stared out the window, watching the sun rise in a glorious ball of orange. He imagined proposing. More cramping. He had never thought about marriage before, not really, but maybe deep inside he had all the same feelings as anyone else—all the romantic illusions of love, hearth, and home. Why else would he be tortured by this feeling of dread?

"Jack?"

He whipped around.

"I didn't mean to scare you," Belinda said, rubbing her eyes. "Why are you up so early?"

She had thrown on one of her silk robes, paper-thin and barely belted. Her hair was disheveled, testimony to all the rocking and rolling they'd done before in bed. She squinted at him—she wore contacts and was nearsighted without them. He smiled suddenly. "Come here."

She came, protesting. "I'm tired. Let's go back to bed."

He pulled her into his embrace. He buried his face in her hair. Yesterday he'd told her he loved her, because it was important he make a declaration before proposing. Now the words popped out in a husky, unpremeditated whisper. "I love you," he said and instantly marveled at himself—at his role-playing. Because it *was* role-playing.

Except—it didn't exactly feel like any role he'd ever played before.

She clung to him, lifting her face for a kiss.

Instead he said, urgently, "Marry me."

"What?"

"I love you. Marry me. Please."

"Jack!" Belinda said, stunned. All remnants of sleep fled.

"Don't you love me?" he asked huskily, persuasively. "Just a little?"

"You have great timing," she said, but she wasn't angry. "Can't I have a cup of coffee first?"

"Not until you answer the question," he said. He couldn't have put a teasing note in his tone if he'd been up for an Oscar. Not then. "Belinda?"

"You know I do, don't you," she said, falling helplessly, a victim of Jack Ford. Hadn't she known all along it would be this way—that she was helpless to resist anything he wanted?

He smiled. Laughing slightly, triumphantly, he cupped her face. "Tell me!" he demanded.

"Yes," she said.

"Yes, you'll marry me?"

"Yes, I'll marry you, and yes, I love you," she said, watching his eyes. There was no mistaking the leap of elation. He hugged her hard, then swung her around until they knocked into the kitchen table, causing a straw catchall with all its contents to roll off and spill to the floor. He hugged her. "Today—we'll get married today."

"Today?"

"Today. We'll fly into Vegas—just you and me and a couple of witnesses off the street. No press. We'll go right away."

When are you going to tell him about the baby? she asked herself. "Why are you rushing?"

"So you don't change your mind," he said, then began dragging her down the hall. "Come on. While you get dressed I'll charter a noon flight out of LAX."

"Jack," she protested, grinding to a halt. "It's not even seven. We have plenty of time."

"You're not going to change your mind?"

She should do it; she couldn't. "No, God help me, I'm not. But maybe I'd better warn you, Jack . . ."

He clasped her buttocks in his hands, pulling her tightly against him. "Uh-oh!"

"*Uh-oh* is right. Your days of other women are over. If we're getting married, this is the real thing—I won't do it half-assed."

He was amused. "Would I ask you to marry me if I wanted to screw around? I don't think any man has other women on his mind when he proposes."

"I'm serious. Marriage means commitment and fidelity."

"I agree," he said, surprising her. "And that means I'll kill you if I ever catch you with the Adam Gordons of the world."

She felt pleased. "Jealous?"

"No. Why should I be? You love me. We're getting married today. I'm very, very happy."

He loves me. We're getting married. I love him. So this is love.

Love and lies.

How could a marriage start with so many unspoken lies between them?

Tell him, Belinda. Tell him now, before it's too late.

She couldn't.

Six hours later they were married in the Happy Day wedding chapel just off the Strip in Las Vegas.

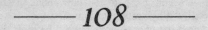

108

"*D*o come in, Miss Griffin," Abe said, smiling.

Melody walked into the spacious, airy foyer that opened onto an even larger and airier living room. Abe gestured her to a couch. On the coffee table was a pot of hot coffee and cups and saucers. "Help yourself," Abe said, his black eyes never leaving her.

"No, thank you," Melody said, primly crossing her legs and folding her hands in her lap.

"Now," Abe said, sprawling comfortably on the opposite couch. "Just what could we possibly have in common with regard to your boss?"

"His worst interests," Melody said, staring back.

"And exactly what do you mean by that?"

"I mean," Melody said slowly, "that if you want to destroy Jack, I can help. I want to help."

"How do I know you're not a spy?" Abe said.

"Because I'm going to give you something that will prove it." Melody smiled. "By destroying Jack."

"And I assume that what you want to give me is in that satchel?"

Melody pulled out the video. Abe's eyes narrowed on the tape, then lifted to meet hers. "It's Jack. Porn."

Abe smiled, then laughed. "How much?"

Melody hadn't thought about selling the information. But now it seemed like a good idea. If she had some money, a nest egg, she could quit and find another job. And be free.

The thought was intriguing—and frightening. "I don't know. I hadn't thought about it. Ten thousand?"

Abe laughed. "Five."

"Seven fifty."

"Deal. Half now, the rest after I've reviewed the goods to make sure it is what you say."

"No," Melody said softly. "All now. Cash."

Abe gave her a grudging look and took the video and walked across the room to a videocasette player. He stuck it in and turned on the TV. And when he saw what he had been promised, he laughed softly, triumphantly. He turned it off and crossed to a safe in the far wall, taking out the cash and putting it in Melody's hands. "Do you mind my asking about the history of this tape?"

"When Jack first came to L.A. he accepted money for sex. Frequently."

Abe stared. "He sold his damn prick?"

"Actually, the cover was that he was an escort. The escort service is still around. It's called Escorts International. He worked for them for two years at least that I know of. I met him in '79, and about a month later he quit."

Abe was smiling.

"He told me about it once. There were lots of parties, orgies. Men and women, together. Jack never did anything with another man, not that I know of. Sometimes there were cameras at these parties. The man who throws them is very big here in town—very respectable. You probably know him."

"Who is he?"

"Bart Shelley, the director."

Abe knew him, of course. "How did you get the film?"

"A private investigator stole it."

"Tell him thank you from me," Abe said.

When Melody left, she was feeling the best she had in years. And she was wondering when Abe Glassman would use the film. And how.

Anticipation was sweet.

109

*I*mpatiently he glanced at the huge clock in front of the store.

Five to five.

Five more minutes and he could take off his red Safeway apron and hit the streets.

Rick was on his knees, stocking the lower shelf with toilet paper. The job was okay. Boring, but that didn't matter. What mattered was that he had gotten it, and Friday he was getting his first paycheck, which according to his calculations would be only for sixty-eight dollars. But that was okay too.

He couldn't wait to see the expression on Jack's face when he handed him fifty dollars.

Jack would probably drop dead from surprise. Rick felt proud just thinking about it, a swelling kind of feeling in his chest. He knew he had really let Jack down by stealing from him, and this was the only way he could think of to redeem himself. He couldn't wait until Jack got back from Santa Barbara.

Five o'clock.

Rick ran into the back, hung up his apron, threw his nametag into his pocket, and half raced, half walked out of the store, saying good-bye to a few of the packers and checkers he knew. On the street outside he paused, glancing around.

"Rick!"

He saw the maroon Mercedes that belonged to Lydia's mom, which Lydia was driving. He rushed forward, leaping in beside her. "Hi," he said, grinning.

"Hi yourself. Hungry?" She was already tooling out of the parking lot.

"Starved."

"McDonald's?"

"Sounds perfect."

Lydia ran a red light, laughing, than squealed around a corner. Rick laughed too. She was a crazy driver. At first it had bothered him but not anymore. At the next light, which she stopped for, he threw his arm around her and kissed her. "You always smell so good," he said, almost complaining.

"Girls are supposed to smell good," Lydia retorted. "No feels in the car, Rick—you'll make me have an accident."

Rick laughed and didn't remove his hand. "Me make you have an accident? That's the funniest thing I ever heard!"

She smacked his hand, which was on her thigh, and hit the accelerator. The Mercedes barreled forward.

"Let's go to the beach after," Rick said.

"Okay."

Rick leaned his head back against the upholstery and once again thought about the expression Jack would have on his face when he gave him the money. He chuckled.

"What's so funny?"

Rick shrugged. "I guess I'm just feeling good."

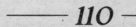

110

*T*wo nights in a row.

And last night he had told her she was a knockout.

Even his Brooklyn accent made her cream.

Mary smiled brightly as Abe handed her a glass of Chablis. The couch dipped as he sat next to her, smiling. "We're gonna celebrate tonight, doll, whaddya say?"

"Let's start right now," Mary said, snuggling closer.

He laughed. "You're the horniest broad I've ever met, Mary. And I like this dress on you."

"Thank you," Mary said. Last night he had given her more money, told her to buy herself another knockout dress. Told her he liked seeing her in dresses, low-cut ones. Mary had never felt sexier or more powerful than she did now. She had even lost two pounds. From all the fucking, she was sure.

"How old are you, Mary?"

Mary looked at him. "Twenty-four. Going on twenty-five."

"You like kids?"

She blinked. "I guess so."

"How come you don't have any?"

"I'm only twenty-four, Abe."

"How come you don't have any?" he repeated impatiently.

"Vince said we couldn't afford it yet."

"Kids are expensive," Abe said in agreement. Then he put down his beer and pulled her onto his lap. "C'mere." He pulled her bodice down, freeing her breasts. He groaned. Mary felt her groin turn to liquid. He crushed her breasts in his two large hands, his mouth on hers, his tongue invading.

He pulled her into the bedroom. They stripped hastily, breathlessly, as if they were teenagers. "Look at us." Abe laughed. "Like a couple of goddamn kids." But his eyes were dark and unlaughing as they moved over her body.

Mary laughed, too, huskily and shakily, lying back on the bed, spreading her legs. Abe loomed over her with his huge red penis swollen and stiff, looking down on her. "I've never given you head, have I, Mary?" he said.

He knelt on the bed between her thighs, pushing them farther apart. "Spread 'em as far as you can. Farther. Come on, bend your knees . . ." She gasped when his thumbs spread her pussy lips and his tongue began a slow, patient journey, traveling back and forth over her hugely swollen clit, washing it devoutly until she came, screaming.

He chuckled.

He shifted around with his head still between her legs

and his cock over her face, dipping for her mouth. She grabbed him and nibbled, then began sucking the huge hammerlike head. He grabbed her cheeks to hold her in place and licked. Mary came again with Abe's face buried in her cunt. When reality returned she became aware of Abe, thrusting deeper and deeper into her throat, half choking her. But she sucked him like a vacuum, and when he started coming in long, thick spurts, she sucked harder, as if to draw every drop out she possibly could.

"Jesus!" he said, panting.

"Mmmm."

A bit later he said, "I don't think you want kids."

She stared. "What?"

"I want to set you up, Mary. As my mistress."

She sat up. Her breasts bounced. For once Abe did not grab one. She stared.

"I'm not in love with you—I'm too old for that—but I can't get enough of you. You know that, don't you, doll?"

"Yes," she managed.

"I don't love my wife and I don't fuck her, but I'll never leave her. I want to make that clear." He grinned. "I'll give you whatever you want, Mary—cars, homes, yachts, furs, jewels. You just have to make me happy."

Mary had a vision. She saw herself stepping out of a private jet in a Russian sable, by Fendi, of course. She was wearing a Chanel dress. Around her throat was a choker of diamonds worth hundreds of thousands of dollars. She descended from the jet like royalty. Below, on the concourse, her mother—clad in blue jeans, without makeup, her hair a mess from the wind—waited, a begging supplicant. Mary looked at Abe.

He laughed. "I know how to take care of a broad, Mary."

"Yes."

"But this is an exclusive thing. No other guys. First off, because I don't ever share what's mine; second, because of AIDS."

"What about Vince?"

"He's a loser. I want to fly you and your husband down

to Vegas. You two will get divorced—I'll pay him off if there's any problems. And when we're through, Mary, you'll see, I'll be generous. You'll be way ahead of the game. Well?"

"Yes," Mary said, breathless, her heart pounding with excitement. Her cunt was so wet and tight she thought she might faint. "Yes, yes."

111

*T*he cunt.

The no-good, rich-bitch cunt.

Canceling on him at the last goddamn minute.

Adam was furious.

To make matters worse, he hadn't been able to stay in town that weekend to take her out even for a single night because he would have looked pussy-whipped for changing his plans. So he'd taken Cerisse to Santa Barbara instead of Belinda—the cunt—and of course Cerisse had been amusing, but he was temporarily stalled. Losing time.

And he'd had to wait a few days before calling her after he got back to town. So it wouldn't look like he was chasing her. And she wasn't in. Or she wasn't answering her phone. Damn and double damn.

He was not going to forget this.

Oh, no.

She wasn't answering her phone.

Either that or she was out every night.

And she hadn't returned his two calls.

Peter Lansing was pissed.

And starting to feel as if he'd been had.

Just when he was becoming furious, realizing he was

right, she called—sounding as sweet as ever, and for some reason Peter felt relief.

"You free tonight?" he asked bluntly. Wanting to see her. Horny as hell. Maybe more. There was something about Melody. Something so innocent. Sort of like the girl next door. It was possible he was starting to have feelings for her that transcended sex.

"Oh, Peter, I'm exhausted. I've been working. I need to have an early night."

He wasn't disappointed. He was angry. He hung up, positive she had used him.

How could he have been such a sucker?

Vince was so angry he put his fist through the living room wall at Ron's.

That bitch had paid him.

Fucked him and paid him.

He had thrown the money back in her beautiful Irish face.

Now he turned to face Mary, who was watching him wide-eyed. "What's the fucking rush?"

"Please, Vince. Why not?"

He couldn't believe she wanted to fly to Vegas for a divorce. "I'm not in the mood to deal with this now."

"Well, you'll have to," Mary said, standing.

He eyed her. Something had changed, and it wasn't just the designer jacket and high heels. She was glowing. She actually looked good. He suddenly had the urge for a farewell bang. And why not? It wasn't as if they were strangers —they were still married.

"You look great," Vince said.

Mary looked surprised. She was even more surprised when he came close and pulled her against him. "Vince!"

"You smell good too," he said, nuzzling her hair.

She pushed herself free. "What are you doing?"

"Old time's sake?"

"Forget it, you bastard! Look, I'm going to be honest with you, Vince. I'm seeing someone. So I want to end this as soon as possible."

"What!"

"I'm seeing someone, and there's no point in dragging this out," Mary said, smiling.

"Who?" he shouted, furious. "Who are you seeing? And how long has *this* been going on?"

"What do you care?"

"Goddammit, who the fuck is it?"

"Abe Glassman," Mary said proudly.

Abe Glassman.

Will Hayward kept repeating the name in his mind, like a litany. It was what kept him going. There were a hundred ways to do it. He had to pick only one.

"Sir?"

He focused on the woman across the counter. "I'd like a round-trip ticket to L.A."

Abe Glassman was not going to kill him.

Will was going to kill Abe Glassman.

—— *112* ——

*A*be had loaned her the silver stretch.

It cruised slowly through the brick-walled entrance and up the long, curved drive of her mother's mansion. Mary sat in the backseat, clad in a blue-and-black print dress by Ungaro, Jourdan pumps, a Chanel bag. She was admiring the ten-carat diamond pendant Abe had bought her this morning, one she had wisely not worn while with Vince. It sparkled and caught even the tiniest, faintest shaft of light. It was nearly flawless.

She realized, surprised and bemused, that she hadn't had the urge for a toot since she had started seeing Abe again.

That man was all the high she needed.

Imagine—she, Mary Spazzio, the glamorous, sexy mistress of a billionaire.

Damn Vince for being so stupidly full of macho pride.

The limo stopped. Mary waited until the driver opened her door; then she slid out. She was disappointed that her mother didn't see her arrival, but then, what did she expect? Celia to be waiting like a maid on the front steps?

A valet, someone new, let her in and told her to wait in the living room. Mary debated ignoring him. After all, she knew this house; she was the daughter; and if she wanted to, she could damn well go where she pleased. But then she decided her entrance would have more impact if she waited. Celia appeared within five minutes.

"Mary?" she asked, as if unsure of her own daughter's identity.

Mary stood casually. "Hi, Mom. I came to tell you the good news."

Unfortunately her mother looked very chic and elegant in a skintight designer jumpsuit. Chic and elegant and thin. Mary started to feel fat. Then she reminded herself that Abe thought she was perfect the way she was—he had said so. He had told her if she lost weight he would be very upset, and she instantly felt better. He thought skinny broads were ugly. She smiled.

Her mother stared at her pendant. "What is that?"

"Oh, this?" Mary lifted her hand. "A gift."

"A gift," Celia Holmes Bradbury Davis echoed.

"Yes."

"Who would give you a gift like that?"

"Abe Glassman."

Her mother's eyes popped.

Mary smiled. Triumph was sweet.

Celia found her voice. "Not *the* Abe Glassman."

"*The* Abe Glassman."

Celia recovered. "Mary—he's older than your father. And what about Vince?"

"We're getting divorced."

"Well, this is news!" She laughed, for once in her life at a loss for words.

"Abe isn't going to leave his wife, but I've decided I like being a mistress. It suits me." She grinned. "Rather, I like being *his* mistress."

Her mother had no response.

Mary started to the door, then paused and kissed her shell-shocked mother lightly, hardly touching her flesh, on each cheek, European-style. "Ciao," Mary said.

Let's see you top this one, Mom.

She laughed.

 —— *113* ——

"*W*ho are you?" Vince said, but he knew.

Abe looked at him and thought, Jesus, Mary is married to this? "Abe Glassman. Let's talk."

Vince scowled. "Me and my buddy are in the middle of dinner."

"Yeah, well, let it get cold. We got a few matters to discuss."

"I believe Mary and I already discussed them." Vince put his hand on the door. "Why don't you go back to L.A., Abe?"

"Listen, punk," Abe said. "Mary told me all about your discussion, and you're lucky I didn't break your head open for touching her—got that?"

Vince drew back. He was big and strong, but he wasn't a fighter and never had been. He instantly recognized the street-tough quality of the man standing in front of him, and his withdrawal was instinctive. He said, but not as hard as before, "She's still my wife."

"Not for fucking long."

Vince was sweating. "Say what you came for, and let me get back to my dinner."

"I want you to take off work tomorrow, and you're all gonna fly down to Vegas so you and Mary can get divorced. Got that?"

"What's the rush?"

"None of your fucking business, kid." Abe reached into his breast pocket and removed an envelope. He threw it at Vince. It hit him on the chest, but Vince caught it before it fell to the floor. "What's this?"

Abe folded his arms.

Vince opened it and looked at a stack of hundred dollar bills. He looked up.

"Count it," Abe said. "That's ten grand for a day of your time. And a no-contest divorce. You're lucky I'm feeling so generous. And if you want to stay healthy and in one piece, you take the money, put it in your bank account, and be at the LAX private terminal tomorrow at eight A.M."

Abe smiled and walked toward the door. "I can let myself out."

Vince watched him leave. He heard Ron come up behind him. Ron whistled. "Jesus! Vince, you'd better do as he says."

Vince didn't answer. He was angry because he was being strong-armed, and even angrier because he knew there was no way in hell he would turn his back on ten grand. Especially since he wanted the divorce anyway.

"Vince, you know he's superpowerful. Maybe Mafia. He'll break your legs or cut off your balls or something if you don't do as he says."

"Shut up, Ron," Vince said. Wondering how in hell Mary had managed to snag Abe Glassman. And why.

He was also figuring out how early he'd have to leave to make it to the airport by eight.

on the important negotiations, which he had been trying
for months... Abe was not several hours... after that
occurring... he worked one more... three weeks left.

114

*T*hey returned exactly one week after their wedding, on a
sunny, warm Monday afternoon. Jack dropped Belinda off
at her house, telling her he'd return that night with some of
his things. They had decided with little hassle that Jack and
Rick would move in with her, although Jack would obviously have to spend more time in L.A. when he was working. Her place was much bigger, and Rick could have the
downstairs without intruding upon their privacy.

He gave her a long, hard kiss before letting her out of
the car. Then, to his surprise, he grabbed her hand as she
was slipping out, pulled her back, and held her tight for
another minute. He nuzzled her hair and released her, gaz-
ing at her, but he found that he couldn't return her smile.

"Sure you don't want me to come and help you pack a
few things?" she said.

"I have some business to attend to first, and I think I
should break the news to Rick alone."

"Hurry back," she urged and he nodded, wondering
how any woman could look so good, so vital, so fit, so compelling. He shifted into first and cruised away.

He thought of Abe Glassman, and then he thought of
Belinda. His wife.

His thoughts strayed to the past week of sheer bliss. He
hadn't intended to spend a week with her. He had intended
to go to Glassman directly after the wedding. But somehow
it had happened—a honeymoon with Belinda Glassman, the
woman who was now his wife.

If he let himself, he knew he could fall in love with her.

He was, in fact, dangerously close to doing so.

He quickly shut off his thoughts.

He blocked out all kinds of emotions and concentrated

on the upcoming confrontation—which he had been living for, probably for the past seventeen years—ever since that cocksucker had had him worked over with brass knuckles to within an inch of his life. He felt grim. His pulse was racing. He had a fleeting image of Belinda standing at the curb, in jeans and a tank top and denim jacket, smiling, eyes shining with love, disheveled from the wind, telling him to hurry back. He imagined Glassman's face, the expression of incredulity, disbelief followed by rage, when he told him.

He couldn't do it.

Rick took the news with bemusement, a touch of indifference, and some surprise. Mostly, it seemed, he wasn't sure how he felt about moving. Jack assured him that it didn't have to be done in a day or even a week. That seemed agreeable to Rick, who finally asked, "What's she like?"

"Gorgeous," Jack said, smiling.

"I guessed that already."

"Well, she seems like a real tough cookie, but underneath she's soft as a kitten. Smart, tough, and opinionated— too damn opinionated. And," he added, remembering the movie *Splendor in the Grass,* "she's a romantic—although you'd never guess, not for a while." He realized he was smiling. He would never, ever have guessed, if they hadn't watched that tear-jerker together.

His thoughts were filled with his wife and the time they had just spent together. He relived every moment. He wondered if it was too late—if he was falling in love with her, if he was already in love with her. He could barely wait to get back to Laguna Beach. And strangely, he felt relief, now that the charade and his plan for vengeance were over.

His agent, Sanderson, called, catching him just as he was about to walk out the door—to her.

"Jack, brace yourself."

He tensed. "What's up?"

"There's an article in *The Star* about you. It's called 'My Life as an Escort.' "

The feeling that plummeted to his intestines was sick

and heavy and dread-filled. "You'd better read it, Jack. And call your lawyer. We'll sue the lousy pricks."

Jack hung up. He didn't have to read it. He knew what the article said.

And he knew who had planted it.

"If you want to see Mr. Glassman, you will have to call for an appointment," his secretary said firmly, big breasts heaving in indignation that he should attempt to storm the fortress.

He ignored her, walked past, heard her protesting, heard her calling security. He opened the door. Glassman was on the phone, cigar in his mouth. He looked up, froze, said, "Hold on, will you?" and put his caller on hold. He leaned back, looking very amused. Jack shut the door behind him and came forward, smiling tightly.

"Well, well," Glassman said. "Another surprise visit? Don't tell me you didn't learn your place, boy? At the bottom of the garbage heap?"

Jack's smile broadened. He said nothing.

Abe stopped smiling, his keen radar noting that his adversary was not afraid, nor was he angry—he was poised like a predator. Abe sat up. "What do you want? You've got about two minutes before security comes and throws you out."

"I want," Jack said slowly, "congratulations."

Abe stared, then gave a short bark of laughter. "For what? Shortest career in history?"

"For my marriage."

Abe's gaze was penetrating.

"To your daughter." Jack smiled. He laughed.

Abe lunged to his feet. *"What?"*

Jack laughed again. "How do you feel about having a grandson with the last name of Ford? Because you can bet we've been working on it."

"You little cocksucker!" Abe roared. "I don't know how you did it, but I'll undo it—before you can even blink!"

"What's wrong, Glassman?" Jack taunted. "Or should I call you Abe? No wait—Dad?"

"You have a lot of balls," Abe yelled, "to dare to use my daughter to get at me."

Jack laughed coldly. "It was a stroke of genius, wasn't it? I knew there had to be some way I could avenge myself. Appropriate, wouldn't you say?"

"You think you can win? Beat me? You think I'll stand for this? You stupid bastard! I don't know how you did it, but your marriage is over before it even begins—I can guarantee that."

Jack laughed. "How does it feel? How does it feel to have your enemy as a son-in-law? Huh? How does it feel, you fucking bastard? And I'll never agree to a divorce—never. You're stuck with me until the day you die." He was snarling.

"We'll see!" Abe growled back. "How could Belinda be such a fool to let herself be conned by you?"

"Does it really matter?" Jack asked. "And if you think you're going to have your thugs work me over again, think twice. My lawyer still has that letter telling everything, only now it's been updated. If I go, I'm taking you with me—old man."

"Get out!" Abe roared. "Get out while you can. But if you think I'll give Belinda a single penny while she's married to you, you're wrong. She gets nothing! Nothing! If she has your son—*he* gets nothing. Not one fucking penny!"

"How does it feel to lose?" Jack said brutally, and then he walked out.

But the elation he had felt in his fantasy of this moment of triumph did not surge forth.

Instead he felt sick.

115

She felt as if she hadn't slept in days. And actually, she hadn't—or not much anyway. But she wasn't tired. Her cleaning lady was coming tomorrow, but she began going through the kitchen, living room, and bedroom like a maniac, cleaning and straightening up. Her mind was on an intimate dinner for two. Contrary to what everyone believed, Belinda could cook—in fact, she was an excellent cook. She decided on pasta primavera and a Caesar salad. By candlelight.

She had an incredible urge to buy something new and sexy, a negligee. She laughed. If she did that, they wouldn't get around to eating—not food anyway.

She was married.

To a man she hadn't known for very long, but being with him was so damn perfect that it felt just like a cliché. It felt as if they had known each other their whole lives. It was *right*. She was impossibly in love, now that she had let her fear go and her emotions run free.

Jack was perfect.

Together they were perfect.

And she had made a decision. She was going to tell Jack the truth. Come clean. He would understand, she was sure of it. He would be pleased. And she was positive he would confess to his past with Nancy. He had to.

She was putting fresh sheets on the bed when the phone rang. She was tempted not to answer it—she hadn't even checked her messages—but what if it was Jack? She picked up and was instantly disappointed. It was Abe.

"Belinda, I have to see you this minute, this goddamn minute! Come down to my office!"

She sucked in her breath. Abe was not going to ruin her

day—her life. "Abe, first of all, I refuse to be ordered around by anyone. Secondly, I'm busy."

"This is fucking crucial," Abe snapped. "It's about that stud con artist you married."

She froze, just for a second. "You mean Jack. Please refrain from calling him names, Abe, or I'll hang up this goddamn minute!"

"I call 'em as I see 'em, and you know it!"

"How did you find out?"

"He came down here to tell me."

Belinda felt a tentacle of dread begin to wrap itself around her. She shook it off. "Look, I knew you would disapprove, but I love him and we're married and you can't do anything about it. I've got to go. Good-bye."

"You wait—"

She hung up. Slightly out of breath. Why would Jack go down there to tell him? Well, when he came home she would find out. She would ask. And as for Abe, he could only ruin the most perfect day of her life if she let him. She finished making the bed.

She was sorting through her lingerie an hour and a half later when the doorbell rang. It couldn't be Jack back so soon—but it had to be. She ran to the door, unable to suppress the wonderful feelings of excitement and delight rushing through her.

Abe shouldered his way in, something small and black in his hand.

"I don't believe this!" Belinda cried, furious at the intrusion and disappointed that it wasn't Jack.

Abe waved what appeared to be an audiocassette at her. "And I don't believe you! Like most goddamn broads, you think with your fucking cunt, not your head."

She was shocked that he would talk to her that way— shocked and angry. "Get out this minute!"

"Belinda, you are a big fucking fool, and I'm not leaving until you hear this tape."

Belinda clenched her fists as he strode to the tape deck and inserted the cassette. She regathered her composure, but that icy tentacle of dread was back, clutching at her vitals.

"I tape every minute of every day in my office," Abe said, "and I want you to hear this conversation." As he rewound the tape, he glanced at her. "Better sit down."

Of course she stood. Then she heard Abe's voice, on the tape:

What do you want? You've got about two minutes before security comes and throws you out.

I want [pause] congratulations.

Belinda tensed. It was Jack, and there was something in his tone that was unfamiliar and frightening and momentarily undefinable.

Her father's rude laugh sounded, and he was saying:

For what? Shortest career in history?

For my marriage. To your daughter.

Laughter followed, and it was malicious. Belinda's dread grew.

What?

[Laughter] How do you feel about having a grandson with the last name of Ford? Because you can bet we've been working on it.

You little cocksucker! I don't know how you did it, but I'll undo it!—before you can even blink!

"What's wrong, Glassman? Or should I call you Abe? No, wait—Dad?

You have a lot of balls, to dare to use my daughter to get at me.

It was a stroke of genius, wasn't it? I knew there had to be some way I could avenge myself. Appropriate, wouldn't you say?

You think you can win? Beat me? You think I'll stand for this? You stupid bastard! I don't know how you did it, but your marriage is over before it even began—I guarantee that.

How does it feel? How does it feel to have your enemy as a son-in-law? Huh? How does it feel, you fucking bastard? And I'll never agree to a divorce—never. You're stuck with me until the day you die.

We'll see! How could Belinda be such a fool, to let herself be conned by you?

Does it really matter? And if you think you're going to have your thugs work me over again, think twice. My lawyer still has that letter telling everything—only now it's been updated. If I go, I'm taking you with me—old man.

Get out! Get out while you can. But if you think I'll give Belinda a single penny while she's married to you, you're wrong. She gets nothing! Nothing! If she has your son—*he* gets nothing! Not one fucking penny!

How does it feel to lose?

Abe turned off the tape.

Belinda was sitting. She was so numb she couldn't think, didn't want to, couldn't move, couldn't breathe.

Abe said, "Jack Ford has been my enemy for seventeen years, and he's using you to shaft me—in case the tape wasn't clear."

His words brought back her ability to think.

Enemy for seventeen years . . .

Using me . . .

Lies. Their love, all lies. She lifted a white face toward her father. "Get out!" she gasped. "Get out, you bastard, before I—" She choked, looking quickly away. She had never hated her father more.

Oh, Jack! Tell me it's not true! *No!*

"Don't worry," Abe said. "We won't let that little prick get away with this. I'll call you tomorrow after I talk with my lawyers."

She couldn't answer—her hold on her self-control was too precarious. She heard him leaving. The front door slammed. She hugged herself hard, shivering.

It was a stroke of genius. I knew there had to be a way to avenge myself. Appropriate, wouldn't you say?

How does it feel to lose?
    I'll never agree to a divorce, never. You're stuck with
me.
    How do you feel about having a grandson with the last
name of Ford?

Belinda got up and ran to the bathroom, but her heaves
were dry. She knelt there at the cold porcelain bowl for a
long time. He didn't know she was pregnant, of course, but
now everything was clear, so clear. The echoes wouldn't go
away.

It was a stroke of genius . . .
    Avenge myself . . .
    Appropriate . . .
    Stroke of genius . . .

─── *116* ───

*T*here was no sweet, sweet feeling of triumph. Just a cold,
panicky fear. And the sickness.
    Jack swung the Ferrari around a curve. He felt the aw-
ful weight of his guilt, and that made him angry. Angrier.
He had been pushed too far.
    He knew Glassman would make a move now. His guts
cramped at the thought. Glassman would try to get at Belinda, try to turn her against him. Maybe even bully her. He
could handle it. He knew he could. Belinda already loved
him.
    If worse came to worst, he would have to come clean,
explain it all. His hands grew white on the steering wheel.
    He had to get to her now.
    Before Glassman.

Before she found out the truth—and the deceit.

She met him at the door, looking ill.

"Are you all right?" he asked, reaching out.

She struck his hand away. "Don't touch me."

He froze. *She knew.* "What's wrong?"

" 'It was a stroke of genius,' " she said, and he felt something sick and cold plunge into his guts. " 'I knew there had to be some way to avenge myself. Appropriate, wouldn't you say?' "

He stared, horrified at hearing his own cruel words coming from her lips.

Her voice broke. " 'How does it feel to lose?' "

"Belinda . . ." he said, feeling desperation uncoiling within him.

She whirled away. She pointed to the stereo system, confusing him. "It's all on tape—every word." She turned to him, her eyes huge and brown in her white, pinched face. "Deny it," she begged.

For just a moment Jack closed his eyes. Dear God, no. Not this. Those words had been meant for Glassman, not for Belinda. Never for Belinda.

"You can't deny it, can you?" she whispered.

His face was agonized and seeking. "Belinda, it's not the way it sounds."

"Just deny it, damn you!" she shouted. "Deny that you married me to get at my father! Deny it!"

He inhaled. "I can't lie to you anymore. I can't deny it."

"All lies!" she said brokenly. Tears swam in her eyes. "All lies—every minute with you has been a lie!"

"No!" he said hoarsely. "No, it's not all lies!"

She looked at him, so stricken with despair, hurt, agony, and hope that he hated himself.

"How much I want you isn't a lie. That's real. You know it's real."

"Oh, good!" she shrilled. "You want to fuck me! Well, buddy, welcome to the crowd and get to the end of the line!"

"Don't make it sound like that," he said. "Belinda, I love you."

"How dare you!" she screamed. "Well, I hate you. Get out! Get out and don't ever come back!"

He felt something twist inside, like a knife. He went to her, placing his hands on the smooth curves of her shoulders, but she turned away with a cry.

"I didn't want to hurt you," he said hoarsely to her back, and God knew, it was true. "Belinda, listen to me—I didn't want to hurt you."

She laughed hysterically. "My consolation prize."

"Let's talk this through, please!"

"There's nothing more to talk about." She turned, lifting a white face and glazed eyes. "Except a divorce."

He was stunned. It took a moment to recover. "I don't want a divorce."

"Oh, right! Because of Abe—you'll never give me a divorce! Well, you just listen good, Jack. You've got another think coming if you think I'm going to stay married to a lower-class piece of ass like yourself. Like I said once before —pricks are a dime a dozen. And I am my father's daughter —or have you suddenly forgotten? How does it feel, Jack, to have another Glassman after your ass?"

At first Jack didn't answer. Her eyes were blazing with fury. And possibly with hate. "I thought you loved me. If you loved me, you'd give me another chance and you'd forgive me."

Belinda laughed. "You've got to be kidding! Love, Jack? It was just the hots—like I said, you are prime meat. Surely you've made that mistake too?"

His jaw tightened. "Don't push me away."

"Nancy was right," Belinda cried. "You're nothing but a liar, a user, and a loser. One big fat loser. Get out, Jack. You're really pressing your luck."

"You are just like your old man, aren't you?" He turned stiffly on his heel. He was at the door, his hand on the knob, when she spat out, "I'll never forgive you."

"Lady," he snarled, "I just changed my mind. I couldn't care less."

"Never."

117

*H*e couldn't stop remembering.

But did he even want to?

Her smile after the first time she told him she loved him, so shy and tremulous, like a child's smile, and how he himself had responded . . . Funny, warm, gargantuan feelings had welled up inside him like a balloon. And he had grabbed her to him and they had rolled over and over and then they had made love . . .

Her laughter when the kite had flown into the tree, and his fear, his own heart in his throat choking him as she climbed after it—practically to the top—while he stood below resolved to catch her if she fell, cursing himself for letting her go after the stupid toy, her every movement terrifying him . . .

How she had looked doing the dishes, how they fought over politics and metaphysics with no end in sight—she believed in past lives, no matter how he tried to explain it was impossible—and how she had finally gotten furious and thrown the wet dishrag in his face and called him a triple Taurus with a dose of Capricorn thrown in. He hadn't understood that insult, but he knew it was bad. He hadn't asked her just what it meant, not until much later, after they had made up with much enthusiasm.

He was not a triple Taurus—because one of his signs was Gemini. She had groaned at that bit of information.

"I'll bet the other is Leo." She moaned in dismay.

"What's wrong with being a Gemini?" he asked.

"I have a fatal attraction to Geminis, and they're all two-faced playboys."

"How do you feel about a reformed two-faced playboy?" he asked, copping a feel. She had giggled. End of argument.

She had cried forever over that movie, and he had been amazed, holding her and comforting her until soft touching had turned into frantic affirmations of love. "I don't ever want to lose you," she had whispered, holding him, stroking him urgently, pulling him down, and he had felt the urgency too, the need to meld and join and dominate and soar.

Maybe it was then that he had fallen in love with her.

He wished he had never used her to get at Glassman. If he could, he would take it all back. And now he had gotten a call from Glassman himself.

"Where the fuck is she?" Glassman had demanded.

"I assume at home—I haven't seen her since yesterday," Jack said coolly, feeling tense and volatile at the sound of Glassman's voice.

"She isn't answering her phone," Glassman said. "Look, why don't you come down to the office and bring your lawyer. I've got a deal for you."

Jack would never accept a deal from Glassman, but he was in the game and he had to play it through. "My lawyer will be in touch with you to arrange a meeting—between him and your lawyer. I'm busy."

Glassman snorted. "Doing what, picking your nose?" He laughed and hung up.

Jack called Brent Baron. Brent, his lawyer, had the letter incriminating Glassman with everything Jack knew, but Brent hadn't read it and didn't know anything about what was going on. He was under instructions to open the letter and take appropriate action in the event that Jack had a serious accident or died from other than natural causes.

"I want you to find out what deal Glassman's got cooking," Jack said.

"Isn't this a job for Sanderson?"

"No, Brent, it's not." Jack filled him in on some of the details.

Baron told him he'd take care of it and get back to him. Jack hung up, then on impulse dialed her number. Her answering machine came on. "Hi, this is Belinda. I'm not in right now, but I'll get back to you when I can." *Beep*.

Jack hesitated, then hung up. They had to talk. After all, they were married. Didn't that give him some rights? Or had he forfeited those by using her so callously? He knew he should wait a few days to let her cool down, but he was impatient and recognized it. He drove over.

Hoping she was home.

Heart thudding wildly.

Jesus, I'm a wreck, he thought, his hands white on the steering wheel.

He knew as he approached the front door that nobody was there. He knew it. But he rang anyway, after walking around the perimeter of the beach house, peering in windows. No, nobody was home. He decided to wait.

He waited two hours and finally left, wondering where the hell she was.

He came back that evening. She still wasn't there.

He wanted to know where she was. Jack prowled around the house again until he found an unlocked window, and he slid it open and entered. He would wait all fucking night—but they were going to talk.

118

*A*dam was not in the best of moods.

He had been calling Belinda all week. Either she wasn't answering the phone or she was still out of town, and if it was the latter, she couldn't possibly be with Ford, could she? It seemed more than possible, and he was consumed with fury.

He had told his secretary to hold all calls. He tried Belinda yet again, with the same results. Maybe he would go over there to see for himself if she was actually back or not. His secretary buzzed. "What is it, Anne?"

"Mr. Gordon, it's Abe Glassman. He says it's urgent."

"I told you to hold all calls," Adam grated, hating having to kowtow to the inevitable—and the inevitable was Abe Glassman.

"I told him you'd just stepped away from your desk. I'll take a message—"

"Put him through," Adam snapped. A moment later he regretted it. Thoroughly.

"Are you a loser or a winner, boy?" Abe shouted with no preliminaries. He didn't pause for the answer. "I pegged you for a winner, Adam, but maybe I was wrong. Have you heard the news?"

Hatred and dread alternated. "What news?"

"My daughter and Jack Ford."

The dread grew.

"That daughter of mine married Jack Ford."

Shock.

"You there? I thought you had her where she belonged —in your bed, making my heir. She obviously wasn't there. What in hell happened?"

Belinda and Ford. He was remembering Majoriis's party and how they'd come on to each other for the whole world to see. He was remembering Aspen—how she'd dumped him to leave with Ford. He thought about the two weeks that they were on location in Tucson together—had they been fucking back then? Playing him, Adam, for a fool?

"Well, the game ain't over yet," Abe said nastily. "I'm going to destroy that little prick—you can count on that. And when I do, Adam, you'd better be there, waiting to pick up the pieces. You got that?"

Oh, he had it, all right. "Yes."

Glassman hung up.

Adam stared at the phone. Then he slammed the receiver as hard as he could on the cradle, cracking it. Just who did that cunt think she was? To make a fool of him? To reject him again? To destroy his chance at Glassman's empire?

Rage, red-hot.

Hatred.

It was hard to think; all Adam could do was feel. But he forced himself to control the burning need to destroy.

And he began to plot his revenge.

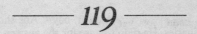

119

"*I* think she's in Tahoe," Peter Lansing said.

Jack was feeling crazed. She hadn't come home that night. And he knew beyond a doubt she was with another guy, to get back at him. Even now, three days later, he was filled with anger and jealousy. "You haven't found her?"

"I'm going to go up there and start looking. She took her Jeep and her dog. From what I found out, that's a typical Tahoe pattern for her. She also took her skis."

"I'm coming with you," Jack said quickly.

"It could still be a few days," Lansing told him.

"I'm coming," Jack said stubbornly. "After all, she's my wife."

Lansing shrugged.

It had been four days since he had gone to Glassman, since she had told him she hated him. Four endless, endless days. He couldn't sleep, couldn't function. He was obsessed. He had to find her, had to explain. Had to make things right. He would, too, by sheer force of will. She couldn't resist him, not this time. And he prayed that, for once, his charm wouldn't fail.

On the flight up to Tahoe he thought about Glassman's deal—with no regret for refusing. Glassman had offered to release him from the North-Star contract in exchange for a Reno divorce. Baron had not asked any questions, but Jack could see that he wanted to ask a dozen. Jack had curtly told him to refuse. Baron had.

It hadn't even been tempting.

He had told Baron he was breaking his contract with North-Star.

Yes, he knew he would be sued, but it was time to bare all. Time to come up head-to-head against that sociopathic bastard and fight to the death. His career was over, as it now was—so what did he have to lose? The answer was easy. Belinda.

If he hadn't lost her already.

He knew she didn't seem to love or even like her father, but he was afraid of how she would react to this development on top of everything else: an open battle with her father. North-Star would sue him and win, Baron said; but when everything came out, the settlement might not be too bad. The settlement, however, was one thing; whether another studio would touch him was another.

Sanderson had had a stroke of genius. "We'll turn it around, Jack," he said.

He hadn't understood.

"The PR. You're the goddamn victim here—and the public loves an underdog. Maybe, with luck—lots of luck and even more careful planning—when all this is over you'll be hot. *Hot!* Jack Ford, poor boy trying to make it big, getting trounced on by a near-mafioso again and again— Jesus, Jack, once he nearly had you killed!" His eyes were snapping in excitement.

Jack felt hope for the first time.

"And you and Belinda, Jack—a love story! After all Glassman did to you, you and his daughter fell in love. Romeo and Juliet." He was triumphant.

"Leave her out of this," Jack said, feeling a shaft of pain. "I mean it. She hates my guts. And I guess I don't blame her." If anything, he felt the same way.

"Can't you pour on some of that old Jackson Ford charm?" Sanderson asked.

"No, Horne, I can't," Jack snapped, furious.

"Jack," Brent had said. "If you've left out anything, I

need to know it—everything there is about you, about you and the Glassmans, so I won't be surprised by any stops he pulls out. Once this thing gets going, it's going to be dirty and we have to be ready."

"I'll tell you how often my mother changed my diapers, Brent, if it makes you happy."

Baron was smiling like a bloodthirsty general about to do battle. "Melody, start taking notes."

Melody nodded, pen poised.

Baron hadn't been smiling an hour ago when Jack had told him he was going up to Tahoe in search of his wife.

"We need you here, dammit!" Brent exploded. "This is fucking important!"

"I trust you, Brent. Whatever you decide is fine with me."

Brent hung up angrily.

Jack wished he could concentrate one hundred percent on taking on North-Star. And Abe Glassman.

But he couldn't.

How could he concentrate on anything until he found Belinda?

He had no choice. He had to come clean.

He couldn't bear her hating him. All he wanted, he told himself, was a chance to explain everything, to make her understand, to make her stop hating him.

That was all he wanted.

120

"*W*hy don't you smile more often, beautiful?"

She glared. "Get lost, bud." She practically threw her skis into the back of the Jeep; then she did throw her poles, and she was conscious of the man walking away, footsteps crunching in the snow. Jerk! she thought vehemently.

And, of course, she thought of Jack.

Her husband.

And wanted to cry but didn't.

Damned if she'd shed a tear over him—he wasn't worth it—and so far she'd succeeded in her resolve. Belinda flipped up the tailgate of the Bronco with a bang, clumped around to the driver's side, fished for furry boots. After she'd changed her ski boots she jumped in. The car had been running, and it was nice and toasty inside.

She leaned back for one long moment, eyes closed. As usual she'd skied herself into the ground, hard, unrelenting, viciously almost; and now every muscle in her superbly fit body was shrieking for rest. And she was starved. Famished. Shifting into reverse, she backed out.

As she sped through the canyon at Squaw Valley toward the little cabin she had rented, she debated about calling Lester. After all, she was professional as far as her work was concerned—what if she was needed? What if, for some reason, the *Outrage* production was being resumed? Of course, she wasn't ready to go back to L.A., not with *him* there. *Motherfucker.* But it wasn't exactly as if he cared where she was. So if she did go back, they wouldn't have to see each other.

She still couldn't believe it.

Still couldn't believe she had been used so cruelly. Nancy had been right—more than right. She, Belinda—the Queen of Man-eaters—had taken the plunge for a stud con artist. Worse—not just the plunge, a free fall with the shoot not opening. Jesus Christ. She had fallen in love with an egotistical, manipulative stud. Impossible. True.

So many lies.

She would have to go back to the real world sooner or later and face everything, including divorce. God! She just wasn't ready. Couldn't face it, bear it. Not yet.

And she would never tell him about the baby. Never.

She thought about the reporter who had appeared on her doorstep yesterday. God, what was that all about? She didn't believe for a minute that Jack had been involved in porn. But if he had, it was the past and his own business, no one else's. Not that she cared he was making headlines—she didn't. So why did she feel sick with worry inside, just thinking about what he was going through? If anything, he deserved to suffer, the way she was suffering. But she knew she didn't feel that way either.

And had he really been with Donna Mills last night?

Don't! she told herself.

She didn't notice the smoke rising from the chimney when she pulled into the drive.

Her Lab barked a welcome. Belinda slid out of the Jeep, hands deep in her pockets. She went cautiously up the icy steps and opened the unlocked door. Then her heart stopped.

"Hi," Jack said very seriously. He was standing in the middle of the small living area before a blazing fire.

For a moment she couldn't speak. Couldn't even get a grip on anything except his presence—and the awful realization leapt out at her that she loved the bastard despite all his lies. Then reality intruded, unpleasant and demanding. "How the hell did you know where I was?" she demanded.

"A private investigator," Jack said, his green gaze never moving from her face.

She gestured to the door. "Get out. Now! Before I call the cops."

"I want to talk to you, Belinda."

"I believe everything has been said—and quite succinctly too." She stared, rippling with tension, and he stared back, his gaze deep and so damn sincere and stricken that she wanted to scream. "That does it!" she said, reaching for the phone.

Jack came up from behind just as she was dialing, and grabbed her small hand with his larger one. "No," he said, quietly.

The contact unnerved her, and she jumped away. "Damn you!"

"Come on," he said, taking her arm and guiding her

toward the kitchen table. "I'm going to talk, and you're going to listen."

She jerked free. "All right," she cried, furious and upset. "Five minutes. You've got five minutes to make your pitch." She slammed into the wooden chair and stared at the tabletop.

"I never wanted to hurt you, and you have to believe that," Jack said intensely. "Please believe me, Belinda."

"You made me fall in love with you so you could play your game with my father, and you never wanted to hurt me?" she snapped.

"I guess I didn't think it through," Jack said softly. "And I never expected him to tape me. Those words were meant to get to him—not to you."

She made a noise of disgust, but it sounded more like a whimper. Jack's hand covered hers. She tried to pull away. He wouldn't release her.

"I love you," he said softly. "I didn't mean to fall in love with you, but I did. Be—"

She wrenched free and to her feet. "How dare you!" she screamed. "How could you do this to me? How dare you even try to continue this lie!"

He was standing too. "I'm not lying! I think maybe I fell in love with you the first time I saw you. I just refused to recognize it. Belinda, dammit! Do I have to talk to your back?"

She strode to the couch and sat, her back still to him, hugging herself. She couldn't handle this, and she hated him for doing it to her. "I don't know why you're doing this. Is it to score more points against Abe?" To her horror, her voice sounded choked, as if she were ready to cry.

"No, no!" He protested vehemently, and he sat on the small sofa next to her, taking her shoulders and turning her to face him. "Belinda, I'm sorry. I love you—I do. I wish I'd never done this."

"Your five minutes are almost up, Jack."

He cursed. "Then I'm making it ten. No! Sit still and listen—*listen,* dammit! If you don't listen, I'll never leave."

She gritted her teeth, looking at the floor. He took her

clenched hands in his. "Seventeen years ago I worked for your father in New York City."

The thought intruded. Would he tell her the truth now? Would he finally tell her about Nancy?

"I drove for him. And your mother. I was only twenty-one, a tough kid trying to make a buck while I was studying acting."

Belinda could hear her own heartbeat.

Jack stood, made a gesture. "It was seventeen years ago."

Belinda didn't move.

"Belinda," Jack said softly, "your mother was lonely and beautiful, and I was twenty-one and the horniest guy you'd ever met. I don't even remember how it happened— but it was the most natural thing in the world. And for a kid like me, a street punk, it was the ultimate fantasy."

"What was the ultimate fantasy, Jack?"

"Your mother and me. We had an affair. It was only for a couple of weeks. And it was seventeen years ago."

Belinda stared at him through a blur of tears. "Is it your conscience?" she asked bitterly. "Or is it because you have no choice—you can't think of any more lies? Any lies I'd believe, that is."

"Belinda . . ."

"I already know, Jack."

He stared.

"I've known since we first met at Majoriis's party. Nancy told me everything. That's the real reason I stood you up that night."

"You married me, knowing I was hiding that from you?"

"Nancy warned me!" Belinda cried bitterly. "She told me you'd do this—use me, hurt me, just the way you did her. She waited for you, Jack, when she was in the hospital, hurt and alone. When Abe started hating her because of you and because she'd lost the baby. But you couldn't even visit her—not as a lover but as a compassionate human being. Is there any compassion in your heart?"

Jack gasped. "I didn't know."

"How could you not know?"

He grabbed her hands and pulled her to him. "There was no way I could know. Listen to me. Your father found out." He took a breath. "Belinda, I don't know how much you know about your father, but you're an adult—*and my wife*—so I'm not going to spare you the details. I used to deliver payoff money—grease money—for him. Envelopes full of cash. Like fifty grand—more. One night after you'd caught me with your mother, Abe sent me to deliver an envelope to Queens. It was a setup." He paused. "I was beaten up with brass knuckles—almost killed. My nose and jaw were broken. My spleen and kidneys were ruptured. I had fractured ribs. Punctured lungs. I was in the hospital for six months."

Belinda was stunned.

"That's why I didn't visit your mother, Belinda."

"Oh, God!"

"It was the end of July in '71." He looked at her grimly. "I'll never forget the date. There's more."

She hugged her knees and looked at the floor, every sense and nerve alert, tense, throbbing. Jack went on. "When I came out of the hospital in New York, your father made sure I couldn't get a job—not even waiting tables. I had no choice—I had no money, no place to stay. I was on the street, thanks to him. I met a woman here and there— rich, older. They paid me afterward, sort of goodwill money. I made enough to get to L.A.

"In L.A. it was the same. I was young, hungry, and good-looking. It was easy to sell it to eat. I worked for a so-called escort service, except the deal always involved sex. I cared but didn't let it get to me. As long as I had plenty of booze and dope in me, all the broads seemed attractive. Eventually I wound up in the drunk tank, and I straightened up fast. I quit the booze. I quit the whoring. I met my manager, Melody, and she got me my agent. Sanderson. He got me my first role—a tremendous break." He stopped, reached out, turned her face to his. "Are you listening?"

"Yes."

"The lead in that pilot. It was instant fame and success.

You know the story. When the show was canceled I signed an exclusive three-picture deal with North-Star. My first flick was great. *Berenger*. Then Glassman took over North-Star. Belinda, your father has canceled release of a major feature, costing him millions, to get me. To destroy me. And this isn't supposition. I finally confronted him, and he admitted it."

She stared at him.

"I know what you're thinking," he said. "But the man's a nut. It isn't just because I screwed his wife seventeen years ago. I didn't even know she was pregnant at the time. Nancy never told me. Her miscarriage"—he hesitated—"it was a boy. And Glassman somehow blames me—says I killed his son."

Belinda said nothing.

"*Outrage* is cancelled." he said. Belinda gasped. "That's right, Belinda, it's definite, written in stone—Abe told me. He's so intent on destroying me that he'll stop at nothing—not even at hurting his own daughter in the process. And I'm stuck—locked into an exclusive deal with North-Star. Until I make two more films for them I can't work anywhere else. And Abe is going to make sure I never make another film for North-Star—which means my career is finished.

"No one knows yet, and my lawyer would kill me if he knew I was telling you this, but I'm going to breach my contract and sign for another TV series—the only work I can get now."

He laughed bitterly. "North-Star will sue. As far as I'm concerned, I have nothing to lose. I'm finished unless I fight. We're hoping that by dragging the whole damn story out into the public eye, I'll be seen as a victim and turn into a hero, and my star will be rising again. But to do that, we're going after Abe with both barrels loaded. No holds barred. All out."

Their gazes met. If Belinda didn't have an iron will, if she didn't force herself to remember the lie that their marriage was, didn't tell herself that this was probably a new part of the game, she would have leaned toward him, until her head rested on his shoulder and her arms went around him. Instead she stood up.

Jack was looking at her anxiously. "Aren't you going to say something?"

"Yeah." She turned. "The door is over there. Good-bye, Jack."

"Belinda, I want you back!"

She walked to the door without looking at him and opened it. She heard him coming. "I'm sorry," he said. "Won't you even think about it?"

She didn't answer, didn't watch him go out the door, didn't even glance up when she heard him pause, giving her a chance to respond, before tramping down the steps. She couldn't.

She wouldn't.

— *121* —

*T*he thing that first brought the magazine to his attention was the *National Enquirer.*

Standing at the checkout counter of his local supermarket, Lansing idly noticed the half-page cover photo of Jack Ford because of its strategic placement. He did a double take, then read the headline: THE SECRET LIFE OF JACK FORD—PORN STAR.

Swearing, Lansing grabbed the rag and read it. Naturally there were none of the incriminating photos within, but they graced a dozen pages of a magazine called *Hard Times* as well as a few in *Playgirl.* The article was devoted to Jack's days as a porn star before he signed with the L.A.P.D. series. The article also revealed the fact that Jack had a wife who was so furious about his secret past that, after an elopement just two weeks ago, she had left him and was filing for divorce. A picture of Belinda Glassman accompanied the article.

Lansing went out and bought both magazines. In *Playgirl,* Jack was alone, merely naked and sporting a massive erection. But in *Hard Times* the photos were intimate and varied—Jack and one or two women at a time, doing it all in many different ways, and the coup de grace was Jack and another man—which, while not showing them in an act of sodomy, suggested it.

He was furious.

As a private investigator he did not believe in coincidence.

Therefore, after these pictures had lain dormant on a videotape for years, having surfaced only since he had stolen the film for Melody, there was just one logical conclusion.

He broke every speed limit on the way to Jack's office. And walked in without ringing. Melody glanced up from her desk in the outer room.

He threw the newspaper and magazines on her desk.

She looked down at them.

"It was you!" Peter said.

Melody gazed at him, her eyes wide and innocent. "What? What do you mean?"

"If it wasn't you, then it was one helluva coincidence, baby!"

"Peter—what are you saying?"

"I stole that video for you. To protect Jack—you said!" He was shouting. "And a few days later these pictures are plastered all over the fucking world! Why, Melody? *Why?*"

She shoved her chair back and stood, enraged. Her face was an unfamiliar mask, which startled him. "Get out, Peter! I don't have to listen to this!" Her eyes were so different —no longer big and vulnerable but cold and ruthless.

Peter unconsciously took a step back. Shocked.

"Get out!" she snarled.

"You little bitch, it was you, wasn't it?"

"Yes!" she hissed. "I sold that tape to Abe Glassman." She lifted her chin triumphantly.

"Why? How could you do this? I thought he was your friend."

"Because I hate him!" she said. "He's an egomaniacal bastard. He deserves everything he gets. After all, I didn't make this up—it's the truth."

She was ugly in her spite and maliciousness.

And Lansing felt sick. Sick at having been used and at having been the instrument of another man's destruction.

He walked to the door of Jack's office.

"What are you doing?" Melody cried.

Lansing didn't answer her. He couldn't even look at her. He knocked.

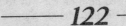

122

*I*t didn't matter.

Nothing seemed to matter.

Jack looked idly at the cover of a magazine called *Hard Times.* Looked idly at himself, naked, probably about ten years younger, but undoubtedly himself, with a very large and very visible erection, poised over a lush female body and with another sex kitten's openmouthed face and large breasts pressed against his buttocks and thighs. "Film Star Reveals All," a red subtitle proclaimed. He pulled forward the *Playgirl,* flipped it open and studied his picture dispassionately. He pushed it away abruptly.

He didn't know who had sent them over, and he didn't particularly care.

Jack could think of only one thing: Belinda was back in Laguna Beach.

He was sure of it. He hadn't spoken with her, but he had called several times. And although he always got her answering machine, the messages were different. She was back. It had been more than a week since he had seen her. And he laughed—bitterly.

What had he expected? That she would fall eagerly into his open arms?

Yeah, he sort of had.

He wished he knew what she was thinking. Did she still hate him? Or did she hate him more now that he was actively engaged in a lawsuit against North-Star, because she knew that was really an excuse to take on her father and drag him through the mud?

He wished he knew what she was thinking. And what about the fact that he had slept with her mother? Christ, that was the least of it, as far as he was concerned—seventeen years ago was another lifetime. But women were funny about things like that, and maybe that clinched it for her. If only he knew.

If only she'd come back.

If only he didn't care.

If only he had felt like laying the bimbo who'd pursued him last night.

If . . . if . . . if . . .

There was a knocking on his door. "Yeah," Jack said.

Peter Lansing came in with Melody at his heels. They both looked angry, Melody a bit frightened. "What's going on?" Jack asked, relieved to have his attention diverted.

"Jack, I don't know how to tell you this . . ."

"What's up?" Jack repeated.

"Melody asked me to do her a favor. To steal a videotape of you from Bart Shelley. She told me she was protecting you—and she asked me not to tell you so as not to worry you. I gave her the videotape the other day."

Lansing pointedly looked at Jack's desk, where the rags were open.

Jack followed his gaze.

So did Melody.

A silence ensued.

"I don't get it," Jack said. He was confused, first looking at Lansing, then at Melody.

"It's not a coincidence," Lansing said harshly, turning an accusing gaze on Melody.

Jack looked at her too, completely bewildered. "I still don't get it."

Melody stepped forward aggressively. "Go ahead, tell him the rest," she said nastily. "I sold the video to Glassman, Jack."

He stared.

"And now I quit!" she said into the heavy pause.

Jack knew his mind wasn't functioning the way it should. "You . . . sold it . . . to Glassman?"

"That's right."

"Mel?"

Tears filled her eyes but not tears of contrition. Tears of anger.

And then Jack understood.

Betrayal. Again.

Unaware that he did so, Jack touched his chest as if to still his pounding heart. *"Why?"*

She turned on her heel and was gone.

Jack sat down, visibly shaken. He looked at Lansing. "Why did she do this?" he said.

Lansing shrugged. "She loved you."

Jack tried to focus, to understand. "She loved me? I love her. She's my best friend. How could she do this to me?"

"A woman scorned," Lansing said simply. Then, "I'm sorry, Jack."

Jack stared at his desk and heard Lansing walk out. A woman scorned. Melody? He loved her. How could she do this to him? When the phone rang he picked it up reflexively.

"Motherfucker, Jack," Brent Baron said. "You see the rags? Is this for real?"

"I got them."

"I mean, Jesus Christ! Should I be expecting more of this shit?"

"I don't think He had anything to do with it."

"I don't think this is funny, Jack, not with you on page ten with a goddamn ten-inch hard-on."

"What do you want from me?"

"An hour of your time—like now."

"All right," Jack said heavily.

Then there was a pause. Baron said, "Is it true? Because if it is, it's more shit we have to deal with."

"Is what true?"

"That you married Belinda Glassman, and she left you because of the porn you did?"

Jack's hand tightened on the phone. *"What?"*

"It's in *The Reporter.* I'm sorry I have to ask—"

"No, it's not true!" He slammed down the phone, momentarily stunned. He didn't want Belinda dragged into this . . .

Seconds later he was out the door, heading for his Ferrari. At the corner newsstand he bought a copy of *The Reporter* and rapidly began reading it. His heart sank when he came to the paragraph about his wife having been interviewed. And then—grim determination.

He had to explain.

He had to.

123

Contrary to what one might think, she admired some of the pictures.

Especially the one in *Playgirl.*

Jack was a beautiful male animal.

The photos in *Hard Times* she found arousing.

Not just sexually. They made her angry as well.

Belinda called her father, but found he was in Las Vegas. Damn him! She knew he was behind those pictures—

he had to be. How dare he! How dare he attack Jack. Even if
she hated him—which she knew she didn't—even though
the pretense of hatred was comforting, attacking her husband was a direct challenge. It was a frontal assault. It was
an attack upon herself. She was ready to do battle.

It wasn't fair.

Jack did not deserve this.

And it proved that all those hateful things he had said
about her father were true. What was Abe, some kind of
megalomaniac? Worse. There was a term for a person without morals, completely self-serving, and she knew the term
from one of her college psychology courses. *Sociopath.* A
synonym for antisocial personality disorder. Of all psycho-
ses, it was the one that was incurable, because the sociopath
never thought he was doing wrong, and was therefore closed
to anyone's attempts to help him make behavioral changes.
Sociopaths felt anything they did was justifiable.

Even beating up a young man to within an inch of his
life.

Even destroying that same man professionally seventeen years later—for the same grudge.

God!

What should she do?

And—how was Jack?

Belinda paced her home, close to tears. She looked at
the phone and wanted to call Jack. Her husband. Didn't she
have the right? But she couldn't do it. Pride. She had so
much of it.

Well, it wasn't as if she wanted a reconciliation.

Or did she? She missed him terribly.

No. She would simply ask—in a casual, friendly way—
if he was all right.

But he was so arrogant, he would think she was weak-
ening.

Well, face it—she was.

Oh, Jack.

124

She had let the dog out, and he was roaming the beach or she would have heard the doorbell sooner, because of his barking. She went to get it reluctantly. A visitor was the last thing she was in the mood for.

She opened the door to face Adam Gordon.

She stared at him in surprise.

He stared at her in fury.

Belinda stepped back. "Adam?"

She wasn't prepared for the blow. Or its violence. He backhanded her across the face, knocking her off her feet and onto her backside in the foyer. Blood trickled from her nose.

"Cunt!"

She rolled to her knees to get up and flee. He yanked her to her feet by the hair, hurting her terribly, almost yanking her scalp off. He pulled her against his body. Belinda threw a weak punch at his face, but it glanced off his jaw.

He grabbed her face with his hand, his fingers digging in painfully. "Rich-bitch cunt."

She clawed his face, drawing blood.

He grabbed her wrists, forcing them behind her back, pressing her against him. She felt a hard-on. She was terrified. "Adam, please! I don't understand." She didn't even recognize her own voice, a whimper of fear.

His face was close. "Me! It was supposed to be me!"

Keep him talking. "You? What was supposed to be you?"

He forced her hands up higher behind her back, making her gasp. She closed her eyes, the pain coming in a black wave. He was going to break her arms . . .

"You were supposed to marry me."

She fought unconsciousness. She blinked. Focused. So much hatred. "B-but A-Adam. We—we were only dating. Please!"

"Your father and I had it all planned. I was to be the son-in-law. *Me!* Not that prick Ford!"

"You're hurting me," she managed.

"Good!"

"Adam, Jack and I are separated. The marriage was a mistake. Surely you know we're separated!"

"Lying cunt," he said, and he dragged her onto the floor.

Belinda bucked as he came down on her. No. This could not be happening. He transferred her wrists to one hand, with the other he unsnapped her jeans. She twisted wildly. He was too strong. "No! No! You fucker!" The last became a sob.

"Cunt. Whore. Slut." He hit her again, but she saw the fisted blow coming and turned her face to the side. The impact took her on the cheek. She felt terror.

Her jeans were skintight. He started cursing when he couldn't get them off her writhing legs with one hand. He released her wrists to pull them down. She went for his eyes with her fingers pointed like talons.

And missed when he ducked.

Her jeans were around her ankles.

And then thrown aside.

She lifted her knee as hard as she could as he was throwing the jeans, catching him on the underside of his chin. There was a crack. He grunted. She rolled onto her hands and knees, scrambling across the pine floor. And then he had her by both ankles and he yanked them up, causing her chin to hit the floor with a thud. He ripped off her panties.

He had both her wrists again, clenched in a bone-breaking grip over the small of her back. She felt the head of his hard penis on the cheeks of her ass. Then she felt his hand, riding between those cheeks, fingers penetrating anally.

Terror.
Helplessness.
Pain.

125

As Jack pulled into Belinda's driveway a Mercedes was pulling out. There was no mistaking Adam Gordon behind the wheel.

Jack turned off the ignition and for one moment just sat, making no move to get out. Terrible jealousy assailed him. He started up the car. Fuck her. He threw it into reverse. He hesitated, then put it back in neutral and snapped the key off. He jumped out.

He had every right to talk to her. They were married, weren't they?

He trotted up the steps. The black dog came running from around the side of the house, barking. "Hey, buddy," Jack said and reached out a hand. The dog stopped barking. It wagged its tail, waiting at the door. Jack didn't knock. The door was ajar.

She was lying on her stomach.

On the floor where the living room met the foyer.

Clad only in a shirt and socks.

Jack rushed forward with a cry, dropping down beside her. "Belinda, what—"

He saw the side of her face. It had turned purple and swollen already. The blood had clotted beneath her nose. "Oh, God!" he said, his hand on her back. "It's me, sweetheart."

She moaned and turned her face away.

He knelt and put his arms around her, his face in her

hair. "It's all right now. Belinda, it's me—Jack. Belinda? How bad are you hurt? Sweetheart?"

She didn't answer. But she made a funny, pathetic noise, like a small animal that is frightened or in pain.

Jack leapt to his feet and dialed the police and an ambulance, then grabbed a blanket from the sofa. He dropped down beside Belinda again, tucking the blanket beneath and around her. He saw blood between her legs and was filled with rage. He was going to kill Adam Gordon. "Belinda. It was Adam?"

She looked at him for the first time. She nodded, tried to speak, whimpered instead. She shifted herself upright, into his lap, to cling. He held her, rocked her. He felt the first slight tremor. "It's all right, darling. It's all right." He shushed her as he would a child.

She started shaking violently. "Jack."

"Yes, yes, sweetheart, I'm here."

"J-J-Jack."

"Yes, what is it, darling?"

"Oh, God!" She trembled convulsively, as if she were feverish. He held her as close as he could, saying anything, his voice soft and warm. But a part of his mind was completely detached, watching from a distance. He was going to kill Adam Gordon. Oh, yes. Soon. But not now. Later. He couldn't leave Belinda now.

"Jack—the baby."

He knew he had misunderstood.

"Our baby," she cried. "I don't want to lose our baby." She was weeping.

His heart had definitely stopped. When it started again, it was in a mad dash for an Olympic gold. "Belinda, why didn't you tell me?"

She wept against his chest.

He was overwhelmed. And horrified. He had seen all that blood . . . Where was that fucking ambulance? What was taking so fucking long? Jesus—Belinda was losing the baby!

It finally came, with two patrol cars. "I think she's miscarrying," Jack desperately told the paramedics. They wouldn't tell him anything. The police asked questions. Belinda clung to his hand as she was moved to a guerney. "R-ride with me."

Impatient and furious, Jack told the police, "A Los Angeles lawyer named Adam Gordon did this. He works at Benson, Hull Harte Industries."

He rode with Belinda in the back of the ambulance, holding her hand, thinking about torturing Adam Gordon before he killed him. And praying for the little soul that was their child. The instant Belinda was wheeled into Emergency at South Coast Hospital, she disappeared down a corridor, and he was stopped from following her.

"I want to go with her!" Jack cried to the nurse who had barred his way.

"You can't go back there, I'm afraid," the petite nurse said, staring at him with awed recognition.

"Dammit, she's my wife! I want to be with her! What's happening?" he demanded furiously.

"You cannot go into Emergency, Mr. Ford," the nurse said in such calm tones. "Dr. Paige will do everything she can to save your baby."

Jack cursed.

"Please relax, Mr. Ford," a detective, Lieutenant Perez, said. "Why don't you sit down? I have a few questions."

Suddenly numb, Jack sat down.

"A certain procedure has to be followed in cases of rape. Your wife didn't bathe, did she?"

Jack cursed. "No! She didn't bathe, for crissake!" He was on his feet, pacing, cursing fluently, fretting, praying.

"You called the police?" Perez asked.

"Yes."

"As soon as you found her?"

"Yes."

"Where did you find her?"

Cursing again, Jack told him, looking past him and down the corridor where Belinda had disappeared.

"Was she alone?"

"Yes," Jack said.

"Where were you this afternoon?" Perez asked.

"In my office," Jack said, straining to look down the hall again.

."You mean, here in town?"

"No. In L.A."

"I see. Do you usually come home in the middle of the day?"

Jack suddenly stared. "What the hell is going on? What the hell kind of questions are these?"

"Mr. Ford, I'm only doing my job. Please answer the question."

Jack's jaw clenched. "I don't live with Belinda—my wife—in Laguna Beach. I live in Westwood."

"I see. What were you doing there?"

"She's my *wife*—I was visiting," Jack said, coldly furious. "Am I understanding this right? You're questioning me while that bastard rapist is running free?"

"Adam Gordon will be brought in for questioning," Perez said. "You and your wife are estranged?"

"Yes." He stared. "I didn't rape my own wife. I didn't beat her up."

"I never said you did," Perez said. "Was anyone at your office with you this afternoon?"

"Yes," Jack snapped. "My secretary."

Perez wrote down her name. "I'm sorry, but I have to cover all the bases. What is your wife's relationship to Adam Gordon?"

Jack went tense. "I don't know."

Perez gave him a look of commiseration—loaded with innuendo.

Jack wanted to slug the moron. Instead he answered the rest of his questions, then turned away. The wait was interminable. His anger at the police started to recede. Worry took over. God, over an hour and a half had passed! What was going on? Please let her be okay!

Thirty minutes later a white-coated doctor appeared, introducing herself as Dr. Paige. "Is she all right?" Jack asked.

"She'll be fine," Dr. Paige began. "In—"

"And the baby?"

Dr. Paige beamed. "The baby is fine. Your wife wasn't miscarrying when she came in."

"Oh, God!" Jack said, and he sank down into a chair.

"She has a few bruises, which will heal. A broken nose. We do have a fine plastic surgeon on staff, but people sometimes want to bring in their own doctor. Your wife was sodomized. The anal tissues are torn, and I put in two stitches. She'll have some discomfort for a few days. I gave her a mild pain-killer. She should take one tablet every four to six hours as necessary. She can go now, but she should rest for the next few days. I want to see her in one week to remove the stitches. Of course, if there's any vaginal spotting, she must come in immediately."

Jack nodded. "Can I see her?"

"In a few minutes," Dr. Paige responded. "She's with a counselor from the rape crisis center."

Jack groaned and turned away. A few minutes stretched into forty-five. Perez approached him and said, "When your wife feels better we'd like her to stop by the station and make a formal statement."

Jack nodded and Perez left.

"Sir? You can see your wife now."

"Thank you," Jack said, rushing in ahead of the nurse.

Belinda looked terribly vulnerable and injured lying in the hospital bed with her swollen, discolored face and the tape over her nose. He took her hand. She opened her eyes.

"Hi," he said with a faint smile. "Ready to go home?"

"Yes, please."

Jack squeezed her hand reassuringly. She looked up at him with hurt in her eyes. He wanted to take that hurt away. He didn't know how.

Getting discharged was another matter. There were more forms to fill out, and he did his best—it was stunning how little he knew about his wife. Then he called a cab and went back to Emergency for Belinda. She was half sleeping, still under sedation. In the cab she sat stiffly against his side, so stiffly he thought it must hurt, while he kept his arm around her and periodically stroked her shoulder reassuringly. She stared out the window.

When they reached her house he helped her into the massive Victorian bed. "What can I do?" he asked.

She looked at him and held out her arms. He sat down and she wrapped them around him, hard. His own arms came up to hold her tightly. "I love you," he said unsteadily. "So much."

He was shocked when her lips found his and took them aggressively and hard. He tried to protest. But she grabbed his hair, almost hurting him, and attacked again, open-mouthed, desperate. She thrust her tongue past his lips. Her teeth caught his. It should have been passion, but it wasn't. Jack knew the difference. It was a physical onslaught, hard and demanding, and he didn't understand what she was doing. He was confused.

She moved her head away. He saw her eyes, wide and surprisingly lucid—not passion-fogged. She pulled off her shirt. "Make love to me, Jack. Now." She attacked him again.

Was this right? He wasn't aroused. She wasn't aroused either, and he knew it. All he wanted was to hold and comfort her, soothe her. But she was a madwoman, pulling him down, her hands like claws on his back, kissing him painfully. For once in his life he had no erection. "Belinda."

"Damn you!" she cried with a choked sob. "Damn you! You don't want me!" She rolled onto her side away from him.

"Honey," he said. "That's not true." He touched her shoulder, she yanked it away. "Belinda, I'm afraid to hurt you—to hurt our baby."

He heard a sob. Her shoulders shook. From behind he wrapped his arms around her. "This is what you need now. Cry. Cry it all out."

She cried. She rolled to face him and burrowed against him and cried. Her sounds were animallike, not human. He stroked her. Caressed her. Whispered endearments. Told her how much he loved her. The crying and shaking gradually ceased. He kissed her forehead, smoothed her hair. "I love you." He kissed her ear. She was very still and very warm against his body.

He kissed her temple, stroked her back. He kissed her bruises one by one, as if to heal them. She lifted her face, eyes closed, lips parted. He kissed them too, gently, tenderly, prodding slowly with his tongue. She clutched his head. He clutched her. And he felt her desire rise just as he felt his.

"I love you," he said, holding her tightly.

She said, "Jack?"

"Yes?"

He looked down, his gaze tender. Hers was bewildered.

"He raped me."

"I know," he said tightly.

"He raped me."

"I know."

126

*F*ortunately Jack never had the chance to kill Adam Gordon.

Gordon was arrested that night.

While Belinda was sleeping Jack phoned Abe Glassman, who had just gotten back from Las Vegas. "What do you want, Ford?" Glassman sneered.

"Your daughter—my wife—was beaten and raped this morning."

There was a stunned pause. "Who did it?"

"Adam Gordon."

There was another pause. "You sure?"

"Belinda says so."

"I want to talk to her."

"She's asleep, and Glassman, she needs to sleep."

"She okay?"

"Facial bruises. A broken nose. Torn anal tissues."

Another silence.

"Just thought you'd want to know," Jack said. And hung up.

Adam was held without bail.

Two weeks later, in the ensuing publicity about his perverted sexual habits, he lost his job.

Exactly five weeks after the rape he was found in his apartment, a gun in his hand, his face blown away.

Suicide, the police said.

It probably was.

127

A hundred ways to die.

Will Hayward sat in the rental car and watched Abe Glassman stride out of his Westwood, California, apartment building and slip into the waiting limo. It slowly cruised away.

Will turned on the ignition and followed.

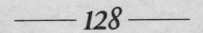

128

"*H*ow are you feeling today?" Jack asked tenderly the morning after the rape. He held a tray in his hands.

"Sore," she said, sitting up against the pillows. "I must look awful."

"Honey, your face is bruised. It'll take time to heal." He came forward.

"I smell my favorite."

"Made by your favorite guy," he quipped, setting the tray across her legs. She was clad in his shirt. Last night she had wanted to wear it.

"Thank you," she said somewhat shyly. She ate ravenously, and he thought it was a good sign. After she had finished he removed the tray, and she got up and went into the bathroom. Jack heard the shower. He went in to help. She sent him away. "My legs and arms are fine."

"Sorry," he said contritely.

Afterward she came out in his shirt and climbed back into bed. Jack had done the dishes, and he came back in to sit beside her. "What can I do?"

"Not much." She smiled slightly. "My face aches. So does my butt. I don't want to take any more pain-killers. They make me too tired."

"Don't be a hero."

She looked at him. "You were a hero last night."

He didn't say anything.

She looked at her hands on the lacy quilt. "You were there when I needed you. I'll always be grateful." She raised her eyes to his.

"I want more than your gratitude," he said quietly.

She stared.

"I want your love again, Belinda."

"You never lost it."

He took her hands, exhilarated. Then he kissed her, gently. "I wish I'd come sooner." He touched the shell of her ear. "Belinda, I want to explain about the porn."

"Oh."

He looked away.

"Jack? I thought the picture in *Playgirl* was hot."

He saw that she was smiling slightly. His relief was vast. "Thank you. I was afraid you'd think badly of me."

"Jack, if you were a paid porn star, I wouldn't care. That was before me. What really pisses me off—can't you guess?"

He was afraid. "No. What?"

"My fucking father."

At his questioning silence she said, "He's attacking you. I guess I knew what you said in Tahoe was the truth. But I have so damn much pride, and you did use me to get at him, so I wasn't ready to listen. And not only is he attacking you he's messing with me—and he couldn't care less. He makes me so damn mad I could kill him. Jack, you're my husband. We're a team. And we have to fight fire with fire. If we win, we win together. And if we go down, well, we go down together too."

He hugged her hard. "Your support means more than I can tell you. Do you know North-Star is suing me for breach of contract?"

"Yes. You told me. I'm proud of you for being so brave, taking on Abe like that, especially after what he did to you."

"It's going to get dirty." He looked at her. "I'm prepared to go all the way with this. If my entire past comes up, so be it—but I'll take your father through the muck with me."

"Fine," Belinda said. "You have no choice. *We* have no choice."

"Belinda, I don't want you involved. He's your father."

Belinda touched his face. "Jack, I am involved. One day I'm going to tell you the awful things he's done to me over the years—to manipulate me, to make me bend to his will. And do you know what the most recent was? Adam Gordon."

"What?"

"Adam told me that he and my father had planned on his marrying me."

"I don't understand."

"Abe has been after me to marry and produce a son for him ever since I was twenty-one. But he wanted to choose the groom. And he chose Adam."

Jack's jaw clenched. "Belinda, he doesn't know you're pregnant, does he?"

"No."

Jack's eyes were blazing. "Now I have a family to fight for. Abe wouldn't hurt a child, would he?"

"No, he wouldn't, not physically. He meant what he said, though—our child won't get a cent from his estate."

"I couldn't care less." Their gazes locked. "When were you going to tell me?"

She took a breath. "I was afraid to, Jack. Before our wedding I was afraid to, afraid you'd think I was trying to manipulate you. And afterward, I was getting ready to tell you when I heard the tape. Then I was so mad I decided I'd never tell you."

He was staring. "Before the wedding? How could you have known before the wedding?"

"Jack." She touched his hand. "The first night we spent together, in Aspen—I never used any birth control."

He blinked.

"Are you angry?"

"I don't understand."

"I just forgot. Except, I'm too smart to forget something like that, and we both know it. I did it deliberately. I wanted to get pregnant. With your baby. Because I love you."

For a moment he didn't move; then he took her in his arms. "Do you know how good you've just made me feel?" He kissed her. "Belinda, no matter what happens—even if my career as an actor is over—what's important is that we're together."

She smiled.

"Besides, my secret dream was always to be a writer."

She hit him.

129

*H*e saw it coming.

And froze.

It was a big green blur that suddenly took on distinct lines. It had been moving slowly, but now it seemed to take on speed. A green sedan. He watched and thought, Jesus Christ, that car's going to hit me!

From somewhere behind him Abe heard Mary scream.

There was impact.

Agony.

Then nothing.

*B*elinda was awakened by the phone. Ignoring it, she turned over, imprisoned by Jack's strong arms and hard warm body. She snuggled against him as the phone stopped ringing, her answering machine picking up the message. Jack moved in his sleep, a nice healthy hard-on pressing against her thigh. She kissed his neck and stroked circles around it, fully awake now, exploding with love and arousal, the most potent combination in the world. He grunted.

She nibbled his earlobe, then traced the shell with her tongue. She felt the moment of his awakening and laughed, looking into his wide green eyes. He smiled then, sleepily, his hands closing around her waist, rolling onto his back and taking her astride him. "I love you," he whispered, closing his eyes, sighing.

"Wake up and make love to me," she demanded, rubbing herself on his belly, already wet.

"Umm," he said, "you make love to me."

She was about to grab him and guide him in when the phone rang again. She frowned, wondering if it was the same caller.

"Tease!" Jack said softly, his hands finding her buttocks, rubbing himself against her mons.

"No, Jack, I think it's important," she said, reaching for the phone.

"Is the honeymoon already over?" Jack asked, one hand sliding from her buttock to her thigh, then back up and between her legs.

"Yes," Belinda said. "Hello? Mom!"

Nancy was barely comprehensible. "It's Abe. There's been an accident. He's at Lewis Memorial. Oh, Belinda—he was hit by a car."

"I'll meet you there," Belinda said, hanging up and leaping off the bed. Grabbing jeans and hopping into them.

"What is it?" Jack said, swinging his legs over the side of the bed.

Belinda zipped the fly, grabbing a black turtleneck. "Abe was hit by a car." She pulled it on. "I have to go to the hospital. Mom's frantic."

Jack was standing, pulling on white jeans. "How serious?"

"I don't know." She pulled on knee-highs and stuck her feet into cowboy boots. "What are you doing?"

Jack was tucking in a shirt. He looked at her. "I'm coming with you."

She stood. "You don't have to."

"I know," he said.

"Maybe you shouldn't."

"I'm coming."

───── *131* ─────

*"H*ow is he?"

"Oh, Belinda," Nancy cried, pale and red-eyed, "he's had a concussion and a broken leg and they won't let me see him."

Belinda found her mother in her arms and held her awkwardly. "What happened, Mom?"

"It was a hit-and-run." Nancy trembled. "He's not a young man anymore, Belinda."

"But he's okay," Belinda said soothingly.

Jack approached with a cup of coffee. Nancy turned and saw him, her eyes widening in fury. "What's he doing here!"

"Would you like a cup of coffee, Nancy?" Jack asked quietly.

"Get him out of here!"

"No, Nancy."

Nancy whipped around at her daughter's firm, low tone. "Belinda, how could you have married him! Don't you understand? He'll destroy you and your life—the way he did me and my life!"

"No I won't, Nancy," Jack said, putting the container down. "I happen to love your daughter. She's the most important thing in this world to me. I almost threw it all away for revenge against your husband. But I didn't—and she forgave me and took me back."

"You ruined my life!" Nancy hissed. "And now, for some reason, you're after Belinda!"

Anger darkened Jack's face. "Untrue, Nancy. It's time we set the record straight. You're not the first married woman to have an affair and get caught. But don't go blaming your megalomaniacal husband's actions on me—not when Abe had me worked over with brass knuckles. I almost died. When you were in the hospital, so was I. Only I was there for six months, and at first it was touch and go."

"Oh, God!" Nancy said.

"Abe ruined your life, Nancy, not me," Jack said. "It's time you put the blame where it belonged."

"Mom," Belinda said, "I know you've hated Jack for a long time. I'm asking you to try and reach a truce—for my sake. And for our child's sake."

Nancy stared.

"You're going to have a grandchild," Jack said softly.

Nancy sat down. She started to weep.

And Mary Spazzio walked in.

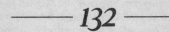

"*W*hat are you doing here?" Belinda was incredulous.

Mary tossed her mane of hair. "I have every right to be here," she said, hands in her Montana jacket. Her glance wasn't on Belinda but on Nancy, sitting and blowing her nose. "Is that *her?*"

Belinda followed her gaze. "That's my mother."

Mary frowned. So that was Abe Glassman's wife. She did an elaborate inventory. Ferragamo shoes, Chanel bag and suit, a couple of emeralds. Mary lifted her chin with disdain. "How is he?"

"Who?" Belinda asked blankly.

"Abe."

"Abe? How do you know Abe?"

Mary grinned. "I guess you could say we're friends." She sauntered away, well aware that Belinda was watching her with amazement. She strolled right over to Nancy.

Nancy looked up, wiping her pink swollen nose with a

Kleenex. She wasn't sure she could make it through this day. Abe hurt, the victim of some crazy driver. Belinda and Jack married, Belinda pregnant. Pregnant! Her insides were twisted into a tight knot, while at the same time she had this recurring image in her head—a tiny blond toddler dressed in white lace and pink ribbons running across Nancy's foyer, shouting, "Grandma, Grandma!" Her granddaughter.

Then there was the shocking revelation that Jack had been too injured to come to her when she had miscarried. And he had cared. He had said so. It hadn't all been lies.

She looked up at the pretty, voluptuous brunette in the purple Montana suit. The girl was smirking. Nancy wondered what she wanted and who she was. "Are you a friend of Belinda's?" She had seen them talking together.

"I'm a friend of *Abe's.*"

Nancy stared, and of course, not being a fool, she knew.

Mary's smirk grew. She had just decided she was going to become the next Mrs. Glassman. It was definitely no contest. Abe would dump this old broad in a second—she had no doubts.

Nancy looked Mary over carefully and sighed. Another just-out-of-the-cradle bimbo, bovine and mindless. Would Abe ever grow up? And when had she stopped caring about his carnal escapades? "It's nice to meet you," she said politely.

Mary gaped, then looked angry.

Nancy did not feel threatened in the least.

133

"*W*hat's he doing here?" Abe roared.

Belinda and Jack stood side by side facing the bed.

Nancy was at Abe's head, trying to calm him. "Abe, please, don't upset yourself."

"That little prick walks in here with my daughter, and you tell me not to get upset!" Abe shouted. "He has some nerve!"

"Stop it, Abe," Belinda said, aware of an immense role reversal occurring. She was suddenly the adult, and Abe the child with the tantrum. "Jack is my husband. He's here because I'm here."

Abe fell back against the pillows, red-faced and out of breath. "After what he did to you, doll, we can have this annulled in no time!"

"We're not getting an annulment," Jack said grimly. "Or a divorce. So just relax."

Abe turned to look at Belinda.

"Jack is my husband," she repeated. "I love him. He loves me. End of that topic. How are you feeling, Abe?"

Abe's eyes popped. "What the fuck's wrong with you?" He snapped. "You're thinking with your cunt again! You heard the tape! He's only using you to get at me!"

"Jack *was* using me," Belinda corrected her father, calm despite the provocation.

"I was pushed into your game, and I was playing by your rules," Jack interjected. "But that's not my style. And even while I was playing, I was in love with your daughter. Your game is over. Now *I'm* making the rules. And the rules say I can take you on and still love my wife. It's going to be hard, but I'm not going to make a sacrifice of my own integrity. And I intend to keep Belinda out of this as much as is humanly possible."

"You marry my daughter and think you can get away with it? You got another think coming!"

Jack leaned over the bed railing. "I'm not a fresh-faced kid anymore, Abe. If I were you, I'd think about that. I'm not afraid. And I'm not going to run. You've pushed me one time too many. *So watch out*— you're in for the fight of your life."

"Good!" Abe grinned. " 'Cause I love a fight."

"Are you ever going to grow up, Abe?" Belinda de-

manded. "For my sake—could you give up this obsession
with destroying Jack? For my sake."

"Just what have you done for me?" Abe shouted.
"You've done everything you could your whole life, to resist
me. Living out in California, writing, for crissake, like some
fucking hippie! What have you done for me?"

She couldn't believe how calm she was. "Abe, don't you
care that when you cancelled *Outrage* to get at Jack, you
hurt me too?"

Abe laughed. Disbelieving. "Sometimes you're not so
smart, Belinda. Your career is the last thing I wanted to see
happen, so it all worked out for the best."

"I don't believe you."

"Believe me. How in hell am I ever going to get you to
settle down if you're some hotshot writer? Settle down and
give me my heir? Huh? I got enough problems keeping you
in line without that added kink. And now this—now *him*.
Jesus!"

"Then if you can't give up this obsession for my sake,"
Belinda said, "can you give it up for my baby—your grandchild?"

Abe blinked.

"Our baby."

Abe stared.

Nervously Nancy interjected, "Belinda's pregnant,
dear."

"Shut up!" he snarled, livid. He jammed his thumb at
them. "Never! I don't fucking believe it!"

Jack put his arm around Belinda, ignoring the furious
man on the bed. "Let's go, Belinda. He's fine. There's no
point in staying."

"One minute. You're really going to hold onto this
grudge against Jack—against the father of your grandchild?" She was disappointed.

"He thinks he's won!" Abe shouted. "He got you pregnant just to get at me! Well, he hasn't won—he'll never win!
Because I'm cutting you out of my will. You won't get one
red cent! And neither will the brat!"

"We don't want a single penny," Jack said, "although I know you won't believe it."

"I feel sorry for you," Belinda said, overwhelmed with pity. "For cutting off your nose to spite your face. For being such a small man. For thinking only in black and white, in terms of winning and losing. This is my child—your grandchild—and no matter how much you hate Jack, you can't change that fact."

"Get out!" Abe roared. "Get out—now!"

"Abe," Belinda said, "you're my father. No matter what you do or what you've done, I can't change that. And despite it all I love you. Even though you've never given me any love back. Love was all I wanted from you, ever—not the horse and the toys and the books. Just love. I do love you, but I love my unborn baby and Jack more. And when you see the light, when you become generous enough in spirit to forgive and forget, I'll be waiting. And maybe then we can start over."

Jack took her arm. They were out the door and in the hall when they heard Abe shout, "It's you who'd better see the light, Belinda—and fast!"

Epilogue

March 1988

*N*ew York City

The sun was trying to pierce the thick layer of clouds. It failed.

Belinda shivered despite her wool coat. Jack threw his arm around her. Even the ground was cold, frozen underfoot, penetrating the soles of her shoes. She stamped her feet; Jack pulled her closer. An icy blast of air touched their faces. "It won't be much longer now," Jack whispered. "Can you make it?"

"I'm only cold, Jack," she whispered back, leaning against his warm hard body. "And I'm only pregnant. Not terminally ill."

He wasn't amused. "We'll stop for a cup of coffee as soon as this is over. Decaf for you though."

He was so serious. Belinda had to smile. The man was going to spend the rest of her pregnancy doting on her—that was very, very clear, because he hadn't stopped since they'd been reconciled. Oh, well. She guessed she could take it.

They watched the casket being lowered into the ground.

Afterward when the funeral was over, Belinda's gaze met her father's from across the grave. He stared; she stared back. Jack was about to propel her with him back to the cab, but Belinda gripped his hand. "Let's go say hello," she said.

"You sure?"

"Yes."

It had been a month since their disastrous encounter at the hospital, and although Belinda was in frequent contact with her mother, she hadn't spoken to Abe once. Holding Jack's arm, she gingerly made her way over the frozen ground toward her parents. It had started to snow.

"Hello, Mom. Hello, Abe."

Abe shot Jack a disdainful glance; then he looked at Belinda. "Hello, Belinda."

"I'm sorry," Belinda said. "I can't believe Will is dead. What a freak accident."

Abe shrugged. "Yeah, a real freak accident."

"You sound like you don't care. He was your oldest friend. He introduced you to Nancy."

"Oh, I care," Abe said with a slight grin. "But even *I* don't have the power to bring him back from the dead."

"Well," Belinda said into the awkward silence, wishing hopelessly, she knew, that Abe would at least acknowledge Jack. "We just wanted to say hello."

"How are you feeling?"

"What?"

"How are you feeling?" Abe repeated.

"Just fine. Ecstatic, in fact. Things couldn't be better."

Abe frowned. Then, gruffly, "So the baby's okay?"

Time stilled. The silence of the winter day became unnatural. Jack said, "The baby is just fine."

Abe looked at Jack. "You really got balls, to think you can break your contract."

"I broke it," Jack said.

"Don't start," Belinda said. "Please."

"Sorry," Jack told her, squeezing her hand.

Abe's eyes had been gleaming during their brief exchange. Now they turned somber. "So." He coughed. "Uh, when is the baby due?"

"Why?"

He shifted uneasily. "I got a right to know."

"Do you?"

"Yeah, I do. After all, he's your son—that makes him my grandson."

Belinda smiled. "Mid-September," she said. "A perfect month to have a baby, don't you agree?"

"I decided," Abe said, "that even if you're out of your mind"—and he glared at Jack—"this is probably my only shot at an heir, so what the hell." He pinned Jack again. "I figure," he said to Belinda, "you'll wise up eventually. You"—to Jack—"I'll see in court."

"Can you believe him?" Belinda asked a few moments later when they were snug in the warm taxi on their way back to Manhattan.

"It's a game," Jack said, shrugging. "He wants to fight me. He wants to keep me an enemy. He enjoys this."

"He does—he really does." She smiled. "Jack, he's accepting the baby."

"Yeah, well, he'd be a real jerk not to. One thing Abe isn't is stupid."

"I didn't think he'd ever come around," Belinda said. "Don't you see though? This isn't the ending, it's the beginning. He's accepted your child—maybe eventually he'll accept you."

Jack put his arm around her. "I'm not holding my breath. And it's not important, Belinda. You know what's important?"

"Of course."

"You and me and our child."

"I already knew that."

"It's funny," Jack said, "but I've been thinking about it. We're closing the circle. It's like a resolution."

"What do you mean?"

"He's wanted an heir for seventeen years. Nancy miscarried his son when I was involved with her. Now you're giving him a grandson—my son." He smiled. "Sort of like fate, don't you think?"

"Fate? Jack! I'm wearing off on you—you're becoming metaphysical."

"I don't know about *meta*physical"—he grinned and nipped her jaw—"but I'm definitely into the physical."

Belinda snuggled closer. "And me looking like a pregnant sow."

Jack chuckled, his hand cupping her hip, his mouth warm on her neck. "A pregnant sow? What does that make me?"

She turned to meet his lips. "A rutting boar."

"Boar? Not bull?"

"What's wrong?" she whispered as he nuzzled her jaw. "Can't your ego handle the epithet?"

Jack groaned. "I think I need my dictionary—why did I marry a writer?"

"Because you love me?"

He laughed as his mouth closed over her ear. She gasped. "Completely. Belinda, there's only one thing that needs handling—and it's not my ego."

Belinda turned so she could put her arms around him. "Why did I marry a superstud?" She gently probed the shell of his ear with her tongue.

"Because you love me?"

"Completely." She ended the word with a long, open-mouthed kiss, her hand stroking the flat planes of his abdomen beneath his shirt.

He growled. "Are you trying to handle my ego?"

Silence.

Jack groaned.

Belinda whispered, "Of course. Do you think anyone else could?"

"Absolutely not."

"You said the right words, Jack."

"Do I get a prize?"

"Absolutely."

"Do I get to pick my prize?"

"Maybe."

"Belinda . . ."

"Say the magic words."

"I love you—witch."

"I guess that will have to do—stud."

"Belinda, I don't think my ego can take much more of this."

"No?"

Reckless abandon. Intrigue. And spirited love. A magnificent array of tempestuous, passionate historical romances to capture your heart.

- ☐ **THE RAVEN AND THE ROSE**
  by Virginia Henley   17161-X $3.95

- ☐ **TO LOVE AN EAGLE**
  by Joanne Redd   18982-9 $3.95

- ☐ **DESIRE'S MASQUERADE**
  by Kathryn Kramer   11876-X $3.95

- ☐ **SWEET TALKIN' STRANGER**
  by Lori Copeland   20325-2 $3.95

- ☐ **IF MY LOVE COULD HOLD YOU**
  by Elaine Coffman   20262-0 $3.95

At your local bookstore or use this handy page for ordering:

DELL READERS SERVICE, DEPT. DHR
P.O. Box 5057, Des Plaines, IL . 60017-5057

Please send me the above title(s). I am enclosing $_____.
(Please add $2.00 per order to cover shipping and handling.) Send check or money order—no cash or C.O.D.s please.

Ms./Mrs./Mr. _____

Address _____

City/State _____ Zip _____

DHR-9/89

Prices and availability subject to change without notice. Please allow four to six weeks for delivery.

"I think it's time for me to start fulfilling your epithets."

"Which ones?"

He managed to laugh—just before they disappeared into the Midtown Tunnel.